THE TRANSPARENCY

James Tindall

Look for the following books from this author:

Jagged Grass (Book I, Seminole Trilogy)

Sun God's Treasure (Book I, Sun God series)

Alas Omega (Book II, Sun God series)

Authors Note:

This is Book II of the Seminole Trilogy.

THE TRANSPARENCY

Book II

Seminole Trilogy

James Tindall

Library of Congress Cataloging-in-Publication Data

Tindall, James

   THE TRANSPARENCY/James Tindall

   p. 335

ISBN: 978-1-7372476-4-7

Published by DTP Publishing, Denver, Colorado

Printed in the United States of America

10 9 8 7 6 5 4 3 2 1

ISBN: 978-1-7372476-4-7

DEDICATION

The Seminole Indians of the

Seminole Tribe of Florida.

The fiercest of all warriors,

keepers of the Glades,

and,

to Jacob Osceola who embodies

the Warrior Spirit of the Seminole,

to my father who taught me the ways of the swamp,

And, to Chiefs Micanopy and Osceola, leaders of the

Second Seminole War — the only war prior to Vietnam that the U.S. did not definitively win.

Disclaimer:

The locations mentioned herein are real, which are a part of the Sovereign Seminole Nation and United States, and other countries. While the many other geographic settings mentioned are also real, any description or likeness of characters that resemble persons living or dead is entirely coincidental.

Authors Note:

Big Cypress Reservation is located just north of Big Cypress National Preserve. Other Reservations that are part of the sovereign nation of the Seminole Tribe of Florida are located in Immokalee, Brighton, Tampa, Ft. Pierce, and Hollywood. The latter is located about 20 miles north of Miami along Interstate 95.

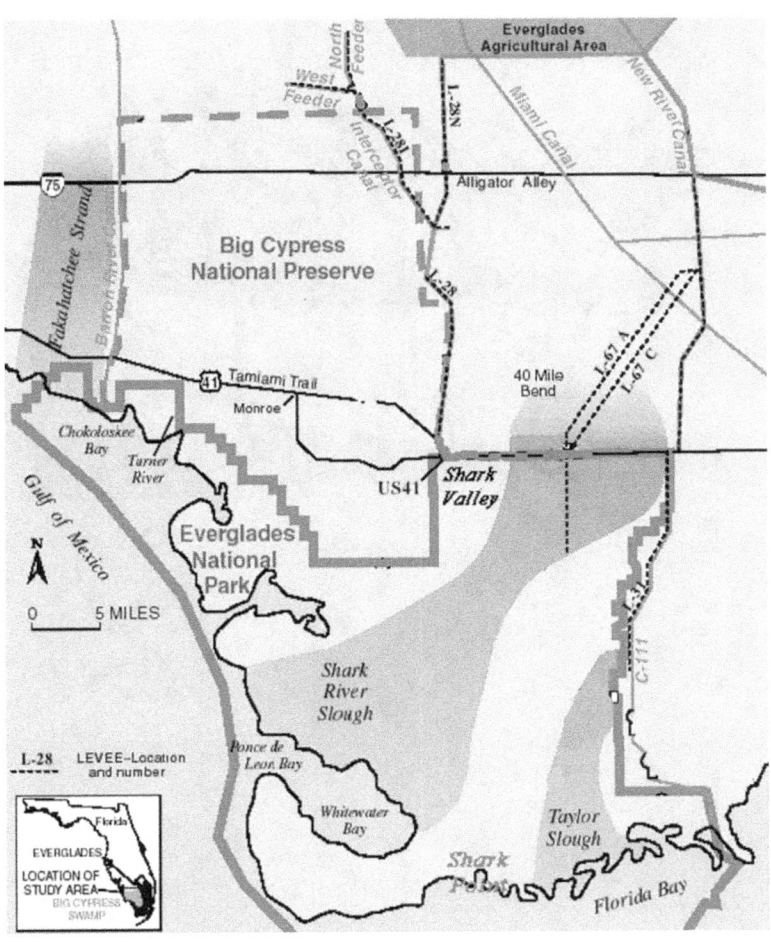

Seminole Chickee

Chapter 1

The isolated docks on the edge of the harbor in Hong Kong were empty. At 2:00 am, only a few prying eyes were up, who knew if they talked, death would visit their door before sundown. The seven figures standing in a semi-circle beneath the dock lamp, which cast a perfect circle of light around them, seemed oddly out of place. Rain drops passing through the light looked like falling diamonds before spattering onto the wooden planks.

The leader of the seven men was easy to recognize, standing in the center of the group, talking to a man on his knees, head bowed, hands tied behind him. He was dressed in a camel hair overcoat and tan Panama hat, wearing a gold watch. His right hand rested atop a straight, ebony, lacquered walking cane with a golden foot tip and a handle shaped like a dragon's head, the body wrapping around the cane downward about six inches. His hands were perfectly manicured. It was obvious he was a man to be reckoned with. One of the seven figures was slowly walking in front of the group and behind the kneeling man. It was obvious she was a woman, hair falling almost to the waist. She stopped and stepped back into the shadows, waiting.

"You have placed the organization in great jeopardy," the leader said.

"That was not my intent."

"What do you call it?" the leader asked. "After all, you were talking to the Hong Kong Police Force. You were giving them information."

"Only to trap them," the man said shakily, knowing there was no satisfying explanation for divulging information to the police.

"We have already taken care of your handler," the leader said. "You know the penalty for what you have done."

"But I have a family,"

"We all have families. If you truly had their welfare at heart, you would have obeyed our rules instead of being so greedy. We have always taken care of you."

The woman stepped out of the shadows. Passing by the leader, he handed her his cane as she continued walking without interruption until she stood behind the kneeling man. Glancing from beneath the brim of his hat, he gave the woman a slight nod. Instantly, she pulled the dragons head and the cane separated into a sword and scabbard. The drawing motion of the sword made a distinctive click and slide as she swiftly drew in one motion stopping with a one-handed high hold. The light had caught the draw, the blade gleaming as it hovered for the briefest instant in the air, rain drops striking its surface before it rapidly descended in an arc. In one motion the sword had been drawn and brought down, the man's head dropping onto the planks as his body collapsed, blood oozing quickly from the neck onto the wood, dripping through the cracks.

Looking at her handiwork, the woman placed the blade on the man's clothing, pulling it toward her, cleaning the blood as she turned the blade over and repeated the motion. Sheathing the sword, she handed it to the leader then, bent over and picked up the man's severed head. The men around her, despite having dealt death themselves, felt squeamish as they watched, wondering why she seemed to enjoy it so. They would be glad when this night was over.

"Ummph," she muttered, as she held the head up and then, dropped it by the fallen body, casually backing away into the shadows, the others looking after. The leader knowingly grinned as the woman's panting decreased, a smile of satisfaction on her face. He was about to introduce to these men who she really was.

The Medicine Man had sent Billie on a critical errand. Only three tribal members had been here before him according to the Medicine Man's history lecture. His teeth were chattering as he sat shivering by the fire, his hands cold as the snow around him while he patiently waited for the sun to emerge from behind gray clouds, the recent snow showers having passed. The sun's rays began penetrating from the blue sky above, the air incredibly fresh. Although only late fall, a couple of snowfalls had bathed the tops of the surrounding mountains in pure white. His view of the Bitterroot Mountain Range was spectacular. It had been a long trip from the swamp to Montana.

Billie had come to retrieve the root of a special plant to replenish the bundle necessary for the completion of the transparency. He was near the end of his final training and only he and Lunadi, who lived in Colorado, were able to perform the ceremony well. The tribal President was also in training but lacked the fortitude the Medicine Man desired and his training had been put on the back burner. According to legend, this was the only place the root existed. Despite the extremely specific instructions of the Medicine Man, after two weeks, he still had not found it. Billie was searching as he had been instructed, on the eastern side of Bitterroot Valley at the very tops of the peaks that ran from north to south. The valley was about one hundred miles long and had a rich history. He was at the northern end of the Bitterroot National Forest, the largest expanse of continuous pristine wilderness in the country. With glaciated, rugged peaks, the drainages had been carved by glaciers long ago to form steep canyons that opened to the valley floor below. The economy of the valley varied significantly from fisheries and timber to minerals, wildlife, grazing, big game hunting and more. It was a plethora of beauty as he stood gazing down the valley. Stamping the fire out, he looked at the hand drawn map written in pencil, comparing it to a more detailed 7-minute map. He sensed he was very close. There was only one problem. The plants grew around a small pool that was a mini hot spring and the only way to find it was within a two-hour window each day, standing in exactly the right location to catch the rays of the sun glinting from the water's surface.

The peaks were as rugged as the canyon walls were steep. Billie had long ventured off the trail used by tourists hiking through the national forest. He had at first wondered how the plant had existed for so long as the foot traffic and visitors to the valley increased each year. After the first three days of searching, he knew why. It would take an act of God to find the pool and the small plants surrounding it and the only time was late fall, after the leaves of aspens and other deciduous trees and shrubs had fallen. According to the Medicine Man, the Great Spirit would always protect the plant from those who would do it harm or reveal its location.

Today, was like the past thirteen days. Billie had come up a main hiking trail and branched off in his search for the pool. About two miles from the main trail, he had set up a small camp. After finally narrowing down the location, whether he found it today or on another day, he would venture out from his camp each morning as he sought the root. Going over the hand drawn map, comparing it to the more detailed one, he began making markings on both. Suddenly, he realized that three of the peaks on the penciled map were identical to those on the detailed map. His heart began to beat quickly realizing how close he might be. Looking at the map, he understood that even if he reached the location today, it would be too late to find the pool. He carefully folded the maps and put them into a waterproof map tube in his small pack. A smile creased his face as he donned his pack, throwing it over his right shoulder, and standing for a moment to watch the shadows grow quickly across the valley floor. He must hustle to make it back to camp before dark.

The former office of Paul Lorio had been converted to one more suitable for power brokers. The floors were made of an alternating pattern of dark iron wood and light-colored mahogany, overlain by a huge Persian rug that matched the horizontal striped walls with alternating six-inch stripes of dark gold separated by a much lighter tan color. Inset in the wall, closest to the large walnut desk at the far end, was a substantial liquor cabinet made of cherry with a chair on either side. Just off to the side of it was a smaller cabinet containing a tray with bourbon and two glasses. In front of the single, large walnut desk, were two gold sofas facing each other, a golden metal coffee table separating them. At the end of each sofa was a polished cherry table. The ugliness of the landfill behind the window where the desk sat was obscured by a wall-sized LED screen that displayed scenes of a magnificent ocean beach, beamed in from the Caribbean.

Sitting behind this desk was a power broker, a well-dressed man in a thousand-dollar suit, silk tie, and Rolex watch. He was immaculately dressed, his hands manicured with precision, and the look of pure focus on his face. It was Don Cilatro, boss of a criminal organization the FBI thought long dead. Though the initial landfill had been a setback, he was already moving forward with his next project.

"Look," Cilatro said. "I don't care what you have to do, get me a meeting with President Osceola. Let's see if we can get him to come up here."

James Tindall

"I'll do what I can and will let you know as soon as I pin him down."

Don Cilatro stood, walked over to the small cabinet, took the tray of bourbon and glasses, and placed it on the small table between the sofas. Walking to the door, he opened it and called for the man in the waiting room.

"Have a seat won't you," Cilatro said, motioning with his hand as he closed the door.

As the man sat, Cilatro took a position on the opposite sofa, tonged a few ice cubes into the glasses and slowly poured them each a drink. He picked up a glass and handed it to the man then sat back on the sofa as he eyed him cautiously, lighting a cigar. The man watched the smoke drift upward, unaware Cilatro was studying him. He knew he had to negotiate gingerly given what had happened with the landfill.

The man, a tribal member, had graciously accepted Cilatro's invitation to come to New York for a weeks' vacation to tell what he knew of the events that took place at the landfill. He had been carefully sought out by one of Cilatro's employees because he was close to the tribal councilmen on three of their reservations. Cilatro knew better than to try to con him, he just wanted to get a feeling for what was happening.

"Before we begin," Cilatro began. "I want to apologize for our employee who went far beyond his scope of authority with the landfill. It has all been such a tragedy. We are still trying to sort things out legally. So, tell me the events as you understand how they happened Mr. Miccos."

"You probably know them as well as I do Mr. Cilatro," Holata said. "Here's what I know from all the gossip on the reservation, talks with various councilmen and other tribal members, and what has been reported in the news. I'll just touch on the important parts. The landfill was voted on and passed to be constructed on BC. The lease was for one hundred years, and it moved forward rapidly. Once the construction

6

was completed, things ran smoothly, and the tribe was happy. Money was coming in for both parties and things probably couldn't have gone better. Then, quite a few children became ill. It was immediately blamed on the landfill. Once that happened, events moved at a rapid pace. They found the shirt of one of the SPD deputies and realized he had been murdered. Genesis blamed Lorio and the deal with the landfill literally collapsed after a gunfight with law enforcement. Your employee Mr. Lorio took a hostage and fled into the deepest part of the Everglades."

"That would be Ms. Christina Jumper, correct? Cilatro asked.

"Correct, only now she is Mrs. Christina Panther. Her and Billie have since married. Anyway, they were cornered on a hammock deep in the Glades and Mr. Lorio was killed by an alligator. The lady working with him, Monique, was arrested and is awaiting trial. There was another woman, I forget her name, who was apparently an accomplice with Lorio. She was also arrested.

When they examined the landfill, they found pipes to dispose of illegal chemicals, but Billie, a trained hydrologist didn't believe the chemical could have moved that fast. Further investigation showed that the benzene had been dumped into one of the feeder canals, apparently the driver had failed to dump all of it at the site. Had he done so it is unlikely any of what happened would have occurred. As far as I know, everyone involved in the illegal dumping has been arrested and charged. The trials will begin in a couple of weeks. From what I've gathered from our tribal attorney there is sufficient evidence in each case to gain an immediate conviction. Some of those apprehended are making deals with the prosecution."

"What is the feeling among most of the tribe?" Cilatro asked.

"Well, they're disappointed," Holata replied. "I mean, we hadn't had good jobs on the reservation for decades, we finally get them and then, they're gone in an instant. But from what

I've been told by the tribal attorney, the landfill will be cleaned up and begin operations again."

"Is there any indication of the time required?" Cilatro asked.

"From weeks to months from what Billie Panther has said. They were going to outfit the landfill initially with the necessary equipment to fuel a methane power plant, but there were insufficient funds to complete the plant. So, while some of the landfill was outfitted with pipes, the rest remains a typical landfill."

"Yes, I recall that from what Paul had told us." Cilatro said, eyeing Holata. "It's really a tragedy that Paul put everyone in such a situation. I appreciate ...., excuse me.

Cilatro walked over to answer the phone on his desk, pushing the speaker to on so Holata could hear.

"Mr. Cilatro, your next client just arrived and will be upstairs in a few minutes."

"Thank you Sally, we're just finishing up." Cilatro hung up and turned to face Holata again, walking over to the sofa.

Holata realized the meeting was over and stood.

"As I was about to say, I really appreciate your candor and honesty Mr. Miccos. I only wish that our employee had not gone rogue on us. Please accept this as a token of my gratitude and enjoy your vacation here."

Cilatro had handed Holata an envelope with five thousand dollars in it.

"Oh, I cannot accept this, the hotel and flight were quite enough," Holata said.

"No, I insist," Cilatro said, pressing the envelope to Holata's chest. "It's so difficult to find an honest man, especially one that I can trust."

"Very well," Holata replied smiling. "But I'll let you in on a little secret. You cannot trust anyone, it's just one of life's rules!"

Don Cilatro froze, looking Holata directly in the eyes, assessing that if he believed this, most other tribal members probably did as well, a keen insight which he would remember.

"Very well," Cilatro said. "I'll keep that in mind. I may call on you again to give me a gut feeling for what is going on with our lost venture. It was kind of you to come. Thank you so much. Sally will show you out; she has a taxi waiting for you downstairs.

As Holata was led away to the elevator, Cilatro watched after him. The man seemed open and had received his excuse for being there well, unsuspecting of the real reason behind the visit.

Holata was walking out of the elevator behind the secretary and had just passed through the doors onto the sidewalk when a motion to his left caused him to look. A limo driver opened the right rear door of his limousine and the flash of ivory pale legs had caught his eye, along with the red bottoms of her shoes. As the woman stood, her jet-black hair fell to her waist, around a black dress that had a wide split with a crisscross design up to about six inches above the knee. The stiff wind blew the woman's hair into her face, which she delicately swept away with her right hand. Even Sally was staring.

The woman began walking, like a model, toward the glass doors. She had an air of confidence and was elegant, built differently than a model. Standing at five feet eight inches plus her heels, her presence was commanding. She was dominating. Her voluptuous breasts looked small on her frame. The muscularity of her flashing legs from behind the crisscross design of the sleek, body-hugging dress, complimented the rest of her taut frame. However, it was her eyes that captivated Holata. They were brown, like the eyes of a tiger, unblinking, noticing everything. She looked directly at him; her stare withering him toward his taxi. As he climbed into the back seat, he couldn't help staring after her.

"Somewhere was a very lucky man he thought."

He was barely aware of thanking Sally as she said goodbye

telling the driver "The Hilton downtown."

As the taxi pulled away, Holata could just see the woman enter the elevator. The incident brought a smile to his face as he looked forward to getting back to the hotel and the fancy dinner he and his girlfriend had planned.

B illie had quickly made a fire once he returned to his small, makeshift camp. Darkness had fallen and with it the temperature. He had made dehydrated chili and coffee as he hurriedly ate and sipped. His thoughts drifted from Christina to the landfill incident to tribal members and how they would fare, the jobs they counted on now gone. The landfill had become a big disappointment, despite straightening itself out. And after additional investigation and reports from various law enforcement and environmental agencies, tribal members realized it wasn't Billie's fault, the President not among them, and no longer blamed him for the results, especially since he was straightening up the mess and had reached an agreement with Lorio's boss for refurbishment of the site and restarting of full operations. The dollar amount wasn't decided on yet but promised to be lucrative.

Thoughts of Christina brought a warm smile to his face as he remembered standing with her on the end of the dock, speaking to the Medicine Man and then watching him slide away in his dugout canoe poled by the strong muscular Indian always by his side and who no one in the tribe knew. Tears were streaming down Christina's face as the sun set toward the western horizon, his son James's arms around both their legs. They had worked out their differences and had moved in together then, had married. The arguments were long gone, and their home was filled with love. Billie pushed the thoughts aside to concentrate on why he was here. He put a few more small branches on the fire, which was close to the front flap of his small tent. He climbed in and began studying the maps yet again, enjoying the warmth. Over and over, he scanned them and began to recognize more details between the comparison. Suddenly, he felt sure he had found the pool.

He turned out the lantern and drifted into a restful sleep, tired from the long day of climbing along the canyon walls. The sounds of a bull elk awoke him, the tint of the sun just bleaching the eastern horizon directly in front of him. Billie slowly stretched as he became more alert. Birds and other animals had come to life in a symphony of sound all around him. He heard a rock tumble not far away. Looking in the direction, a small herd of deer were moving down toward the valley, likely out of the high country before the next heavy snow trapped them. Most of their food sources were now gone at the higher elevations. He wished that people were as smart. He started a fire, putting several limbs on it to get it going so he could warm up. His teeth were already beginning to chatter. The fire was roaring as he made coffee in a metal can and fried bacon. The bacon had almost finished when he put in a couple of eggs and scrambled them. From his pack, he pulled the last two slices of bread and placed the eggs and bacon between them. Slowly he ate his sandwich and sipped his coffee, enjoying the rays of the early morning sun that bathed his face.

He made sure his pack was ready as he finished his coffee and sandwich for the arduous climb down the wall of the finger canyon. It would take him about two hours to reach what he thought was the general location of the pool. Studying his maps once more, he felt more certain than ever that this would be the day. Billie pulled the bundle from his pack and carefully unwrapped it making sure the three artifacts and two pieces of wood inside were not touching. He must be careful not the let the new roots touch any of the current bundle, which one of the new roots would complete. He rewrapped the bundle and put it into its sealed metal container before he began his trek downslope.

Walking about one quarter mile, he picked up a little used game trail that took him over a ridge where he cut across the

James Tindall

end of another small canyon and then, walked about two miles to the spot he had marked on his map. Using his compass as a straight line, he triangulated the landmarks around him and began to wait. It would be about an hour before the sun would be in a position for its rays to reveal the pool if he were indeed in the correct spot. As he waited, he used his compact binoculars to scan the valley below. To the north on his left that he couldn't see was Missoula, Montana where he hoped to leave from tomorrow. Off to his right were some small towns and scattered farms and ranches. The valley went as far down as he could see before bending left and out of site behind mountain ridges. In the distance he could hear elk bugling, a light breeze bringing the sound up from the valley floor. The blue sky was cloudless as he took in the awe-inspiring view. Bright yellows and oranges of aspens and other deciduous trees were mixed among the green of the pine forests and pastures of farms surrounded by peaks capped with pure white snow. The temperature slowly rose as he continued to take in the beauty of this pristine forest. Able to keep the sun in his face, its warmth flooded over him. Glancing at his watch, the hour had passed quickly.

Billie turned back so that he was facing in a northwest direction and began scanning the area where he believed the pool would be. It was about three to four hundred yards away and he was about one hundred feet above the pool's elevation. There were no game or other trails in this area of the forest. It was so rugged even staunch hikers and climbers wouldn't likely venture into it. All the deciduous shrubs and trees had already lost their leaves, which lay scattered on the ground, some frozen in brown layers within the shadows of the trunks from whose branches they had fallen. He had been panning the landscape for about thirty minutes when he caught a glint. Like a small shiny object. Focusing his binoculars more carefully, he could see the base of a large shrub surrounded by several others, as well as a few adjoining pines. Looking through their bases where all the branches joined, he could see several glints then, between a shrub on the far right and the base of the tree next to it, the pool was barely visible. His heart began beating faster as he looked closely at the pattern of trees surrounding the pool to make sure he could identify it when he got closer. He stood to get a better look and the pool was no longer visible. Stooping once more, he could see it again.

"Small wonder no one else had ever found it," he murmured.

Billie got to his feet, gauged the best path to the pool and hurried as fast as he could over the rock strewn, tree thick forest. Nearing the pool, he had to drop about forty feet in elevation and then, climb back up. He recognized the shrubs near the top of the climb instantly. Carefully making his way through them, he discovered a small pool about fifteen feet across. The plants the Medicine Man had described grew profusely around the perimeter of the entire pool and several feet into it. They were surrounded by low growing shrub oak giving way to ponderosa and lodgepole pine whose height prevented view of the pool from the ridgeline above. Billie wasn't a gardener, but realized the pool received about five hours of sunlight each day, which was plenty for most plants to thrive.

He knelt and put his hands into the crystal-clear water. Anticipating it to be very cold, he was surprised to find it warm to the touch. Pushing his hand further down into the water it became warmer with depth. "Surely, this was not a hot spring," he thought. On the far side, directly across from him, a steady stream of bubbles reached the surface, making a slight gurgling sound; it was. Making his way around to them, he knelt and smelled the bubbles as they burst. There was an almost undetectable odor of sulfur yet there was no pale-yellow color on any of the surrounding rocks. Billie knew there were always fault lines along mountain ranges, perhaps far below was a fissure with molten lava that allowed the heat to generate slowly toward the surface. "Anyway, time to quit playing geologist and botanist," he mused. For whatever reason, the pool was warm throughout the year and sustained the plant whose roots he was here to collect. He retraced his steps back to the opposite side of the pool from whence he came and carefully began to uncover the roots of one of the plants. The Medicine Man called the plant *oshasha* and said it meant love healing. Billie had did some research and found no naming or history of it. He took out a small gardening spade from his pack and slowly began to remove the rocky soil from around the base of one of the plants. It took only a couple of minutes to discover the nodules the Medicine Man had told him to look for. They resembled peanuts but were about three to four times longer and felt more like a light cork wood. He took out his knife and collected three of the nodules, each from a different plant and meticulously recovered each plant, dumping a few handfuls of water around the area he had dug so that the soil was formed again around the roots.

Next, he washed the three nodules in the pool as he had been instructed and let them set for a half hour before he dried them further and then, placed them in direct sunlight. As the nodules dried, Billie stood and gazed about his surroundings. He couldn't believe he had found the plants and felt lucky it had only taken fourteen days. He relaxed as he sat down, laid back on a rock and soaked in the sun. His goal accomplished; he was pleased with himself.

His thoughts drifted back to a phone call he had received a couple of weeks before.

"Are you Billie Panther?" the voice asked.

"Yes, how can I help you?"

"You can help me by dying. You cost me a great deal of money because of the landfill fiasco. I will be paid whether by your life or another!"

The phone slammed down on the other end, the memory jolting Billie out of his thoughts. He looked at his watch. Time to collect the roots and head back to camp. He looked at them;

they appeared well dried according to his instructions so, he placed them into a small tin. In no time he had the root portions in his backpack and was on his way to camp. Thoughts of the phone call nagged at him. "Wasn't it always the case?" Billie thought. "Someone else had made the mess and yet he was blamed for the results. It seemed to be a narcissistic trend in society anymore. They muck it up and you pay! The voice sounded eerily calm and ominous." Because of the call, he had taken extra security precautions for him and his family.

Thoughts of the call subsided as he arrived at camp, uncovered the live coals in his firepit and stacked on more wood. The sun was just setting as he took the roots from his pack, placing the tin about two feet from the fire to slowly dry the roots over a two-hour period. He was doing everything according to the Medicine Man's instructions. While the roots dried, he took out both the penciled map and the detailed map and tossed them onto the fire. They were completely burned and had turned to ash, which Billie broke up with a stick as he stirred the fire. He no longer needed them, and it would prevent anyone from finding the location of the *oshasha*; it must remain protected. He made cornmeal hoecakes and bacon along with coffee and sat cross-legged in front of the fire, feeling content about finding and collecting the roots. With them, he would be able to complete transparency training and help his people further. He had no idea it would be in ways he could not yet imagine. Billie slowly drifted to sleep as the roaring fire turned to embers. He was awakened by a stiff wind coming from the north. Crawling into his small tent, he took out his light and opened his bundle then, lay the newly collected roots next to those inside. He kept peering at them as if something would happen. Sleep got the better of him as he turned off his light and again lay his head down.

As he slept, thoughts of the phone call kept recurring. The sound of the receiver slamming down haunting him as he began to realize it must have been a pay phone. He could detect a faint bell, like a ships bell in the background. While sleeping, he tossed and turned, going in and out of a tortuous sleep. In doing so, the bundle, along with the three new roots mixed and began to touch. A huge lightning bolt striking a nearby tree, followed by clap of thunder brought him instantly to a sitting position. The pieces in the bundle had merged and a storm of epic proportions was brewing. Lightning strikes were occurring across the entire valley, unrelenting as a driving rain began, which quickly turned to snow. There were so many lightning strikes the landscape was bright as midday.

Ominous black clouds filled the sky. The lightning strikes becoming so numerous that a blue flame began to dance across the ground as the snow changed back to a horizontal rain driven by a fifty mile per hour winds. Instantly Billie realized what was happening. He had forgotten to put his bundle away and all the parts of it had merged, electrical spikes jumping from it. Rapidly, he took two small sticks and began prying the pieces apart. Occasionally he was shocked by the charges emanating from the pieces. Blue flame on the ground had restarted his fire, as tree after tree was split by lightening. It took him a couple of minutes to separate the pieces. Almost the instant he separated the last piece, the clouds and lightening dispersed and a bright moonlit sky returned. He couldn't believe he had forgotten about the bundle pieces touching. Billie carefully rewrapped the bundle and stored everything back in his pack. Morning found him erasing any trace of having been there before he headed toward the main trail.

L i Na Liu stepped off the elevator and entered Don Cilatro's outer office. Sally was right behind her.
"Come in Li Na," Cilatro said. "It's a pleasure to see you again. Sally make sure we're not disturbed. Oh, and let Morgan in when he arrives."
"Yes sir."

When Cilatro closed the door, he wasted no time getting down to business.

"I gather you have spoken to our friends in Hong Kong?" Cilatro asked.

"Yes," Li Na said. "They are willing to fund the remainder of the money. Per our calculations, the landfill will be capable of generating 300,000 megawatt hours (MWh), which is substantial. The approximate value is $33 million in revenue annually."

Cilatro had been eyeing her as she spoke. One thing he knew was that she was as deadly as she was beautiful. Her name meant delicate, logic, and destroy, in that order – Li, Na, Liu.

"That's quite a sum and legal," Cilatro said. "What are your employers demands?"

"Given we will put up 60 percent of the funds, they want a proportional return. The revenues should pay the construction costs off the first year and after that, we split the proceeds. This means that no party pulls profits until the plant is paid off."

"That's a hard bargain given the construction costs," Cilatro replied. "Also, we will need to pay a portion to the tribe. I've been thinking ten percent, but they may want more. Are you willing to budge any on that?"

"Because this is a joint venture and legal, our intent is to double production or more, up to $70 million per year," Li Na said. "After the first phase, we begin construction enlargement and pay off build costs over the next ten years for the second phase. We will work up the numbers on that. We believe that you should give up seven percent and we will be willing to cough up another five percent."

"Hmmmm," Cilatro mused, realizing there was no flexibility, but that was the cost of getting into bed with a viper. "That is doable, if we can keep their expectations down."

"The landfill is back under their control," Li Na said, staring into Cilatro's eyes. "They will get all the funds from that and since we are fronting all power plant construction costs, I think it's a gift."

"Agreed," Cilatro said. "I'm amenable and ...."

Sally interrupted with a knock on the door, letting Morgan pass.

"Thanks Sally," Cilatro said. "Morgan, good to see you. This is Li Na Liu from Hong Kong, working with our colleagues there."

"So nice to meet you," Morgan said, extending his hand as they shook.

The stare he received back from her tiger-brown eyes was unnerving. Instantly he knew he must stay on his toes. He took a seat beside Cilatro.

Morgan Stanton was a well-dressed man in his late forties, fit, broad shouldered, and six feet in height. He was college educated and a formidable fighter. A handsome man with dark hair and blue eyes. And yet, he could move about unnoticed in a crowd or on the street, which was often needed in his ling of work. He was Cilatro's fix-it man. If something went wrong or needed to be done, he got the call. Unlike other thugs in the organization, Morgan was intelligent and a strategist. He thought through every aspect before making a move.

"We were just going over the figures," Cilatro said. "I see nothing we cannot live with. This brings us to you. We need you to set up a meeting with the tribal President as soon as you can."

"This must go unnoticed," Li Na said icily. "My employer will not tolerate the same mistakes as before."

"The problem we have is that we are being watched," Morgan said. "I have anticipated your needs and tentatively set up the meeting in four days. In case you haven't noticed, there are feds across the street in their car making notes. The landfill fiasco is at the top of their list. They are convinced you had something to do with it."

"What are you suggesting?" Cilatro asked.

"The meeting will be offshore in the speed yacht we have. I've arranged for it to station beyond the 12-mile limit so it will be in international waters. As you recall, it can reach seventy knots. I've ensured the boat cannot be traced back to us through an offshore firm serving as a rental agency. It will be rented to a friend of ours that has no known ties to anything remotely related to our interests. He will be on board pretending to fish should be we stopped. I've kept him clean for a reason."

"That sounds wise," Li Na said. "How do you propose getting me and Don Cilatro to the boat for the meeting?"

"The problem is not you; it is Cilatro. I have arranged two ways. First, the President will be riding in our speed boat, the cigarette boat. It can do 100 miles per hour. So, even cruising at lower speed, it'll reach the yacht in fifteen minutes, depending on wave conditions. However, we will slow down and take countermeasures to determine if it's being followed. We may switch boats a few times to make sure. Second, Don and you will be flown by helicopter from an obscure location staying below radar detection levels to the meeting. Once all are present, you'll discuss what you need to and leave the same way. Excepting you, Li Na."

"Why?" she asked.

"It would not be good for any of you to be stopped together," Morgan continued. "Thus, you will remain on board the yacht until being dropped off at an intermediate location or onto another speed boat."

"That sounds like a lot of effort for a meeting," Cilatro said.

"Given the nature of what has happened, my employers would expect nothing less," Li Na said. "Thank you, Morgan, it sounds a bit elaborate, but well thought out."

"You are welcome," Morgan said. "However, the problem we have is getting Don to the meeting from here. Everywhere he goes he's being watched. So, tomorrow, you'll be driven around until we are sure there are no tails, and you'll go down in our tour bus to Miami. It's about a twenty-hour drive; there will be two drivers taking turns. They will obey all traffic laws so that no suspicion is aroused. You can work from the bus doing whatever you need. I'll be with you to further ensure no mishaps."

"Alright, I guess that takes care of the basics," Cilatro said. "Figure out a place for us to rendezvous in Miami before the meeting. We will go over numbers again and fine tune the details. Li Na, Sally has arranged a taxi for you back to your hotel."

"Very well. I have already checked out and the bellman is holding my bag. I checked into another hotel and have a back way out. The feds will run into a dead end. Before I leave, I wanted to remind you of the other project. We'll discuss the strategy later."

Morgan was carefully watching her. He began to realize how cunning and ruthless she was. There would be absolutely no trust with her. He visualized making love to her but knew instantly that if it were necessary, she would do it for fun and then kill him. Best to give her a wide berth.

"It's settled then," Cilatro said. "Our next meeting will be in Miami. This information goes no further."

The day promised to be awfully long and tiring. The tribal President stood, staring out his office window, watching white egrets on the lawn. It had just rained heavily, and they were feeding on grubs, worms and other prey escaping the waterlogged soil. He was thinking about the five meetings he would have that day. One of them was with the tribal attorney to discuss the landfill issues. A feeling of dread crept over him. He didn't think that anyone could have implicated him but there was always the chance. He sighed heavily as the phone rang, wondering what now?

"President Osceola. How may I help you?"

"President," Morgan said. "It's good to hear your voice. We need to have the meeting as scheduled in three days. Is that going to be a problem?"

"No, I have it on my calendar," President Osceola said. "Let me know the location and I'll be there."

"Due to the circumstances, I'll have someone discreetly pick you up," Morgan replied. "You understand, and of course we will reimburse you for your time and expertise, the usual amount."

"I understand. Call me with the time and location for pickup."

"I will let you know in two days," Morgan said. "And by the way, this is completely legit, but no need to tell anyone at this point. If you can help us pull it off, you will be well rewarded."

"Understood."

The President grinned at the thought of another $10k coming his way for a meeting. Although legitimate, he needed to make certain that no one saw or even thought he was meeting with Don Cilatro and his people. Being the employer of the demised Paul Lorio there would be too much perception of another project going bad. He remembered the earlier discussion of the power plant before the landfill was constructed. He wondered who Cilatro had found to front the rest of the money? It didn't matter because it would be a straightforward business deal excepting his under the table cut. His day had just gotten a little brighter.

Christina was so excited at Billie's return. They had not been apart for more than a day or two since they had gotten married and she had missed him terribly, especially not being able to contact him by phone. James had missed him too, crying for joy when he walked in the door. They had made sweet love most of the night and finally fell asleep — exhausted and content. Even now, as the airboat slid across the sawgrass, she couldn't keep her eyes off his handsome face and flashing smile that always put everyone at ease. Billie slowed the boat at they neared their favorite fishing spot that he had discovered one day after training with the Medicine Man. It was encircled by cypress heads except for a narrow passageway where lily pads floated on top of the water. These always signified deeper water than found in surrounding areas of the swamp. Most people did not know that the lily leaf does not really float but each leaf or lily pad is attached to a system of stems and tubes. The tubes are connected to openings called stomas in the top of the leaves and help the lily pad float and to collect oxygen. The oxygen is transferred to the water lily's stem and down to the plant's roots, carrying up to almost three quarts of air each day. Their white and yellow flowers bloom profusely through the summer adding charm and beauty to the swamp. They also serve to absorb harmful chemicals in the water and often form a natural riparian zone.

Billie had noticed the small channel surrounded by bromeliad, called air plants by the locals, and draping Spanish moss and had gingerly guided his airboat through it, discovering that the channel opened into a five-acre pond filled with lily pads. The pond was about six to eight feet deep with some areas much deeper. He could not believe all the fish he had seen — brim, speckled perch, small-mouth bass, and others. He assumed the many species had migrated during the wet season and made the pond their home. The day he discovered it he had sat for several hours on his boat watching fish jump while alligators lay in the sun around the edge and otters played in water that was almost clear compared to other areas of the Glades. The place was a cornucopia of fish and wildlife, including a lone panther.

"Let's go over there," Christina said, pointing.

"Yeah," James said, beaming from ear to ear.

Billie steered the boat and slowly slid around the pond until he was on the west side, about one third of the way into the deepest part. He stopped and threw his small anchor over the side so they wouldn't drift.

"This is going to be great," Billie said. "Let's bait our hooks."

Christina and Billie helped put a worm on the hook of James's cane pole.

"Yuck," James said. "The worm guts are squishing out."

"That's okay," Billie said. "It's supposed to do that so the fish will be attracted to it."

"Why?" James asked. "Can they smell?"

"Hmmmm," Billie murmured. "I don't really know, but it doesn't matter because they like to see the worm squirm."

Billie was smiling at Christina as she looked at him askance, nodding her head.

"Why don't we use our rods and reels?" James asked. "They are easier to work with."

"Yes, they are," Christina said. "But if you cast out and reel back in, the hook will get stuck on the lily pads and if a fish bites it and runs, you'll also get hung on the pads. Using a pole, you can place the hook and bobber directly between the pads and lift it straight up, so you don't get hung up."

"Okay," James said glumly, not seeming convinced.

In just a few minutes, all three had baited their hooks and dropped them between the pads surrounding the boat, the red and white bobbers floating serenely on the surface.

Five minutes passed and James yelled, "Yay, I caught one." Christina held out a small hand net to catch it and get it into the boat. It was a nice sized brim, which they stuck into a cooler. In no time, James had put another worm on his hook and lowered it and the bobber back into the water, giggling and happy, his face glowing. Christina and Billie watched him for a moment, thankful for the smiles and laughter after what they had recently been through.

"What do you think about losing your job?" Christina asked.

"It's been eating at me for the past few weeks," Billie replied. "I want to help our people, but I also need to work."

"You were saying you had an offer," Christina said. "I'm not sure you should take it."

"Yes," Billie said. "It's a good offer from the Water Management District. I asked them to let me think about it for a few days."

"I've heard they're a good group to work for," Christina responded. "But how are you going to help our people if you're working off the reservation?"

"That's just it," Billie said forlornly, staring at his bobber. "There won't be much I can do except vote in tribal meetings and do volunteer work."

"I have the pulse of the community," Christina said. "Everyone knows that what happened was not your fault. They also know if you had not acted as fast as you did, some of our children would be dead. And that you have and always will have their best interests at heart. Although the council stripped you of the councilman position at the request of the President, the tribe will need to vote for the new councilman or councilwoman to replace you."

"True," Billie said. "But I will not be in the group."

"That's not true," Christina said. "This is why I do not want you to apply for jobs off the reservation. Although the water group would be lucky to have you, there is something you need to know."

"What's that?" Billie asked.

"I think the President doesn't want you there because he envy's you and is afraid you'll displace him. I wasn't sure of it myself and so talked to the tribal attorney Sam Longfellow about the entire council matter. It's up to the people, not the President or council."

"What do you mean?" Billie asked.

"It's simple," Christina said. "The rules state tribal members select the councilman or woman from each reservation. They have sixty days to elect one from among those who put their name in; the council could also come back before then and reinstate you saying they had acted hastily or for any number of other reasons. Either way, you need to put your name in because my sources say if you do, you'll win. Everyone but the President is behind you Billie. You can win and stay in a position to help our people. He certainly isn't."

"Sam told you all this?" Billie queried. "It seems in opposition to tribal government issues."

"It is not Billie," Christina said. "I'm telling you that the rules and policies do not prohibit it. Of course, the minute you announce your candidacy the President will likely bring all his powers against you to keep you from winning, but the people are on your side. Furthermore, we're in a good position, and I make enough for us to get by until things work themselves out one way or the other."

"Hmmmm," Billie mused. "I'd need to hastily put things together because the election is only two months away."

Billie had no idea he could run again. His heart began to beat faster as he quickly devised a strategy on how to get his name on the ballot and convince tribal members to vote for him. His thoughts ran to a counter strategy on what the President would throw in front of him as a stumbling block and was in a deep trance when an excited James caught a speckled perch and Christina helped him land it. The President would blame the entire landfill incident on him, but it was the President that signed off on it through Solomon's advice because Solomon, like Billie, understood that it would be good for the people and had put political differences aside to make it happen. There was sufficient ammunition already to go against the will of the President.

President Billy Osceola had left his office and headed south on I-95. As he came to the outskirts of Miami, he began taking side streets, wandering in different directions and even parking in three separate locations to ensure he was not being followed. About an hour later, he pulled into the parking area on the north side of Simpson Park. Only a few cars being present, he chose an isolated area away from them on the north side. He was contemplating the amount of money he would ask for to make this deal go through. Although legitimate, the characters were a bit shady, even for his liking. More importantly, he knew as well as they did that without his buy in, the power plant would be a no go. "I'll wait for them to make an offer first. If it's to my liking I will not push them." He sat and waited and began sweating so cranked the car and ran the air conditioning as he watched people walk in and out of the park, cars also coming and going. Long shadows cast their forms across the parking lot as the sun set. He had been waiting for over two hours. Although he knew the meeting was clandestine, the wait was getting to be a bit much. He rolled down the window of his car and lit a cigarette, blowing soft plumes of smoke into the dark night. It was 8:00 pm when a car pulled next to him. The driver got out and walked over.

"We are ready sir," the man said politely. "Please get into the back of my car and I will take you to the rendezvous."

The President did as he was instructed. The driver closed his door and headed northwest on SW 15th Road through Triangle Park then, up SW 5th Avenue and right onto highway 41, merging back onto I-95 heading north. They crossed the Miami River and after a couple of miles, the driver began taking random backstreets and headed toward the Atlantic, picking up Biscayne Boulevard heading north, pulling up at Bayfront Park Path.

"It is time for you to get out sir," the driver said quietly. Follow that path to the fountain. Look for a man in a red shirt."

The President exited the vehicle as it slid into the darkness. There were a couple of people here and there as he headed toward the shore. He had walked about six hundred feet and was at the back of the fountain when he saw the person he was supposed to meet, the man walked straight to him.

"I'm Blake, go to that boat and get in," he said, pointing.

A cigarette boat had pulled up to the rocks just beyond the

fountain, idling its engines, barely audible from the distance. It was a mere twenty-five yards away. As they were about to get in, a driver at the wheel, a man sauntered toward them from the fountain area.

"Say, what are you guys doing here with that boat?" he asked. "Got a light?"

"Sure thing," Blake said, looking around.

Without hesitation, Blake drove a six-inch blade under the man's chin and up into his skull. The President looked on, aghast.

"What did you do that for?" Billy asked.

"We can have no witnesses say anything about what they saw. Cops are too good at linking things together anymore."

"You've implemented me in a murder," Billy said.

"So, I have," Blake responded calmly. "Time to go, move quickly."

The two jumped aboard as the driver gently increased the rpm's and began slipping past Dodge Island on the north side and finally past Fisher's Island beyond into the Atlantic. The boat quickly disappeared into the darkness cruising about eighty miles per hour. Here and there were lights from other boats as they began a meandering course north, then south, back, and forth. The driver finally headed out to sea, keeping an eye on his GPS. The President estimated the boat was doing about ninety having picked up speed as it continued its course, bouncing across the waves as the mist from the tops flew skyward and then, descended on them, chilling them due to the speed. Blake was using binoculars to scan the dark waters all around them to make sure they were not being followed. The lights along the shore behind disappeared with only a glow in the sky to signify the presence of Miami. After about half an hour, the boat decreased its speed, continuing its back-and-forth maneuvers then, slowly headed further out into the ocean. The driver had long ago cut the lights. Some distance away, Billy could see lights from a larger vessel, which they headed for.

The cigarette boat pulled up next to the yacht on the starboard side. The crew lowered a ladder and motioned the President to climb aboard. Apprehensive, he slowly climbed the ladder to the deck as the boat took off. Once aboard, a crewman escorted him to the main salon. He was flabbergasted by the opulence of the room before him. Not being an expert, he had glanced from bow to stern as he had stepped onto the deck. This was one of those mega yachts he had read about in the boating magazines in his office. It was at least two hundred feet long and looked like it had been designed for speed. Looking at the salon before him, he could see the foredeck stretching toward the bow. It was very long with no obstacles and could be used for various purposes, including landing a helicopter, which was just arriving.

"Wait here for the others," the crewman said. "Make yourself at home. Have a drink or snack, whatever you'd like."

"Can I ask you a question?" the President asked.

"Certainly," the crewman replied.

"How big and fast is this boat or ship?"

"We prefer to call it a yacht," the crewman said. "It's 220 feet long and we've had it up to 64 knots."

"That's incredible for such a large boat," the President said. "Thank you."

The crewman nodded as he walked away. The President began to survey the room more carefully. It had coffered ceilings that were polished, along with the walls. He wasn't certain but it looked like teak wood. There was a built-in bookshelf, seating area with a large corner sectioned sofa, seating area with a round table and white tufted chairs, a bar, and what appeared to be a gaming area. He was in awe. His assessment was quickly interrupted.

"Quite a setup, isn't it," Morgan stated, entering the room.

"It certainly is," the President responded. "I'm impressed."

"Yes, it never ceases to amaze me," Morgan said. "Can I get you a drink?"

"Sure, how about a margarita on the rocks?"

"No problem."

They both heard the helicopter lift off and watched it through the front salon windows.

"The others will be here momentarily," Morgan said. "I'll make them drinks too."

No sooner than he had verbalized his statement than in walked Li Na and Don Cilatro. Both were immaculately dressed. Cilatro wore light, khaki-colored pants, white silk shirt, and a blue blazer with gold buttons. He tossed his white hat onto one of the sofas, which exposed the gold watch he was wearing. Directly behind him was Li Na dressed simply in blue jeans and a long-sleeved tan blouse. She was ravishing, neither Morgan nor the President could keep their eyes off her until she looked at them. Her gaze cold as ice and aloof, as if they didn't exist. Instantly they were uncomfortable. Morgan had finished making drinks, knowing what each preferred and brought them on a tray, sitting it down as they shook hands and introduced themselves.

It's good to see you again President," Don Cilatro said. "Let's get directly to the point. You will remember that when the landfill was put in that there were insufficient funds to couple it with an electric generating methane plant. We now have the necessary capitol with our partner based out of Hong Kong."

"Yes, Don," the President responded. "But, given the way things worked out, we thought it best not to pursue the venture at that time."

"Agreed," Cilatro said. "This brings up the split. We have lost a great deal of money in this endeavor because of Paul. Now, we need to make things straight. You know who we are and our capabilities. What are your thoughts?"

"Having been kept apprised of the investigation and pending

charges, it appears law enforcement has an iron-clad case against all those at the landfill. This includes that lady working with Paul, Ms. Phenning I believe, and as a result they face serious jail time. Given what has happened, you will need to keep not a low, but an invisible profile. Also, the tribal attorney has informed me that the tribe now completely owns the landfill outright due to breach of contract. Because of this, I am not sure how to make up for lost revenue to you on that end. I will not be able to shift funds for payment without notice."

"We anticipated this," Li Na broke in. "Mr. Cilatro and his group would like something in return for their loss. Having discussed it as partners, we feel that the best way to ensure pay back, since they fronted the money and because we are both fronting the money for the power plant, that we get it in a percentage."

The President looked Li Na directly in the eyes. This time he did not flinch. She was cold, her voice level. He perceived she had a set figure or percentage in mind and would be unwavering in demanding it.

"I can support this, but given recent events, tribal members will want to make sure the business is legitimate, and that the tribe gets a fair share. I have a figure in mind, but you won't like it," the President said.

"Before it is set in concrete, let us tell you what we're going to do," Cilatro said. "If I'm not clear, Li Na will fill in the blanks. First, we are putting up all the funds. Our group will put up forty percent and Li Na's group will put up sixty percent. There will be no funds required from the tribe. We foot the entire bill from start to finish."

"That sounds very good," the President said, already feeling better about the deal.

"Also," Li Na began. "We are going to pay for the initial build outright. Once the plant is in, we will double the output, but the second build phase will be disbursed yearly until it is paid in full. This means that you'll get the full percent on net for phase one each year and once the second phase is complete, construction costs for that phase and payback for costs will be lessened until the second phase is also paid in full."

"That makes sense," the President said.

"One more item," Cilatro said. "The groups funding the project will be completely legitimate and will hold up under scrutiny, but we will be behind them. However, there will be no links back to us. Does that sound acceptable?"

"Certainly," the President replied. "As long as there are no ties to the original group, I can get it passed in council and through tribal approval."

"The big question is how much do you want for the tribe? Li Na asked, leveling her cold gaze on him.

"Originally I had thought eighteen percent," the President said. "Now, that may be somewhat high. I will be under scrutiny if I go too low in presenting the deal. I believe fourteen percent may be more appropriate."

Li Na and Cilatro stared at him, quiet. He could tell they were thinking. They did not speak; the silence began to grow uncomfortable.

"That seems a bit stiff," Morgan said, diving into the middle of the conversation. "Mr. President think of it this way. The tribe will get all the landfill jobs back, as well as many more positions at the power plant. And you do not need to put up one dime for a business that will be completely legitimate garnering substantial revenues for the tribe. How can you help us here?"

Morgan's comments broke the ice enough for Cilatro to gather his composure as he spoke confidently.

"Billy," Cilatro began. "We've discussed business issues before and we have always reached an agreement. I believe we can reach an agreement now. I want you to remember that the percentage given back to the tribe is coming from each of the partners shares, which means we get considerably less."

"Would you mind if I walked out on the deck for a moment to

think?" the President asked.

"Not at all," Cilatro said, Morgan and Li Na nodding affirmatively.

The cool ocean breeze hit him in the face as he closed the door, stepping onto the deck. This was a great opportunity for him, but he knew the figure he presented was not one they would consider. A compromise was necessary. If he could pull in enough of a nest egg for himself, he could go lower without raising the eyebrows of the tribal council and members. Looking through the salon windows, he noticed the three others were likely discussing options.

"It's time he thought."

"I propose giving him a nest egg and then a percentage," Li Na said, watching him through the window. He's politically savvy and we can make millions if he will go along. After all, he is the only one that can make it happen. Since we do not need to pay for the land, but only lease it, that will be a huge dividend in the end."

"What do you think Morgan?" Cilatro asked.

"I am not sure what you would propose as a cash bonus for him once the tribe passes the resolution, assuming they do," Morgan said. "I would offer a lower percentage, say 9.5 percent and watch his reaction."

"Excellent idea," Li Na said in approval. "Let's offer that and Don, if our group fronted him $400,000, could you match with another say, $350,000?"

"It's a little steeper than I wanted to go," Cilatro said. "But yes. It'll come out in the wash long term anyway."

"Good, let's spring the initial percentage Morgan suggested and add a potential large bonus without telling him up front," Li Na said. "Shish, here is comes."

"I have been thinking what the council and tribal members would think appropriate for the venture," the President said. "I'm not sure I can go much lower."

Reading the reaction in their eyes, he knew that fourteen

percent was too much. But they would counter, there was too much to lose for them. Li Na was staring at him, her gaze colder than before, a kill look. Billy swallowed briefly.

"If I may," Cilatro began. "We were thinking a bit lower due to the fact we are taking all the risk and paying all costs. The three of us have gone over the figures again. Somehow, we need to come to agreement. Morgan has been doing a lot of analysis on the project and has suggested a percentage and a private stipend to you once the resolution is passed."

"What's your number?" the President asked, hoping it was better than anticipated.

"We are thinking 9.5 percent for the tribe," Li Na said, scrutinizing his face. It was poker, no sign of good or bad. "Also, we were thinking of a $300,000 stipend for you at passing.

"Interesting," the President mused. "I won't be President forever and meanwhile; your groups will be raking in the dough from my efforts for a long time. You need to do better."

"Let's adjust upward," Morgan said. "We all know you are key to this approval. I suggest, 10.5 percent and $500,000."

"Let me propose a counter," the President said, knowing they could go higher having been in this chair many times before. "I suggest eleven percent and $650,000."

The other three stared at him. Li Na had given a secretive thumbs up to Cilatro and imperceptible nod to Morgan. They had shaved 1.5 percent off the maximum offer for the tribe and $100,000 in stipend to the President. A good deal for all.

"Mr. President," Cilatro said. "You drive a hard bargain. We can all live with that. Your stipend will be transferred to your choice of banks or given in cash by end of business day the resolution passes."

The group stood, shaking hands, smiling. They were relieved. The President had already earmarked his money, along with several million more he had stashed for a private residence far from the reservation.

Realizing it could all blow up in his face, he needed a scapegoat to pin things on if it did. He knew the perfect candidate.

Chapter 2

Sawgrass scraped the sides of Billie's airboat as he slid as quietly as he could through the vast expanse of swamp. He was taking the roots he had collected to the Medicine Man who he hoped would be happy to see him. It was early morning as he sped across the marshes, veered near hammocks, and enjoyed the vast array of wildlife — Anhinga birds, turkeys, alligators, deer, wild pig, an eagle here and there, large flocks of egrets, cottonmouth moccasins, quail, otters, and more. He never got over how diverse the swamp was and how deadly it could be. His thoughts drifted to the day he had barely managed to overcome his adversary Paul Lorio and how the Medicine Man and several warriors were watching. He had learned a lot about himself that day. More importantly, he realized that the Medicine Man could see for at least a short period into the future. He knew what the outcome would be, and Billie wondered if it was because of his abilities with the transparency. The Medicine Man was going to show him how to do it well but had admonished him that the true secrets of the ceremony would not be forthcoming for some time. It was a matter of complete trust and honesty. He had said that the Great Spirit would tell him when those things should be shown. The Medicine Man had told him to get his affairs in order because he would be in another dimension for more than one or two days. He had become apprehensive.

Billie pulled his airboat up onto the edge of the hammock where the Medicine Man stayed. He had tried to explain what one of these small islands were to some visitors a few weeks back.

"Essentially," he said. "A hammock forms a sort of ecological island in the swamp, which biologists call a contrasting ecosystem. Hammocks are elevated islands or areas within the surrounding sawgrass. But the elevation may only be a few inches above the water level in the Glades. While many of these treed islands are populated by hardwoods, almost as many are populated by palm trees as well. They serve as a haven for deer, wild pig, and other wildlife."

The tourists to the swamp safari had finally understood. Billie was quickly brought out of his thoughts.

"The Medicine Man is waiting Panther," the warrior said.

Billie looked up to see two muscular warriors directing him down the path in front of the boat. As always, no one would gain audience without being admitted by these two men. They were not overly friendly, but not unfriendly, rather professionally courteous. Billie followed the lead warrior into the hammock as the second warrior walked behind him. He could smell the mustiness of the swamp as he walked along the meandering path. Every thirty yards or so they would pass another warrior standing stoically as sentinels, barely seen seeing that they blended into their surroundings. Although Billie had been here often, these warriors who served the Medicine Man always impressed him.

They had been walking through cabbage palms that cast dark shadows on the Spanish moss hanging from hardwoods mixed among them. The dark shadows disappeared as they entered a small pine and palmetto flat. Directly in front of them were several small chickees set in a shallow triangle several small fires, mostly embers, burning between. The Medicine Man motioned the warriors away. They moved to the edges of the flat into the tree line. Barely discernable, they turned, looking outwardly for potential dangers.

"Sit, young warrior," Medicine Man said. "Did you bring what I sent you to collect?"

"Yes," Billie said, retrieving the roots from a small possibles bag hung over his shoulder. "Here they are, all of them."

He held out his hand, which contained a red bandana wrapped around the roots.

"Did you have any trouble finding them?" the Medicine Man asked as he laid the bandana on the ground and gently peeled back the edges to reveal the roots.

"It took me two weeks," Billie replied. "I narrowed it down from the hand sketch you gave me as I kept comparing that to a professional quadrangle map. It was as you told me. Honestly, I don't know how anyone could find the place without directions. Even the location prohibits accidentally stumbling upon it."

"And the maps?"

"Burned to ashes and stirred into indiscernible pieces; also, as you instructed."

The Medicine Man, leaning forward, peered into Billie's eyes, their faces only inches apart. His once dark brown eyes, now a hazel gray as he stared without blinking, were piercing Billie's soul to its center.

"You are an honorable man, Billie. Our tribe is better for you being here."

"Thank you," Billie said. "But I fear my ability to help the people has diminished since I lost my council seat."

Seconds felt like hours as the Medicine Man gazed across the palmetto flat, into the dark shadows of the cabbage palms. He glanced further across the palmettos as a quail called and then back at Billie.

"Do not let such things worry you. You will be reinstated. I have seen it."

"But how?" Billie asked. "The council voted."

"There is one among them who will convince them. But take care my young warrior, it is not what it seems. Be observant less the reappointment be like an albatross around your neck. The burden is heavy and incessant, and, in the end, he will answer for it. But enough of such talk. Today is a great day for you because you will walk among the spirits of yesterday. Where is your bundle?"

"Here," Billie said as he took it from his bag and laid it beside the other.

The Medicine Man sorted through the bundle and gently took the smallest root from the several and placed it at the end of the other artifacts of Billie's bundle.

"This is the order you should always have them in young warrior. I gave you the smallest root because your spirit is strong. It is the strongest in the tribe and always will be if you remain a man of honor and of your word. Observe."

The Medicine Man laid the roots on a light-colored piece of buckskin in a short row.

"The first is abalone shell, it represents water. This second piece is the fossil of a feather, which represents the wind. The third piece is the iron medallion you have always treasured. You do not remember it, but I gave it to you when you were but a young boy of eight; it represents earth and fire, left is earth, right is fire. Notice the halo impression in the middle; it signifies the earth is the Great Spirits footstool. This piece is the foundation. The fourth piece is of the ancient Kauri tree, the oldest workable wood on earth; it represents time past. It will always be able to be worked and carved. Fifth is iron wood, it is hard, never changing. It is like your word; if you give your word, you must fulfill it as a man of honor and a warrior. And this last root is what you obtained. I will tell you the name of it once you take my place. Not now, but in years ahead."

"I did not tell you what happened when I was retrieving the root," Billie said. "The bundle became mixed, and a great lightning storm arose. I pried the pieces apart and it stopped."

38

"Ah," the Medicine Man smirked. "You learned by experience. Look carefully at the piece's young warrior. It is required that you remember the order. Let us make an experiment.

The Medicine Man waved his hands in an outward circle. When the warriors saw what he was doing, they lashed themselves to the nearest tree. Certain they had protected themselves, he laid the feather fossil atop the abalone shell then, slowly pushed the root Billie had collected closer to them until static electricity began emanating from the three. At once the blue sky turned to dark, blue gray towering cumulus clouds as the wind picked up to a speed of almost fifty knots. Rain began falling, the wind blowing it horizontally as lightning bolts began to strike trees on the far side of the palmetto flat. The storm was all around them, but like the eye of a hurricane, they were peaceful within its center. Billie noticed the clouds had become towering and was panicked as he looked about. He could see the warriors clinging to palm and oak trees, fearing for their life. The Medicine Man was very calm. Looking at him, Billie slowly relaxed as the Medicine Man pulled the root away. The wind, rain, and lightning stopped instantly, and the sky turned blue again.

"That was incredible," Billie said. "Is that part of the Transparency training?"

"Yes. Now let me explain how this works. If you make a mistake, it could mean your life or worse."

"What could be worse than death?"

"Being trapped between dimensions unable to protect yourself from the demons around you. You have the strongest heart I have ever known young warrior so, pay attention. This root is the key because it holds the Great Spirits power so only the pure in heart may wield it successfully. You see the order; that order must be kept and none of the pieces must teach each other. The buckskin does not conduct a current so keep the bundle this way. Rolled out, it is as it will be needed. This is how you roll it back into a proper bundle. Begin at the first artifact. Note that it is a couple of inches from the edge; roll the edge over it and then, keep rolling over the next in turn giving about one-half more roll before going over the next artifact. Once you have rolled over the root, which you may call dii potentia meaning God's power, the true name will be revealed to you later, you will have an inch or more excess. Tie each end of the bundle and bind it in the center. Use buckskin lacing. Now it is safe and harmless."

Billie looked at the bundle. It resembled a protective covering one would place over an expensive watch or other valuable item. Nothing about it stood out as being important. No one seeing it would give it a second thought. As a matter of fact, it would likely be tossed out as if it were of no importance.

"How do I use it properly?" Billie asked.

"That is the correct question," The Medicine Man said as he carefully unrolled the bundle to reveal its contents as before.

"It will take some practice. You will need to go to a very isolated spot to do that. But first let me give you some instructions. Do not forget them. If I were to ask you what you would like to experiment with first, what would you inquire?"

"Could you call fiery hail from the sky?" Billie asked.

The Medicine Man was taken aback wondering why Billie would want such a thing.

"Yes, I can," the Medicine Man said. "Why would you want to do that?"

"I was thinking that if we were surrounded by enemies or being chased by enemies, it would be a good way to stop them."

"And so, it would. What you ask is not difficult. Watch and learn."

He took the feather fossil and then the iron medallion and laid them next to each other in an upside-down V-shape and then laid the Kauri at the bottom to form a triangle. Next, he took the dii potentia and placed it at the top. One end of the root was larger than the other. He pointed the small end toward the farthest side of the palmetto flat and slowly lowered it until once again, static electricity began to engulf all the pieces. Almost immediately after it began, the sky clouded over, almost black; as before, towering cumulous clouds grew and began glowing red on the outer edges; burning hail began to fall. After a moment, the Medicine Man pulled the dii potentia away from the other pieces and everything returned to normal. Billie's eyes widened in disbelief.

"How did you do that?" Billie asked.

"It is no great mystery," The Medicine Man replied. "Look at the pieces and what they represent. What combination would you use if you wished to make a hurricane?"

"I suppose the abalone, feather fossil, and dii potentia," Billie said.

"Close, but you missed one piece."

"Which one?"

"You missed the ironwood. It would need to sink below the water's surface. So, you would need to be in a place with access to water, in a pinch, even a cup would suffice to place the ironwood in and the others atop it. Just remember the ironwood would need to be submersed so it is just below the surface."

"I noticed that you pointed the smaller end of the dii potentia toward the far edge of the palmetto flat," Billie said. "Is that how you control the direction."

"Very observant, the Medicine Man quipped. "Yes, that is the direction, but let me explain how to bring the events closer to you or move them farther away."

For the next several hours, the Medicine Man explained all that Billie could absorb as he taught his protégé what he needed to know. He trained him to look for patterns and to develop a strategy rather than to memorize what he was learning. Billie caught on quickly and seemed a natural at it.

The Medicine Man observed him with a twinkle in his eye. He was pleased.

"You learn well, young warrior," the Medicine Man said. "There is only one other that has caught on as quickly as you."

"Is that Lunadi?" Billie asked.

"Yes. What do you know of him?"

"I have heard that he is a warrior and working out west, but little else."

"Good," the Medicine Man said. "It is my intent to keep him away until needed. He was a threat to the President but had no interest in politics. You see, Lunadi is a true warrior. Not that you are not. But he took a path I put him on and when the time is right, he will return to help you. Until then, he has another calling that he must fulfill."

"Why is he a different kind of warrior?" Billie asked.

"Again, the right question," the Medicine Man said, gazing into the distance as if he were in a trance in some far-off place. "Lunadi is a true warrior because he has no empathy; he is thorough, meticulous, cold blooded when necessary, and the best of the best in the past and now. You see, he trained the Great Spirits warriors before this world was and now, he is training others. He will have no mercy on those who stand in his way once the Great Spirit unleashes him. When he does, he will be the rider on the pale horse and death and hell will follow him. You will reveal this to no one. He has been through the training that you are about to receive and only he, has been as trustworthy as you. Remain a man of honor no matter what happens. Now that you know the basics of using the bundle, it is time to begin your training in the Transparency."

The President was in his office about to go to the tribal meeting. He was thinking about the discussion on the yacht with Cilatro and his colleagues. There was something unnerving about the three of them. He knew that Cilatro was cold and ruthless. Morgan surely was cunning, manipulating, and obviously had no qualms about doing what was needed to get the job done for the pleasure of his boss. A shiver ran up his spine as he remembered the coldness in the eyes of Li Na. She had been courteous enough, but her eyes were like those of a shark, filled with death, unwavering and fearless. Instinctively he knew that she could become a serious threat. He needed to get his money as quickly as he could and leave office when the time was right, away from the greed and corruption that he was master of. He walked out the door in deep thought, strategically weighing his options.

The first thing on his agenda this morning was meeting with the tribal council before introducing the legislation for the power plant. Some would welcome his news; others would not be happy since they had candidates of their own to push for the office Billie Panther had been in. He envied Billie and most knew that, but if something happened, he would be the perfect candidate to pin the blame on — the scapegoat. As he walked into the council chambers, the others were already present. After a few pleasantries and taking his seat, he wasted no time getting to the point.

"As most of you know, we received the final report on the landfill debacle yesterday from the FBI, SPD, BIA, and U.S. Marshals. What I'm about to say will please some of you and anger the rest. Have all of you had a chance to read the report? The group nodded affirmatively. Good, then you know that we made a mistake in relieving Billie Panther of his council position. Every day I have complaints via letter and email, as well as by phone from angered members who have promised to vote me and you out of office."

"I told you it was a mistake," Solomon said. "Although Billie isn't my favorite person, he has the peoples interests at heart. We should have never voted him out and might I remind you President that your vote was the deciding factor."

"I am fully aware of that," the President said, glaring. "That brings me to my point. Although we had originally scheduled an election, I have talked about my intent with the tribal attorney Sam Longman who informed me that my current intent to correct the problem we created is viable. He urged me to do so due to both legal precedence and potential lawsuits."

"And what is your intent?" Solomon asked.

"Well, first, let me say that I am sorry and that I apologize for leading all of you in the wrong direction," the President began. "I beg your forgiveness in the matter. My intent is to reverse my decision and I urge you all to do the same."

"We accept your apology Mr. President," Solomon said. "We were just as hasty as you were, but you unduly influenced other council members. Looking around the table, Solomon could see that most of the members were not quite certain what the President was getting to. What do you mean reverse your decision?"

"I will state it as clearly and succinctly as I can," the President said, feeling they would be on his side. "We voted hastily in taking Billie out of his position. This report, holding it up, proves that. Therefore, I vote that we reinstate Billie to his council position and cancel the election, which remains far enough away that no one has put much effort in."

There was shock among the members as they talked between themselves. They were quickly interrupted.

"I was almost killed as you all know by those landfill thugs," Solomon said. "It was Billie who saved my life, along with Genesis, not to mention the lives of our children. I therefore support the President and demand that we reinstate Billie. All in favor?"

There was still murmuring and dissatisfaction among two of council members. They quickly realized they were outnumbered.

"We agree," the council member from Brighton said, raising his hand to cast his vote.

All the other council members raised their hands as well.

"Mr. President," Solomon said. "The vote is passed. The

decision to reinstate Panther is unanimous."

"Excellent," the President said, thinking they were clueless as to why. "Billie Panther is reinstated and will be informed this afternoon. Because I am aware of his vote preference, I will cast his vote for him later at the tribal meeting for the power plant. Further, we will make it the first item of business to state that we were hasty in relieving Panther. Agreed?"

All the council members nodded yes.

"Good," the President said. "I have already talked to all of you, and you have agreed to the plant. It makes perfect sense, and we can use the money. The attorney has done due diligence and the partners involved are completely legitimate."

"Who is going to run the landfill to work with them?" Solomon asked.

"Billie is the natural choice," the President said. "He is a master at the landfill and related operations and will be a boon to the new partners. Besides, knowing the project so well. He is the natural choice don't you agree?"

The council members nodded in agreement.

"Good," the President said. "Let's go do this thing."

Mabel was sitting at her sewing table making an intricate ceremonial jacket for Billie, which she hoped wouldn't go to waste. She was stitching the sleeve at the cuff when the phone rang.

"This is Mabel."

There was silence and then she heard a muffled sob.

"She passed Mabel," Dakotah said. "I thought I was ready, but I wasn't."

Mabel had a sinking feeling in the pit of her stomach. She knew Dakotah to be an honorable man and that no matter how much he loved her, he would never leave his wife for her or any other woman. Now, she was gone. Her heart reached out and yearned to be close to this man who was much more than a friend. She never had gotten the knack about what to do at times like these.

"I am so sorry," she said. "I don't know what to say at such a difficult time. You have my deepest sympathy. Is there anything at all that I can do for you? I know how difficult this time must be."

"No," Dakotah replied. "I'll be okay. I just needed to hear the voice of a dear friend. It's hard, but I will make it through."

"I am here if you need me," Mabel said, a tear trickling down her cheek as she gazed across the swamp. The moment she had known would come was upon them both, but much needed to be done before they could be together after so many years. "If you need me to make some calls, help with the funeral or anything, just let me know."

"That's very kind of you," Dakotah said. "If I need anything, I'll contact you. I may call you in a few days if that is okay."

"Certainly. Whatever you need. Don't hesitate to ask."

"Thank you, Mabel. Take care and have a good day. I'll be thinking of you."

The line went dead. Her heart was aching because she knew the pain he was going through. At the same time, she felt a joy descend upon her because she knew that as time passed, and not a lot, that the two of them would be together, if only as friends. She walked out of her chickee onto the walkway, looking down into the coffee-colored water, her reflection took her back to years before. His smiling face seemed so close; she reached out to touch it, her own reflection shown back at her. Life was strange she thought. She had some friends in DC that she could reach out to and have flowers and meals sent to Dakotah's home to lessen the stress. The pain, well, that would take time. She knew he had prepared for this day, but no one is ever really prepared as they watched a person they had loved for so long, slowly wither and die a pitiful death from a ravaging illness out of their control. It was like a living agony. Tears began to stream down her face, dropping into the water.

The anguish of his pain engulfed her, and a lifetime of memories came flooding back.

A great many members of the tribe had gathered to listen to the President and the Council. They had read about the power plant and the potential jobs it would bring. More than a few wanted to escape the shadow of casinos and tax-free cigarettes for a more noble way for the tribe to earn money. The room was buzzing at what the council might say.

"Let's bring this meeting to order," the President said. "Order please."

The room became quiet as the President stood at the podium, everyone looking directly at him in anticipation. In the back of the room was Li Na and Morgan. Dressed in jeans and tee shirts, they had gone unnoticed. There was no need to draw attention to themselves until the time was right.

"I'm going to cover two topics today as briefly as I can," the President said. "As many of you know, the council and I relieved Billie Panther of his leadership position after the landfill problem."

"Yeah, and most of us didn't agree with you," a member shouted out, many of the rest murmuring agreement.

"I understand how you feel," the President said. "First, as a governing body, we want to apologize to all the tribe's members for what we did. The council members nodded their agreement. We acted in haste because of the stress and pressure of the moment. During the last few days, after receiving reports from various agencies regarding the landfill incident, including the FBI and SPD, we realized our gross error. After speaking among ourselves, the tribal attorney, and others, we hereby reinstate Billie Panther to his council position."

The room burst into yells of approval and clapping as the members, looking at each other, felt relieved that for once, the governing body of the tribe was doing something that was right. They rarely back peddled once they decided an issue. There now seemed to be honor restored where it had been lost. Li Na and Morgan looked at each other, not sure if this would affect the deal or not.

"Now, let's get on to the other topic," the President said. "As you know, we have been discussing joining a power plant to the landfill operation. The methane generated by the landfill can produce much power. Initially, the funds were not available to make it happen. Now, we have the needed partners who will make that investment. Two of them are standing at the back of the room. Li Na and Morgan raised their hands and waved at the members, receiving nods of approval. Their companies are going to invest the money and will move the project forward pending approval by the tribe today."

"This isn't going to turn into another landfill fiasco, is it?" a member yelled out.

"No," the President said. "I can assure you of that. The tribal attorney and BIA attorneys have performed their due diligence and everything, including the companies investing the funds is completely legitimate."

"Who's going to be in charge of merging the landfill with the power plant operation?" a member asked.

"We have thought long and hard about that," the President replied. "The logical choice is Billie Panther. As you all know, he has both hydrology and law degrees from Yale and knows this area better than anyone else. Plus, you all know him. He will bend over backwards to help our people. While we may have personal disagreements with him occasionally, there is no doubting his intent for all of you."

The members clapped their approval. At the back of the room, Morgan and Li Na realized this could affect their plans to a degree, which they would discuss later.

"Before we vote on this," a member said, standing. "We would like to know about the funding process and the revenue generation back to the tribe."

"You are more than entitled to that information," the President said. "Nothing will change much, but the gist of the process is that the investing companies will provide all funding for construction and related issues, including permitting and getting the legislation through the counties, state and other agencies. The tribe will lease them the land for one-hundred years, but we will remain in control through the inspection process and related activities. We do not need to put up any of our own funds."

"That is amazing," a member yelled. "What is our cut?"

"All of this will be documented and issued by Sam Longman once final agreement is reached," the President said. "Since the investing partners are putting up all funds, we are looking at approximately eleven percent. I know that does not sound like a large share, but each of the partners are paying for everything, which is coming from their shares."

One of the members had been placed in the audience as a shill by the President and now was his time.

"You're right Mr. President," the member said. "It does not sound like a lot, but I think we could live with it."

As he spoke, he looked around, getting nods of approval from most of the others.

"There's not only the percent return," the President said. "Don't forget the many good paying jobs that will be coming from both the landfill and the power plant. As you know, we need these jobs and they are right on BC, which will require minimal transport costs for those employed."

The room burst into applause as they roared approval.

"If you approve, perhaps we should vote."

As the resolution was read, the vote was taken, and the power plant project approved. Li Na and Morgan stayed for a few minutes as they shook hands and talked with various members then they discreetly left. They had been working for this day for a long time. Their operational strategy had paid off and for the first time in their lives, their money would be legitimate.

The Medicine man was staring at Billie who seemed to be in some far off spot.

"Quit drifting on me young warrior," the Medicine Man said, snapping his fingers in front of Billie's face. "Now is the time for the transparency. You must pay strict attention. On the first trip, I will be with you. After that, you will traverse the other dimensions on your own. One of the most important things that you must do is to protect your body from environmental and human dangers. If your body is killed while in the transparency, you will forever remain locked within the dimension, wandering as a lost soul."

"How do I protect it?"

"You can protect it using others to watch over it or you can perform the ceremony from within a location that is safe such as a house, shipping container, cabin, building, or similar place. Caves can be used as well, but you must be sure they are not being used by a wild animal."

"How do we begin?"

The Medicine Man waved his arms at the warriors who encircled them from a distance, watching over them. Next, he bade Billie lay down and built a small fire just away from his head and another at his feet. Opening Billie's bundle, he placed the dii potentia root in Billie's right hand. He then built two more small fires next to Billie so that he would be between them as he lay down next to him. He took his bundle and retrieved the largest dii potentia root Billie had brought back and grasped it in his right hand as he lay flat next to Billie.

Moss hanging from nearby oaks began to sway as a breeze started to blow.

"Mimic me young warrior in every aspect."

Ever so lightly, the Medicine Man began to hum, and Billie joined in. The hum changed to a staccato rhythm and abruptly stopped. There was a sound in the air, indeterminable yet pleasant, almost like a woman's voice whispering. A white mist began to gather atop and immediately around their bodies, growing thicker and brighter, hovering over them in an undulating fashion. Abruptly, there was what sounded like a sigh and the mist separated and took the form of each, respectively hovering above their bodies. The mist slowly turned from white to a darker gray and then a black color, fading as it moved quickly into the dark undergrowth of the hammock and then, returned, dissipating into the air above their physical forms.

Billie opened his eyes and was astounded to see a giant tree directly in front of him across a large lake. The Medicine Man watched him closely to gauge his reaction. A look of surprise and awe swept across his face as his mouth opened to say something but couldn't quite get the words out. The tree was massive. Its trunk seemed the size of a mountain, dark around the bottom changing to a brighter orange as it reached upward, as if an unseen flame was burning within. There was something peculiar about the tree. Instead of it just going up like a normal tree, it was like separate sections with a new trunk emerging from the one below, gigantic branches of its own replicating up the height of it. There was a burning halo that formed an aura around the entire tree.

On the left side of the tree were a couple of ships in the vast expanse of water that surrounded its base. They appeared dead, with no crew. Around him here and there were arrows that protruded from the ground as if someone had been shot at and missed. He slowly rotated his head to take in the entire scene before him. Steep mountainous walls led down to the water, standing as bastions to protect the tree. But why? It was so massive that it appeared indomitable. At first the whole scene had appeared dark, but suddenly, Billie noticed the aura and flame were growing much brighter. It was then that he noticed the small white fruits, which had been hidden before. He noticed what he had not before as he stepped back. Across the largest branches of the first section, there was a set of eyes staring at him, as far apart as the trunk of the tree was wide. He felt a fear he had never known. Then, he realized the eyes projected compassion as they looked down from either side of the trunk that was so large even the dead ships appeared small.

Billie started to step back again, but the Medicine Man held his hand behind him so that he could not retreat.

"Fear not," he whispered.

"Who is it that comes before me?" a booming voice asked, the earth shaking beneath their feet.

"It is I, with my young apprentice, from the Seminoles," the Medicine Man said.

"So, this is the young warrior you have spoken of," the voice from above the tree said, the earth shaking again.

"Yes, Great Spirit," I ask that you accept him. He is well trained, and his cares are for the people only. There is no greed or malice within him."

"Very well, Medicine Man of the Seminole," the Great Spirit said. This time there was no shaking of the earth, but the voice was as a whisper that penetrated to their very core. "Train him well. And young warrior, if you fail to do your duty, your life will be forfeit. The people come first."

The eyes disappeared, but the tree remained lit from the fire within, yet the branches did not burn. Billie was at a loss for words, his knees shaking as he was overcome by some unseen power. The Medicine Man helped him sit down. It was then that he felt something on his head. It was a headdress. Where had it come from. The Medicine Man had one too. Finally, Billie was able to speak.

"Was that the voice of the Great Spirit?" Billie asked.

"Yes," the Medicine Man said. "Those were his eyes as well, at least an image of them."

"Why did he not reveal his person?" Billie asked.

"Ah, my young warrior," the Medicine Man said. "None on earth, no tribal warrior, except Lunadi has the honor and strength to gaze upon him. If you saw him with your natural eyes, your body would burst into flame. Do not ever presume to do so if you value your life."

"I understand, I think," Billie said. "Why does he reveal himself from within the tree?"

"He is not from within the tree, but without. Those fruit that you see, never eat one under any circumstances. Those on the ship did. A Medicine Man caught by the Spaniards of the White Mountain Apache brought them here. It cost him his life, but it was the only way to save his people. He violated the laws of the Great Spirit, and they all paid the price. He forfeit his life for his people."

"What is so special about this place?" Billie asked.

"This is where his spirit resides during rest, out of his physical form," the Medicine Man replied. "More importantly, that is the tree of life. Many scriptural accounts from different tribes, bibles, and books on religion speak of it, but they are inaccurate as you can see."

"It's incredible," Billie stuttered. "What would happen if I ate the fruit?"

"Oh, you wouldn't have a chance to bite it," the Medicine Man said. "The instant you reached for it, you would be immediately killed. Look there."

Billie looked toward where the Medicine Man pointed and saw a group of men and a few women that appeared to be warriors with golden eyes, staring down on them from their perch high up the side of the mountain that encircled the tree. They had on silver breastplates and gloved hands that reached to their elbows, with a quiver of arrows on their backs and spring steel bows. Instead of a traditional moccasin, they wore boots that extended to the knee, and a cape that hung almost to the ground, a golden hue in color. Their hair was as flaming fire so that they blended with the aura surrounding the tree. On their wide leather belts hung long knives with exposed blades, gleaming from the light bouncing off the water. They were without fear as they looked upon them.

"I will teach you the rules once we return," the Medicine Man said. "For now, follow me and do not touch anything. If you are curious about something you must first ask, not act. Acting wrongly here in this hallowed place will quickly result in your death. To begin, I will take you around the tree. It is a long but worthwhile journey. Also, those warriors you see are everywhere; accept that fact. You see, there are portals from other dimensions that reach to this place, but only the pure in heart and obedient can enter them. It is the tradition of the Medicine Men before you. Those from many tribes come here to gain inspiration and to talk to the Great Spirit. And it is those portals that you must learn. Each has a different purpose, and it is the portals that allow you to travel, almost anywhere you wish if you violate no laws. Look over there. Do you see that cave-like opening in the shape of a wave?

"Yes."

"That portal will allow travel to any wet area on the earth. You need to learn how to use it. I will help you."

As the two continued walking, the ever-present warriors watched over them; a few were walking directly behind them, shadowing their movements. The Medicine Man showed Billie all the portals and explained what they represented. He also explained a deeper purpose for the tree of life and the reason that he was able to come to this place. They had spent a total of three days around the tree. For food they ate white berries with a taste sweeter than honey that grew profusely on the steep slopes and drank water from the lake surrounding the tree. It was the purest water Billie had ever had.

"What would happen if someone like the President came here?" Billie asked.

"He knows enough to come here, but is fearful of it," the Medicine Man said, gazing across the lake at the tree, its fiery glow reflecting from his eyes. "I fear he did not learn well and that he would do something stupid, almost immediately, and those warriors, nodding his head toward them, would perform their duty. Come, we must return."

The Medicine Man did not want to alarm Billie. Although the President had learned enough to reach the tree of life, he had stopped training him because of his projected spirit; it was too dark. It was only when he had shown his bad spirit that the instruction had ceased. The Medicine Man intuitively knew that greed would create an insatiable lust within their leader. Time would be the measuring stick for what the President would do, but the Medicine Man felt a strange foreboding. He shook it off as they were translated back into their bodies.

As he hung up the phone, a small smile creased Cilatro's lips. It appeared everything was going as planned. The resolution had been passed and the power plant would soon begin construction. Already palms had been greased at the county, state, and federal levels to pass it through. Besides, there was no way for any of those entities to learn that he was involved.

"What are you smiling about father?" Dianna asked.

"The power plant construction has been approved by the tribe," he replied. "I want you to get involved. You have studied this and worked with lots of our construction firms. You will be the accountant and project manager. Communicate nothing to anyone before you pass it by me."

"I understand father," she said.

Dianna had never known about her father's business until she had finished her MBA at Harvard. She was a head turner. Everywhere she went men couldn't keep their eyes off her. She had a lithe body that exuded confidence and sexuality. Her raven hair was accentuated by a constant, friendly smile and blue eyes. She had always had an air of confidence and innocence. Directly after graduation, her class had a party and two of her classmates decided they would take her and do as they pleased. Their fathers, both extraordinarily rich, had raised them to take what they wanted. Unknown to them at the time, Cilatro had sent two of his men, Frank and Kelly, to keep an eye on Dianna until she made it back home for a family celebration in her honor. As Dianna left the class party, two of her male classmates followed her, shoved her into the backseat of their car and drove to a secluded area next to Kennedy Park along the Charles River. They dragged her out of the car. One held her while the other started slapping her then, punched her in the stomach to knock the wind out of her so she would submit to their demands. They threw her to the ground and began licking her neck and kissing her. She fought back ferociously but they were too strong. She had a split lip in multiple places, two black eyes and bruises on her cheeks where she had been beaten. She was sure she would have bruises everywhere if she survived, attempting to fight them off.

"You may as well give up," one said, climbing atop her, ripping her skirt and panties off. "You can't win. Just relax and enjoy it."

"She can identify us," the other said. "We cannot let her live."

An ominous feeling overcame Dianna. If she didn't fight back now, she would have no chance. She fought even harder, to no avail. The second assailant pinned her shoulders to the grass as the first ripped off her blouse and bra. She lay naked and helpless beneath him as he unzipped, ready to penetrate. A hatred she had never known welled up in her as she head butted him and at the same time grabbed his balls and yanked. He slapped her hard across the face in return with his left hand, dazing her as his weight sank on her because of the pain. Without warning the scene was lit up by headlights from a car. Somehow, it had driven right up to them without being noticed. Frank and Kelly stepped out either side of the car, invisible in the darkness behind the lights.

"Step away from her, now!" Frank said.

The two assailants stepped back toward the rear of their car.

"Grab her and wrap her in the blanket," Frank told Kelly. "You two. Do not move."

Kelly, from the passenger side, big and burly, approached Dianna and gently helped her to her feet, wrapping a blanket around her, trying not to stare at her lithe, athletic body. She began lashing out at her assailants as Kelly moved her away and back to the car.

"There, there," Kelly whispered. "We have it all under control. They cannot hurt you anymore."

Dianna was standing by the car, shaking uncontrollably, slowly getting into the back seat as she strained to regain her composure. It was only then that she could clearly see her attackers in the headlights. They had always given her a hard time.

"If I only had a gun," she thought, "I'd kill them both."

Kelly gently assisted her in sitting down on the back seat, motioning for her to stay as he closed the door and walked back to the front of the car.

"Do you have any idea who this woman is?" Kelly asked.

"No," the two classmates stuttered back, fearing the two men they couldn't see.

"She is the daughter of the most powerful organized crime leader in the northeast," Frank said. "We have no choice in what must happen now."

"We didn't mean to do it," one of the classmates said. "She is just so attractive. All she ever said to us was no and tonight we thought we would get a little pay back."

"I see," Kelly said. "So, she said no!"

"Yes," the classmate said arrogantly.

"And still you forced her?" Frank asked. "Don't you understand college boy that no means no? Tell me the truth. What did you think would happen once you had your way with her? You were going to kill her, weren't you?"

"We didn't think that far ahead but realized we would need to kill her to protect our identities."

"We thought as much," Kelly said. "You have admitted your

guilt, now for the punishment."

The two men stood helpless, the lights from the car illuminating them against the blackness of the night. There was no warning as Frank and Kelly, armed with suppressed 9mm pistols, shot each with a double tap to the chest and once to the head. They were dead before their bodies hit the ground. Dianna, from the back seat witnessed the entire incident. In her moment of hatred she smiled, knowing the two men had gotten what they disserved. She began to wonder who these two men were that had saved her from humiliation and certain death. They were always around her father, and she knew their names, but that was about all. She realized that if the two assailants lived, some other woman or multiple women would later become their victims. Frank stepped forward and placed his fingers along each of the victim's necks to make sure there was no heartbeat then, nodding affirmatively to Kelly, they climbed into the car dimming the lights, and made it back to the street. After a minute or so, Frank turned the lights on as they sped through the night.

That night, Dianna lost her innocence, and had quickly gravitated to the dark side of the businesses her father ran. Frank and Kelly became her personal bodyguards, as well as her friends. She had no qualms about who she was or where she was going and would remain forever grateful to her father who knew the vices of men and had the strategic foresight to protect her.

"Is there anything I need to know before I begin?" Dianna asked.

"Hmmmm," Cilatro mused. "They have a council member you will need to work with. Don't try any wiles with him because he is happily married. We need him on our side. Be strictly professional and courteous, be friendly too, but not overly so."

"Who is he?"

"His name is Billie Panther, and he is all about his people,"

Cilatro said. "I curse Paul for mucking things up. Had it not been for him, we wouldn't need to be so secretive, and we would already have a built trust."

"I will restore that trust father," Dianna said. "I will befriend Billie and his wife."

Cilatro looked at his daughter and remembered the sweet innocence she had before that night. Even though there was a hardness about her, she hid it well and to those she met, she was as friendly and smiling as ever. He had no doubt that her smile would win their friendship and trust.

"Yes, befriend them. Let's get this project off to a good start. You shall be the bookkeeper for the partnership. Beware Li Na, she is dangerous and cunning. Give her no information about yourself. Morgan will help you with that. It is his job to work directly with her."

"Very well father," Dianna said, as she arose to leave. "I will make it happen."

A smile was on her face again. If anyone could be charming and disarming it was Dianna. More importantly, she could do it without malice. She was more like a man in her thoughts, compartmentalizing everything.

President Billy Osceola was on the phone speaking with Cilatro, staring out his office window as was his daily habit, smiling, gloating about the payoff he had received. Don had been true to his word; the money was already in his offshore account.

"I have talked with the other decision makers for the state and feds," Cilatro said. "Everything is a go. When can we get access to the site?"

"As soon as you want," the President said. "Send one of your people down and we will get everything going. We have already begun setting up several construction trailers for your offices and other needs."

"Very well," Cilatro said. "I will be sending down our partners accountant initially, along with Morgan whom you met. They will get everything ready to begin as soon as the feds give us final approval."

The President noticed Billie walking down the sidewalk outside.

"Look Don," the President interrupted. "I'll keep you posted. I have to go; something has come up."

The President hastily walked out of his office and into the lobby. He didn't want Billie snooping around his office because he was just too damn observant.

"Billie," the President said, extending his hand as they shook. "I'm glad you're here, there's something I'd like to say," the President said, Billie eyeing him warily.

"Good," Billie said. "There something I wanted to ask you anyway."

"Go ahead."

"Why did you strip me of my council position?"

"Well, that's what I wanted to talk to you about Billie. I want to apologize to you personally. Although we have not always seen eye to eye, we both have the best interests of our people at heart. I wish you had been here earlier for the power plant resolution."

"Did you pass it?" Billie asked.

"Yes, we did," the President said. "That's not the half of it. The council and I looked over the law enforcement report from the landfill incident. Along with that, Solomon told us how you had saved his life and how your quick actions saved the lives of our children. Billie, I don't know how to say this, but I am profoundly sorry for what we did. The council and I acted in haste. Too much haste. We realize that mistake and I have been asked by the entire council to extend our apologies for putting you in a precarious position after all you have done. We recognized after reading the reports that you were not at fault in any way. I hope you will accept our apologies in good faith. This morning, we corrected the mistake we made. The election was canceled for the council seat. We canceled it because we voted unanimously to reinstate you. Billie, you have your position back. Again, please accept my apology and those of the council."

"You did that for me?" Billie stammered. "I don't know what to say."

"Don't thank me yet Billie," the President said, chuckling. "I sort of put you back in the hot seat. Because you were not here, I voted in the affirmative for the power plant because I thought you would do that, but also, you have been placed in charge of it and the landfill due to your scientific and legal expertise. I hope you don't mind."

Billie was watching the President as he spoke. The apology seemed sincere, as if the President really meant what he said. Taking things at face value, there seemed no reason not to accept it.

"I accept the apologies," Billie said as they shook hands. "Tell me more about the power plant."

"Thank you, Billie," the President replied. "We came to an agreement with the partners who are investing the money. You can get the documents from Sam and look them over. He, along with the feds have vetted these partners and you'll be happy to know that everything is on the up and up. There are no skeletons in their closets, only honest businessmen seeking a new venture."

"How will the funding work?"

"They, the two partners, are putting up all funds. In return, we lease the site for one hundred years and the tribe gets back ten to eleven percent, maybe more. The numbers on that are not fixed in stone yet, but it's a good deal. After the initial plant is constructed, we will have the same deal, but the second phase will be paid for out of generated revenues unlike the first phase which will be paid up front."

"You put that together?" Billie asked.

"Yes, as much as I could," the President said. "Sam and the

James Tindall

council members helped but I did all I could to make it happen."

"Thank you," Billie said sincerely. "I underestimated your skills. What a boon this will be to BC for both money and jobs for tribal members. With the landfill and the power plant, we can erase some of the tarnish our other money-making ventures have given us."

"Thank you for the compliment, Billie," the President said. "Coming from you it means a lot. I just got off the phone with one of the partners. He's sending two people down in a few days and the other partner will be sending someone as well. They've asked for construction trailers and related items to be on site for offices and such. I got the process going, but you have much more expertise. If you could get those matters attended to, I would be grateful. And you will be happy to know that they have already deposited thirty percent of the funds that we can begin drawing down on. You can work with them on the process. Please keep me and Sam informed so we are aware of progress."

"I'll get right on it," Billie said, standing. "I won't let you down and will keep you abreast of everything."

"Thank you, Billie."

The two shook hands, the President watching Billie get into his truck. He knew that the project could be very successful with Billie on board, but he would keep his options open.

No sooner than Billie had gotten into his truck than he called Christina who wasn't expecting him back. He was lucky to catch her. Teachers were not allowed phones in the classroom. Fortunately, she had just broke for lunch.

"Hey baby," Billie said. "You won't guess where I am."

"I assumed you were with the Medicine Man," Christina said. "What's up?"

"I was with him, but we finished early," Billie said. "I decided to go to the tribal offices to confront the President and find out

why he axed me. You'll never guess what happened."
Christina could hear the excitement in his voice, the seconds
seemed like minutes.
"Well?" she asked.
"First," Billie said. "They passed the power plant resolution
and its already beginning. They put me in charge of it."
"That's great," Christina said. "Now you don't need to take
that water job. You will at least have a paycheck."
"That's not all baby," Billie chattered excitedly. "Are you
sitting down? They reinstated me to council and apologized
for removing me, saying they had acted in the heat of the
moment and asked for my forgiveness."
"That's wonderful," Christina said, tears starting down her
cheeks. "Come home and we'll talk more. I want to hear all
about it. I need to get back to class."
"I need to go back to see the Medicine Man for one day," Billie
said. "Is that okay?"
"Yes," Christina said. "Do what you need to do, and we will
talk tomorrow or the next day. This is exciting."
Christina had a lightness to her step as she returned to class.
She knew because of Billie's heart the Great Spirit would
always watch over them.

The airboat thudded into the hammock as Billie, killing the
engine, jumped from the boat into the company of the two
warriors as they led him to the Medicine Man. He was sitting
among seven equally spaced fires in a circle, smoke from the
burning a green palm leaf rising from each.
"Sit, young warrior. I am ready to begin."
Billie assumed a cross legged sitting position directly in front
of the Medicine Man as he began to hum, which turned into a
soft chant, almost like a song. The elder's eyes were open
staring toward Billie, but not at him, it was as if they were fixed
on some unseen object.

A scene appeared before the Medicine Man as he tested Billie's heart. There was a hapless fawn struggling to get out of the marsh to its mother on the hammock. It still had a few spots as its coat changed to the typical buckskin type of color of a Florida whitetail deer. A large alligator was closing in on its would-be prey and was opening its jaws when a panther sprang from the hammock floor, biting the alligator on its neck behind the eyes then, clawing it across the eyes as it leapt right in front of the fawn, guarding it. The alligator, one eye missing and bleeding from the neck, glided away through the water and sawgrass. This prey would not make a meal today. The Medicine Man instinctively knew that the panther represented Billie and the hapless fawn the tribe. It was unclear what or who the alligator represented. The Medicine Man exhaled a long sigh. Here in front of him sat another true warrior, like Lunadi, neither would budge when it came to protecting the people, neither would give up. His heart was as pure as could be found, unlike that of the President.

The faraway look in the Medicine Man's eyes disappeared as his gaze focused on Billie. He would have his warriors watch over this one because he would be the tribe's salvation. "Tell me young warrior," the Medicine Man began. "What has happened? You seem to be very excited today."

"The President and council reinstated me to my council position," Billie said. "They apologized and said they acted in haste and put me back in charge of the landfill. Also, the power plant resolution passed, and I will be working with that too."

"So, you see, it is as I told you," the Medicine Man said. "They need you Billie and they know that. The tribe needs you too. It is fitting that you retain the seat. Stay cautious. Keep your eyes open for those who would stab you from behind. Remember politics. There is always a tradeoff less you become the scapegoat."

"But enough, today, I will show you how to enter into and out of the body with your spirit," the Medicine Man said. "You

must be able to do it quickly and efficiently. Take the dii
potentia from your bundle and place it in your right hand."
Billie had already practiced several times and was able to grab
the correct piece immediately.

"Mimic my rhythm and intonation," the Medicine Man said.
"You will need to do it yourself without my assistance and
sooner than you think. The key is to focus on where you want
to go. Remember the portals on our previous journey and how
you can manipulate them. Our first trip will be to a location
that will overlook Shark Key. Focus on it; the place I have taken
you before."

The Medicine Man began to sway imperceptibly, chanting
softly. As the chant grew in intensity, they each squeezed the
dii potentia root and a white mist began swirling around them,
changing darker as it had before and then, racing across the
palmetto flat faster than the eye could follow. Almost instantly,
they were standing on the edge of a mangrove marsh near
Shark Point, overlooking Florida Bay. To the south were low
lying islands that dotted the bay and the area surrounding it;
they also could see US1 meandering its way to Key West and
past it, the Atlantic. To the west and southwest was the Gulf of
Mexico. Billie was excited as the stiff ocean breeze blew his hair
back. A huge smile was on his face as he looked at the Medicine
Man and at the spectacular natural view around them. Almost
instantaneously they had traveled eight miles. It was
incredible and exhilarating.

"Is it always this easy?" Billie asked.

"Yes, for the most part," the Medicine Man replied. "It is a little
more difficult if you're under a lot of stress so you must
practice staying calm and alert. And, like I told you before,
your body must be protected while you're out of it. Let us
return in the same fashion and I will practice it with you a few
more times and then, you must do it alone."

The two men practiced it over and over the rest of the day
going to different places including Key West, Naples, West

Palm Beach, and Cuba. Because the travel time was so short, the practice session did not take as long as Billie had planned. Before long, the day had waned, and sunset was upon them. They walked to the west edge of the hammock to watch the setting sun, sitting quietly eating hoe cake and fried fish as they enjoyed the calm of nature.

"Tell me about the power plant," the Medicine Man said.

Billie rehearsed all that he knew, including the legitimacy of the funding companies and the tribal revenues, speculating on both the landfill and the plant.

"Watch carefully," the Medicine Man said. "Although the companies appear legitimate, someone could have looked the other way to make it appear so. Greed has always been our undoing. What you have told me sounds like a boon for our people, but you can never be too careful."

"Understood."

Billie stayed the night and left early the next morning. His first order of business would be to stop by the landfill.

Chapter 3

Li Na was sitting on a tour boat in Hong Kong harbor, her boss next to her. They blended with westerners and other tourists as they discussed the new venture.

"Are you sure this is a safe place?" Ki Luo asked, looking around.

"I am certain," Li Na said. "No sound can be picked up and you have your security."

Ki Luo was the leader of the largest Chinese Triad in Hong Kong. With salt and pepper hair, a slim yet fit physique, and business suit, he would easily be overlooked in a crowd and always underestimated by others. Ki was as ruthless as he was cold and had zero empathy. Everything was business and anyone who stood in his way didn't live long to tell it. He took what he wanted and had no loyalty to anyone except his organization. Many had tried to kill him, but he was crafty and kept his finger on the pulse of everything in Hong Kong, the U.S., and other countries. He traveled with a minimum of a dozen bodyguards no matter where he went. They were the best of the best in guns, knives, and swords. As he sat with Li Na, they were dispersed around him in such a way that even a professional wouldn't detect them all. Ever observant, they would forfeit their life for their master if required.

"What is our exposure on this venture?" Ki asked.

"None," Li Na said. "The offshore traces go seven deep. I constantly watch for investigations. If they get to the fifth offshore company, I extend another seven deep. We are secure and untraceable, even to the FBI."

"Good," Ki said. "I don't want this coming back on us. What do we need to worry about from the tribal side?"

"Their President is in our court," Li Na said. "He doesn't know anything about us, just that our company is legitimate. With the money we paid him, he's ready to slip off into retirement and not be bothered further with politics. I checked him out thoroughly. He's for his people, but also greedy. He will not finger us."

"What about others?" Ki asked.

"There is a councilman they reinstated when I was there," Li Na said. "You will recall the information I gave you on the landfill issue that went sideways that was controlled by Cilatro. The men that caused it got greedy and none of it spilled back on him. The councilman that stopped the entire thing was who they just reinstated. His name is Billie Panther."

"I remember the name from the reports," Ki said. "Is he going to be a problem?"

"My estimation is no," Li Na replied. "My sources say he is a stickler for the law. Everything is done legitimately, and he will be able to find no fault with it. Besides, if he becomes a problem, I'll take care of it."

Ki looked at her through narrowed eyes, knowing exactly what she meant. He remembered back to that night on the dock when she had removed the head of an informant as casually as if she had swatted a mosquito. Then she had picked up the head looking into the face as if she expected to see recognition of some sort. With a shake of her hair, she had dropped it and walked away. It sent a chill up his spine; he was glad she was on his side.

"You need to get there as soon as you can to represent us," Ki said.

"I'm leaving first thing in the morning."

Billie had just left his meeting with the regulators at the Florida Public Service Commission about the new power plant. They had gone over all the regulations. The approval of new power generation in Florida is governed by the Power Plant Siting Act and the meeting had confirmed that the tribe was adhering to all procedures and policies. Normal inspections and related issues would be prevalent, but nothing that would be a problem if construction was up to code. All the construction offices had been set up and they were awaiting the arrival of the partners representatives.

As Billie headed back home, south along Interstate 95, his thoughts turned to the dream he had of the spider web that he had related to his mother and the Medicine Man. In the dream as he got stuck in the web, an unseen force would get him unstuck and he would meet leaders from the various clans. In the background he could see lightning bolts, but they were weird because they were heading from the ground toward the sky. Between him and the bolts was his bundle, laying open on the ground, static electricity flowing from it. The background looked familiar, but he couldn't make it out. Perhaps it was nothing as most dreams were not. He shook it off.

While driving south, he decided to make a detour and get as close as he could to the St. Lucie Nuclear Power Plant, a twin nuclear power station on Hutchinson Island, near Port St. Lucie in St. Lucie County. The station was commissioned in 1976 and was continually updated for safety and potential hazards. Billie got off I-95 and headed over to the A1A cut off near the island, which was only eight miles south of Ft. Pierce. He pulled off onto the edge of the highway as far as he could, not being a hindrance to traffic. Retrieving his binoculars from the center console, he focused them on the twin nuclear reactors, standing like sentinels before the expanse of the blue-green waters of the Atlantic beyond. As he looked at them, his dream of the spider web and the lightning bolts unfolded before him. The lightning wasn't coming from the ground, but from these plants that were now clear in his dream. He was brought back to reality by the sharp yelp of a police siren from the cruiser pulling up next to him.

"Are you having difficulty?" the officer asked.

"Oh, no," Billie replied. "I was just admiring the power plant."

"Understood," the officer responded. "You cannot park here. Please move along."

Billie smiled and waved slightly at the officer as he pulled forward and back onto the highway. The patrol car followed him for a minute before making a U-turn on the median and heading back in the opposite direction.

Many thoughts began to race through Billie's mind as he contemplated the dream and pondered it over and over in his mind. Was the plant going to be attacked? If so, would radiation escape? Maybe the lightning bolts going toward the sky was an omen that something was going to happen to it. He had so many questions and suddenly it dawned on him. If the plant went down, the energy from other plants, because of the shortfall, would be much more valuable. He shook the thought from his mind as he drove. No one would be that devious and Sam had assured him they had done due diligence and that the partners of the power plant were strictly legitimate. Still, Billie had a hard time shaking the sinking feeling in his stomach.

It was late afternoon when he drove onto BC. He walked into his office and began setting up files and white boards to keep track of the landfill and power plant projects and was just about to head home when there was a soft knock at the door.

"Ah, Genesis my brother," Billie expressed. "How are you doing?"

"I'm doing well. Trying to get over my depression of Mary Jane's passing."

"I'm so sorry about that," Billie said. "If we had only known."

"We are not fortune tellers," Genesis said. "But that brings me to a point. I've been looking at the paperwork and costs of the power plant. I know it's out of my realm of responsibilities, but how it the tribe going to afford that."

"Second thoughts, eh?" Billie asked. "I've had similar, even today. However, Sam says the tribe and state has done due diligence and even kicked it up to some federal agencies who helped them. The partners are honest from everything they could find, and they are putting up all the funds."

"Why would they do that?" Genesis asked. "There are lots of other businesses they could do that with."

"True," Billie replied. "From our conversations, these people are strategists, and they say that water, energy and food are the best things to invest in for future earnings."

"I guess that makes sense," Genesis mused. "More people results in more of each, a great demand, and a higher price. Pretty shrewd of them."

"I thought so too," Billie said. "You know, Sam and other attorneys from the state, as well as the FBI investigated these guys. From what they tell me they are completely legit, clean as a whistle."

"My mom used to tell me there is always a skeleton in the closet," Genesis said. "If you don't mind, I'll poke around some myself. I have a few friends who can go deep without drawing attention."

"Alright," Billie said. "If you find anything, let me know. Otherwise, it's business as usual at the landfill site as we ramp up construction of the power plant. Keep this strictly between us."

Billie watched Genesis walk out the door. He knew there was a bad taste in his mouth from the loss of Mary Jane and who could blame him? According to the reports, the bad apple was Lorio who got too greedy. Billie couldn't help thinking that in a business of that scale, no one did anything without the tacit authorization of his employer. That meant Don Cilatro or someone between him and Lorio approved what was going on. But he didn't want to dwell on it. Unless proof was forthcoming it was a moot point. He let his thoughts drift back to his conversation with Christina. They were both very happy at the new turn of events. Both the job and home front were in cruise control for the moment. Things couldn't be better.

Genesis had contacted two friends, one from the DEA and the other from the Florida Bureau of Investigation who were able to run global checks on various groups and had set up a neural network analysis to check for links between the partners. They were meeting at Horatio's home who had his equipment set up in his hobby shop off the garage. It was lined with AR-500 steel and was impervious to break in, at least from anyone but a total pro. He didn't want to add to the tally of dead DEA agents.

"What is this?" Genesis asked.

"This is the fault tree showing the communications from the deceased Paul Lorio to everyone he talked to," Frank said. "There is nothing out of the ordinary that is obvious. We'll go deeper, but I don't believe we will find anything."

"That's right," Jonathan interjected. "All the calls were made to people who were listed in the investigation, as well as calls from them. Neither of our groups could come up with calls to Cilatro, at least not from the cell taken from his body."

"Is it possible that he had another cell or contacted him some other way?" Genesis asked.

"Absolutely," Horatio replied. "However, we haven't found that yet. That would be the smoking gun if it exists."

"Also," Jonathan joined in. "Every call traced was among the group. There appears to be no link to Cilatro or the other partners out of Hong Kong. And, as far as we know, Cilatro is not involved in this. The other partner is a holding firm in the Cayman's."

"Come on guys," Genesis said. "You got to give me something."

"What are you getting at?" Jonathan asked.

"We have two groups of partners who are investing millions into a power plant," Genesis said. "I still believe one of them was hooked into the landfill that went south and we don't know anything about the other."

"That's not entirely accurate," Horatio said. "Both of us have dug through what we could find with a fine-tooth comb. We have reached a quagmire."

"What do you mean?" Genesis asked.

"The partner out of Hong Kong, although appearing legit is slippery to say the least," Jonathan said. "They appear legit, but their accounts are offshore and every time we try to narrow it down, we run into a stone wall, another company we cannot verify."

"That proves they are up to no good, doesn't it?" Genesis asked.

"Not necessarily," Horatio said. "All organizations now, even legit ones get tired of the governments they are under spying on them. It's difficult to keep out of their reach with all the new technologies tracing them at every turn so they deliberately try to ensure there is no trail of their financial activities except what they need to show for tax purposes."

"That doesn't help me," Genesis said, exasperated.

"True," Jonathan said. "But what we suspect is that the Hong Kong partner is involved deeply with the Chinese triads or the Yakuza. Proving it is something else. The Cayman partner is for all purposes invisible. A dead end."

"Even if they are involved in criminal activities," Horatio began, "the venture has been vetted by the tribe, county, state, and feds. The money invested would need to be proven dirty, especially since the power plant construction has been approved and the partners vetted."

"What he's saying Genesis, is that as of right now, everything appears legal," Jonathan said. "We will keep digging and see what we can find out and keep you posted."

James Tindall

"Okay," Genesis said. "I guess that's the best we can do."

"Wait," Horatio said. "Before you go there is one thing."

Horatio and Jonathan were hesitant to bring it up as they looked at each other nodding.

"This woman, Li Na Liu," Jonathan said. "Take care how you deal with her. Our friends on the Hong Kong Police Force tell us she is as cunning and cold blooded as they come."

"I'm not worried," Genesis said.

"You should be," Horatio said. "My field contacts say she has been apprehended multiple times, but no law enforcement group has been able to produce any evidence for prosecution. I have a hunch she may have been undercover Hong Kong Police, but that's just a guess because of her background."

"Dare I ask what she was arrested for?" Genesis queried.

"Murder," the two said in unison.

"Supposedly, the individuals she murdered were beheaded," Jonathan said.

"The witnesses also disappeared," Horatio quipped.

"Then we have them," Genesis said.

"No!" Horatio said emphatically. "All we have is inuendo's. This information comes from field agents we know personally and they're not about to come forward and expose themselves. There are no records anywhere of her being arrested. If there were any, they have been scrubbed."

"Hmmmm," Genesis murmured. "Sounds like she is undercover. Keep digging."

The two nodded as Genesis walked out the door to his vehicle. Across the street sat an inconspicuous champagne colored sedan. The Chinese driver had been watching and listening in on their conversation with a laser microphone. He waited until Genesis was most of the way down the block before he pulled out to tail him. After making a few turns he dropped back even further because he knew where Genesis was headed. Settling back, he made a call.

"I followed him as you instructed," he said. "I'll send the

recording shortly."

"Are there any problems?" Li Na asked.

"They are digging but have come up empty. They are however aware of your arrests by field agents but unable to verify anything."

"Keep me posted."

About two hours later, Li Na sat listening to the recording. This Genesis was suspicious, likely driven by his girlfriend's death. The question was who was driving the backdoor inquiry, himself, or Billie Panther? And how long would they keep it up? The mere fact it was happening did not bode well for them. She must protect Ki and his organization despite the costs if she were to reach her personal objective.

The Medicine Man sat stoically, cross legged in front of a small fire, the smoke rising gently in front of his face. He had heard Billie's airboat approach and thump into the bank at the edge of the hammock. He appeared momentarily accompanied by two warriors.

"Sit, young warrior," the Medicine Man said, pointing. "Now that we have used the roots once, it is time to purify them so that the energy of the Great Spirit is in harmony with each one."

"How do we do that?" Billie asked.

"Unroll your bundle and remove the root and place it in the container with the rest of them."

Between the two was a small new, empty coffee can, the inside shiny the outside a bright red, potentially good to the last drop. Billie placed his root in it along with the others. The Medicine Man was humming, gently swaying back and forth, motioning for Billie to join him. The warriors took up their places as before. Seconds later, the smoke on the fire disappeared as the fire turned into a blue flame that blew toward the can and the roots. As the flame touched the can a bright white, blue light radiated across the entire palmetto flat.

The warriors shifted to an at-the-ready-stance. Incredibly, the blue flame danced across the palmetto tops as the entire hammock was encircled by angelic spirits circling around the outer edge of the flat as more and more of them appeared. They began circling so fast that a mighty wind blew. Billie was aghast at what he witnessed. The blue flame engulfed the entire hammock and as the wind picked up. It took the shape of an inverted tornado with the spout going as far up into the air as he could see. It was directly above him, and he saw the tree of life where the Medicine Man had taken him. It was no longer in the bottom of the canyon, but atop a green, grassy hill higher than the tallest mountains and behind it he could see directly into the cosmos as if a giant portal had been opened.

Suddenly the portal closed as the blue flame and the angelic hosts dove into the can. The blue flame washed across the palmetto flat again and was in turn sucked back into the can so quickly that a thick white mist arose then, zoomed downward into the can. Billie jumped away from instinct as if the can were going to explode.

"Do not be so jittery my young apprentice," The Medicine Man said. "There is no need to fear. Observe the contents."

Billie leaned over to look into the can. It was no longer shiny on the inside but appeared as gold and on the outside was as crystal.

"I do not understand," Billie said.

"Of course not," the Medicine Man laughed. "No vessel in this world can hold the spiritual gifts of the Great Spirit or his angels, only one that has been tempered and purified. This has now been tempered for that purpose. Look at the roots."

Billie peered to the bottom of the container. The roots glowed as if they were a crystalline light.

"The roots are now prepared to work as a mediator between you and the Great Spirit," the Medicine Man said. "They are now a light unto the world though the world will see them not."

Billie reached down to touch them. Almost at the same instant the Medicine Man screamed.

"No!"

"You must not touch them; there is one last step for purification."

The Medicine Man took the old roots in his bundle and placed the metal medallion face up then, took the feather fossil and placed it across the top. A great wind began as he placed the abalone shell next to the feather fossil, forming a shallow upside down 'v', a heavy rain began to fall but did not touch the ground. The wind shaped the rain into an inverted vortex as before. The dark gray blue clouds that had formed disappeared as the sky become an azure blue and the rain vortex shot down into the can. The instant the rain met the crystalline roots, a great spout of steam shot toward the heavens and disappeared. The entire palmetto flat, along with Billie and the Medicine Man and warriors were engulfed in a white mist that quickly dissipated into the most beautiful day of sunlight and temperature they had ever seen.

The warriors looked on with awe for never had they experienced such an event. The spirit that remained seemed filled with love and calm as they bowed down and prayed.

"You may now touch the roots," the Medicine Man said softly.

"They do not feel like a root anymore," Billie said, holding one in his hand.

"Indeed, they are not. They are now in crystalline form but quite unbreakable and are filled with the light of the Great Spirit."

"Will they always glow like this?" Billie asked.

"Yes," the Medicine Man said. "They will glow brightly as long as they are held by one pure in heart. It is difficult to explain. When you used the root without purification you saw the tree of life in its altered state as it appears to those who would use it to thwart the power of the Great Spirit and, because the root was in its earthly state. You were not killed because you were accompanied by me. The root is now in its spiritual state. When you see the great tree from now on it will be as you saw it a few moments ago with the cosmos behind it."

"I am honored," Billie said.

"No, you are accountable because you have been chosen," the Medicine Man said. "Now you have an even greater responsibility. The chief has been required to choose a place of worship off the reservation and he has not. You will keep the dii potentia in your bundle, I will keep one, and the others must be placed upon a small altar in the place of worship that the chief has supposed to have constructed. They will be placed there in this purified container."

"I will speak to him about it," Billie said.

"No, the responsibility is now yours," the Medicine Man said. "He is torn between the treasures in the next life and the lust for power and money in this one. It is a tug of war he has likely already lost. You will build the place of worship here, drawing a map in the dirt, and you will place the container atop the small altar. It need only be large enough for two to kneel in front of it, but it must be made of natural material. Use cypress for the legs and top and bind it with switch grass to hold it together, just like the bowls we make. There must be a tree on each back corner. You will never divulge the location to anyone."

"I understand," Billie said. "When do you want it done?"

"It is not I that wants it done but the Great Spirit," the Medicine Man said. "It needs to be constructed as quickly as you can. That is all."

Billie new it was time to go. He placed the crystalline dii potentia in his bundle and was escorted back to his boat by the two warriors. As he slid through the sawgrass, the sound of the Lycoming engine lulled him into deep thought, wondering why the President had not complied with the wishes of the Medicine Man. Having seen them together on a couple of occasions, he knew there was an animosity between them, but still, you didn't go against the Medicine Man's wishes. Glancing at this watch, he knew that if he camped the night, he could prepare the place of worship by the next afternoon. He had the necessary tools in his kit on the boat. All he needed to do was harvest some switch grass. He made a call to Christina and told her he wouldn't be home until tomorrow as he sped across the glades looking for the cypress head that was in such an obscure and out of the way location that it would never be visited except by the Medicine Man or a designated emissary. He also knew that the Panther Clan would control the place of worship. For now, that meant him.

Don Cilatro had walked out of his office, his two bodyguards a short distance behind him as he pulled out a burner phone, he used for only three days at a time.

"Cilatro," he said.

"We may have a minor problem," Li Na said, as she explained to him in detail, as was her nature, the purpose of her call.

"Can they find out anything?" Cilatro asked.

"It is not likely," Li Na replied. "It would be best if we could make this go away."

"Let's not do anything drastic," Cilatro said. "I have a man on the inside in the FBI. I will have him do a follow up and talk to Genesis and convince him that Karla was the one behind the greed of Lorio and that no one else was privy to it."

"Okay," Li Na said. "And if that does not work?"

"We will make a plan B," Cilatro replied.

Cilatro was thinking quickly as he called Morgan.

"I just had a conversation with Li Na," Cilatro said. "Speak to Karla's attorney and have him tell her to go along with the fact it was only her and Lorio. We need to buy some time to keep this back door inquiry off our ass. Have our agent follow up with Genesis and suggest he visit her in jail, along with Monique who doesn't know anything. She's been paid to keep quiet. The two of them should be able to convince him it's a dead end."

"Very well," Morgan said. "And if that doesn't work?"

"The three of us will develop a separate strategy to deal with it."

This could turn out to be a mess. He could call Ki, but that would make him look inept. Best to handle this in house.

In an administrative security federal detention center near 4th street in Miami, the guards buzzed in Curtis Malone of the FBI. He was led to a small room where Ms. Karla Phenning, Monique and their attorneys waited.

"Good morning," Curtis said. "This should not take long. Your statements have been typed up. The Bureau needs you to go over it and make sure it is accurate. Then, you need to sign it."

"Are you keeping your end of the bargain to charge Ms. Phenning with a lesser sentence since she is cooperating?" the attorney asked.

"Yes," Curtis said. "Here is a copy of the agreement. You need to look it over and sign it as well."

"What about Monique?" her attorney asked.

"Yes, her as well.

The attorneys and two women looked over the cooperation agreements first and signed them. Then, they began looking over their statements.

"There are a few minor errors here," Karla's attorney said. "I will make the correction and initial it and do so throughout the document. At the end, I will put my initials and signature and you will witness it agent Malone."

"I will do the same," Monique's attorney said.

"That will be sufficient," Curtis said.

"He has no idea we have been paid to keep our mouths shut and tell them what they want to hear,' Karla thought. "At least we won't be poor when we get out."

It took over an hour, longer than Curtis had anticipated before they wrapped everything up. Finally satisfied, the agreements were signed, and Curtis was on his way. The attorneys had made copies of the agreements in the warden's office before they left the detention center.

On the way back to the FBI regional office Curtis phoned his boss, updating him on the completion of the paperwork. As far as the FBI was concerned, the investigation was closed. No leads came forth indicating other accomplices. The information was passed along to Seminole PD, Miami-Dade Police, and several other law enforcement groups.

It was a beautiful sunny day as Ki watched the ships pass up and down Victoria Harbor. His office on the 84th floor of Two International Finance Centre on the south side of the harbor had a commanding view. Almost directly in front of him was the China Ferry Terminal across the harbor, Kowloon Bay to his right and Breakwater just kitty corner past West Kowloon Nursery Park. A stiff breeze was blowing the spray from the tops of the small waves as they peaked. It was like the bay was full of diamonds. Ki never tired of the view. He was looking at Central Piers nine and ten adjacent to the Hong Kong Maritime Museum when his phone rang. Like all others in his organization, it was a burner.

"Yes," he answered.

"We are working on the problem we discussed," Li Na said. "I do not believe they will discover our plans, but we are keeping a close eye on them."

"Are you and Cilatro working on it together?" Ki asked.

"Yes, each of our groups have aligned our resources."

"What is your first option?"

"We know that Genesis is working with some DEA and FBI personnel off the books. They are currently downtown and any moment our men will pay the workshop a visit."

"Workshop?" Ki queried.

"It's the DEA agents place, next to his garage," Li Na said. Based on where it is, we know this is not a formal search they're doing."

"Still, we must take no chances," Ki said. "Remember our goal."

"I do and will keep you apprised."

Ki put the phone in his pocket as he thought about the next steps. His organization had been planning this for several years and they would be well paid once the power plant was in operation and other plants in the grid went down, especially the St. Lucie Nuclear Power Plant. He wondered aloud what the going rate for electricity would be when the plants in the south Florida area crashed. After all, it had not been that long ago when the winter freeze in Texas caused almost $200 billion in damages. One electric company served almost seventy percent of customers in the state, not unlike Florida. Texans had suffered extended outages of power and water. Most people had no idea that the U.S. power grid is just a huge electrical exchange where one company sells power to another, which creates a volatility in and of itself in supply and demand. Power is also the Achilles heel of critical infrastructure for every nation. When power goes down, water distribution and communications infrastructure suffer proportionately. Large portions of Texas were below freezing for more than a week after the winter storm hit. Ki couldn't help but smile as he remembered an electrician telling him once of the adage they lived by, "the cold of winter often severely damages electrical components; the heat of summer kills them."

He continued to work the strategy of the power plant. They had more than sufficient time to complete sabotage the power plant being targeted.

Genesis had decided to take a trip to the detention center himself and was waiting when the guard led Karla Phenning in and seated her at the table.

"I'm not supposed to talk to you without my attorney

present," Karla said. "But we've already signed our statements and agreements with the FBI.

"If you prefer not to, we can wait," Genesis said. "I just want to clarify what's in your statement."

"If we stick strictly to that, I'll give you some leeway."

"Just a couple of quick questions. You said that the illegal dumping was between you and Lorio. There were no others involved?"

"No," Karla said. "It was just he and I. My customers wanted chemicals disposed of and it seemed like the perfect way to do it."

"Rather than legally," Genesis asked.

"Do you know how much it cost to dispose of chemical waste?" Karla asked.

"No," Genesis replied.

"For the lowest level waste, it is about $800 per gallon," Karla said.

"Wow," Genesis whistled. "I didn't realize it was that much."

"Now you know why we did it," Karla said. "Think of how much money I could make charging a quarter of that by the tanker load."

"So, you're saying it was all about the money?" Genesis asked.

"Everything is all about the money," Karla said sarcastically. "It was a straight up business deal. We saw the opportunity to make the money and we took it. Does that satisfy you?"

"Yes," Genesis said. "Thanks for your cooperation."

The guard took Karla away. Genesis couldn't help thinking how greedy people were. At the same time, such a lucrative undertaking would be hard for most to resist, better money almost than drugs. Her answers corresponded with her statement. He was satisfied. His thoughts were interrupted as the guard led in Monique.

"What do you want from me?" she asked.

"Just to clarify a couple of points in your statement," Genesis said.

"It's all there in black and white."

"In the statement you inferred you had no knowledge of the illegal dumping."

"It's not inferred, it's a fact. My only job was to keep Billie away from the site and out of Paul's hair. I did not know he was planning on doing what he did. Look, I'm just a paid woman."

"Hmmmm, so, you didn't know about the dumping, and you didn't know about the death of the woman in the car, or the kidnapping of Christina?"

"No. I didn't know any of those things. When they decided to leave the landfill site, I was basically kidnapped as well."

"Why did you go along with it?"

"I had a gun to my head. If you had a gun to your head and were looking at jail time as a would-be accomplice, what would you do?

"I'm not sure," Genesis responded. "I'd try to dig myself out."

"I did. Now, look where I am. I was paid to do what I did. I kept Billie out of Paul's hair and was awfully attracted to him. I was hoping something different would happen."

"You mean like living happily ever after?"

"Exactly. Christina was a bitch to him, and he had more than an attraction for me. It was going my way until Paul pulled his stupid stunt."

"You wanted to marry Billie?" Genesis asked.

"A girl could do a lot worse."

"I suppose you're right. Thanks for your time."

Genesis pondered what both women told him as he drove back to Hollywood. Everything they had said made perfect sense. After thinking about what Jonathan and Horatio had divulged, everything seemed to fall into place. Like everyone else, they were just trying to make an extra buck; they just did it the wrong way. With the facts in about what happened and justified by evidence and witnesses, it appeared the women were both telling the truth.

84

Rain had been pouring down all evening as the pickup truck pulling the 250kW generator pulled up next to the fence adjoining the street of Frank's hobby shop. As luck would have it, the power panel for the shop and home were on the outside of the structure, adjacent to the fence. The dark clad shadowy figures deftly pulled the cables from the generator over the vine covered chain-link fence. One put a cover over the panel to keep off the rain and bypassed the main electrical input as they hooked up the cables. A soft whistle signaled to the dark-clad figure operating the generator to start it and bring it to full power for sixty seconds. The generator started quietly; once running the operator rapidly increased to full throttle and then flipped the power switches on. The lights in the house, including the outside door lamps, instantly went dark. A surge of 250,000 watts and 330,000-volt amperes surged through the residence and hobby shop frying every electrical circuit, device, and computer plugged into the outlets. The entire electrical panel was fried, turning cinder black. Most of the GFI circuit switches were also completely damaged. The men hastily rolled the cables up and were off. They had come and gone in under four minutes, the pouring rain serving as the perfect cover. Just as they turned the corner, the entire neighborhood went dark from a massive lightning bolt. They had pulled off a perfect sabotage.

Li Na was sitting across the street watching, making sure her men were not interrupted. They were efficient. With the heavy rain, few cars were out on the road. Before she knew it, they had loaded up and disappeared into the rain-soaked night, lightning bolts dancing across an ominous black sky. As they turned the corner and she pulled out, a smile spread across her face. Frank would think it was a power surge that had taken out all his equipment and household appliances. This indeed was good news. Even if they continued their backdoor investigation, it would be a couple of weeks before he could get everything up and running again. It was plenty of time to begin the next phase of the operation. She was excited at the prospects of closing in on her goal.

Frank returned home to find all his appliances inoperable and his electrical service panel inoperable, cooked like a fried fish. He had burned candles all night. Up at dawn, he called an electrician to check things out. Suspicious by nature, he had walked all around the inside and outside of his house, garage, and hobby shop. There was nothing out of the ordinary that he could see. He was checking the armored door of his hobby shop when the electrician called him to come to the electrical panel.

"It looks like a lightning strike took out everything," the electrician said. "See all that black area? That's where it fried everything. There's some power lines down and look over there; that tree was struck by lightning."

"But that tree is twenty yards away," Frank said.

"Yes, but lightening can arc from one object to another, taking strange paths to a ground. This chain link fence five feet from the panel doesn't help. A bolt could have arced and traveled down the line and then arced again."

Frank's eyes had a distant glaze as he thought back to basic training at Ft. Jackson, South Carolina years past when they had been on the rifle range shooting at four-hundred-yard targets. The sky had filled with clouds so dark gray and blue that they were almost black. Lightning bolts had begun to fly, rain falling horizontally, drops as big as one's thumb, the wind driving them unrelentingly. The storm had rolled in so fast they had nowhere to run. They were ordered out of the firing pits, permanent fox holes, and commanded to discard their rifles, helmets, ammunition belts and anything metallic. The drill sergeants had them run fifty yards into the firing lanes and commanded everyone to get into a prone position, face down on the ground.

The rain fell in torrents, running across the clay soil and

grass like one fluid sheet, almost an inch deep. Frank was grinning at his fellow soldier thinking it was a lot of hoo-ha about nothing. It was then that the lightning bolts began to dance around the firing lanes in the edge of the tall pines, one after another. Suddenly, he was frightened as it looked like blue flame moving across the ground toward them. He and his fellow soldiers were terrified, frozen in place, they dared not run despite the urge to do so. Holding their breath, it was as if time had frozen. Blue flame danced scant inches from his face as he shut his eyes and prayed, every muscle in his body tensing. Directly behind him, they heard a large bolt of lightning strike something. A strange foreboding overcame him as slowly, the storm moved off and the rain stopped. They were ordered up and gathered their gear. Then, the drill sergeants yelled for them to come over. Everyone crowded around, looking down into one of the fox holes. They saw the charred, smoking remains of two of their friends with their helmets on, holding their rifles in blackened hands. It was sickening. He would never forget it.

"This is why you obey orders," drill sergeant Cook had said.

A passing car on the highway jolted him back to the present. Looking at what the electrician had pointed out and the burned out, cinder black panel, Frank passed the episode off as an act of nature.

"Can you fix it?" Frank asked.

"Yes," the electrician replied. "I'll pick up the parts and begin later today. Better call your insurance company because this may become a bit pricey."

"Ok," Frank said glumly. "I'll get on it right away."

Frank busied himself around the house making calls. When he had gotten on top of things for the day, he unlocked his hobby shop. Walking around he could tell no one had been inside. He began checking his surge protectors and turned them on one at a time. There was no response. As he fumbled with his desktop computers, they were unresponsive, as well.

Obviously, the motherboards and circuits had all been fried.

"Make a note dumbass," he thought. "From now on when done, unplug everything."

He was reluctant but pulled his phone out and informed Jonathan then made his next call.

"Genesis, I have some not so pleasant news."

"What's going on?"

"Looks like a lightning strike took out all my computers."

"Could it have been foul play?"

"You're as suspicious as me. At first, I thought it might be, but after walking around with the electrician, it looks like a lightning bolt did them in, including all my household appliances."

"What will this do to our investigation?"

"It will take a few weeks to get it up and running again, but the information gathered so far is gone, not that we had found anything of importance anyway. You know my friend, I think we both may be getting too paranoid. These people have been vetted by the county, state, tribe, and the feds. No one found anything and we didn't either. Did you get the FBI report?"

"Yes," Genesis said. "I also went to the detention center and interviewed the two women. The more I think about it the more I am inclined to agree with you."

"Then there are no other identifiable accomplices," Frank said.

"Only those we already suspected."

"Yes," Genesis sighed. "I realize it may be a dead end. Let me know when it's back up. We'll make a decision then."

Dingy as they came, the lounge sat a half block from A1A, about one-hundred feet back from a small frontage road. The engineer frequented it on almost a daily basis after work, probably because it was cheap. He had no idea it was owned by a friend in Cilatro's organization. He had been sitting at his table for about two hours, drinking. He was slow and his thoughts confused. Normally, he wouldn't have drunk so much but an extremely sexy blonde at the bar kept raising her glass to him. The man to her right, finding it difficult to sit on his stool, was obviously annoyed.

Most of the patrons in the bar had long gone, leaving only the bartender, the blonde, her friend, and a couple of men behind the engineer. One of them slowly slipped around to the dark end of the bar closest to them. Standing in the shadows against the wall, only a small, imperceptible red light denoted his presence. The man he had been sitting with stayed at the table. It was then that the blonde's friend slid off the stool and staggered up to the engineer.

"What do you keep looking at my woman for?" the man asked.

"She keeps raising her glass to me," the engineer replied.

"She's celebrating the soccer score you twit," the man said as he bent over and hit the engineer so hard, he fell off his chair.

Getting to his feet, the engineer swung back; the fight was on. The engineer was no match for the boyfriend but was too drunk to care. The boyfriend hit him again and knocked him away from the table, where he fell at the feet of the man behind him.

"Perhaps this will even the score," Morgan said, handing him a loaded .38 revolver.

The engineer regained his feet and pointed the gun at the man.

"Come on asshole," the engineer said. "This will take care of you."

"I'm not afraid of that pea-shooter," the man said, staggering forward.

He tried to hit the engineer, but the engineer managed to block the blow with his left forearm, kicking the man in the groin in the process. He sunk to his knees looking up.

"Talk to my friend."

The engineer leveled the gun at the man's chest and pulled the trigger, knocking the man backward where he lay still upon the floor. The bartender had slipped around the engineer and hit him over the head with a beer bottle. He was out cold. No one moved. It was so quiet you could hear a pin drop.

"Got it," the man at the end of the bar said.

The assailant stood, removing his bullet-proof vest, his blonde friend standing beside him.

"That was like a scene right out of the movies," Morgan said, laughing. "We couldn't have planned it better. Here's your money. Thanks. Get the hell out."

The two scurried out the door as Morgan and his friend pulled the engineer into a chair. He had sobered just enough. Morgan slapped him hard across the face to sober him some more then, the bartender threw a picture of ice water into his face.

"Show him the surveillance video," Morgan said.

The other man showed the engineer the video of the shooting. It had been staged so perfectly that anyone who watched it would see the engineer had shot the man in cold blood. After all, he was on his knees holding his groin. The engineer would have no protection under the law and would spend the rest of his life in prison.

He started crying as he watched the video. Then, Morgan explained everything the engineer would do for them to make it all go away. Morgan stood and started walking out, turning he said, "If you don't comply, the video goes to the police. I'll call you tomorrow."

Ki Luo kept enjoying the view from his office. Li Na had just informed him that the backdoor investigation was stopped for the moment and likely finished.

"What did you say the power prices were in Texas after the freeze?" Ki asked of his assistant.

"There was a variance in prices, but on average, they went up 10,000 percent, about $9,000 per megawatt hour for a week or so," his assistant said. "They leveled off, but prices remained quite inflated for some weeks. One woman charged her electric car. Guess how much it cost?"

"How much?"

"Eight hundred dollars," his assistant said chuckling.

A smile passed across Ki's lips as he began thinking about the venture. This was going to be the first trial run. If successful, the partnership would begin working with other reservations, particularly the Navajo and the Navajo Power Plant. If they remained cautious, thorough, and methodical, they would become the dominant controller of electricity across the U.S. offering price guarantees to consumers, as well as other incentives. His assistant had devised the plan because Native American Reservations could act independently, to an extent, within the U.S. avoiding many SEC, FCC, foreign ownership, and other regulations. They were not immune, but more flexible.

"What would you recommend based on your research?" Ki asked. "I mean in terms of pricing and getting consumers to go with us."

His assistant, Akio was mixed Japanese and Chinese and one hell of a numbers man. Slim with small glasses and a quick wit, he was as bright as they came, and money was the most important thing in his life!

"Considering the domino effect and interdependency of the infrastructure, it's something we need to study a bit more," Akio said.

"What do you mean?" Ki asked.

"During the Texas freeze, the maximum number of generators and the unavailability of fuel caused outages and derates that affected 6.1 gigawatts of capacity. Considering fuel limitation, this applied to thermal plants, especially gas ones given that nuclear fuel is not affected by weather conditions and coal should also be largely shielded unless it gets wet or frozen. Boiling it down, it is likely most of the fuel outages were gas plants. Their share of total outages affecting the gas fleet comes to about thirty percent, which is significant."

"So, you're saying the outage heavily affected gas prices for cars and trucks?" Ki asked, his eyes widening.

"Exactly," Akio responded. "The main problem they had was that the major electrical supplier could charge anything they wanted when the interruption occurred. Many in the state were furious because they were left unprotected against the price increases."

"Hmmmm," Ki mused. "We could get around that by stating we won't increase prices over some percentage if a similar disaster like the one in Texas occurred."

"That was my thoughts as well, especially given the prominence of hurricanes in the state," Akio said. "If we do not get greedy, the consumer will support us. This is what I propose. Lots of power companies are doing it anyway. We make it easy for the customer to go solar because we can sell the excess energy. At the same time, to avert the fiasco of what happened in Texas, we guarantee our prices will not exceed eighteen percent in event of a natural disaster. And for the first three days after the disaster, perhaps a week, the consumer gets free emergency electricity."

"Hold on; that's a lot of profit down the tube," Ki said.

"Perhaps," Akio replied softly. "But the consumer would see that we were trying to help them at the expense of profiting ourselves and position us to become the dominant supplier through sheer customer loyalty thus, growing our customer base. Remember, this is the first of many, all legit."

Ki grinned broadly, as if a light had gone off. "You're much brighter than I thought. I see how you are thinking strategically. Very well. I want you to propose several scenarios with costs and let's present them to the partners."

"If I may suggest sir," Akio began. "The tribe has a member who knows the ins and outs of cascading failures and critical infrastructure, better than anyone from what the President told me. Why don't we get the tribe to ask him to make a presentation about it? I can be there along with Li Na, and we can ask pertinent questions and make everything look even more legitimate."

"Who is this person?" Ki asked.

"His name is Lunadi, and he has presented to some of the highest officials in the American Government but hates them with a passion although always willing to share his knowledge."

"Alright," Ki said. "Work up the numbers and I'll contact Li Na to make it happen."

Morgan was diligently working with the engineer they had compromised. The man was Fred Clubine, head engineer for the Port St. Lucie nuclear power plant. Already having gone through three marriages and heavily in debt to his ex-wives for child support and alimony, he had been an easy target. The video of the shooting at the bar, a threat to kill his family, and a cash bribe of $500k, insured Fred's cooperation and loyalty.

Working on the dark web and through Middle Eastern contacts, they had purchased the plans for a remote-control countermand device that could intercept any electrical signal, which could then be recoded to perform the commands coming from the device instead of the commands issued from the system. It was quite ingenious and would work with any type of system, even ballistic missiles. Morgan didn't understand the complexity of it but thought of it as a Pandora's box that could wreak havoc on the adversary; it was quite ingenious. But Fred thoroughly understood its capabilities and was able to encode it.

"Where will you place the device?" Morgan asked.

"It needs to be placed on the condenser," Fred said.

"Why?" Morgan asked.

"We are working with a boiling water reactor," Fred began, happy to display his knowledge. "It cools the exhaust steam from the turbines to below the boiling point so that it can be returned to the heat source as water. In this case, to the reactor core."

"What happens if the water is not below the boiling point?" Morgan asked.

"The reactor core will slowly rise in temperature and the rods could begin a meltdown," Fred said.

"We don't want a meltdown," Morgan said. "We want enough of a snafu so the plant will be closed temporarily for inspection. Can you do that?"

"Yes. I can place the device and control it and then, remove it before anyone is the wiser," Fred replied. "Just hope that we don't lose control of it."

"What do you mean?" Morgan asked.

"If the device gets too hot, it may not accept our shutdown commands."

"Then shield it so it doesn't," Morgan said. "Get on it so we can test it."

"Right, . . . "

Morgan's ringing phone cut the engineer off.

"Morgan."

"Have you looked into whether or not Genesis is working for Billie?" Cilatro asked.

"Yes," Morgan said. "I've been working on that. Li Na has been helping us and eavesdropped into their conversations. What I have determined is that most of this is directed paranoia due to the death of his fiancé. Because of that, everything happening on the reservation has become a red herring. He does report to Panther and discusses his concerns, but we know that Panther isn't buying into it without proof. He's got more of a scientific mind so, facts are important to him without going off halfcocked."

"Where does that leave us?" Cilatro asked.

"We are cooperating with them and so far, so good," Morgan said. "Neither Panther nor other tribal officials have given us anything but what we need. Li Na said Genesis had some outside sources looking into legitimacy of the partners, but they found nothing. And apparently an electrical storm the other night has shut their three-man operation down. I doubt they found anything damaging since the feds didn't, nor state or tribe. As a matter of fact, the FBI, just released their final report which states that Lorio, Phenning, and the others were operating on their own. No other accomplices were found. Essentially, the case is closed. Besides, you're not shown as a partner, so I think we're in the clear."

"Let's not get too complacent," Cilatro said. Keep an eye on them. How is the project going?"

"I'm working on it now," Morgan replied. "It looks well in hand. We should be testing the apparatus in a couple of days."

"Good," Cilatro said. "Remember, just enough to force an inspection."

"Yes sir."

Cilatro and Ki were on the same page. If they could pull this off without a hitch, a continual stream of revenue would be theirs for years. More than they could have ever hoped for. He frankly wondered why they had not thought of this before. "I guess short-term profits had a way of obscuring strategic paths."

Billie had put the finishing touches on the place of worship. True to what the Medicine Man had said. He found the cypress head and had made a small altar from split cypress and bound together with switch grass to which legs were fastened onto it. Sitting down, his 185-pound weight didn't seem to faze it. There were two cypress trees near each back corner of the altar, so he placed the altar edges against them, marked where the legs were pressing the soil and began digging each leg down about six inches. Once he had the holes for the legs dug, he sat the altar back in place and filled around them with the soil he had removed, leveling the altar as he went, continually tamping the earth around them. Again, he sat on the altar to make certain it was secure, tamped the legs some more and smoothed the earth all around the altar for a space of about twelve feet by twelve feet in front of it. Around the edges he transplanted some ferns he had dug up on other hammocks.

The project had taken him most of the day. As he sat looking across the cypress head and sawgrass beyond, a feeling of peace washed over him. The sky over the horizon began to turn orange as the sun sank lower in its orbit. He suddenly was aware of a presence., the hair on the back of his neck standing up. Coming around the edge of the cypress head, he noticed the Medicine Man poling a dugout canoe. He was alone. It was the first time Billie had ever seen him without his warrior bodyguard.

"Greetings my young warrior," the Medicine Man said. "I assume you have finished?"

"Yes, it is as you requested."

The Medicine Man's keen eyes swept the area behind Billie, noticing how clean and ordered the altar and its surroundings were. As the bow of the dugout touched the edge of the head, the Medicine Man held out his hand. Billie grasped it and helped him atop the hammock floor.

"You have done well," the Medicine Man said.

"How did you know I was here?" Billie asked.

"I knew you were you," the Medicine Man said. "I knew the young warrior apprentice would do what needed to be done and would waste no time doing it. Indeed, you have not. Fetch me the bundle out of the canoe, it's in the leather possibles bag."

While Billie retrieved the bundle, the Medicine Man stepped off seven paces directly in the middle of and in front of the altar. He pressed a small cypress branch into the soil to mark the spot and began gathering some dead palmetto fronds, root fibers, and dead cypress branches, placing them in a neat pile off to the side. Then, he took a portion of them and built a small fire where he had pressed the branch into the ground. Billie laid the bundle gently atop the altar. The sun had set, the orange glow in the horizon fading quickly. The two men sat cross legged from each other on either side of the fire as Billie pulled some hoe cake and water from his bag, passing them to the Medicine Man. They both sat quietly, the gleam from the fire in their eyes as they watched the orange tint in the sky turn to a faint blue and then black as the stars in the heavens twinkled brightly.

The Medicine Man turned his face to Billie, not speaking. His face was calm, not judgmental.

"The Panther Clan will always have control of the bundle from this point forward," he said. "The reason is because you did as you were asked, the President has had two years to do what you were asked to do only yesterday."

"Why did he not do it?" Billie asked.

"Because his heart is of the world and the wealth it contains," the Medicine Man said. "He does not truly care about the people unless something is in if for him. Like most politicians no matter where, he is about power, control, and money to the detriment of all else, especially the welfare of people. Let us not talk about him further, he has chosen his path. Tonight, is about our people, you, and the clan."

"What is so special about tonight?" Billie asked, watching the Medicine Man's face intently.

"We must purify this place," the Medicine Man said. "You have a bundle, I have one, the people need one. It will always be here on the altar. And you are the chosen one of the clans, the undisputed leader of the tribe, even though you are not the President. Everyone looks to you for the way to go, the path to take. As we purified the dii potentia, we will purify this altar for the people, and you will be their intercessor. Upon you is placed a great responsibility. Your oath is to always protect the people, no matter what!"

"I understand and will do my best to always help our people."

"I know you will," the Medicine Man said. "It is your nature;

it has always been. Come, let us begin."

The Medicine Man put a few more branches on the fire. As it burned brightly, he went to the alter and unrolled the bundle. He placed the artifacts from the bundle onto the alter and arranged them in a circle. The now golden and crystalline can was placed on the far-right corner. Billie sat watching with great curiosity.

"Note the order of the artifacts," the Medicine Man said. "When petitioning the Great Spirit for the people, the order must not vary. Now, close the circle until the artifacts touch each other, like a five-pronged wheel. Hold the root, the dii potentia until last. Now we must pray."

The five pieces of artifacts began to glow blue and then gold, a wavy gold mist, like the flickering of a flame shooting up about a foot into the air.

"Oh, Great Spirit," the Medicine Man petitioned. "We come before thee to make this place of worship sacred, so that it's ground may be hallowed, a place of worship for the people and those who would help us."

Billie, his head bowed, but eyes opened, had been observing everything. He felt so inadequate as he watched the Medicine Man.

"Now young warrior, the final touch. Place the dii potentia here like this so that one end is atop this artifact and the other atop this one. Never divulge the order. It completes the circle of six parts. The seventh part is the Great Spirit, which the purified root beckons, it being a part of the first foundations of life. Bow your head and watch, but do not turn your head outwards lest you die!"

Billie laid the dii potentia in place as instructed. The golden flame atop the bundle of artifacts grew until it reached the top of the cypress trees thirty feet above and began to swirl outward, emanating in a circle from the alter to several hundred yards around it. The color burst from gold to emerald green as it shot across the top of the sawgrass. Next, the burst was orange then a faint purple. There were no sparks, just a perfect circle of color, lighting up the sky as if it were noon. Purple was followed by red, then ruby, then a crystalline sky blue. Billie kept watching the dii potentia. Each time it changed color, that color was the burst of brilliance that shot outward from the altar. Almost instantaneously, the color bursts began changing every second, beginning with royal purple, followed by red purple, dark red, bright red and then, changing so fast Billie couldn't keep up. Without moving his head, he glanced upward with his eyes through the cypress head. He saw individuals, like spirits encroaching the alter. As they did so, the next flash of color caught them and they burst into a yellow, blue-green flame, exploding like a firework. At the far edge of the circle, several hundred yards away, a great many more spirits waited, moving forward after each flash. Suddenly, the color changed to blue white, producing an eerie, humming sound as it shot for over a thousand yards outward from the alter, catching all the spirits as they encroached. The color began to fold inward like petals of a flower closing as darkness fell. The spirits attempted to escape, running up the sides of the flower then, all at once, exploding like a crystalline glass into millions of tiny pieces; they faded to nothing. The color closed completely like a flower and fell straight onto the altar, turning to the original gold flame as a few sparks shot outward. Billie assumed it was the remnants of the spirits he had seen.

"Look up," a voice said. "This place is now hallowed and sacred. See to it only the faithful and pure in heart visit."

Both the Medicine Man and Billie looked upward. They saw a pair of eyes inset in what appeared to be the shape of a Shaman's head bones. The gaze was fierce and determined, yet soft and loving. Billie wanted to look away but could not. The eyes faded into the darkness leaving the altar intact, the artifacts of the bundle now separated. Billie and the Medicine Man could scarcely move as they retreated away from the altar and sat once again by the fire.

"What were the spirits or what looked like spirits I saw through the cypress trees?" Billie stammered.

"They are those who desire the light of the Great Spirit but are condemned to darkness because of their actions in our previous life," the Medicine Man said.

"Were they killed again by the colors?"

"No," They saw the light and migrated to it, the colors represent the many realms of the Great Spirit and when they caught the spirits, they were cast back into darkness."

Billie sat, deep in thought at what he had witnessed. It was overwhelming. He didn't know if he were up to the tasks the Medicine Man was going to require of him.

"It is not I that require the tasks," the Medicine Man said, discerning his thoughts. "It is the Great Spirit. Conduct yourself as you have, with honor and commitment and you need not fear."

"If I do not?"

"Then you will be like those you just saw," the Medicine Man said. "You must keep the path. Come, let us think about this and sleep."

The fire burned down to embers as Billie thought profoundly on what he had seen. Everything about his life and relationships seemed to pale in comparison to it. His sleep was an uneasy one as he tossed and turned throughout the night. He awoke to the smell of hoe cake and frying venison. The Medicine Man was glancing as him as he cooked. His warrior bodyguard had returned, watching over them.

"Why didn't he come with you yesterday?" Billie asked.

"He is pure of heart," the Medicine Man said. "However, purifications can only be done by those who control a bundle. He can also visit this place, as can others as the Great Spirit told us."

"What happens if someone comes who is not pure in heart?" Billie asked.

"There are two types of people young warrior," the Medicine Man said. "There are those who try to survive and try do the right thing. The other type is evil, who do evil continually, as is their nature because they chose the wrong path. If the first type comes, the Great Spirit will work on their intuition, and they will have no interest and veer away from the place of worship. If evil comes, once they hit the boundary of several hundred yards as you observed last night, they will be consumed and become like the spirits you saw, instantly changing from physical mortality to a confined spirit."

"So, who can come here?" Billie asked.

"The pure in heart and those that control the bundle."

"How many is that?"

"You, I, and Lunadi," the Medicine Man said. "The President could have, but he has pursued another path. If he comes here, he will be accounted as evil. The pure in heart are many but will likely not come unless directed by the Great Spirit."

"Did you train Lunadi?" Billie asked.

"Yes, I did, under the direction of the Great Spirit."

"Will I get to meet him?"

"Yes, he has been summoned by the council to make a presentation. He will come and do that and then, he will leave again. As I told you before, his mission is not on the tribal lands, but to assist those who will help save us all elsewhere."

"I will be happy to meet him," Billie said, not wanting to ask more. "Why are there so few of us with the bundle?"

"The work of the Great Spirit is done by all, even the evil though they know it not," the Medicine Man said. "But few are chosen to the task. It is a great honor and an awesome responsibility. Always remember, many are called; few are chosen."

The Medicine Man's bodyguard walked over to the fire, picked up some hoe cake and fried venison, and returned to his position. He made absolutely no sound. The glance he gave Billie froze him for an instant. Though the glance was non-

James Tindall

threatening, it pierced Billie to the center. He watched the warrior as he resumed his place, putting the meat between the hoe cake and chewing it, washing it down with water. If anyone had a great responsibility, it was this warrior who protected the life of the Medicine Man. Billie's eyes lit up as he thought of a question, again the Medicine Man was aware.

"If someone chases you here or you bring someone unworthy, they will be stopped. Their punishment will be in proportion to what they would do to you."

His eyes were watching Billie to make sure he understood.

Chapter 4

Morgan had come down from his project working with the engineer to meet with the President. They had decided to meet at a sidewalk café adjacent to South Beach. Making sure they were not followed, it was early morning as the sea breeze blew in from the Atlantic, gulls screeching as they floated in the air. When the waitress set the food on their table Morgan glanced furtively about to determine if anyone was close enough to overhear them. Both sipped Cuban coffee with milk; it was strong enough to float a horseshoe. The President wasn't too fond of it but tolerated it for his guest. The common Cuban breakfast platter — tostada and a fruit bowl with sides of bacon and eggs, helped him get the coffee down. Both men dressed casually to blend in with the crowd, only this morning, people were sparse. The light breeze blowing through the sidewalk café felt good as the temperature climbed by the minute.

"I'll get directly to the point," Morgan said. "Genesis seems to be snooping around with a couple of his friends from various federal agencies. It appears that he is trying to vet us further. What can you tell me about him?"

"Genesis is about the law," the President said. "Much like Billie, only he is very paranoid of late."

"Because of his fiancé's death?" Morgan asked.

"I believe so," the President replied. "If you wish, I could talk to him."

"It would need to come from you," Morgan said. "You must not indicate that we have made any inquiries of you."

"Understood," the President said. "I'll have a casual chat in the next day or so, as a matter of fact, we have a scheduled meeting with him tomorrow about some SPD policies. I'll pull him aside privately."

"Great," Morgan said. "You know, this power plant will be a boon to all of us."

"Yes, it will," the President said, thinking it already had been.

The report in her hand was not good. She was trying to figure out who had given the information as she picked up the phone.

"We have a serious problem," Li Na said. "The friend of Genesis, Jonathan, was able to leverage some information from an islander in the Caymans. He listed the next couple of companies the accounts are in."

"How far ahead of them are we?" Ki asked. Hold, I have a call. I'm back, it's Cilatro, he is on with us."

Li Na described the situation.

"I do not see that we have a choice," Cilatro said. "First, we need to stay ahead of these guys; second, we need to stop the prying."

"Agreed," Ki and Li Na responded in unison.

"I think the FBI report will do that," Li Na said. "This was found before that was issued."

"Can we stay ahead of them?" Cilatro asked.

"Yes," Li Na said. "I have our best tech guy on it and he's jumping way ahead. They won't be able to track us. The problem is that Jonathan got someone in his agency to loan a computer with more sophisticated search software on it than he had access to previously."

"So, this is coming again from their backdoor investigation?"

Ki asked. "I thought we had stopped that."

"It was only a temporary fix," Li Na said. "We assumed errantly that they would just stop with the lack of equipment. Their persistence was not anticipated."

"We need leverage on them somehow," Cilatro said.

"I have a way, but I don't think you'll like it," Li Na said.

"What are you proposing?" Ki asked.

"We have no leverage on Genesis or his two friends short of killing them," Li Na said.

"We can't do that," Cilatro interrupted.

"Yes, agreed, hear me out. I propose leveraging Billie Panther by kidnapping his son who will then put pressure on Genesis to lay off. It will occupy all his time."

"But that would point a direct finger at us," Ki said. "The project would end before it gets started."

"Perhaps," Li Na said. "But what if it was us who saved the day, found the boy and returned him back to Billie?"

"Hmmmm," Cilatro said. "That could work, but how could we carry it out?"

"Subterfuge and terrorism," Li Na said. "One of our enemies wants to put pressure on our company by sabotaging a current project. I can have it all worked up by our intelligence officer who could contact the FBI and drop a bread crumb that they think something is afoot and give them information on a couple of individuals we suspect. It will not be traceable back to us, and we will help them escape when law enforcement closes in."

"It seems a bit dramatic," Ki said.

"It has to be," Li Na replied. "That's the only way. If we kill Genesis and his friends, the trust will be gone, and the tribe will naturally blame us, whether we did it or not. They did the same with Lorio and if that driver had not dumped the remaining part of his load into the creek, we wouldn't be in our current predicament."

"I would tend to agree with the plan," Ki said thoughtfully.

James Tindall

"What do you think Cilatro?"
"We cannot afford to be stopped at this juncture," Cilatro said.
"Make it happen Li Na and ensure we are not connected in any way."

It was school day at Miami Seaquarium, one of Florida's best sea attractions located on beautiful Biscayne Bay only minutes from downtown. Buses from quite a few schools were lined up to give the teachers a break, while they escorted the kids around to have fun with the many attractions. Christina was feeling great as she walked around with the kids in her class talking to other teachers. The kids were screaming, yelling, laughing, and having a great time. Despite the effort, it was difficult to keep the kids separated into classes as they crowded as close as they could to the exhibits. Other parents with their kids were mixed in, overrun by large groups of students here and there.

Two men, well dressed, escorting a young teenage girl in a wheelchair, mixed in with the groups. Like the kids, they were laughing and smiling, appearing to all around them to be having the best day of their lives. It was Li Na's men, waiting for the perfect opportunity to nab James and quickly escort him out of the park. The kids were not sticking to the tour, but began to wander toward the killer whale show, dolphin harbor, and tropical wings exhibits on the east side of the Seaquarium. It was nearing lunch, and everyone was finishing up at the manatee exhibit and gathering around the nearby hot dog stand. James asked to go to the restroom on the other side of Sharky's. The men knew this would be their best chance as they separated and caught James in the restroom, all alone. The teenage girl in the wheelchair they had been pushing was a mannequin. They put the mannequin in a stall as they covered James's face with a rag doused in desflurane, a fluorinated methyl ethyl ether. A common drug used in the medical industry to cause general anesthesia, and loss of consciousness, both before and during surgery in adults and for maintenance anesthesia for children during surgery. Very rapidly, the kids blood solubility was reduced as vapor pressure increased and James passed out almost instantaneously. The men put him quickly into the wheelchair, covered him with a large beach towel and hat and wheeled him out of the restroom toward the south entrance of the Seaquarium. A small van was waiting into which they loaded the unconscious boy and wheelchair. The driver merged quickly onto highway 913 heading southeast. About one mile down they pulled into Hobie Island Beach Park and drove to the furthest end of the parking lot adjacent to Rickenbacker Causeway.

They hurriedly unloaded James and the wheelchair and pushed it briskly toward the causeway. The van had already exited the parking lot and was back on the highway. A speed boat was waiting patiently for them under the causeway, engines idling, out of site to passersby. The two men looked around to make sure they were not being watched. Fifteen seconds later the boat was speeding north toward Ft. Lauderdale where they would stash the boy until they received further instructions.

Christina was overwhelmed with the number of kids and decided to take a break to wait for James outside the restrooms. She had been waiting a few minutes, wondering what could be taking him so long. After another five minutes, she decided to yell into the men's side to find out what he was doing, calling his name several times. No one had come in or out of the bathroom, so she barged in, beginning to breathe heavily, realizing that something was wrong. No one at all was in the bathroom. Then, she saw some feet in one of the stalls.

"James," she said. "Is that you? Come on, we need to go."

Receiving no answer, she knocked. The stall door swung open. Sitting on the toilet was the mannequin. Her heart leapt into her throat. Panicking, she called park security who arrived on scene within a couple of minutes. The Seaquarium entrance was closed as security checked everyone going out. Now on lock down, security decided to tape off the scene until officers from the Miami-Dade Police Department (MDPD) could arrive. Christina was frantic as she called.

"Billie, get to the Miami Seaquarium as fast as you can," she said.

"What's going on?" Billie asked.

"I cannot find James," she said, sobbing. "He went to the bathroom, and we found a mannequin sitting on a toilet."

"Okay," Billie said. "I'm in Hollywood at the Tribal offices. I'll bring Genesis. Don't panic. Has security locked down the park?"

"Yes. They did so immediately."

Billie ran to find Genesis. Within a couple minutes they had jumped into his SPD vehicle, sirens blazing, heading down I-95 south to Miami Seaquarium. It was about thirty miles away. Christina updated the two as much as she could. They arrived on scene to find MDPD already setting up perimeters, checking parking lots, cars, and exhibits — every part of the park.

Genesis noticed a sergeant nearby as they looked around the restroom. He was in uniform and thus, well received.

"Sergeant," Genesis said, extending his hand. "I'm head of the Seminole Police Department. Billie Panther, one of our tribal councilmen is the father of the missing boy James. Can you tell us anything?"

"Nice to meet you both. I'm Sergeant McAllister of MDPD. We have set up perimeters and are checking everyone going out, including all cars and every part of the area. One of our corporals is going over security recordings. Any ideas you have would be of great help."

"Sounds like you're doing all you can," Genesis replied. "What, …" His voice trailed off as a corporal from MDPD came running up, out of breath.

"You need to see this sergeant," the corporal said. "It's definitely a kidnapping."

The corporal held out a laptop, playing a video of two men with a wheelchair, pushing it into the bathroom right behind James. The video showed the men coming out about two minutes later. The clothing on the figure in the wheelchair was obviously James. Billie and Christina were trying to keep their cool.

"Who would want to kidnap our son?" Billie asked. "Genesis, what do we do?"

"Currently, the MDPD has jurisdiction of the case," Genesis said. "Even though the FBI could take over, I recommend you let MDPD keep it and the FBI can work with them on an advisory capacity and pull in their extensive resources. That way we have two large law-enforcement groups working together and more manpower. I don't need to tell you finding him will be like trying to find a needle in a haystack."

"I agree with your thinking," sergeant McAllister said. "As parents, you can help us sift through the security videos and help us identify James throughout the park. We will trace all his movements throughout the day and see if we can identify the people who took him. They had to follow him until that point to pick the time to grab him."

"Very well," Billie said. "We will help all we can."

"This way please," Sergeant McAllister said.

Genesis pulled out his cell phone as he followed the group. Jonathan answered and he explained everything.

"Alright," Jonathan said. "I'll contact my counterpart at the Miami field office, and he will get someone over there right away to help out and start their side of the process. I'll tell him you want MDPD to keep jurisdiction for now. I think that's a smart move."

"Thanks."

As day turned to dark, law enforcement turned the park upside down and sifted through the security videos. The men who had abducted James were pros. There was never a clear enough picture on the security videos to identify who they were. Genesis had called back to tribal headquarters and informed the President who held an impromptu meeting with SPD to lend all the assistance they could. Next, he called Morgan and explained what had happened. Morgan, playing his role, acted as if he were in complete shock. The sting was in play. After much thought, they had the President call Genesis who suggested they meet. Genesis, being a bit paranoid had his guard up.

Morgan and Li Na arrived at the park to find it cordoned off and swarming with law enforcement from various agencies, including the FBI. They were directed to a command center just inside the front gate, which wasn't much more than a party tent with open sides. Officers were manning phones and calling out questions and orders. Quite literally it was a mad house. Hovering around a table were Genesis, Billie, Christina, Sergeant McAllister, and FBI Special Agent Phil Austin. They all stopped what they were doing when Morgan and Li Na approached.

"I'm Sergeant McAllister and this is Special Agent Phil Austin with the FBI. We received a call that you may be able to shed some light on this situation. Anything you can tell us could be a great help."

"Please, take a look at these photos and see if you recognize them," Phil said.

As the two looked over the photos, a gleam of recognition registered in Li Na's eye.

"Do you recognize something?" McAllister asked.

"This man," Li Na said, pointing. "He looks like he may be familiar, but I don't see the front of his face anywhere in the videos."

"That's because he is a pro," Phil said. "What can you tell us about this type of situation with your company?"

"Our company is involved in water and energy projects, such as the power plant we are partnering with the tribe, all over the world. This type of thing has been happening with us and with our competitors throughout Asia. They kidnap someone and use them as leverage for blackmail or to sabotage a project so that it does not come to fruition. Our intelligence officer says it's spreading around the globe."

"Do you think it is possible this is one of those incidents?" Genesis asked, watching her closely.

"I'm not sure," Li Na said. "Here is the number of our intelligence officer in Hong Kong. He's tied in with law enforcement all over the area. I have already called my boss and he is standing by to help you in any way he can."

"Thank you," McAllister said as he took the paper and handed it to Phil.

"Sam," Phil yelled. "Call this number and get these pics over there to see if they have any information that may help us."

Genesis couldn't tell what Li Na was thinking. Outwardly she was gracious and kind, but her dark brooding eyes showed no emotion. Perhaps Chinese people all had that look. After all, Native Americans were portrayed as being emotionless. Maybe they were not so different after all. And, despite the fact he wanted to find dirt on them, multiple agencies and his small operation had yielded nothing.

"Thank you," Billie said. "Any help is appreciated. With all the children here today, there has to be a reason why they took James."

"I suppose we all have enemies," Morgan said. "I'm not in law enforcement, but I do not believe in coincidence."

"I agree," Phil said. "This has to be either personal or, as Li Na suggested, it may be targeting the company to sabotage your power plant operation."

"Sir," Sam said, panting as he rushed over, handing him some papers. "You need to see this."

As Phil and Sergeant McAllister scanned the papers, they both smiled.

"Talk about a break," McAllister said.

"What's going on?" Billie asked.

"We hit a gold mine of information," McAllister said. "This is the rap sheets of the two men in the security video. It turns out with the side profile pictures that Li Na's intelligence guy and the Hong Kong Police were able to positively identify them."

"That's a good start then, isn't it?" Christina asked.

"Yes, very good," Phil said. "However, identifying them and finding them are two different things."

"Put an APB out on these guys right away Sam," Phil said.

"Do you think you can apprehend them?" Li Na asked.

"In time yes," McAllister said. "But time rapidly becomes a luxury we do not have."

"All of you have been a big help," Phil said. "It's time for us to get down and dirty. If you don't live nearby, perhaps you should get a hotel. We have your numbers and will keep you posted. Call us if you need or want to."

Sergeant McAllister and Phil turned back to their men as they began the search in earnest. They had no car or other information to go on so their first target was Asian bars in the downtown area to see if they could get a lead. The group was already out the front gate getting into their cars.

"Li Na," Billie said. "Thank you for your help. If your intelligence officer can dig up anything else to help us . . ."

"I understand," Li Na said, interrupting him. "I will call my boss and keep him working on it."

No sooner than Li Na and Morgan were in the car and out of the parking lot than she contacted Ki.

"Everything is going as planned," Li Na said. "The only problem is that the Hong Kong Police were able to positively identify the men. We cannot help them escape; they must be eliminated."

"Can you arrange that?" Ki asked.

"Leave it to me," Li Na said smiling. "I'll take care of it."

After hanging up, she called the two men.

"You did great work and left no physical trace," Li Na said. "The other safe house has been stocked with food and supplies. Go there now and await my call. We need to squeeze these guys for a few days."

"Do you think they bought it?" Morgan asked.

"Yes," Li Na replied. "They are paid servants for lack of a better term. They will do as they are told. We are taking care of their families and they will give their lives if need be. How long do you think we should squeeze Billie for?"

"Two to four days should be sufficient," Morgan said. "The problem is how do you tell Billie to lay off the search Genesis is doing when this is not supposed to be about sabotaging the company?"

"That is easy my friend," Li Na said smiling. "That search is what gave these guys the information they needed to target us. He will immediately tell Genesis to lay off, especially since he knows this is a routine occurrence in Asia and other places."

"Damn you're good," Morgan said.

A sly smile crossed Li Na's lips as she thought what she would do if Morgan did cross her, but he was too smart for that. Like herself and the rest of them, it was all about the money and for her, the money would lead her up the chain for those she pursued. She had already decided to eliminate the men who had taken James, but she needed to throw off Billie and she needed to keep the men involved so they would believe that things were going according to plan. She made the call.

The hotel room wasn't a suite but was comfortable. Christina sat, trying to gather her thoughts. Even though she was not James's biological mother, she loved him as if he were her own son and spent more time with him than most mothers were able to, both at home and school.

"I know it's hard for you," Billie said. "But we'll get through this just like we did the landfill fiasco."

"It's just that I keep thinking what I could have done to make sure James stayed safe," she said.

"Do not make it hard on yourself," Billie said. "Who would have thought that such a venue would result in this? It's not your fault. The restroom wasn't fifty feet away and you had a whole classroom to look after."

"Aren't you distraught too?" Christina asked.

"Of course, I am," Billie said. "I'd like to get my hands on those two. The Medicine Man told me to not stress about things I cannot change, but to move forward and work on those things I can. This is one of those times. People with much more expertise than we have are looking for James. I feel certain we will find him. The best we can do is give them whatever information we can and stay the course. Getting upset and divided is a waste of energy that will help no one!"

Christina sat on the edge of the small sofa staring at him. She knew he was right but could not believe how calm he was. But it was only outwardly; Billie's mind was racing. He kept wondering why of all the children at the park that it was James who had been taken. It had to be linked to what Li Na had said was going on in Asia and around the globe. He turned to say something to Christina when there was a soft knock on the door. Billie looked through the peep hole; the person in the hall looked very official, so he opened the door.

"Are you Billie Panther?" the man asked, taking off his hat.

"Yes."

"I need a moment of your time. May I?"

"Yes, come in," Billie said.

Christina was wondering who the gentleman was. He was dressed in a black shirt and deep purple tie, with black slacks, pricey Italian shoes, and black leather belt. He had a soft smile, nice tan, and penetrating eyes as he gazed around the hotel room.

"Good evening, Christina," the man said as he took up an

empty chair across from the sofa. "Please, Mr. Panther, sit next to her."

"How do you know my name and who are you?" Christina asked, a sinking feeling in her stomach.

"I know a great deal about both of you," he said. "Who I am is unimportant. I thought we could have a little chat. First, I want you to thank Genesis for this little chat. If he had not been poking around, we would not have found out about your energy project."

"What do you mean?" Billie asked.

"He decided to do further vetting of your partners and Walla," here I am.

"You mean looking into the background of the folks in Hong Kong?" Billie asked.

"Yes, they are our archrivals and now we're going to make them pay."

"You have James," Billie said as he started to reach for the man. The visitor pulled a suppressed 9mm from behind his waist, waving the barrel directly at Billie, motioning for him to sit back down.

"Now that we are clear," the man said. "I'm not here to harm you but I will if necessary. Yes, as you have surmised, we have James. He will be okay as long as you do what you are told."

"Is he hurt?" Christina asked, her eyes glistening.

"He is perfectly fine and will remain so as long as you cooperate. You see, you two have the most to lose, a life; our rival will lose only money. It is unfortunate we need to use James as leverage, but life has its twists and turns. Now it is time for you to listen. Can you do that?"

Billie and Christina looked at each other and then back at the gentleman. He looked slightly Asian, but it was difficult to tell though his English was impeccable.

"You will be our mediator with Li Na and the police. If you do as we command, James will remain unharmed. Your role is simple. We will pass demands through you to them with instructions via phone. If they meet our demands, everything will be fine."

"And if they don't? Billie asked.

"Convince them," the man said as he walked to the door, pistol in hand. "Make your calls and we will be in touch. Here."

The man tossed Billie a cell phone and was out the door without a sound.

"Call Genesis," Billie said, "Get him here now. I will call Sergeant McAllister and Phil.

Within minutes, Genesis and about a dozen law enforcement officers were on scene as Billie and Christina explained what had happened. The police checked the security feeds and had clear pictures of the visitor from various angles, but not his face. It was evident he was not one of the men from the theme park. He had arrived and exited the building at the front entrance in a luxury sedan. The plates, clearly visible, had already been run by MDPD; they were stolen.

"This guy is very smooth," Phil said. "There are no direct facial pictures of him and the plates on the car were stolen. A dead end on that account."

"Is there any way to track him when he calls?" Billie asked.

"Susan, come here please," Phil called out. "Billie, this is Susan Hill our communications specialist."

"Pleased to meet you," Susan said. "May I have the cell phone he gave you?"

Billie handed it over. She used it to call the main network number, which displayed the cell number on caller ID.

"There's your cell number," Susan said. "I will use that to track the caller when he makes contact. We'll need to set up in here for the time being. After today, we will be doing it from headquarters."

"Can you track him?" Billie asked.

"It depends on how long he stays on the line," Susan said. "Let me explain to you how all of this works. You've seen in many movies how people on the run are hunted down because of their cell phones. Unfortunately, it's not that easy. A novice could try to allude us by putting their phone into airplane mode but that doesn't really work because every phone has two operating systems. One of those systems connects to cellular networks and the other one interfaces with the consumer. Generally, airplane mode only disables features in the consumer facing operating systems that is used between the phone and the carrier network. So, your phone could be giving out a ping and you would not know it. This cat is slick, he knows this.

Communicating with a cell tower can expose you because you do not need to be giving out GPS coordinates. You see, the communications network compares the signal strength of your cell phone on multiple cell towers, and we can approximate your location via triangulation. In rural areas, where there are fewer towers, we could probably get a good fix on you and find you quickly but in urban areas where there are more cell towers, we can only get an approximate location, more definite if you can keep this guy on the phone. I'm guessing he is too smart for that.

Let's look at this from his end. He could remove his SIM card, but every phone has a built-in feature set of identifiers that can often be detected via tools like Stingray devices now used by the police and military, as well as fake 2G cell towers put up by the NSA. Forcing a phone to 2G means no encryption and it's easily detected and tracked. You're going to ask so, I'll explain. Stingrays are also known as cell-site simulators or IMSI catchers. They mimic cell phone towers and send out signals that can trick a cell phone into replying with its location and data that can be used to identify the user. These are surprisingly widely used. Again, I think your guy is too smart for this and we are not going to be able to get close enough to get a visual.

The ACLU has a map and list of federal agencies known to use cell-site simulators. This list includes the DEA, Secret

Service, FBI, U.S. Marshals, U.S. Army, Navy, Marine Corps, National Guard, DOE, and many more. We can use Wi-Fi to track him if we can get close enough because it sends out your MAC address, a digital fingerprint. Although stores use it to track your movements, it is not ideal for tracking due to limited range."

"Wait," Billie said. "You mean if I walk into a store, they can track me by my cell phone."

"Yes," Susan said. "If you leave your Wi-Fi on and it connects to the stores Wi-Fi, which it usually does unless the system is secure. The simple solution for this is to avoid unencrypted public Wi-Fi, in other words, turn the Wi-Fi on your phone off. But trust me, from what we know now, this guy is too smart for that as well. To be honest, everyone should turn their Wi-Fi off in public because of man-in-the-middle attacks and fake 'trusted' routers. Fake Wi-Fi access points are sometimes called 'evil twins' that are designed to look legitimate but are actually operated by an attacker. Connecting to one can allow eavesdrop or it can direct you to a fake website where the attacker or hacker can obtain sensitive passwords and other information. Using HTTPS, TLS, or SSL sockets help greatly, but even they are slightly vulnerable. So here it is in a nutshell.

There is a difference between something being probable or possible. This guy knows what he is doing so he will likely remain ahead of us, which puts him in control and makes my job more difficult. Try to keep him on the phone for at least seven seconds or more. That will allow us to get an approximate geographical location. As soon as he hangs up, he will likely either remove the battery from his phone if he can or put it in a privacy case that blocks all signals in and out. Worst of all the phone will likely be a burner which he will replace. We will do all we can, but I cannot promise you anything. Also, I doubt he will be anywhere near where James is being held when he calls."

"Understood," Billie replied.

"Genesis," Phil said. "MDPD and the FBI will be canvasing local bars, especially those that are more Asian oriented. It's a long shot, but we have a composite of the guy based on side profile videos. Apprehending him from a phone call as you heard Susan's explanation will probably not happen. If we can get someone from a local bar or restaurant to identify him, it will allow us to focus our efforts more narrowly. Until then, we need to wait for his call."

Genesis was leaning against the wall outside tribal headquarters smoking a cigarette the next day. He had quit but this kidnapping, his fiancés death, and other issues were putting a great deal of stress on him. He was obscured by a short palm tree and couldn't help overhearing one side of the conversation of the President on the phone. His ears perked up when he recognized the President's voice.

"You should not have put me in the middle of this," the President was saying. "I will have no part of it. Return the item at once. Yes, I know the place it's that hotel near South Beach. Okay, I will be there at 10:00 pm."

The President didn't notice Genesis as he made his way to his office. Genesis watched him disappear around the corner and hastily strode to his cruiser. He called Billie and picked him up outside his hotel then, traveled to a nearby park where they could talk privately.

"I do not know what is going on," Genesis said, looking about. "Given what is happening, we can't be too cautious. I overheard a private conversation this morning."

"What kind of conversation?" Billie asked.

"It was the President on the phone with someone. He didn't know I was there. Essentially, he said he would be no part of something, and that they would have a meeting here at 10:00 pm, pointing to a location on a map laid between them."

"You think he meant James?" Billie asked.

"I don't believe in coincidences," Genesis said. "It has to be

James Tindall

about him in my opinion."

"What can we do?" Billie asked. "Should we bring the Feds and MDPD in on this?"

"My mind tells me yes," Genesis said. "My gut tells me no. This is thin information to set up a tactical operations raid. Look, I'm aware of the transparency and some of the things that it can do. Can you use it to gain access and find out more?"

Billie looked Genesis, unaware that he knew that he was in studies with the Medicine Man about the transparency.

"How do you know about that?" Billie asked.

"I have my eyes and ears," Genesis said. "I only know tidbits."

"Ok," Billie said. "Your small insight is true. I have just learned how to negotiate my way around but haven't practiced much yet."

"This will be your first test then," Genesis grinned. "I can help you with what you need to do."

"The only thing I need is for you to guard my body from harm," Billie said. "Let's devise a plan."

Genesis and Billie found a secluded construction building not far from where the meeting would occur. Billie prepared for the transparency by building two fires and laying between them. In his hand was the dii potentia. He had instructed Genesis on what to do and then laid down between the two small fires, they were positioned about a yard away from his head and feet.

Billie began to hum softly and then an imperceptible chant. The dii potentia in his hand began to glow a bright white. As Genesis looked on a golden mist engulfed Billie's body, slowly floating upward, transforming into bright sparks as it disappeared.

Almost instantly, Billie found himself on a grassy hill, the tree of life on his right. Beyond it was the cosmos. The eyes that watched over the tree, those of the Great Spirit were not present. On the horizon, the cosmos stretched before him, galaxies, nebulas, stars, and planets, floating in a vast array of deep red, blues, orange, black, and yellows. It was almost like a painting, but the planets and galaxies were in constant motion. He remembered what the Medicine Man had told him of the differences between where he had gone without the purified dii potential. There had been tunnels there; here it was the green grass of a huge hill where stood the tree of life dropping off into the deep cosmos.

"Think he thought, as he walked along. How do I find the portal to take me where I need to be?"

As he continued walking, there was no change in his surroundings, no people, only the sweet silence of nature. Billie sat down on the grass to gather his thoughts. No sooner had he sat down than he heard a voice.

"Think whereon thou would go."

He looked around and saw no one. It was then that he remembered what the Medicine Man had said, which was to think about where you wanted to travel. When he remembered this, he thought about the hotel where the meeting was supposed to take place. Immediately a portal opened before him, and he arose and stepped into it and was instantly whisked away as he saw stars flash by so rapidly it was as if there were millions of them surrounding him all at once. It was like being on a roller coaster. In a flash, he found himself in the hallway of the hotel. A couple walked right by him but didn't notice. Billie was in a purified spirit form.

He walked down the hall listening at each door. As he leaned against the third door, his head penetrated it while his body remained in the hallway. It startled him. He realized he could just poke his head through the door, or even walk through the walls from one room to the next. The problem was that he didn't know what room the meeting was in. Billie quickly hurried to the end of the hall near the elevators and began walking through the rooms, right through the walls. He was halfway back up the other side when he walked into the meeting.

The man who had visited him and Christina was sitting on a sofa, the President was opposite in a chair.

"You had no right to involve me . . .," the President said, suddenly stopping, standing, and looking slowly around the room.

As the President looked around, Billie got nervous. The President had been involved in the transparency. He could feel the spirit in the room.

"Where is the boy now?" the President asked.

"In a safe house in Ft. Lauderdale," the man said. "Don't worry he won't be harmed, not yet anyway."

"See to it he is not," the President said. "A spirit is in this room, you must go."

"What do you mean?" the man asked.

"Go now, say nothing else."

The man became nervous as the President picked up a pitcher of water and in one fluid motion, cast it in an arc around the room. Billie saw it coming and jumped. Too late, the water hit him from the waist down and the President and the man could see his form where the water hit, the spirit emanating a golden color. The man immediately charged for the door and ran down the hallway. The President stood his ground.

"I don't know who you are," the President said. "You should leave and not return else we will battle."

There was no point in remaining since the man had left. Billie had garnered two small pieces of information as he squeezed the dii potentia and he was gone in a flash of light, reentering his body, and standing erect in front of Genesis.

"You've been gone longer than I anticipated," Genesis said.

"Because I had to search through the hotel to find the right room," Billie said. "I found out two things, the President didn't know anything about it and James is somewhere in Ft. Lauderdale in a safe house."

"They're going to use him as leverage, like the guy told you," Genesis said.

"Correct," Billie responded. "The question is, can we find him and end this thing?"

"I'm guessing you'll be contacted shortly with their demands," Genesis said. "That's probably our best bet. We're not going to find him this way. We need more information."

"Yes, we do."

Christina was fraught with grief, stress, and anger. Tears were rolling down her cheeks as Billie explained to her in the bathroom what he had found out.

"We need to tell the police," Christina said through her tears.

"I normally would agree," Billie said. "But we really don't have anything to go on. It's the same man who obviously is not going to go anywhere near the safe house. We need to keep monitoring as much as we can."

"Meanwhile James could get hurt, even killed," Christina sobbed.

"Woman up Christina," Billie said loudly. "We are in a situation that we are not able to dictate. James will be okay. Somehow, we need to get more information. Until we are contacted, we really do not know what is going on. The police don't know either."

Billie's phone rang. He exited the bathroom and waved to Susan who was counting down with her fingers from four. When she hit one, she pointed to Billie.

"Panther," Billie said.

"Do you have a pen and paper, Mr. Panther?" the man asked. "You need to write this down and follow instructions to the letter."

"Yes, go ahead."

"Go to 1635 South Sycamore in Ft. Lauderdale. Look in the newspaper box for a manila-colored envelope. It has the necessary instructions. You have three days to comply."

"We have an officer a couple of blocks away," Sergeant McAllister said. "Have him pick it up and bring the envelope here as quickly as he can."

"What do you think the demands will be?" Phil asked.

"I have no idea," Sergeant McAllister said. "Better get Li Na over here and Morgan. Whatever the demands are, maybe they can shed some light on them."

Fred had constructed a heat shield around the countermand device and placed it in a fire resistance test furnace. He slowly increased the temperature of the furnace as he watched readings from the datalogger inside the countermand device. The temperature climbed to 750° Fahrenheit. He tested the device five times and each time it reached the same temperature before failure. He randomly selected another countermand module and tested it, each time getting the same results. The device was ready and would perform flawlessly. As an additional precaution, he suggested to Morgan that they sabotage a water supply to the main feedwater pump that provided water to the steam generators where it absorbed the heat produced by the reactor core. The pipe was already corroded and more than twelve hundred such incidents occurred every year in nuclear power plants. The pipe contained water at 370 °F and was pressurized to 450 pounds per square inch. Once the pipe broke the water would flash to steam as it jetted from the ends. There was also a high likelihood that the steam would actuate the fire suppression systems and water from the system would damage electrical components such as computer card readers at the locking doors and impede first responders, trapping them on the wrong side of the doors which they could not open with their keycards. The fire system, along with the ruptured pipe would also flood the building section where it was housed. If his calculations were correct, the plant would be shut down for at least two months or more before inspections cleared it for operations. Fred enjoyed working on the project. Despite its hostile use, it kept his mind of the bar scene.

Victoria Harbor is classed as a natural landform harbor that separates Hong Kong island in the south from the Kowloon Peninsula to the north. The deep sheltered waters and strategic location on the South China Sea was instrumental in the establishment as a British colony and its subsequent development as a global trading center. It also gave birth to many notorious criminal enterprises. Today was one of those days where the air was without pollution, having been blown away by a stiff breeze coming from the South China Sea. Ki admired the beautiful cloudless sky. He took great pleasure watching this natural splendor and was always irritated when a ringing phone interrupted his serenity.

"The situation is set," Li Na said.

"You had better hope this works," Ki said. "If it does not, we will answer to the bosses. Do you know what that means?"

"Yes," Li Na replied. "We will lose our heads."

"Only after they torture us and kill everyone we know," Ki said. "I will leave it in your capable hands."

Li Na knew he was right, but she could not afford to fail her mission. She was so close to completion. It would take months more, but the result would be one of the most successful criminal operations in history. All she needed to do was play the cards she was dealt and do whatever it took to be on the favored side of the tribe. The only way for her to succeed was for the tribe to succeed. Her ringing phone snapped her back to the present.

"Hello Morgan," Li Na said.

"I just received a call from Sergeant McAllister," Morgan said. "They want us at Mr. Panthers' hotel room."

"I assume they are expecting a ransom call," Li Na said.

"Yes," Morgan replied. "They want us on hand to hear what the demands are. They assume it will be about the partners involvement."

"Understood," Li Na said thoughtfully. "I'll meet you there in twenty minutes."

The hotel room was buzzing with activity when Li Na and Morgan arrived. Everyone was busy with specific tasks as they prepared for an imminent phone call given the intelligence they had received from Li Na's man in Hong Kong.

Billie watched the two enter the room. He had no reason to distrust them but remained wary. Looking at the two, he noticed that Li Na was leaning slightly on a cane she held in her right hand. It was one of the best-looking canes Billie thought he had ever seen. The handle was a pommel type, rounded and flattened at the top to fit easily into the palm of the hand. The entire cane appeared to be made of ebony with a non-slip fitting at the end of the cane; fittings made from hand-engraved brass. The brass fittings were just below the pommel, another about four inches below that and the non-slip one at the end of the cane. They appeared to be engraved with dragons and tigers circling an unseen prey. Li Na had an elegance about her, a graceful athletic demure. Billie had no idea the cane contained a sword with a double edged, Damascus steel, twenty-one-inch blade that had been folded over 8,000 times, and that Li Na was expert in its use.

"Thank you for coming, both of you," Billie said. "I never noticed you with a cane before."

"I use it on and off," Li Na said. "Mostly when my knee is acting up. I injured it in a motorcycle accident a couple of years ago. Right after the accident I used it all the time, now it's an off and on thing."

"I remember from my studies that women in Hong Kong like to ride fast bikes," Christina said, smiling.

"Yeah, we need something that can keep up with us," Li Na said.

They both laughed. The joke wasn't lost on the men who looked somewhat embarrassed at the hint they couldn't keep up physically with women.

"Our intelligence officer thinks he may have identified the man you met," Li Na said. "Even if they did, it will not be easy to find him. As in Hong Kong, there is a vast underground Asian network in Miami."

"How can we find him?" Billie asked.

"It will take trained personnel and would be best if they were Chinese and spoke fluent Mandarin."

"I just found out that you formerly worked with the Hong Kong Police Force," Phil said, interrupting.

"I did," Li Na said. "I worked with them for several years with the Organized Crime and Triad Bureau. My specialty was investigating triad societies and their involvement in organized crime. I answered directly to the commissioner of police due to the sensitive nature of my work. One night I was ambushed by several triad members and managed to escape. Once my identity was compromised, I was of no value to undercover field operations. I could not just be in mundane police management and so I quit the force and joined the private sector where I can work on long-term strategy, security, and intelligence protocols."

"That explains why there was no record of the charges of murder that Genesis had told him about," Billie thought.

"Very interesting," Sergeant McAllister said. "With your experience, I'm sure you can be of assistance."

"I will do all I can to recover James," Li Na said.

"Do you have any idea what they will demand?" Phil asked.

"I'm guessing they will want us to leave our partnership with the tribe," Li Na said.

"But that doesn't make sense," Sergeant McAllister replied.

"It makes perfect sense," Billie said. "Look at the interdependence of water, energy, communications, and other critical infrastructure. We know energy is our Achilles heel and whoever controls that will gain a lion's share of the wealth in that sector moving forward."

"Excellent," Li Na said. "You have seen the strategy correctly."

"Yeah, but they cannot just have you drop the partnership and them move in," Phil said.

"Oh, they wouldn't move in quickly," Li Na said. "They would wait for a period and then approach the tribe as a new partner. They are so embedded you would never find out they are operating beneath the law."

"But others would come forward to be our partners," Billie said.

"Yes, they would," Morgan replied. "However, correct me if I'm wrong Li Na, these guys would threaten, intimidate, and potentially kill any competitors."

"Correct," Li Na said. "That is why we must get James back and negate the outside influence."

"Phil," Susan called across the room. "It's him."

The room fell silent as Billie walked to the phone.

"Are we ready Susan?" Phil asked.

She gave him a thumbs up.

"Keep him on the phone as long as you can Billie."

"Hello," Billie said.

"This is your friend," the man said. "I have a deal to offer."

"First, I want to talk to James," Billie said.

"All in good time," the man said.

"Now, or no deal," Billie said. "Very well, I will merge him. Put on the kid."

"Hello, Dad?" James said.

"Are you ok son?" Billie asked.

"I'm fine," James said. "I am..."

"Your son is safe for the moment," the man said, cutting James off. "Now for our offer."

Susan was motioning to Billie with her hands moving outward along an invisible string to keep the conversation going.

"What are you proposing?" Billie asked.

"Your partners are to drop out of the power plant project," the man said. "Morgan's company and Li Na's employer. In addition, Li Na's employer in Hong Kong is to remove itself from all energy projects in the Hong Kong area. That is all. You have seventy-two hours to initiate."

"What, . . ." Billie began as the phone went dead.

Li Na and Morgan were looking at each other. Morgan knew this would be the end of the line if they gave in. Li Na knew that from what was said that her main employee in Miami had turned on them. She was no longer in control of the situation. The strategy of kidnapping James had backfired. Ki would be displeased. She must not show any signs of her lost control to Ting. She would say nothing to Ki until she could resolve the matter.

"We have the location," Susan said. "He's on 163rd Street, just east of I-95."

"That's the unofficial Chinatown area," Sergeant McAllister said. "Let's get some cars over there now and begin a sweep of the area."

"What does he mean unofficial Chinatown?" Li Na asked.

"Unlike other cities of its size, Miami has no real Chinatown," Phil said. "There's a movement underway to establish one, but 163rd Street is as close as we have come to a formal designation. It's the single largest group of people from Chinese descent in one area. It's in North Miami Beach."

"Are there Chinese bars and similar businesses there?" Li Na asked.

"Yes," Phil said. "Quite a few of them."

"Any suggestions on how we approach this?" Sergeant McAllister asked.

"I have a proposal," Li Na said. "I am Chinese and speak the language fluently. If you send your typical officers in, all the employees, patrons, and business owners will shut you out. Let me go in with one of your Chinese male officers. It will be to collect intelligence only."

"I'm not sure I can authorize that," Phil said. "I am not allowed to put civilians in harm's way."

"I do not need your permission," Li Na said, looking him directly in the eyes. "I extend the invitation for you to let me help you otherwise, I'll do it myself."

"You would put your life in danger for our son?" Christina asked.

"In China, an employee is an extension of the company," Li Na said. "He or she is like one of the family. So, James is my son too."

A single tear trickled down Christina's cheek, understanding what Li Na had said.

"Dispatch send Detective Yuen up," Sergeant McAllister said. "Li Na, we have a young detective that will go with you. He'll be in civilian clothes and knows that area quite well."

"Thank you," Li Na said. "We have little time and much to accomplish."

"What are your plans?" Phil and McAllister asked in unison, as they looked at each other, surprised.

"The man we're looking for has class and style," Li Na said. "The first thing we need to do is find where he frequents. It will be upscale."

"How do you know that?" Phil asked.

"If you go to a low-class establishment the clientele is poor and looking for a score," Li Na said. "Any chance to turn someone in for money would be heaven sent. At upscale locations, the clientele does not worry about money; they simply seek a good time. And if they do not know you, they will not talk to you because you are considered beneath them."

"I've never thought of it like that," McAllister said. "It makes sense. Maybe we should make modifications to our investigation protocols."

"Culture is irrelevant in such situations," Li Na said. "It is just one of life's precepts."

The group was amazed at her wisdom. Morgan felt more

at ease. Somehow, he knew she would find and likely eliminate this threat. He had the inkling that she was no longer in charge of James. A small smile spread across his lips.

"Detective Yuen," McAllister exclaimed. "Come meet our new acquaintances. Everyone, this is Detective Yuen. He's been on the force about five years now."

Detective Yuen was a handsome man. A blue-eyed blonde rich girl had already scooped him up and saw to it that he didn't wear the common suits that most detectives wore and were easily spotted by criminals. He was dressed in an immaculate gray suit and black leather shoes and belt with a pink shirt and multi-colored silk tie with orange, blues, and light greens as the predominate colors. On his hip, barely visible was a 9mm pistol in a leather burgundy, concealable side holster. He had salt and pepper professionally groomed hair, a great tan, and beaming smile. Sergeant McAllister introduced the detective to everyone. When he was done, the detective got directly to the point.

"I'm told I'm to accompany Li Na to some local Chinese bars and other places," Yuen said. "When do we need to start?"

"I'd like to cruise the area first in midafternoon," Li Na said. "We will choose a few locations we believe will be frequented by our perp and return for surveillance about 5:00 pm."

Detective Yuen had cruised the 163rd street area earlier and parked while Li Na walked into several establishments. They had been looking for over an hour, scrutinizing the front of each store. They almost passed the business without realizing it.

"Pull over," Li Na said. "Look at that establishment."

"Yes, I see it," Yuen said. "I have been in there before, but so long ago I forgot. We were investigating the death of a Chinese restauranter. The door is the only sign of an entrance. Note that it is inset into concrete with no windows on the outside. It is two floors and only the wealthy go there. Anyone deemed inappropriate is denied entrance. Upstairs is a massage parlor and private cigar bar, as well as several well-dressed security personnel. The bottom is the bar."

"How can we be admitted?" Li Na asked.

"Let us come back about 6:00 pm," Yuen said. "We need to be appropriately dressed; that means rich. So, wear nice jewelry and attire."

At 6:00 pm, the two returned. Li Na was wearing a pale pink silk dress, sleeveless, with a slit up the left side. She had her hair up in an exquisite bun and wore red bottomed shoes and a Rolex watch. Yuen had changed into a black dinner jacket and white shirt with gold cuff links, expensive watch, and gold rings. Looking like a billion bucks, they walked casually to the door, fashioned in deep jade. It looked like it had been freshly polished. Above a small window in the door in one-inch-tall gold letters were the words "Opium Den" in Chinese.

A security guard just behind the door, wearing a tailored suit with white shirt and tie, greeted them in Mandarin. "What is your pleasure this evening?" he asked.

"We wanted to check out your establishment and enjoy ourselves," Yuen replied in perfect Mandarin.

The guard inspected them and what they were wearing. Feeling satisfied at both their dress and language, he motioned them inside and led them to a small round table with two chairs.

"A waitress will be with you soon."

The two watched him walk back to the door where he resumed a standing position, much like a statue. Li Na gazed around the room. It was a labyrinth-like speakeasy bar, hidden away from the bustle of the outside world. It was obvious that it was a Chinese establishment. A foreigner would not be well received and likely not admitted.

The vibe of the establishment was vintage décor meets exotic parlor, set over two floors with four distinct areas that included an apothecary, upstairs massage parlor, Peony and Academy. The Apothecary showcased a long bar, painted in orange-red, Chinese-firecracker hue, housing uniformly labeled medicine bottles that contained an arsenal of alcohol. The top floor housed the massage parlor and cigar bar along with several private rooms. Upon entering, one was instantly transported back to 1960s Hong Kong, where much of the interiors were inspired by the former colony. The Peony area was exclusive and nestled deep within Opium's Den. It was a drinking den; a bar within a bar, where those with an adventurous spirit and money could experiment to the utmost without hassle or haste. The Academy was no less spectacular for in it a drinker and budding mixologist could check out the masterclass.

Li Na and Yuen were impressed. It made her feel that she was back in Hong Kong having a casual drink with Ki after a long day.

"This is definitely the type of hangout our target would seek," Li Na said. "It is very private and will be difficult to gain information."

"I was thinking similarly," Yuen said. "Perhaps our best bet is just to surveil the place from across the street."

"Is there another way in or out?" Li Na asked.

"I do not think so," Yuen said. "I know there is a back door, but only for kitchen staff. Also, it has two guards if I recall my last visit."

"If our target befriends them, they may let him in," Li Na said. "I would watch both doors."

"I will set it up," Yuen replied. "I'll go to the restroom and check things out as casually as I can."

"Alright," Li Na replied. "I'll wait here and order a drink for each of us."

The waitress arrived shortly after. Li Na ordered drinks for them called 'gunpowder' which was ironic since history has taught that the Chinese invented gunpowder during the Tang

Dynasty in the 9th century. The drink was a combination of spiced rum, lemon oil, and black tea that added bang.

"I managed to get into the kitchen," Yuen said upon his return.

"Is the door open?" Li Na asked.

"Only for deliveries and taking out trash behind the bar," Yuen said. "One of the waiters told me no one is allowed in because of a failed robbery a couple of months back," Yuen said. "I heard about it so that's credible. It is unlikely our perp can gain access that way. Like the front, they also have a security guard just inside the door."

"Let's just hang out for a while and see if he shows," Li Na said.

The two sat and chatted as they absorbed the surroundings. It was evident to Yuen that Li Na would not say any more than she had to. She was very private, but also very alert.

"Tell me more about your service with the Hong Kong Police Force," Yuen said quietly, making sure he was not overheard by others around them.

"There is not a lot to tell other than what I said earlier," Li Na said. "I was forced to end field work when I was recognized. And as you well know, law enforcement has become very political. I didn't want to become one more bureaucrat that managed police departments and personnel and so, I opted for the private sector where I could use many more of my skill sets."

Yuen watched her carefully as she spoke. Her explanation had merit because he knew only too well the bureaucracy and politics involved in his own job. There was something else. He could see it in her eyes but could not determine what it was. She was hiding something. It was none of his concern, so he let it slide. They had been sitting for a couple of hours with no results. Both wanted to ask a waitress or bar tender if their target had been in recently, but it would arouse too much suspicion. They decided to go to another bar on their list, which was on the north end of South Beach and had a more mixed crowd. There they had asked a bartender who didn't recognize the description or picture they had of their supposed friend. They retired for the evening.

Controlling bosses who were not constantly apprised of situations tended to become a bit fraught. Such was the case with Ki when he got the call from Miami about 11:00 am. "I've been waiting for an update," Ki spoke without waiting. "I realize that sir, but remember you are twelve hours ahead of us," Li Na said, attempting to subdue his hidden anger. "I keep forgetting," Ki said. "What news do you have for me?" "I just finished scouting two places with one of their detectives," Li Na said. "I have gained their trust. They do not realize we are the masterminds behind this." "What is the next step?" Ki asked. "I have a strategy to divulge some information to them, so that they get closer to the kidnappers," Li Na said. "Once they are, I will intervene and save the day." "Will that be enough?" Ki asked. "Yes," Li Na replied. "It will save the boy and endear the tribe to us. Then, the project will continue as planned." "Very well," Ki said. "I will inform the others."

James Tindall

Chapter 5

Dianna was meeting with Morgan at the power plant. Construction was moving along smoothly as they coupled the landfill with the gas inlets.

"How long before we are operational? Morgan asked.

"If we keep moving at this pace, about two or three more weeks," Dianna said. "The tribe has helped us jump through quite a few hurdles that would have bogged us down."

"Yeah," Morgan mused. "They want the money too."

"Hey, it's a good deal for all," Dianna said. "The problem from what you have explained is whether this will blow up in our face because of that boy being kidnapped."

"You don't think Don had anything to do with it do you?" Morgan asked.

"Of course not," Dianna replied. "That would be stupid, and he is not. Besides, we all know it would destroy the income stream."

"You know, we could always do this on another reservation," Morgan said.

"Yes, but few are near such an energy consuming population," Dianna said. "And we are going to do that anyway, but we need this one up and running so it's our shining star — proof to the others. More importantly, all our money is tied up. Is there anything we can do to help find the boy?"

"I have some men out scouting quietly," Morgan said. "I don't think we should offer their services to the police. They're not the most law-abiding group if you know what I mean. All we can do I'm afraid is keep our eyes and ears open. Li Na has more intelligence resources and is working with the police. They seem to be getting closer."

"Then help her all you can," Dianna said.

A ring interrupted their conversation.

"Hi Dad," Dianna said.

"Any news on this kidnapping thing?" Cilatro asked.

"No. I was just talking to Morgan about it. He suggests we help Li Na all we can because of her intelligence resources."

"What do you think?"

"I agree with him. Miami is a big place, and she seems to have great resources for digging things up on people."

"Agreed," Cilatro said. "I was just on the phone with her boss. He says they have things as much under control as possible for now. I want you to continue construction as fast as you can. Don't worry about the kidnapping, just get the project completed."

"Yes father. I understand."

"Let me speak with Morgan."

Dianna handed the phone to him.

"Yes boss."

"I want you to help Li Na as much as you can. Dianna will continue completing construction. Do not hinder her. She needs to focus. You and Li Na handle this other issue. I do not need to remind you that time is our enemy. Get it done!"

Morgan handed the phone back to Dianna.

"Your dad is getting antsy," Morgan said.

"I know. This kidnapping could throw a monkey wrench into his entire plan."

"Yes indeed," Morgan said. "Look, I need to run. Keep up the good work and we'll talk later. Hopefully this other issue will be resolved soon."

The irony was that Cilatro, and Morgan had no idea that Li Na had organized the kidnapping and that it had now gotten out of control.

There wasn't a breeze stirring when Mabel, sitting at her sewing machine, sweat dripping from her brow, heard the airboat in the distance. She listened for a moment and realized it was headed her way. Standing up, she wiped the sweat from her face as she walked outside onto the elevated wood walkway. She could see the boat as it quickly drew closer. It was Genesis.

"Hello Mabel," Genesis called as the boat bumped into the walkway, the propeller stopping.

"Genesis, so good to see you," Mabel said. "What brings you out this way?"

"Billie sent me. He is in the middle of something particularly important and wanted me to convey this message in person."

Mabel at once recognized something was afoot and led Genesis to a table at the end of the walkway under the shade of a large cypress tree. She walked into the chickee and gathered a tray with two glasses and a picture of lemonade. Walking slowly back to the table, she sat the tray down and poured each of them a glass. As she took a seat, she looked in Genesis' eyes. She saw apprehension.

"Speak to me."

"The news is disturbing, but we have everything in hand, at least as much as we can," Genesis said. "James has been kidnapped."

Mabel, her hand shaking, put her glass down.

"How can you ask me not to be alarmed?" she asked. "My only grandson has been kidnapped."

"It was done for a reason," Genesis said. "It's about the power plant project."

Genesis explained to Mabel all that had happened. She didn't like it but understood that if the partners went along,

James was a mere formality to them.

"Damn!" she exclaimed. "People will do anything to make a buck. What is society coming to?"

"I feel the same," Genesis said. "I feel certain we will get him back but at the same time, the tribe will lose this financial opportunity. Not that it's a tradeoff because James' life is more important than the project. I keep asking myself why it happened at this particular time?"

"You think something is up?" Mabel asked.

"I think that something is about money," Genesis replied. "Who will gain? What are your thoughts?"

"From what you have said, both the tribe and current partners would lose. The question is, who would become the new partner? They cannot just swoop in if this current scenario comes to fruition. These are some very cunning people. Assuming the events unfold as you suspect, the next partner, who will likely wait a while to approach us would probably be the culprits. Quite a conundrum."

"I was wondering if we could find out some other way?" Genesis asked.

"A thought just hit me, and you will know better than I do," Mabel said. "Doesn't something this big need to go through the government and BIA in Washington?"

"Yes, it would," Genesis said, his eyes widening in surprise. "They would need to sign off on it. However, given the nature of this, we cannot call someone in DC and bring it to their attention. Billie would never forgive me if I did that. We need to keep this under wraps."

"What if I told you we have a high-ranking BIA insider?" Mabel asked.

"Then we should definitely use them. At least to look into the policy of the project being signed over to other partners."

"Give me your phone," Mabel said.

"Billie, this is your mother. Genesis has explained everything. Go somewhere you can talk freely."

Billie was surprised at his mother's call.

"Susan," Billie said. "It's my mother. I need to take this."

He motioned for Christina and they both went out onto the balcony.

"Mom, Christina is with me, you're on speaker."

"Billie, listen to me. This issue is critical to the tribe, which you know. We need to get someone in DC involved that is on our side. You know who that is."

"Yes mom. I do."

"Who are you referring to?" Christina and Genesis asked at the same time.

"Billie, it's going to come out eventually and we can trust Genesis and Christina. Let me explain please."

"Okay," Billie said, his shoulders sagging.

"Christina and Genesis, this is to go no further than the four of us."

Mabel explained all that had happened from the time she was a young woman on the reservation and hooking up with Billie's father. Then, she explained who he was and what he did. Christina and Genesis were both surprised, remaining nonjudgmental but understanding. At this point, regardless of how things had happened, Billie's father could be a godsend to the entire tribe.

"You must promise not to divulge this information and I will contact Dakotah."

"We promise," Christina and Genesis said.

"Billie, with your permission, I'll make the call," Mabel said.

"Alright mom," Billie said. "Fill him in and tell him to be discreet. Have him inform us of any measures we need to put in place."

The airboat pulled away from the walkway, Genesis turning in his seat to wave goodbye, Mabel waving back. She felt a peace come over her that she had not known for a long while. She smiled to herself as she walked back to the small table and began sipping her lemonade again. Looking at her watch, she pulled her phone from her skirt pocket and sent a brief text.

```
"Important you contact me as soon as you can about
tribal matter."
```

Dakotah Pillan was taking his lunch break about a block and a half from BIA headquarters in DC. He had exited his office building and walked east down the sidewalk along D Street NW and crossed 17ᵗʰ Street NW into the President's Park. He found his favorite bench overlooking the Ellipse, a large oval lawn area. He had made a couple of tuna sandwiches on wheat bread and pulled them out of his paper bag along with a bottle of water. He savored the taste as he washed the sandwiches down. Then, for his treat, a small chocolate bar that he tore into small sections and let melt in his mouth, beneath his tongue, one piece at a time.

This place, as hectic as DC was, had given him solace during the past weeks. Rain or shine, he was always sitting on the same bench at lunch. Having been born on a reservation, he had come far, reaching a GS-15 level in the federal government. He was well respected in his agency because people knew he looked at things through a strategic lens and not a political one. Whenever a critical issue arose, his colleagues and other managers would consult with him about his opinion and other concerns they should look for to make the projects a success.

It had rained earlier, the clouds giving way to a brilliance Dakotah rarely saw in the city. The sky was a deep azure blue, the grass a brilliant, luscious green. Birds were chirping and squirrels were playing around them. The pain he felt at his wife's passing had slowly diminished and this setting had helped soothe the ache in his heart. He still had occasional waves of grief, but he focused on the good memories. The pain had become more infrequent. His wife had never been able to bear children, but they had a life of travel and leisure, both work and vacation. They would take impromptu trips up the coast on the weekends exploring nature and the sea and eating one of their favorite dishes, spiced shrimp, common around the area. He was far from his reservation upbringing and felt he had adapted well to the white man's culture in DC. He loved it because of what it had brought him compared to reservation life of which he was reminded every day when he dissected projects that would attempt to help the reservations they were destined for. At the same time, he hated it because of the political corruption and greed.

He had indeed come far, and he was not finished yet. After twenty-five years of service, he had been promoted to the Deputy Bureau Director of Field Operations. The promotion would take effect in ten more days. His immediate boss would be the Director BIA. It was unfortunate his wife was not here to witness it. Tears began rolling down his cheeks as they sometimes did. Unable to control his grief, he slowly wiped them away. It was a difficult time. He had watched his wife for several years while she withered from colon cancer, dying an undignified death, and losing almost eighty pounds.

He had bathed her every night, at first in the bathtub and finally, near the end, atop the bathroom counter; she had become so emaciated. Each night he would cry himself to sleep knowing the pain she was going through. He had reached a point at which almost anything was a welcome respite to take his mind off it. There had been an outpouring of support from people at work, even the director and his wife. Family always brought people together whether they were the perfect or the dysfunctional type. There was far too many of the latter. He had immersed himself in his work with a fury. It seemed to his colleagues that he could do the impossible. Maybe that was why he was getting the promotion. He somehow knew all would work itself out in time, despite the fact that it didn't make things any easier.

He pulled his vibrating phone from his pocket and read the message. As a manager, he dissected its potential meaning. Although Mabel had not attended the funeral, some of her friends had brought him meals, sent flowers and cards, and invited him out for weekend brunches and activities to keep his mind off the tragedy. She had been so gracious. As he read the message, he knew it was not a ploy to get him to talk to her, it was about the welfare of the tribe. It would be another half hour before he needed to be back at his desk.

"Hello Mabel," he said. "How have you been?"

"I should be asking that of you my friend," Mabel said. "I can only hope you are handling the tragedy as well as you can."

"It's been difficult, but I'm making it through. The grief is subsiding as you said it would and I am able to come to terms with what happened. What's up?"

Mabel explained all that had happened and what was going on. Because James was his grandson, he would become involved whether he wanted to be or not.

"This is not good news," he said. "The BIA will greatly frown upon it if it becomes known to the agency."

"What can we or what should we do?" she asked.

"First, never call my work phone," he said. "Use this number only. It is best if you text me and let me call you discreetly. Second, send the partners document to my private email. If the agreement does not mention that selling or transferring partners responsibility and or sale requires tribal approval, redraft the document to include that and get all parties to sign it again with the same date as the initial one. This will throw a monkey wrench into the hostile takeover ploy if that is what it is. Third, I want to be kept updated daily on the progress. It may be wise for you and me, as well as Christina, Billie, and Genesis to have a personal meeting in Miami. Discuss it among yourselves. Meanwhile, I will investigate the policies required for these issues. Be careful who you talk to."

"Thank you Dakotah," Mabel said softly. "We welcome your input on this."

"No, thank you Mabel. It's good to hear your voice."

Dakotah walked back to his office with a spring in his step. He was excited and concerned at the same time. Whoever these people were, they had serious clout. He would discreetly do a search and see what he could find out. It had been good to hear Mabel's voice. As he walked beneath the trees along the street, his thoughts drifted back to years before when they had first met. Those tender and love-filled memories began to replace the grief as he thought of the happy times they had. Although he had been riddled with guilt about cheating on his wife, he had a son and a grandson now. He must do all he could to ensure they were protected. He was not without means to do so.

The Medicine Man was concerned. He had felt an evil energy that was constant, but he could not put his finger on it. It was like an omen and had troubled him for several days. He instructed his warriors to surround the hammock, letting no one in. Looking across the palmetto flat, he knew what had to be done. He prepared the way of the transparency. The outstretched shadows of the trees as the sun sank below the horizon began to touch his two small fires as he lay down with the dii potentia in his right hand, squeezing it harder than normal. The root began to glow a bright white as it flashed across the palmettos and surrounding oak and palm trees. A strong wind began to blow in a circle, like a hurricane and then calmed directly around his body. The Medicine Man was standing beside the tree of life. He did not come here as often as he should to receive instruction from the Great Spirit, but this time something was different. He could not shake the feeling of darkness. In the distance he could see a blackness in the cosmos, another bad omen.

A set of eyes appeared, as far apart as the tree was wide,

looking down on him. The outline of a face barely discernable. "Fear not my servant," a voice said. "All is as it should be. The path of the young warrior must not be altered, for I have set it."

"He is in a precarious position," the Medicine Man said. "Should I not help him?"

"You may help, and you may protect him as you can, but you must not interfere."

"How far am I allowed to go?"

"You should do all you can. However, you must not alter his decisions. He is to remain accountable before me."

"Yes, Great Spirit. I understand."

The day was a typical Florida day in Port St. Lucie. A nice breeze was coming in from the Atlantic. The smell of the ocean was in the air as seagulls floated alongside the two walking men, waiting for a morsel of food, none coming, they flew on down the beach gliding effortlessly on the wind currents.

"As I told you, the device is ready," Fred said.

"You're sure it will not cause a melt down?" Morgan asked.

"Yes, positive. It has been designed as you wished. It will create a critical scenario for which they will be forced to shut down the plant for inspection."

"How long?" Morgan asked.

"Based on similar scenarios at other nuclear plants it should take them three to four weeks to complete the inspection and do a safety sign off. Perhaps twice that is, if the political pulse changes."

"That doesn't give us much time to orchestrate our marketing campaign."

"That is not something I can affect," Fred replied. "Perhaps you should have the campaign ready to go as soon as you give me word to trigger the device."

"I had thought about that, but if we move too soon suspicion might be cast upon us."

"Look, you have me in a bind," Fred responded. "I don't dispute that, but we cannot go so far as to create a meltdown. If you wait for two to three days before you make any announcements, it will work."

"What would you do if you were in my shoes?" Morgan asked.

"It's simple," Fred grinned. "It doesn't matter when we trigger it because it's about timing on your end. Make sure that your plant comes online before this one goes out or, a few days after. In the meantime, start a media campaign about how you will operate on the consumers side based on what happened in Texas. Advertise you're a new kind of energy company focused on the needs of the people in good times and bad. I'm not a marketing specialist, but people will be watching. Give them an incentive to join you."

"That's not a bad idea," Morgan said. "How soon can you trigger the device once I contact you?"

"I can have it in place and ready almost immediately," Fred replied. "Once I trigger it and the overheating and domino effects occurs, I'll remove it so there is no trace."

"Very well. I will tell my boss that we are ready to move forward. For now, no more contact. Here's a new burner phone. Keep it with you. It has one programmed number in it that will show up as 'Me.' Don't answer it unless you see that on the caller ID. Once this is over, our deal will be complete, and you can go back to living your life as if this never happened. Actually, it didn't."

As Morgan walked off, Fred watched him. Sticking the phone in his pocket, he continued down the beach, wondering if this man would keep his word. But it didn't matter. If he didn't cooperate, the images on the tape would send him to prison, perhaps for a lethal injection.

James Tindall

The beach side restaurant had few patrons and those that were present were tourists; flowered shirts, pale skin, and cameras all attested to the fact. Li Na had taken a seat at a corner table behind a palm tree as she staired down the beach. She had been waiting for over an hour, watching to ensure she had not been followed. The man in the photo the police could not identify was her man. But she had sensed something about him that made her wary and uncomfortable, as if he were playing her instead of the other way around. The phone call essentially told her he was working for another group. Her eyes went immediately to the movement as she saw him enter the restaurant and cautiously but quickly look around. He saw her almost immediately and strolled over, taking a seat. Li Na noticed that he was dressed more casually, like a tourist, but not as loudly in khaki trousers, tan shoes, and a pale salmon colored shirt with hat and sunglasses. He melded perfectly with them.

"Good afternoon," he said, as he sat down observing her reaction.

"Hello Ting."

"Li Na."

Ting Zhang had previously served in the Ministry of State Security (Guó'ānbù) for the People's Republic of China (PRC) and still had strong connections with them that neither Li Na nor other triad groups he worked with knew about. The Guó'ānbù serves as the secret police agency of the PRC for security, civilian intelligence, and other obscure, off the book operations. It is responsible for counterintelligence, foreign intelligence, and political security with close ties to the Intelligence Bureau of the Joint Staff. Ting was deeply embedded with them and both sides of the aisle were constantly scratching each other's back. There were over fifty triads operating out of Hong Kong, but only about twenty were involved in criminal activity and Ting worked off and on for most of them if the money was right, which was his only loyalty.

"We have a small snafu," Li Na said. "The tribe just re-drafted the partnership agreement that states tribal authority is required, full council vote, for any partner to sell or step out of the original agreement."

"Then, the boy is not as valuable as we had hoped," Ting said.

"No, he is," Li Na replied. "He is our key to cementing our relationship with the tribe so that they trust us."

"What do you propose?" Ting asked.

"We need to draw this out a little longer," Li Na said. "I want them to sweat some more before he is found. It will serve to strengthen our partnership."

"As you wish," Ting said.

"Keep him well hidden. I'll let you know when to begin the exit strategy for him."

"I will do as you request," Ting said, rising to leave.

"One more thing," Li Na said. "This stays between the two of us."

Ting nodded affirmatively as he walked away and out of the restaurant. Li Na had detected a slight downward motion of his eyes. He was up to something, and her intuition told her it was not good.

No sooner had Ting reached the sidewalk than he was on the phone.

"Xu Lo," the voice answered.

"We need to alter our strategy," Ting said.

"Why?"

"The tribe altered the partnership agreement requiring a full council vote for anyone to replace current partners."

"Did all the partners sign it?"

"They had no choice if they want to stay in the deal," Ting said.

"Of course," Xu Lo replied. "It makes sense. Thank you. I will discuss options with my partners. Continue following Li Na's commands for now. Make her believe you remain her ally and employee. We'll keep the boy longer than she wants. She is shrewd so plan ahead."

Xu Lo was leader of the third largest triad in Hong Kong. When China resumed sovereignty of Hong Kong in 1977, they had applied a 'united front' tactic to recruit the triad societies to the Communist camp. This had allowed triad leaders to set foot in mainland China and bridge up with both state enterprises and officials. Merging with the political dynamics, the traditional structural and social network approaches were insufficient for the triads to succeed. Because of the triad's influence they leveraged and converted the great social capital they developed in the mainland into economic capital through illegitimate means in the stock market. Xu Lo and Ting had a great deal to do with that and were respected among all the triads for their cunning. Now, through attempts to break into more profitable and legitimate long-term businesses, participating triads were constantly running into snags.

The partnerships, based on the agreement re-draft, were more solid than ever. The only way to pressure a deal to get one out would be to leverage one of the partners. Ki would not be easy, and neither would the organization of Don Cilatro. However, Cilatro was more vulnerable. A plan would need to be devised, a careful strategy.

The power plant construction was proceeding rapidly. Multiple subcontractors had been called in and progress was visible daily. Dianna was a master at project management and attention to detail. She gave reports to her father every afternoon, updating schedules and completion deadlines. In turn, Cilatro kept Li Na and Ki informed. Dianna glanced up to see Billie driving into the site as she walked over to greet him.

"Good morning," Billie said.

"Good morning, Billie."

"I cannot believe how fast you are getting this plant completed."

"Well, you know what they say," Dianna replied. "Time is money and the faster we can get this project completed, the faster everyone will get some."

"We could all use some bucks," Billie grinned.

"As could we," Dianna said, smiling. "I know it may be a stress point Billie, but any word on your son yet?"

"No, the FBI, MDPD, and Li Na are all chasing leads. We are hoping something breaks soon."

"Is there any chance these people will give up their demands?"

"Perhaps. As you are aware, we have all agreed to a redraft of the partnership document that requires a full council vote for a partner to sell their interests. According to Li Na and Sergeant McAllister, the leverage of James isn't as valuable now."

"I'd like you to keep me posted."

"I will do that," Billie assured her. "Also, we have tied the landfill into the plant induction system. If you had to make a guess, how much longer do you think it will be before the plant is operational?"

"You have probably noticed that I've called in multiple crews," Dianna said. "The partners, including the tribe want it done as soon as feasible. The crews are working around the clock, and we are paying inspectors extra to inspect as we go. I think about two weeks, and we may be able to turn the key."

"That's awfully fast," Billie said. "You're not cutting corners, are you?"

"You know me better than that," Dianna smiled. "All the inspectors are from different departments and double check everything. We cannot afford to cut corners based on what the costs are. After all, insurance doesn't pay for stupidity."

Billie laughed. "I understand completely. If there is anything you need do not hesitate to call. I'll be in my office down the road if you want to drop by."

"I may just do that," Dianna said with a laugh, feeling a stirring within her. Billie was an attractive man with a beaming smile that just seemed to light up the room. Despite her knowing he was happily married Dianna had her private thoughts about him.

She went back into the construction office and sat down. Going over project details she began to have a feeling of accomplishment. Looking at the schedule, completion would be much sooner than expected. She decided to add another contractor and picked up the phone. Her father and the other partners would be pleased.

The balmy New York day found Don Cilatro finishing his 5:00 am jog through Central Park. He stopped to sit on a bench at the ringing of his phone. His four bodyguards positioned themselves out of ear shot.

"Good morning," Ki said. "I trust our plan is going according to schedule."

"Yes," Cilatro said. "Everything is ready. The device has been tested and is ready to deploy. Morgan says once we give the go, phase one can be implemented at once. I would suggest eight to twelve hours once we initiate."

"Agreed," Ki said. "What of our strategy?"

"Your accountant modified what we had initially thought, and I am inclined to agree. We would lose money yes, but we would gain on solar energy sales and amass a larger customer base utilizing the guarantee of no more than a temporary eighteen percent increase during the month of the disaster, giving the customer three to five days of free energy directly after and then, lowering our rates back to normal the next month."

"Yes, that will work well I believe," Ki responded.

"I would like to make another suggestion," Cilatro said. "The other power companies will be suffering. To remain a competitor, they will need electricity that we can provide. I would suggest that we increase our sales to them by twenty-five percent. They will have no one else to turn to."

"Hmmmm," Ki murmured. "That would ensure a large generation of cash."

"Not only that," Cilatro began, "We can embed ourselves with them deeper through negotiation so that any time they need more power, we can provide it on a contractual basis."

"I don't follow," Ki said.

"You know they will balk at the price increase, so we lower the price through a longer-term supply. They'll be happy and we'll have very large legitimate customers."

"That's brilliant, Don," Ki said. "I'll have Akio work up the numbers on that. This is looking better every day."

"Perfect. I'll keep you informed from our side along with Li Na. Work your magic with the numbers."

It had been too long since Lunadi had visited the tribe and home. Despite living in the west and enjoying the rugged beauty of the mountains and the splendor he viewed each day from his upper deck, the Everglades would always be home to him. He just didn't enjoy the humidity in the summer and the sweltering heat. It was like walking into a greenhouse with the doors closed and the fans off, sweat oozing from every pore. No sooner had the plane landed than he quickly made his way to the airport and to the pick-up area where Genesis was parked in his tribal police SUV to take him to headquarters in Hollywood. Quite a few people were waiting for his presentation.

"It is good to see you again my brother," Lunadi said.

"And you," Genesis replied. "I think it's time you gave up the west and moved back home."

"They don't need me here," Lunadi said. "I can always give my opinion and share my expertise from my phone and laptop. More importantly, I can avoid politics and don't have mosquito's the size of giraffe's knocking on my door every evening begging admittance."

Genesis laughed. "I must say, I wouldn't miss that either."

The two had known each other since their days in service. They were like brothers. It was fun catching up as they drove the short distance to headquarters. Genesis found a shady spot in the parking lot then, they made their way to the conference room where everything was set up as Lunadi had requested.

"Hello President," Lunadi smiled, shaking hands.

"It is good to see you again," the President said. "How is the west treating you?"

"I can't complain," Lunadi said. "How are you and politics?"

"Don't ask," the President laughed. "Look, I need to talk to a couple of these folks. Check the equipment and make sure it's what you requested. Let me know if you need anything else. And Lunadi, these folks are very important to us."

"I understand. I won't let you down."

Lunadi began checking the equipment and put in his thumb drive, flashing quickly through a few of his slides, checking his laser pointer, and making sure the focus was sharp. Satisfied that everything was ready, he gave Genesis a thumbs up who conveyed it to the President.

"Ladies and gentlemen," the President said. "Please take your seats and we will get on with the presentation. I would like to introduce you to Lunadi, one of our tribal members who resides in the mountain west. A valuable asset who assists us in times of importance. Once he gives his presentation, you can meet him personally afterwards. He is only known to a few of the tribal members. Let me give a brief introduction. Genesis, and I served alongside Lunadi in the Middle East. He saved our lives several times. He is a decorated war hero and has several college degrees including a PhD, which we welcome in his service to us. I won't get too personal, but he is a true warrior and in him specifically, the warrior spirit never dies! Lunadi."

"Thank you, Mr. President," Lunadi said. "I am always

honored to be with you and among our people. I am aware of the power plant project and what it means to the tribe and partners. Today I will give you a presentation about critical infrastructures and their basic interdependencies. You can ask questions as we go, or hold them until the end. With that, I'll begin."

There were several in attendance who, unknown to Genesis, Lunadi, the President, and Billie, were there to learn how they could gain by creating havoc among the interdependencies. These included Li Na, Morgan, and Akio, as well as several others.

"I'll begin with this image," Lunadi said. "It is what I call the U.S. Threat Schema that denotes basic interdependencies between our critical infrastructure key resources. You will notice there are three levels of infrastructure with level 1 being the most important, followed by the remaining two levels. These are our most important infrastructures."

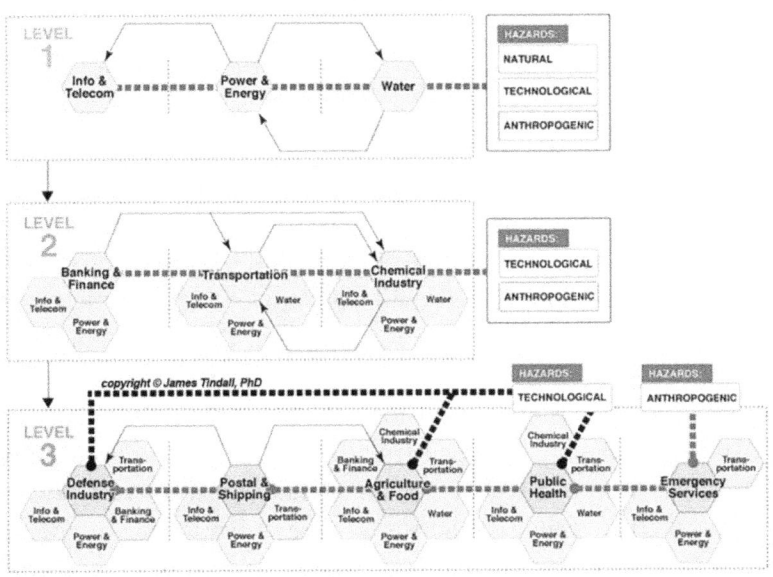

"Excuse me Dr. Lunadi," Akio interrupted. "So, looking at

your figure, are we to understand that power, water, and telecom are the most important?"

"Exactly," Lunadi responded. "Our Achilles is heel is power. If you cut power, every other infrastructure is affected in a proportionate manner. For example, cutting power halts water treatment and distribution and within twenty-four hours, will greatly affect communications or more immediately, especially if the power supply is cut to all. As an example, cut power and trace that cut through the other infrastructures in levels 2 and 3."

"Why?" Morgan asked.

"Cutting power immediately affects the commercial community such as gas stations, retail, etc. Most community and city policies require that retail stores shut down due to potential health problems. As for communications, while some are immediately affected, especially computer networks, the cell phone, which most of us live by, will be inoperable within twenty hours due to low battery issues, unless you can recharge it."

"But what about cell towers?" Akio asked. "Won't they die out before our cell batteries?"

"Not typically," Lunadi said. "This is because all of them by law has a fuel generator back up. If they cannot be refueled, the tower will cease operations in about twenty-four hours, but in larger cities that have more of them, that is a minor nuisance. This because other towers will pick up the communications load and attempt to balance it. However, the increasing load will cause problems getting calls through because of overloaded bandwidth. Let's look at something closer to home, hurricanes. If you recall, Hurricane Katrina devastated New Orleans. Why? Because water killed power and every infrastructure failed. Hurricanes are a constant threat to Florida and its infrastructures. Our power plants around the area are vulnerable to storms whether by wind, flooding, or lightning. A large enough storm can create havoc."

"What do you mean?" the President asked.

"Let's look at an example," Lunadi continued. "Suppose the nuclear plant in Port St. Lucie went down for some reason. It doesn't matter what the reason is. When a power plant goes down, the electricity must be rerouted through other plants and substations so that customers can get electricity. Too often that rerouting carries too much power and blows out transformers, substations, and related infrastructure. The 2003 New York City blackout created just such a scenario. Over ten billion dollars in damages occurred when several substations and transformers were blown out because they could not handle the surge of electricity being rerouted. In other words, they were overloaded, and the system stayed down for three days. If several power plants had been similarly damaged, consumers could have been out of electricity for a month or more."

Akio, Li Na, and Morgan were looking at each other. They understood clearly that this was exactly what they needed to know. They each had a silent smile on their face as Lunadi continued to brief them, giving them information that was proving more and more valuable.

"This is extremely interesting," Akio interrupted. "You mentioned the New York City blackout. What would happen if multiple power plants went out such as the nuclear plant you mentioned and one or two others?"

"The power grid is a giant electrical exchange where one group buys power from another to distribute to their customers," Lunadi said. "If two or more plants went down, the main power lines would be checked first to ensure safe transmission while the plants were each brought back online. This could be a slow process, but other plants further up the grid would send electricity down the line to provide power. That power would be purchased by your power provider, and you would still be paying them your bill."

"Is that what happened in Texas?" Morgan asked.

"Exactly," Lunadi replied. "Texas lost quite a few nodes in their grid and got power from outside their region to supply homes and businesses. It took longer than they expected to repair their substations, transformers, and generation plants. However, the major supplier bought power from other parts of the grid and charged enormous rates to the customers. Due their policies, the consumer was ripped off but could do nothing about it. It is something for you to consider if you were to get caught in a similar scenario. Being transparent to the consumer will help you fare better during and after a disaster."

"How much electricity do you think will be needed in the next few decades?" Akio asked.

"I may be a little rusty in my numbers but according to the Energy Information Administration, about ten years ago they estimated the population of the U.S. would increase by about seventy percent. Most of this increase is slated for the west coast, Arizona, Texas, Florida, and other parts of the southeast. Consequently, the demand will grow at least fifty percent. In my opinion more because so many more cell phones, laptops, and other vampire appliances, and technologies are continually added to the mix."

"If you were in charge of the power plant, how would you incorporate it into a future scenario?" Li Na asked, scrutinizing his reaction.

"If I could come up with the funds, I would triple its capacity to be ready for ramped up demand."

"Anything else?" Dianna asked.

"One major suggestion, never trade water for energy; it's a very bad idea. One reason is that in the future, the demand for water will drastically increase as many hydroelectric dams become inoperable due to water levels, which will place a greater demand on coal fired and other power plants, as well as much more energy that will be required for water treatment and distribution."

The presentation continued as those present feverishly

took notes. Lunadi had given them a gold mine of information that would not go wasted. The President was always amazed at Lunadi's knowledge and was pleased as he witnessed the wealth of it being dispensed to this group. It was obvious by their notes they were impressed with this man's gift to them. Before they realized it, the two-hour presentation was over. Most of the tribal members had left, clapping loudly at the end. The group representing the partners stayed to ask more questions.

"Thank you Lunadi for the wonderful presentation and so much information," Li Na said, recognizing that this man was a warrior of high caliber. It was in his mannerisms and easy style, which most would not recognize.

"You're most welcome," Lunadi replied softly, his eyes staring into the depth of hers. It gave Li Na a nervousness she had not experienced for many years. "Let me know if there is anything that I can do for you. Contact me anytime at the phone number I put on the last slide."

After a few more questions, the group departed, leaving only Genesis and Billie remaining as they watched the last person, Li Na, exit the room.

"Watch her," Lunadi said.

"Why?" Genesis asked. "Did you detect something?"

"She is not what she seems," Lunadi responded.

"You mean not as docile or as innocent as you would suspect?" Billie asked.

"Yes," Lunadi said. "She is masterfully cunning. Let not her demeanor fool you. Keep your wits about you unless her beauty entices you both."

"When's your flight?" Genesis asked.

"It leaves in about two hours," Lunadi said.

"I'll go start the car so it will cool down," Genesis said, walking away.

"The Medicine Man says you know the transparency well," Billie said. "Is there a way we can talk? He has told me much about you."

"I would have stayed over had I known," Lunadi said. "Has he taught you how to meet near the tree of life?"

"No, I am at the stage where I have gone through process where the tree is protected by the lake and warriors. Afterward we have been to the tree where you can see the cosmos behind it."

"Then you have the knowledge required," Lunadi said. "You have my number. When you want to meet, call me and we will plan a time to meet there while in the transparency."

"Is it that easy?" Billie asked.

"Only if you know the transparency," Lunadi said. "The only ones who know it are the Medicine Man and those he has taught. Usually, he will not reveal those to you. Each of us has a responsibility, a mission if you will. Yours is to serve and protect our people. Mine is similar, but in a different way. For you see, the Medicine Man has also told me about you and your calling as well."

"Why does he do that?" Billie asked.

"Because, like today, we can help each other," Lunadi said. "There will always be times that we will need to do so. This is only the beginning. I must go for now."

"When should I call you," Billie asked as Lunadi walked away.

"Call me whenever you wish," Lunadi said, reaching the door and turning. "I am here for you, my brother. Let us talk when you think it appropriate."

Billie nodded affirmatively. A calmness had come over him as he stood near Lunadi. He could not describe it but believed he had felt Lunadi's spirit. Despite his being a warrior spirit, he had a spirit that touched others in a positive way. He walked slowly out the building into the parking lot and was just opening his car door when his phone rang.

"Panther," he said.

The wind along South Beach was picking up as Li Na stood on the balcony of her hotel room. The waves had begun to cap, pushed by a strong breeze that blew mist into the air, which caught the sunlight and displayed hundreds of tiny rainbows. She sat down in a chair and watched with curiosity the splendor of the ocean as it turned from light aqua green to dark blue far out toward the horizon. It was filled with activity from small boats fishing to sail boats headed toward unknown destinations, several cruise ships, and windsurfers. There were both young and old couples walking along the beach sharing their hopes and dreams and love. For an instant she let herself dip into self-pity wishing she had a significant other, but it was only a fleeting whim. She was happy because she was her own boss serving as a consultant to the wealthy crime bosses who needed her knowledge. Unknown to them, she was slowly working her way up to find the murderers of her family. They would lead her to the prey she sought. An hour had passed as she grudgingly pulled a cell phone from her purse.

"The presentation was great," Li Na said.

"Did is shed light on our problem?" Ki asked.

"Perfectly," she said. "We are fine tuning what we need to do so that everything will coalesce at the right moment. Coupled with the knowledge we already had, we can ensure success."

"How long will you need to develop final strategy?" Ki asked.

"It will be ready by the end of the week, perhaps sooner," Li Na said. "Everything will be in place before the power plant becomes operational."

"I'm not sure about that," Ki said. "Cilatro told me Dianna put on extra crews and the plant could be completed significantly ahead of schedule."

"That could be in the next week," Li Na responded, surprised. "I'll work with Akio and Morgan, and we will have the final strategy ready in four days. However, I have a suggestion. Let's not rush into this as soon as the plant is completed. I think we should make sure the plant is running well. We need to do it at the right time."

"What would you consider the right time?" Ki asked.

"We are in hurricane season and will likely have several make landfall in the next three weeks. If we wait until they hit, we can execute right at that time or just as one passes. It would conceal our movements and almost everyone would have the perception that the hurricane or hurricanes caused the damage. It wouldn't be difficult to introduce lots of disinformation on social media."

"I like it. Let's make it happen. We can have no delays. Make sure everything is ready."

The light pink-colored, cinderblock home looked like hundreds of others in the area. It had a single car, open carport behind a four-foot-tall chain link fence that bordered a shell-rock road. The area was full of retirees with single mom families here and there. The two Chinese men sat patiently in the living room watching an Asian comedy show on TV while the air conditioning ran full blast. The house was small, about six hundred square feet. In the second bedroom sat James, reading a book. He had a bruise on his right cheek and his eye lid was black and blue. Enough to tell that he had been treated a little rough. Unlike most kids his age, he was accustomed to encounters that didn't always end well and was smart enough to know that until he could get away or someone found him, cooperation was his key to survival. The captors had nailed the window shut with plywood from the inside and out and had a clear view of his room from where they sat. So far, they had treated him okay. Initially, they had roughed him up on the speed boat. But seeing he was cooperating, had since left him alone. Sitting on his bed reading, he kept thinking about how to get away. The time was not yet, but if he stayed alert to his environment, sooner or later an opportunity would present itself. This was the third place they had been since his abduction. As the Medicine Man had taught him since he was five, he practiced patience.

Almost nine thousand miles away Xu Lo kept working on developing a strategy that would end successfully. He knew that Ki had discovered he was up to something. The two triad leaders were suspicious of everything, and spies were cheap in Hong Kong. Xu jumped at the sound of the phone.

"Lo."

"I do not think having the son will help us now," Ting said. "We need to go for the girl. It's the only way to get leverage on Cilatro who the weakest link of the partners is."

"Are you certain?" Xu asked.

"Quite," Ting said. "I suggest we get the girl and hold them both, so we have some leverage over the tribe and more over the partner. We should do it now."

"No!" Xu said emphatically. "She is the key to completing the plant. Wait until it becomes operational. How is the boy?"

"He is safe and well treated," Ting said. "I have him moved every few days. So far, we are completely under their radar. Once we have the girl, we will continue to move them until a decision is made by the partners."

"What are you thinking?" Xu asked.

"As soon as we gain control, we get rid of them," Ting replied. "Eliminate any possible connections."

"I tend to agree, but let me think about that," Xu said. "How long will it take for you to grab her?"

"We have a plan in place," Ting said. "Once we have the go ahead, we can be ready within twenty-four hours."

"Very well," Xu said. "Let me complete my strategy and I will get back to you. Do you think Li Na knows that you are working for us?"

"She doesn't expect at all," Ting replied. "I'm sure of it."

"Keep me informed."

Unknown to the two men, the conversation had been recorded. It was transferred to a digital recorder so it could be held next to his phone.

"You need to hear this," the man said then, played the recording. "Do you know who the second man is?"

"Yes," Li Na said. "I know them both quite well. Feed me any information you discover. Thank you. A well-deserved gift will be sent your way."

Li Na's suspicions had been confirmed. Now she knew Ting was double dipping in the triads. It was always a dangerous game. Taking Cilatro's daughter would be a major blow to the partnership but with this information she was almost certain she could preempt Xu Lo's plan. If Xu Lo got what he wanted, war between the two triads was a certainty. It was important to get the information to Ki as soon as they could. She turned in her chair and leaned over to Akio, whispering in his ear.

"What's up?" Morgan asked.

"Oh nothing, just some company business," Li Na said. Now was not the time to tell Morgan about Dianna potentially being taken. "Excuse me for a moment," Li Na said. "I need to talk to my boss."

She slowly walked toward the restrooms. The two men looking after. Morgan knew something was up. He would talk to Cilatro but wasn't sure if anything would come of it.

"I have bad news," Li Na said.

"What is it?" Ki asked.

"I cannot talk about it now," Li Na said. "The accountant will contact you on line two and fill you in."

Line two was their code for a secure satellite phone. Akio would call from the private jet and inform Ki. Things were about to get very interesting between two powerful enemies in Hong Kong. Interactions would become difficult and dangerous.

Ten days later, the tribal council, many tribal members, as well as members of the press had gathered, along with the partners and their representatives at the power plant. It was ribbon cutting time as the plant powered up, lighting strings of lights that had been placed around as the crowd clapped at the sight of money. That's what the lights really meant.

"Our partners are with us today for this historic occasion," the President said from the temporary microphone. "This is a momentous day that will be a boon to the tribe and our relationship with our new partners. Let's hear from them."

"I want to thank you Mr. President," Morgan said. "Our other partner couldn't make it today but wanted me to extend his thanks to be able to work with the tribe and congratulate you all on an outstanding accomplishment. I must second those sentiments. It's an honor to work with you and partner with the tribe for this long-term investment. As you all know, this is just phase one of the projects. In the next couple of years, we will double the output which will provide more jobs and generate more revenue for the people. We all look forward to a long and prosperous relationship. And we promise to be a new kind of energy company, one that works with our customers not against them, especially in times of disaster. Thank you, Mr. President. Thank you all."

The crowd roared its approval as everyone present mingled together, eating food from the buffet tables, drinking, and having a good time. The press mingled with the crowd getting stories for the next day's release of the local papers.

"Excuse me, aren't you Billie Panther?"

"Yes," Billie said.

"I'm Susan York of the Herald. Could I ask you a couple of questions on the record?"

"As long as you accurately report my comments," Billie grinned.

Susan chuckled nervously.

"The plant is quite impressive," Susan stated. "Will the tribe benefit from it? I ask this because it seems so many projects like this one don't do as well as they should."

"I would agree with you," Billie said. "Project success is

dependent on choosing the right people to help run and stay focused on it. For this one, we have chosen the right people and it will be a huge success."

"In what way?"

"We promise to be a different kind of energy company," Billie said. "If you recall what happened in Texas, the residents were gouged severely by the power companies. I shouldn't tell you this, but I don't see how it can hurt now that we are operational. Because of what happened in Texas and the long history of electric companies, we will be giving three to five days of free electricity to our members, which will help them recover after a disaster."

"Wait a minute," Susan said. "You're telling me if we had a major hurricane, I would get free electricity for a few days after to help my pocketbook."

"That's right," Li Na said, interrupting as she walked up.

"This is one of our partner representatives, Li Na," Billie said. "Meet Susan York of the Herald."

"Where do I sign up as a customer?" Susan asked. "I can't wait to get this in the paper. You might be swamped with new customers."

"We welcome all," Li Na said. "It's why we created the partnership and want to expand even further."

"What do you mean?" Susan asked.

"Well," Li Na began. "This is the first plant of our planned expansion in Florida, the southeast and out west eventually.

"Will you implement the same free policy after a disaster?" Susan asked.

"Yes," Li Na said. "The policy will be the same throughout our network."

As the two continued to talk, Billie caught Genesis walking by.

"Any news on James's whereabouts?" Billie asked.

"Apparently Li Na, her intelligence man and the MDPD, as well as the FBI are working together on several leads they have. Detective Yuen is helping, and they found one safe house where James was, but they had already moved him."

"That's not good news," Billie said, sighing.

"Actually, it is," Genesis replied. "The fact that they found a safe house means they're beginning to follow a growing trail. It may be sparse so it will take a little longer, but more importantly it means James is okay, at least for now. Trust me, we're working on it. Do not give up hope."

"Working on what?" Christina asked, walking up.

"Like I explained to Billie," Genesis said. "We found one of the safe houses where James was held. They have moved to another, but we are getting closer. Keep your hopes high. You've handled this much better than other parents. Don't stop or give up now."

"Is there anything we can do?" Christina asked.

"Not now," Genesis said. "If they call, contact me immediately or Sergeant McAllister and Phil. Otherwise, it is a law enforcement matter. We won't stop until we find him."

"It's hard to be patient," Billie said. "We miss him and fear for him."

"I feel the same," Genesis said. "A lot is going on behind the scenes. Li Na and her intelligence man in Hong Kong have been a big help, which is how they found the first safe house. Now that we know what to look for, it will help. Hang in there."

"We will," Christina sighed. "It's just hard and each day it seems to get harder."

Genesis looked at her knowingly as he put his hand gently on her shoulder, nodded and walked off. They both knew he was right. They gritted their teeth, determined to follow it through.

Because Li Na now knew that Ting was working for another triad, she had implemented stricter security and communications controls with her intelligence officer. She had one of her men shadowing Ting everywhere he went. Their initial plan had backfired now that another triad was involved. Getting James back would not be so easy and there was no way she could protect Dianna without giving away her strategy, in which case the partnership would dissolve, and the tribe would take over everything. She had overheard Genesis telling Dianna about their culture and the transparency, which she had investigated. Perhaps she could work with Billie to resolve the damage done by Ting and avoid a real mess for the tribe and her boss. Her phone began to ring, it was one of her men. "Hello," Li Na said.

"I think he is suspicious he is being tailed," the man said.

"Okay," Li Na said. "Back off. If you lose him, we will pick him up later."

If Ting thought he was being followed, he would be too suspicious to give away the location and shift to extreme measures to prevent intelligence gathering. "Damn it," she thought. "Why did I let him hold the cards here? Because she had trusted him to be working for her. I won't make that mistake again."

Rain was falling in large drops and lightning flashes lit the sky over Miami just after 10:00 pm as the two dark clad men swiped a key card against the reader on the hotels side entrance door. One of them had lifted it from an old couple as he helped them into a taxi out front. Rather than take the elevator and risk the chance of running into other patrons, they entered the stairwell and cautiously made their way to the thirteenth floor. The weather outside had driven most guests inside. As the two silently crept past one door after another, keeping their heads down to avoid camera recognition, they could hear TV's blasting from inside most of the rooms. The hallway was convenient for stealth since columns jutted from the walls at regular intervals hiding doors until you were directly in front of them. They finally reached room 1322, softly knocking on the door.

"Who's there?" Dianna called out.

"It's Miami Dade Police ma'am," the man said, holding an MDPD badge up to the peep hole.

The door swung wide open revealing Dianna in a pair of jeans and tee shirt. Before she could say anything the two men rushed in. One of them hit her on the back of the neck at the bottom of the occipital bone with an outward hand sword, knocking her out cold. She at once collapsed to the floor as the other closed the door. Within a half-minute they had secured her hands behind her back with a police zip tie and taped her ankles together with duct tape, as well as her mouth. They searched the room quickly for her cell phone, putting it in a privacy bag then, one of the men hoisted her onto his shoulders as the other checked the hallway. No one was visible. They quietly exited the room and dropped the key car in the middle of the hall a few doors down. Someone would find it and return it to the front desk; the older couple and the hotel desk clerk would be none the wiser. They quickly made it down the stairwell and out to a waiting car. Throwing Dianna into the trunk and slamming it shut, the two jumped in, the car sliding out of the hotel parking lot, disappearing into the stormy night. Quickly out of site they headed north on I-95. About thirty minutes later, they pulled under the open carport of a non-descript house in south Ft. Lauderdale where Ting awaited them. The door to James's room was closed; he was asleep. The men quickly lifted Dianna from the trunk and brought her inside. She was still unconscious.

"Do you have her phone?" Ting asked.

"Yes," one said, handing it over. "It was placed in the privacy bag before leaving the hotel room as you requested."

"Good," Ting said. Wake her up."

One of the men went to the kitchen and poured a cold glass of water from the refrigerator, walked back, and threw it in Dianna's face. She jerked awake instantly, trying to determine where she was and what was happening. Already gagged, her words were just an angry murmur.

"It is time to listen madame, not talk," Ting said. "I have your phone and will be contacting your father. If you do as these men direct, all will go as planned. If you fight them, you will not see your father again. Nod if you understand."

Dianna nodded, as the memories from her graduation night came flooding back. Again, she was in harm's way through no fault of her own.

Ting looked down at her. He could see the fear in her eyes. "Good," he thought. "He had gotten through. Being the daughter of a crime boss, he was sure she understood the circumstances she found herself in."

"Take her and lay her on the bed in the other room," Ting said. "Treat her well. Do not let her escape. She is key to our plan. I will stay in touch."

D on Cilatro was sitting in his office when he received the call the next morning.

"We cannot find Dianna," Morgan said.

"What do you mean you cannot find her?" Cilatro asked.

"Frank and Kelly were rooming on each side of her and when they knocked on the door this morning, she didn't answer," Morgan said. "Her bed wasn't slept in, and the room is undisturbed. The only things missing are her and her phone."

"Have you called it?" Cilatro asked.

"Yes, multiple times," Morgan said. "It says out of range or turned off."

"Something is wrong," Cilatro said. "Keep checking and calling. I will make some calls. Let's touch base later."

Just like the night of her graduation, Dianna was in jeopardy again. Cilatro knew instinctively what this was about — leverage. He was already dialing.

"Ki," Cilatro said. "We have a problem. My daughter is missing."

"I was just about to call you," Ki said. "My accountant has told me that another group is attempting to become the main partner. You know what that means?"

"Yes," Cilatro said. "Things will get bloody. Do you know who they are?"

"Yes, I believe so," Ki said, not wanting to identify them specifically, at least not yet. "We are looking into it now. I have informed Li Na and she has her intelligence officer on it."

"Let me know the moment you have something."

Cilatro was cold hearted as they came, but his daughter was all he had. "Curse the son of a bitch who did this," he thought. "He's already dead."

"Mr. President," Cilatro said. "Dianna has apparently been kidnapped."

"I heard," the President said. "The FBI and MDPD are at her hotel room now. I will pass along any information that I hear about. Is there anything you want me to do?"

"I would never ask this because I'm not a man of faith," Cilatro said. "However, I've been talking to my daughter, Morgan and Li Na who have told me of a practice among some of your tribal members where their spirit can exit the body and do good."

"That is true," the President said. "Very few have that ability and training."

"Are you one of them?" Cilatro asked.

"Yes," the President said. "I have the training, but it was not meant to find a person."

"I need you to do all you can to find her," Cilatro said. "If you are successful, I will reward you greatly."

"I will do all I can and let you know," the President said.

"No," Cilatro said. "Work with Li Na and Morgan. I have other things to attend to. Spend your efforts working with them to find my daughter."

"As you wish."

Miami Dade Police officers and the FBI were combing through Dianna's room. There was no evidence of foul play as they searched. They had already questioned Frank and Kelly and dismissed them as suspects since they were Dianna's bodyguards and good friends. They were wringing their hands and frantic because they had lost the bosses daughter.

"Susan, do you have anything?" Phil asked.

"Nothing," she said. "We keep calling the phone, but it is not transmitting a signal. I'm thinking the phone is in a Faraday bag."

"Check this out," Sergeant McAlister said, panting as he raced through the door. "The security feed caught the criminals."

The three looked at the security footage, which showed the criminals enter the building then, making their way down the hallway to the room and haul Dianna away. As the car drove through the parking lot, the plates were barely visible, too distorted to get a tag number.

"She was indeed kidnapped," Phil said. "This proves it."

"Do you think its related to the boy?" Susan asked.

"It's very likely that once the tribe signed the modified partnership agreement that James was no longer the bargaining chip they hoped he would be," Sergeant McAllister said.

"Agreed," Phil replied. "Now they have a tribal member and a partner member."

"I smell a squeeze coming," Susan said.

"Okay," Phil said. "Susan, work with McAllister and MDPD. Check every traffic cam, ATM, and any other cameras you can find and see if we can track where this car went. It's our only hope of finding them quickly."

"Yeah, until they make another demand," McAllister said.

Chapter 6

Jagged grass gave way to the airboat as it moved through the water to a hammock that only the President knew about. It was his haven and security location. Most of his valuable possessions, especially his cash were stowed on the small island that protruded from the sawgrass, so secure that only he could find them. The hammock was small enough and miles away from frequented areas that it would not attract attention. He even had a landing pad in the middle for a helicopter. As both a rotary and fixed wind pilot, he was a capable man and had devised a plan to disappear at a moment's notice.

The President had jumped from the boat before it stopped and jogged quickly to the inside of the hammock where he had constructed a small, raised platform behind the chickee where he experimented with the transparency. As he prepared for initiation of it, his thoughts raced over recent events. He couldn't help thinking that whoever this was trying to barge in and take control was a ruthless group. Only such a group would have the nerve to kidnap Cilatro's daughter. If they had the daring to go after Dianna, nothing would stop them from leveraging any tribal member, especially the President. "It may be time to begin preparation of a quick exit strategy," he thought.

Darkness had begun to fall as he completed his

preparations. The two fires he would lay between were piles of hot embers as he threw another small log onto each. He lay down and grasped the dii potentia in his right hand as he remembered the teachings of the Medicine Man. A black mist engulfed him as his spirit left his body. He gasped, finding himself before the tree of life that lay across the lake, the ever-present eyes looking down on him. He looked around and could see the warriors staring, their golden arrows, ready to defend the tree. The Medicine Man had warned him not to try to reach the tree or he would be killed. He slowly worked his way around and found the first tunnel, trying to remember the instructions.

As he walked along, the lessons learned slowly came back. He chose a tunnel he thought was the correct one and found himself on a cliff, overlooking rolling green hills with a castle and the ocean in the background. He immediately stepped backward into the portal and chose another tunnel finding himself in the middle of people fleeing for their lives as a pyroclastic flow streamed down mountain slopes from an erupting volcano. Stepping back into the portal, a frantic man ran past him and stopped at the edge of the lake surrounding the tree of life. Still panicked, he ran along the shore and found a small boat and began heading for the ships. The guardian warriors shot him with a half dozen arrows before he made it ten feet. The fear was still in the man's eyes as he fell backward into the boat, which slowly drifted across the water.

The President sat down, having watched in horror what had happened to the man. Now he understood why there were arrows here and there sticking out of the ground and edges of the lake. He tried to calm himself as he once again attempted to remember what to do. He was out of his league, and he knew it, but he had to try. A boy's life was at stake. For once he was thinking about someone other than himself. Almost like a bolt of lightning, it hit him. He walked along looking for a circle of rocks with a triangle shaped rock in the middle.

Finding it, he walked into the tunnel and reached the portal at the end. Stepping through, he saw a long, graveled road in Ft. Lauderdale lined with evenly spaced houses. An aqua-green house caught his attention. Like watching a television through a tunnel, he could see James and Dianna sitting on a bed. He crept closer and just as he could see them more clearly, he was swept back through the portal.

The mist gathered around his body and his spirit returned. He at once sensed something was wrong; danger was present, the hair on the back of his neck tingling. He laid on the raised platform without moving. When he had constructed the platform, security was a priority since he believed he would have no one around to protect his body when he was out of it. The aura of the root would sense danger when it returned him to his body.

Opening his eyes to just a slit, he let them move upward and downward and side to side trying to detect the as yet hidden danger. Close to him, just out of reach, on the corner of the chickee hung a razor-sharp bush axe with a double edged, sixteen-inch curved blade. Beneath his left hand, he had constructed a small trap door with short two by four-inch boards. All he had to do was press downward and grab the 9mm pistol, which he slowly did, his movement almost imperceptible. It was then that he saw it. They said they didn't exist in the Everglades. His years of experience of people in the metro Miami area releasing their pet snakes when they became too big told him otherwise. In front of him was proof. An anaconda raised its head above and to the right of his feet, positioning itself to find his head and attack.

The President rapidly stood, getting his feet beneath. The snake, sensing the motion, raised its head above the platform again, drawing back to strike and hold its prey. Multiple rows of sharp curved teeth were visible on the top and bottom of the snake's mouth. They were used to hold its hapless victim, while it wrapped its body around it, suffocating by constriction until dead. Then, it would swallow it whole.

The President raised his pistol, emptying the magazine at the snake, wounding it just below the head. In one fluid motion, the President grabbed the bush axe and swung it from right to left like a baseball bat, severing the head from the body as the snake fell, lifeless to the ground, writhing from brain signals sent at the time of death.

"The only good snake is a dead one,' the President muttered.

Pacing it off, the snake was just over twenty-one feet long. He was still breathing hard, sweating profusely from the ordeal. There was no use attempting the ceremony again and it would be too dangerous if there were other snakes such as this one about. He had brought some fried chicken and biscuits with him that he had picked up from a local fast-food joint on the way out. Rekindling the fire, he sat down and slowly ate, drinking a soda and contemplating his situation.

The FBI and MDPD had converged on tribal headquarters in Hollywood. Don Cilatro had flown down to meet with the President who had informed him of what he had found out during the transparency. Li Na, Morgan, Billie, the President, and others were present in the council chambers. It was a blur of activity as they prepared for the inevitable phone call.

"Okay, Billie and Mr. Cilatro," Phil said. "We do not know who they will be calling. Whoever they ask for, keep them on the line as long as you can so we can attempt a trace, at least we can determine the basic area."

"What makes you think they'll call from where Dianna and the boy are being held?" Cilatro asked.

"Because this time, they need to assure you they are still alive if you're going to try to meet their demands," McAllister said. "It's called proof of life. Detective Yuen has been combing the neighborhoods where we think they may be. There is a good chance they will be in one of them."

"Quite everyone," Susan said as the phone began to ring.

Counting down from four to one, she pointed at Billie to answer the phone.

"This is Panther," Billie said.

"Pass the phone to Cilatro," Ting said.

"I want to talk to James first," Billie said. "I need proof of life."

"Very well," Ting replied.

"James, are you okay?" Billie asked.

"Dad, I'm ...," James began as he was cut off.

"As you can see, he is okay. Pass the phone to Cilatro."

"This is Cilatro."

"We have your daughter. If you want to see her you will comply with our demands."

"I want to talk to her."

"Say hello to your father."

"Dad, is that you? They, . . .,"

"As you can see, we have them both," Ting said. "Comply or they die!"

"What do you want?" Cilatro asked.

"We want your partnership," Ting said.

"You must know our agreement prohibits that," Cilatro replied. "If we sell, the tribe has first right of refusal. There is no getting around that. And even if we did sell our shares, the people taking over would be immediately arrested."

"Let us worry about that, just figure it out. You have little time to comply."

The phone went dead as Ting hung up. Li Na recognized his voice.

"We have a general area of a couple of square miles," Susan said. "It is here."

She outlined an area on a map set up on a large easel.

"That's a lot of homes to cover," McAllister said. "We need to narrow it down somehow."

"The call came from Dianna's cell," Susan said. "Now it is dark again — no signal."

"Do what you can," Phil said. "We have no choice but to begin surveillance operations in the area. A grid search."

"You cannot do it during daylight," Genesis said. "You will tip them off if you do. Also, I suspect they are even now moving to a new location."

"You may be right," Phil said. "What do you recommend."

"Sergeant McAllister," Genesis said. "Didn't you tell me you have some drones with FLIR sensors?"

"Yes," McAllister said. "I see where you're going, and I like it. They are small and at a couple of hundred feet, invisible and unheard."

"We also have similar equipment," Phil said. "Susan will help. Let's develop a grid area for each to search and get them up in the air. Each pilot in command will have a specific area. Sergeant, what do you think about having a couple of swat teams standing by?"

"Good idea," McAllister said. "Place them here and here, at these coordinates."

"President," Phil said. "How does this guy think they can take over since we are aware of the deception?"

"I'm not sure," the President said. "The agreement is iron clad. It can only be modified by the BIA who would need a substantial reason to do so. Do you think they are stalling for time or some other reason?"

"Hmmmm," Phil mused. "That is possible. Let's concern ourselves with that later. The good news is we know both Dianna and James are okay. Our priority is getting the operation going and finding them."

Billie and Genesis gathered into a corner with Christina. Li Na, who had remained quite during the exchange, nudged Morgan and Cilatro, pulling the President into a corner.

"What do you think?" Cilatro asked.

"I attempted to find them through the transparency," the President said. "I was unable to get the address, but I know what the street looks like and the house."

"I have dealt with such things with the police before," Cilatro said, glancing toward Phil and McAllister. "I think we can handle this better ourselves if we can find the right location. What do you think Morgan?"

"Yes, I agree," Morgan said. "With Li Na's expertise and people, we can handle it."

"If we get you pictures with a street-level view, do you think you can identify the house?" Li Na asked.

"Definitely," the President said.

"Very well," Li Na said. "We will get our men on it right away scanning the area and getting photos back to you. Keep your phone handy."

The room was so busy no one noticed Morgan and Li Na slip out. Remembering the area on the map, they retraced the boundaries on the map app on their phones. Within an hour, they had a dozen men taking pictures from the end of every street and intersection in the area Susan had pointed out. In attempts to narrow the search, they were looking for an aqua-green house.

Li Na drove through the area slowly, pulling to the edge of the gravel roads here and there. The neighborhood had very mixed cultures, which made it difficult for any one group to stand out and be noticed. Whether the police found them first or not didn't matter. Li Na would personally take care of Ting. Ki had expressed an interest in having him brought back to Hong Kong and she would if she didn't kill him first. In a couple of hours, it would be dark. They would search for another hour and call it off for the day. As each of their men took pictures, they sent them to Li Na and Morgan who forwarded them to the President and Cilatro. The cross streets where each photo was taken was logged by Morgan, so they knew precisely where to go if they located the safe house.

Rain from the night before had dried up when Dakotah reached his office. Unaware of what was happening in Florida, he was caught off guard when he answered his phone.

"Dakotah Pullin."

"This is special agent Randy Moss of the FBI."

"How can I help you agent Moss?"

"Are you aware of what is going on with the Seminole Tribe?"

"I'm not sure what you mean."

"A group is trying to displace the partners who signed the original agreement for the power plant. They have kidnapped the daughter of one of the partners and the son of a tribal member."

"Oh my," Dakotah said, anxiety gripping his stomach. "I was aware only of the boy, which I thought the police and FBI had well in hand. How can I help."

"We would like the BIA to ensure that no other party can be brought in."

"I am almost certain they cannot, but will need to check on it," Dakotah said. "As you know, our policies are very strict with such issues."

"Could you look into it and call me back?" agent Moss asked. "A copy of the policies would also help us. This whole thing is a bit strange since they know that we know what they are attempting."

"I will look into it right away and get back to you," Dakotah said. "Give me your cell for immediate contact. I will call you shortly."

Dakotah did not like the sound of what he had heard. Anyone could tell that by kidnapping the daughter that James was not enough to bargain with. Something was up. He accessed the agreement with the tribe and partners on his computer. Next, he pulled up BIA policies regarding such transactions and sent a copy to agent Moss.

"Agent Moss," Dakotah said. "I sent you the policies to read over. After reading the agreement and comparing it to our policies between the agency and tribes, the only way a partner can step away is to sell or exchange his interest to the tribe."

"Is there no other way?" agent Moss asked.

"There is one other way," Dakotah said. "The partner can sell to another group or partner. However, that transaction requires full council approval of the tribes governing body."

"How likely is that to occur in this case?" agent Moss asked.

"Not," Dakotah said. "The entire council would probably reject it because they would rather the tribe have a greater interest, especially in a case with such a valuable resource. The only way, . . .," his voice trailing off.

"What, what are you thinking?"

"The only other way is they would need to bribe the entire council and I don't see that happening, but you would know more about such tactics than I would."

"I need the BIA to take action on this now," agent Moss said.

"We cannot take any action until the tribe attempts to modify the partnership," Dakotah said. "Until then, our hands are tied. Our goal is to approve or disapprove of their actions, which we seldom override. I'm afraid we need to wait until and if they try to modify the agreement."

"I understand," agent Moss said. "I will stay in touch. It appears we have a conundrum on our hands."

A mixture of thoughts began running through Dakotah's mind. Whoever this was had a brazen attitude. What could they want? Surely, they knew this was not going to be fruitful for them. As James's grandfather, he was not going to let the police handle the matter anymore. He would get involved and stay involved until the situation was resolved. His hand was shaking slightly from the adrenaline rush as he reached for his phone.

"Mabel," Dakotah said. "I need to speak to Billie. Things appear to be getting out of hand."

"What do you mean?" Mabel asked.

"Did you know the other person that was kidnapped?"

"No, I didn't know there was another."

"It happened two nights ago," Dakotah said. "They took the daughter of a partner. My guess is for additional leverage."

"Billie didn't tell me that," Mabel said.

"He likely has his hands full," Dakotah replied. "Have him call me directly. We need to talk."

The wheels of the plane thumped onto the tarmac of Ronald Reagan Washington National Airport. The hub of the nation, the airport was extremely crowded as officials, military personnel and individuals scurried toward their destinations. It was 7:00 am. Billie made his way to the taxi's lined up outside the terminal and told the driver to take him to BIA headquarters, which was barely five miles away. It would be the first time Billie had ever met his father. Despite the circumstances, he was in an elated state. The trip was short as he exited the cab, entered the building, and picked up a visitor pass where his dad's secretary waited to greet him. They walked upstairs and the secretary admitted him to his dad's office, quietly closing the door. Dakotah was smiling at his son from across the room. Walking around his desk, he shook Billie's hand, which turned into a warm, hard hug.

"You have become a man son," Dakotah said. "Mabel has told you about everything?"

"Yes," Billie said.

"Good," Dakotah replied. "We will catch up later. Since we are both short on time, tell me how I can help."

"Are you aware of the power plant and what is going on?" Billie asked.

"I am," Dakotah replied. "What concerns me is how bold these people are knowing that we know they cannot get another partners share. I have been trying to figure out what angle they have."

"Me too," Billie said. "Nothing makes sense. I thought they could be stalling for time as a competitor, but the competing power plants are already in place and their ownership has not changed."

"I had thought along those lines as well," Dakotah mused.

"Regardless, I have been going over policy here and talking with Randy Moss at the FBI. The current agreement is not going away, and they have no course of action regarding the partners. I am sorry about James, is there anything I can do?"

"No," Billie said. "It's become a waiting game hanging on new demands and like you imply, the demands make no sense. Maybe when this is all over you can come down and visit."

"I'd like that," Dakotah said. "It's been a long time since I was on BC."

The two talked for a couple of hours, catching up on Billie's life and family and what had happened to Dakotah as he worked in Washington. The more they talked, the more they realized that their journey was melding together. Dakotah took great pride in Billie's accomplishments. Like most fathers, it made him feel like he had done something right, his son having graduated from a prestigious Ivy League school. Even though he could not be there all the time, it was his money that had paid his way. The other side of him felt guilty for betraying his wife. That was in the past. All they could do was move forward. Dakotah opened the drawer of his desk and pulled out a photo.

"Look at this," Dakotah said, his eyes moistening.

"This is me and mom at my college graduation," Billie said. "How did you get this?"

"I took it Billie," Dakotah replied. "I've always been there in the background and kept up with all you have done. Given the circumstances it was what it was. I'm always there for you son."

"Here, you will want this," Billie said, retrieving a picture from his messenger bag.

Dakotah took the picture, his hands trembling in anticipation. It was Billie and Christina with James and Mabel. He sat staring at it and it reminded him of all the things he was missing.

"This is recent, isn't it?" Dakotah queried.

"It was taken during last year's Green Corn Dance," Billie said. "Mom thought you may want one. This year's ceremony will happen soon, maybe you can come down."

"I will treasure it," Dakotah said, trying to conceal his emotions. "Yes, if I can get free it would be fun."

There was soft knock at the door.

"It's time sir," the secretary said.

"I'll be right there," Dakotah replied.

"I will keep digging on my end son. I have a few people I can run this by. Maybe they can make sense of it where we cannot."

"Thanks, dad," Billie said. "I'll keep working on it also. Something is definitely not adding up here."

"Keep me posted on James," Dakotah said. "I'll keep you posted as well."

"Okay then," Billie sighed. "We will talk more later."

Dakotah watched Billie as he left his office, escorted by his secretary. Walking over to the window, he looked down to view him climb into a taxi. He thought back so many years before to his love Mabel and yearned to have the time back to make changes. But alas, the time was gone. The decisions had been made. It was ironic that both had wanted to stay together, but that both had known it was not the honorable thing to do, despite their lapse in judgement during their time of lust that had turned to love. It was perplexing how sex clouded one's judgement. He watched the taxi until it disappeared then, slowly walked to his meeting.

A few hours later found him making calls to the BIA regulatory group, Florida Power and Light, the senate finance committee and a few others. These were people he had helped in the past and who all helped each other when it came to policy and related issues. Dakotah was too smart to tell them what was going on, but instead used hypotheticals that sounded like real situations. Despite his efforts, they all came up short in attempting to uncover a motive for such actions.

Dakotah remembered his years in the military serving in special operations in Latin America and began to wonder if this was a ploy for something else? It would explain the basic demands and behavior, but what could the ploy be?

The conversation was getting heated as Cilatro paced back and forth. He was furious that his daughter had been kidnapped and was dressing Frank and Kelly up and down.

"How the hell could you let this happen?" Cilatro shouted. "You're supposed to protect her."

"Everything seemed okay boss," Frank said. "It was raining hard outside, and we had just checked on her to see if she needed anything."

"That's right," Kelly joined in. "We offered to get her some ice and she said she was fine and was about to go to bed. We even had her lock the door with the knob and safety door lock. Our rooms had adjoining doors and neither of us heard anything."

"Okay, let's think this through," Cilatro said, calmer. "If that is the case then whoever kidnapped her posed as a police officer. Otherwise, she would not have let her guard down. That is a certainty. We also know that whoever took her knows as well as we do it is a useless gesture."

"These guys have everyone, including the police banging their heads against the wall," Frank said. "What are we not seeing?"

"Let's keep at it," Cilatro said. "Have Morgan get a ten-man crew down here right away. Maybe the extra manpower will help in the hunt."

Privately Cilatro wondered if it was as simple as extortion.

Neighborhoods around south Florida tended to look much the same once you were away from the hustle and bustle of downtown. There were lots of cinderblock style homes painted in vibrant colors typical of those used in the Caribbean. These were not the new homes of the upper middle class and wealthy with their pools and multiple car garages, but those of the blue-collar working class. They were small, efficient, and ageing, with open carports if they had one at all, surrounded by pressed shell-rock roads instead of asphalt. People struggled to get by as prices for food, electricity, gasoline, and other necessities continued to increase under the dreadful management of the current administration. Many turned to selling drugs to make ends meet. Li Na and her men had been over the entire area the FBI had traced the phone to and there was no sign of the house the President had seen in his vision. Law enforcement had come up empty too and were broadening their search. As she walked along, trying to act as casual as she could, one of her men trailed just over her shoulder.

"I want you to get the drones up with the FLIR and have them comb the areas on each side of this one, all sides."

"What do we look for?" the man asked.

"Look for houses with groups of four or more people," Li Na said. "Make a note of where they are, and we will check each of them out in the morning. Go quickly and get on it."

"Aren't you coming?" the man asked.

"I'll be there in a while," Li Na said. "I want to finish up this block and will return on the other one."

"This is a dangerous place," the man said. "Are you sure?"

"Yes. I'll be fine. Go."

The sun had set an hour before; darkness had quickly engulfed the neighborhood. There were few lights, and no one was on the rock roads. Li Na turned right to go up the next block and back to her car, her cane touching the ground as she walked. She reached the corner on her final round. The streetlight was out, barely able to distinguish her surroundings, which were mostly shadows of hulking cars, old boats, and camper trailers. Suddenly, she sensed danger.

"We'll take the cane bitch," the man said. "It should fetch twenty or thirty dollars. We'll take your purse too."

Li Na instantly whirled, coming face to face with three

assailants. They were scraggly type men in their young thirties. Drug addicts from the looks of them. The leader lit a cigarette, blowing smoke in her direction. The glow from it as he drew each puff was enough to outline all three men.

"Yeah, maybe we'll take something else too," the man on her left said.

She was not afraid. The men would have run if they had been able to see her smiling face. They stood about four feet away, in such a manner that the leader was just behind the shoulders of the other two men on either side of him, their formation forming a shallow oval.

"You heard me bitch," the leader said. "Hand over the cane and purse."

Li Na pretended to be nervous as she pulled the cane up with her left hand, slightly turning the handle with her right, her fashionable purse, dropping off her right shoulder into the crook of her arm. Framed against a distant streetlight, the men watched her silhouette in anticipation.

"Don't hurt me," she stammered, appearing afraid. "I'll give you what you want."

"You'll give more than that," the third man said.

When the purse hit the crook of her arm, she let go of the top of the cane while the purse slid down, tossing it at their feet, re-grabbing her cane top with her right hand. The purse landed directly in front of the leader. All three men glanced down when it thudded onto the road.

"Pick it, . . .," the voice suddenly stopped.

The sound of the sword being quickly pulled from the sheath was frightening. The men's eyes began to widen as the blade arched through the air severing the head of the first assailant on her left. The single arc continued, cutting the jugular veins and throats of the other two men who fell gurgling to the ground. A few seconds later Li Na shook her sword off and wiped each side of the blade on the pants of the first assailant then, stooped down and picked up her purse.

She was careful to avoid the pools of blood. Looking carefully about, ensuring no one else was around, she slung her purse back over her shoulder and walked casually down the street to her car, humming and smiling.

E arly the next morning, Dakotah had just gotten to his office when his phone rang. He thought it strange since he always arrived early and no one else was usually in.
"Dakotah."
"You need to quit asking questions," the voice said. "It will make us look bad if you pursue this."
"I'm just making sure that we don't get caught in something unawares."
"We won't. Let the policy group handle it. Stay out of it. The superiors of those you called have called me. Our hands are tied. Understand?"
"Yes sir, I understand."

As the phone clicked dead, Dakotah wondered why the Director, BIA would concern himself with such matters? There were usually only two explanations, politics or money, typically both. Staring out the window as he swiveled in his chair, he began to believe that whatever this was, it was larger than they fathomed grasped. He had better warn Billie. Time to tread lightly.

T he Green Corn Dance celebration was going well. Most of the tribal members were present and having a great time. It was a good time for council members and the President to mingle with the tribe on a more unofficial manner and let the members know that they were being considered and that their best interests were at heart. Whether true or not the perception was what counted. It was one of the few times that members of the tribe were able to greet the Medicine Man and learn more about him. He gave his wisdom freely to all but remained aloof from most of the trivial affairs of the people. It was his chance to feel the spirit of each member of the tribe and work on his longer-term strategy for training those considered worthy. Their hearts were an open book to him wherein he could see the character of the individual.

Knowing he would be there, Billie managed to find a private time to talk with him, which didn't go unnoticed by the President.

"Medicine Man," Billie said. "It is good to see you. Do you have a moment?"

"Yes, Billie," the Medicine Man said. "Sit down please."

As he sat down, two warriors stood behind Billie a few feet away so that no one could approach the Medicine Man and interrupt the two. The Medicine Man gazed across the crowd as members passed. Because Billie's back was toward the celebration and people, he did not see the President staring across at them, but the Medicine Man's keen eyes missed nothing.

"What is it you wish?" the Medicine Man asked.

"Are you aware of James and the missing partners daughter Dianna?" Billie asked.

"Of course," the Medicine Man replied. "It is not the obvious you seek, but the hidden plan."

"You knew what I was going to ask?"

"Yes. There is treachery afoot. Look not toward the obvious."

"To what should I look?"

"The person contacting you has two bosses. Find out who the other boss is, and you will have your answer."

"Do you think the other boss is here?"

"No, the Great Spirit confirms he is across the deep."

"A competitor of one of the partners?" Billie asked. "That has to be it."

"More than a competitor," the Medicine Man said. "Such a lust for control and power you have never met. It is that lust that will expose him. Follow the money. Do you understand?"

"Yes, I understand."

"Good, go; enjoy yourself."

Billie nodded in respect and began to mingle with others attending the celebration. Finding Christina, he pulled her aside.

"He has pointed me in the right direction," Billie said. "It will not be easy, but we may have a chance."

"I'm very frustrated with the progress of the search," Christina said. "Something needs to happen. Law enforcement has gotten nowhere."

"That is why it is up to us," Billie said. "We need to be persistent and focused and, we need to be patient. I know this is pulling our heartstrings, but they will not harm James as long as they can use him for leverage."

"That doesn't make it any easier for me," Christina said, a tear rolling down her cheek."

Billie put his arm around her and held her close.

"We must hang in there," Billie whispered. "Come enjoy the celebration. I'm going to talk to Genesis."

Christina watched him go, gazing around the crowd. Near one of the event tents that had been set up she caught the eye of the President and strolled over. She didn't know that he had been watching her and Billie.

"Mr. President," Christina said. "How are you doing today?"

"Well, thank you. How about yourself?"

"I'm frustrated over James," Christina said. "Do you have any more news than Billie? I'm really worried, sick to my stomach and ready to pull my hair out."

"I'm afraid not," the President said. "As you know, we are all working with law enforcement and the partners. I don't know if Billie told you or not, but right now we are waiting on the next demand from the kidnappers."

"He mentioned something about that," Christina said. "What is it they want?"

"It's becoming less clear," the President said. "They know there is no path by which they can oust one of the partners. It may be as simple as a ransom demand, but that's just a guess or, a ruse for something more sinister. Who knows?"

As he spoke, the President was feeling guilty about his part in getting the power plant going. He was hoping that it was not the partners who were involved in this fiasco. The woman in front of him was heartbroken. As much as he tried to be stalwart about the circumstances, his eyes moistened in compassion for her. He was not an evil man, but like many, had a weakness for money. He gently placed his right hand on her shoulder.

"Have faith Christina. I know it is difficult, but we will find James. We are closer than we were."

"I hope you are right. Patience is a difficult virtue for me now."

"I understand. Look, I must talk to someone. Don't give up hope."

The President walked away stopping and talking with members as he went. She hoped he was right, but it was getting more difficult each day. She was beside herself and became unaware of her surroundings as she walked. Suddenly, she heard someone calling her name. It was the Medicine Man.

"Christina, come sit with me," the Medicine Man said as she drew near.

Walking between the two stoic warriors, she sat cross legged in front of him.

"You look so discontent," the Medicine Man said. "Fear not, all will be well."

"How do you know that?" Christina asked. "Do you have a crystal ball or something?"

She realized as soon as the words fell from her lips that she had misspoke.

"I'm sorry," she said bitterly. "I had no right, please forgive me."

"My child. We all have heartaches in this life, it is part of our journey, along with the joys. Be not ashamed of your words. You are bitter and that is understood. To answer your question. Yes. I have something better than a crystal ball. I have the guidance and visions of the Great Spirit. All will be well with your son, but others will suffer in this part of our journey. I know this for I have seen it but am forbidden to give details. But I tell you now to build your hope. All will be well in the end."

Tears began rolling softly down Christina's cheeks as she reached out both hands and clasped the Medicine Man's hands in hers.

"Thank you. I will try to do as you say."

"Be faithful and of good heart. Go now and set your gloom aside."

Genesis and Billie had separated themselves from the crowd at the ceremony and were beneath a palm tree in earnest conversation. Everyone knew what was going on with the kidnapping and could guess what the two were talking about without hearing it. In a small community, nothing was kept secret for long.

"Did you hear what happened in the area where the MDPD and FBI thought the kidnappers were?" Genesis asked.

"No," Billie responded.

"They found three men dead," Genesis said. "One had his head removed, the other two had their throats cut."

"That's gruesome," Billie said. "It doesn't have anything to do with James, does it?"

"We don't think so," Genesis said. "It looks like a robbery gone bad. Sergeant McAllister said they men appeared to be addicts looking for a score. His officers found sick humor in it."

"I guess they didn't get the score they thought," Billie said. "But isn't that kind of death odd?"

"Not necessarily," Genesis said. "They think a Columbian took a machete to them. What was odd was that it appeared to be one long cut that took all three down."

"Hmmmm," Billie mused. "That must have been one sharp

machete or someone with skill, lots of skill."

"Exactly," Genesis said. "At any rate, the entire area was checked, and they have widened the search."

"What are you two in such deep conversation and whispered tones about?" Christina asked, walking up.

"I was just filling Billie in on the latest update," Genesis said.

"Then fill me in please."

"The police and FBI did not find James and Dianna in the planned search area. They have widened it and continue to investigate."

"Are they getting any results?" Christina asked.

"Yes. They found the house where James and Dianna had been held."

"That's good news then, right?"

"In many ways. It means we are hot on their trail and hopefully, they will find fingerprints and other evidence that will help us narrow where they may go next. My guess is they have a series of safe houses and move frequently."

"Finally, some hope," Christina sighed.

"Don't worry, we will find them," Genesis said. "The longer they keep making demands, the greater the chance we have of closing in."

A third safe house in as many days. The men holding James and Dianna were getting tired of moving but knew it would keep them out of the clutches of law enforcement and prison. They kept James and Dianna in a bedroom together, door open, tied to the bed unless they had to go to the bathroom.

"Why do they keep us?" James asked.

"They are trying to pry money out of the partners," Dianna said.

"What partners?"

"My fathers' company and another are partners with the tribe in the power plant, which is now operational. Because it is up and running, they think they can extort money from us."

"Can they?" James asked.

"Yes, but it will not be that easy for them to collect," Dianna said.

"What will happen to us?" James asked nervously.

"They will likely exchange us for the money," Dianna replied.

"But won't' they get caught when they do?" James asked.

"It depends on how well they have planned," Dianna said. "Don't worry about that, let's keep playing dots."

Dianna knew the police were not far behind them based on the frequency they moved from one safe house to another. She began to make notes in the very back of the note pad as James kept watch. She kept them hidden under the mattress in case they moved again. The two were being well treated and the men holding them didn't seem overly concerned. It was just a job and when they were finished, they would move on to some other job. Dianna didn't worry about them, but about the well-dressed slender man that came once to each safe house. She could sense his killer instincts and knew that the two of them meant nothing to him.

Dark gray towering cumulus clouds heralded the approach of severe thunderstorms as they transitioned from the cumulus stage to the mature stage. The forecast was for rain all day. With the Green Corn Dance over, everyone was back to work. Billie drove back and forth from the power plant to his office as he assumed some of Dianna's tasks, as well as his own. A sheet of water was flowing across the parking lot when he picked up his ringing phone.

"Billie, we need to meet privately," Dakotah said.

"When?"

"As soon as possible. Do you have a private place?"

"Yes. How soon can you be here?"

"I'm boarding now and will be there in three hours on BC, about noon."

"Okay, don't come to BC. I'll grab my airboat and meet you at the I-75 fishing park about twelve miles west of Andytown along Alligator Alley,"

"Roger that."

B illie hooked his airboat to his pickup and was on his way a couple of hours later. He had stocked it with snacks and water and filled it with fuel, including the reserve tank. He kept wondering what his dad wanted and why they needed to meet in private. The thirty miles to the fishing park passed quickly. He took the eastbound exit and negotiated his way to the boat ramp, backed up and put his airboat into the water. He quickly parked in the almost empty lot and maneuvered his boat through the water into the Miami Canal and under the freeway then, turned right past the north side of the freeway, along the bank close to the western most restroom. Twenty minutes later he noticed a small silver rental car pull into the lot. It was his father, who noticed him and quickly parked. Running to Billie, he jumped into the boat. Billie grinned as he took a seat next to him., the boat heading north into the deep sawgrass.

"Where are we headed?" Dakotah asked.

"It's a surprise but you will like it," Billie said. "What is so important that we need to meet?"

They were yelling at each other over the sound of the engine as they slid through the deep sawgrass. With the recent rains the water in the Glades was deep and the airboat moved along effortlessly. They decided to stop talking because they were getting hoarse from yelling. Dakotah relaxed and let past memories come flooding back. It had been too long since he had been on the reservation. He began to relax as the natural surroundings lulled him into a peace he had not felt for a long time. Wildlife, flowers, sawgrass, and hammocks were all around him. He gazed in wonder at the anhinga birds sitting on branches of long dead trees waiting for their prey to stir the water before diving in for a meal. Alligators' heads appeared to float in spots of open water as the boat sped by, huge drops of rain falling onto the tranquil, dark surface. Despite the rain, the ride was exhilarating as Dakotah continued to be immersed in his surroundings, giving Billie an occasional grin, and putting his arm around his shoulders. The boat slowed as it negotiated around a couple of hammocks and pulled up to an elevated walkway.

Billie hooked the boat to the railing.

"This is the place," he said. "It's the most private place I know besides the Medicine Man's hammock."

"When did you build this?" Dakotah asked.

"About ten years ago," Billie said. "But she lives here."

He nodded to the chickee a few yards down the walkway. Standing in the doorway was Mabel who recognized Billie right away. She kept trying to recognize who the other man with him was. Then, Dakotah turned.

"Oh my god," Mabel screamed as she ran toward him, almost knocking him off the walkway. She wrapped her arms around him, tears of joy streaming down her face.

"Mabel," Dakotah gasped. "It's so good to see you."

The two stood hugging, hands around each other's waist, leaning backward and looking deep into their eyes.

"Billie," Dakotah said, looking up. "You didn't tell me you were bringing me to see your mother."

"That was not the initial goal," Billie said. "You wanted to meet somewhere private. This is one of two places I know where we can do that."

"I'm glad you chose this place," Dakotah said as he put his arm around Mabel's waist and walked toward the table at the end of the walkway.

The rain had stopped, the clouds dissipating quickly to reveal a blue sky. Mabel hurriedly retrieved a washcloth and dried the table and chairs off.

"Would you like coffee?" she asked.

"That would be great," Dakotah said. "He stood looking across the sawgrass. The peacefulness he always treasured came back as a calm swept over him, the mustiness of the swamp mingling, playing with his sense of smell. He breathed deeply as he enjoyed the expanse of nature before him.

Billie watched him. The gaze on his face was so distant, slowly turning into a smile. It was a smile of wistfulness as they sat down. Mabel poured coffee for them, grinning as she looked down into Dakotah's face. A beaming smile greeted her.

"Well, since this is a private meeting, I'll leave you two at it," Mabel said.

"No, please stay," Dakotah said. "You are not interrupting, and you need to hear this too. Your thoughts can be valuable."

"First, did you do what I told you to?" Billie asked.

"Yes," Dakota said, reaching into his pocket and holding up a cell phone in a privacy bag.

"Good," Billie said, putting his finger to his lips and laying his phone on the table. "Mom, place yours here."

Mabel laid her phone beside Billie's and watched while he placed both into a privacy bag. "Please put all of them in the chickee," Billie said.

When Mabel had returned, she sat down next to Dakotah. "Why all the secrecy?" she asked.

"Most people are unaware that a smart phone acts like a receiver," Billie said. "What you say around it can be heard on the other end and this, we do not need others to hear."

"What have you found out father?" Billie asked.

"It's a red flag," Dakotah said. "That is why we need to keep this between ourselves. "The director called me. He is never in so early. Essentially, he told me to lay off my assistance to you and let our policy group deal with it. I would not have thought anything about it, but the issue isn't seemingly that important."

"Seemingly?" Billie queried.

"Yes. All I was doing was checking the agreement against our policies to determine the procedural way to handle the potential conundrum."

"Why do you think he called you?" Mabel asked.

"That's the problem," Dakotah said. "It doesn't make sense. What we were doing would go through him within a day or so anyway. It is almost as if he was pressured by someone."

"The question is for what and by who," Mabel blurted out.

"Yes, what and who indeed," Dakotah said. "As I told you before, the partnership agreement is ironclad. No one can come in and change it or take it over. There has to be another explanation."

"Do you think this guy making the demands is blackmailing the director somehow?" Billie asked.

"That was my first thought," Dakotah said. "However, I don't think he would need to. The more logical course would be that he is blackmailing one of the partners. And I presume it would be Cilatro since his daughter was kidnapped. There is no reason I could see why the director would be in such a position."

"I must say all of this is very odd," Mabel said. "Nothing makes any sense. The kidnapped girl could be more easily ransomed unless, . . ." Her voice trailed off.

"Unless what?" Dakotah asked, he and Billie leaning forward.

"Unless there is a multiple ploy going on here. Think about it, a partner's daughter is kidnapped which as Billie suggested earlier would give them more leverage. They know that they cannot become a partner. I think they knew that all along. In my opinion, this is not just about money, or you would have heard from them already with a ransom demand. My intuition tells me this is more insidious."

"That would make sense," Billie said. "But it still doesn't explain what it may be."

"Maybe it's not about the present," Dakotah said. "Maybe it's about the future and behind the scenes control. How much money will the power plant generate?"

"Not as much now but moving forward it will be in the billions of dollars over the next decade," Billie said.

"Wait a minute!" Mabel exclaimed. "Didn't you tell me that this was one of many power plants the tribe and its partners were going to put in?"

"Yes," Billie said. "They will all be on tribal lands and ours serves as a model for the rest. Showing it is successful will make other tribes want to in, just like they did with casino's that we started."

"Hmmmm," Dakotah mused. "I think Mabel is onto something. Suppose for a moment this is about leveraging the future power plants for a cut of the take of each or more insidious goals. Even ten percent of ten plants would be in the billions."

"Perhaps more," Billie said. "Lunadi just gave us a presentation on critical infrastructure and how electricity was our Achilles heel. As a matter of fact, he gave me a link to a report and told me that I should read it."

"Did you?" Mabel asked.

"Yes, because his presentation was so fascinating," Billie said. "The gist of the report was about more than energy shortages, it was about how it was intertwined with water. A federal agency over twenty years ago projected the needs of electricity for today. They indicated that due to population growth and economic expansions that the U.S. would need almost 400,000 megawatts of new generating capacity by 2020. That's 400, one thousand MW nuclear plants. Not one has been built during that time. Because vampire appliances have grown that were never anticipated, the demand is overwhelming, much more than anticipated. Lunadi suggested back in 2006 that rolling national blackouts, much like those in California would be commonplace within ten years. We are at that threshold."

"That means that electricity prices will rise substantially," Dakotah said. "They've gone up almost one hundred twenty percent in the last decade. It's beginning to make sense."

"What do you mean?" Mabel asked.

"I believe the strategy is long-term extortion," Dakotah said. "It they can leverage the partners who will be the companies going to other tribes, they can extort huge sums in the future, perhaps even leverage control of these plants. And, since many of those tribes are likely near large urban areas the power plants located on tribal lands will become exceptionally valuable, especially where they are coupled with water resources such as BC. And they may even be able to control larger blocks of the power grid."

"It would be a gold mine for them," Billie said.

"It would appear that whoever is behind this, has surmised the strategy of your partners," Mabel said.

"You are likely correct," Dakotah replied.

"But we don't know who is behind this," Billie quipped.

"Not yet," Dakotah said. "It would take a lot of digging to find out. And the Department of Energy wouldn't take this lightly."

"Genesis has dug into it some," Billie said. "I had to ask him not to because the enemy is within. Besides that, he has no jurisdiction outside reservation boundaries."

"Didn't he work previously with the DOE after the war?" Mabel asked.

"Yes," Billie said. "What are you getting at?"

"I think I know," Dakotah interrupted. "As I recall he was with the Federal Protective Forces of DOE. Most consider them a clandestine group. These are the FPF; paramilitary forces of the DOE that are responsible for the protection of Category I nuclear material. It's a demanding job. Each of the members hold law-enforcement status even though they are classified as security police. They are equipped and trained to respond to serious incidents at DOE facilities by armed adversaries and to reacquire any nuclear materials that may be stolen. Essentially, they are elite fighting forces designed to operate in combat environments. They are trained to repel such elite forces as

Navy Seals."

"But how does that help us?" Billie asked.

"We need someone on the inside," Dakotah said. "This could be our shot. If we draft an MOU with DOE, I can get Genesis sworn in as a provisional member for as long as he and the director wish. He would then be able to enforce tribal law on the reservation, but also off since he would be a sworn federal officer with the same national authority as the FBI and U.S. Marshals. More importantly, this could be classified by DOE as a terrorist act, and they would have sophisticated equipment to conduct computer and other searches with that you do not have, including surveillance."

"I'm not sure you could get them to go along with this," Billie said. "We wouldn't be a high priority."

"Let me handle that," Dakotah said. "I know the director personally and he owes me a favor. Not only that, he also commanded Genesis during the war, not to mention Genesis worked with FPF before landing here. They have a good rapport."

"You make it seem so easy," Mabel said.

"When you know Washington politics, some things are not as difficult as you would suspect. It's all about watching your back and exchanging favors. Besides, he owes me a big one and this is a small one. He's also been itching to do more with local energy groups on potential terrorism issues to expand his network. This will fit his requirements exactly. Not only that, both he and Genesis have a great trust and he can provide additional resources other law enforcement groups cannot."

"This would allow us to have an inside man," Billie said. "And we could trust him. How soon could we make this happen?"

"As soon as I get back, I'll talk to him. His office is not far from mine. You need to talk to Genesis and make sure he is okay with it."

Billie stared off across the swamp contemplating what his father had said. It seemed a bit complicated, but he would do whatever it took to get James back.

"He's my grandson, you know," Dakotah said, as if sensing what Billie was thinking. "We will get him back. I will call in every favor owed if I need to."

"Thanks dad," Billie said. "We're just beat up with this problem. There is not much we can do but rely on the local police and FBI. At this point, we have few leads."

"I understand," Dakotah said. "We must remain hopeful and do what we can."

Mabel had been making lunch for them, the smell beginning to make their mouths water. It helped shift their attention from the matter at hand. As they ate fried fish and hush puppies, they talked about the past. Laughing and smiling, they caught up on twenty years of missed time.

"I hate to spoil the party," Dakotah said. "I have a plane to catch and duties to perform. We need to get this operation initiated as soon as we can. Mabel, it was an honor."

The two stood hugging each other for a couple of minutes and then kissed. Mabel wanted to melt into his arms. The passion was so great that memories of their lust years before instantly flooded back, engulfing them in a momentary bliss that both were in dire need of. They began to part, not wanting to let go of each other's hands.

"I will be back sooner than you think," Dakotah whispered.

"I'll be waiting," Mabel said hoarsely, choking back tears of joy.

As Dakotah made his way to the airboat, Mabel slipped up next to Billie, pulling his shoulder down with her hand, she kissed his cheek.

"Thank you, son," Mabel said.

Billie squeezed her hand, nodding in understanding as he climbed aboard. The motor roared to life, and they were off.

Continuing to look over his shoulder until they were out of sight, Dakotah waved back at Mabel who watched them leave. It would not be long he thought, and they would be together again. The ride back to the car was too short as Dakotah said goodbye to Billie and was down the freeway toward the airport.

Shouting was coming from Ki's office. His secretary cringed at the sounds as she heard a chair crash against the window. She had never known her boss to be outwardly angry and knew something was very wrong.

"How the hell could they have guessed our strategy?" Ki asked. "No one but the two partners and you and Li Na knew."

"I don't think it is as difficult as you would suspect," Akio replied. "Energy prices keep soaring, along with water and basic commodities. The increase in power prices during the Texas incident likely tipped them off, as well as the backdoor investigation by Genesis."

"Have they made any demands yet?" Ki asked.

"Other than the partner sell, which they knew wasn't going to happen, no, they have not," Akio said.

"What do you think we are looking at?" Ki asked.

"As Cilatro and Li Na suggested, we have developed partnerships with a dozen more tribes eager to work with us," Akio said. "The President has been great at selling the concept and they're on board. All the partnership documents will be signed by tomorrow. Because we have everything in place, their only play is extortion. With Cilatro's daughter caught in the web, he is under a lot of pressure to cave."

"Li Na told me that Ting is working for Xu Lo," Ki said. "He leads a powerful triad, but he knows he doesn't have the resources to pull this off."

"It is likely he is working with two triads," Akio said. "I am digging as is Li Na. If there is something there, we will find it. Right now, their only play is Cilatro. Potentially, he could sign an agreement with them for a share of his percentage. However, according to Li Na, he is pissed and not inclined to do so, daughter or not. He is as the American's say, a hard-core son of a bitch!"

"Call Li Na and tell her to do all she can to find the package," Ki said. "I have a couple of personnel to bring in. Tell her to expect them in three days and make arrangements for their stay."

"It's done," Akio said as he rose, closing the door behind him.

Ki stood looking out the window then, bent over and placed the chair he had kicked over to its original position. He glanced at the tempered glass as he picked it up, which had not been damaged. He felt confident that Li Na could work out the situation, but he wanted to be sure and was sending his best two men to help her. They were assassins of the first order, with experience from the Chinese army in counterintelligence and special operations. Li Na would know exactly what to do with them. Her latest report was optimistic, but Ting was crafty. He would be dealt with soon enough. The two men would take as much technology as they could with them. The most important being a dozen drones that had been networked into a swarm with dual FLIR cameras and a twenty-five-kilometer operating range. Ting would not stay out of their grasp for long. They had both trusted him and he had turned on them, working in the service of the other triads. They were planning something larger than he was currently aware, there was no doubt.

Ki drug a chair to the window, grabbing a pad and pen. He began to sketch out his strategy from the beginning through the next twenty years. Then, began to fill it in with energy prices that seemed to increase every day. Looking at the link between water distribution, energy costs and economics, he began to see how his enemies had picked up on what he and his partners were attempting. He had to give credit to Akio because he believed he was correct. The prices, along with completion of the power plant, had created a large red flag and the partnership with the tribe had been all over local and regional news. Small wonder they picked up on it, not to mention Ting. The other tribes would follow suit because they wanted the attention and within the next few days, his enemies would have the bigger picture. If Cilatro sided with them, it would only affect his money and not the triad's. However, it would create an enemy within. They needed to get the daughter back and eliminate the triad leaders as an example. It was that simple.

It was a beautiful day in Washington. The air was clear of pollution and Dakotah was taking in deep breaths sitting on the park bench.

"Be careful there," a voice called out. "You don't want to suck in too much of our foul air."

Both men laughed at the notion. Washington was foul, there was no doubt about it. If there was a master of the DC scene, especially in terms of understanding politics and keeping secrets, it was Jonas Rothman, Director of the Department of Energy. He had more power than anyone could conceive and with his FPF, was a formidable leader to deal with. He must have power, having already served two presidents. Jonas had better trained guards than the secret service, two of them standing about thirty yards away. Jonas never went anywhere without them. Dakotah wouldn't be surprised if there was an entire tactical team a block away. Jonas never took chances, not even with friends.

"It's been a while," Jonas said sitting down, pushing his right hand out for his agents to back further away then, shaking Dakotah's hand. "Tell me what's on your mind."

"Do you remember Genesis?" Dakotah asked. "How can I forget him, he saved my life at least a half dozen times, a debt that I am unable to repay."

"Would you like to command him again?" Dakotah asked.

"Hell yes," Jonas said. "You have my full attention."

"This is what is going on and we need your help, your advice at the least," Dakotah said. "If you agree, this is Genesis's number. The only ones who would know are the three of us and Billie Panther."

"You mean your son?" Jonas queried.

"How did you know that?" Dakotah asked. "I thought only three people knew. Never mind, I'm sure you have your resources."

"It doesn't matter how I know," Jonas said. "Just know that I protect my friends."

Dakotah explained over the next half hour everything that had been developing in south Florida and what they were up against. The problem was more than they could handle. Jonas was looking across the park, listening intently and planning at the same time. When he finished Jonas was staring at him, a huge smile on his face.

"What?" Dakotah asked.

"I'm not smiling because of your troubles my friend," Jonas said. "It's because of the opportunity you have brought me. You see, the case you have laid out is like one that I have proposed before. It describes the potential infiltration of our nuclear and major power plants from embedded terrorists from other countries, specifically China. Over a period, they could very well infiltrate leadership at these plants or their owners and even commit sabotage. My fear and probably paranoia, is the why, which you have not been able to figure out. That is because it is probably a long-term strategic plan to threaten U.S. energy and demand a ransom for one or more of our nuclear plants."

"Why would they ransom them when they could have a percentage of multiple plants through extortion?"

"Because a nuclear plant costs about $20 billion to build, not to mention ten years to vet. Ransom only one and the demand would easily be many times more than from your current conundrum."

"So, you will help us then?" Dakotah queried.

"I've been hoping for an opportunity like this for years," Jonas said. "Not only will I help, but I'll also make sure it is done right. If Genesis is on board, we can begin at once."

"I'm sure he is," Dakotah said. "Here is his number, handing over a piece of paper."

"This will allow us to work with many more power groups on the sly side. And it will allow us tribal access through Genesis that we have never been able to gain. Again, my suspicion is that what you have laid out is a long-term plan that will not stop with your plant. It will extend to the nuclear plants and bribed politicians in this town that are more than happy to make a buck at our expense. I think this may be a trial run."

"And here I was thinking I'd need to call in a big favor," Dakotah grinned.

"It is I that owes you a favor," Jonas said. "Here, take this. It's a burner phone. Protect it. When I call it will display 'D' on the screen. You'll know when to dump it. Later my friend."

"That was easier than I thought it would be," Dakotah thought to himself." He watched Jonas walk away, his security detail following him, secretly wondering if what Jonas had said was all there was to it? It made sense given the bureaucracy on the Hill. Now for Genesis and Billie to do their part. He looked at the burner phone Jonas had given him, removing the back to uncover the battery, hoping what he thought may be there wasn't. It was clean. No tracking device. That showed a level of trust. Good. Dakotah slowly pulled his own phone from his breast pocket.

"Billie, great news," Dakotah said. "I just spoke with Jonas. It's on. Have you spoken with Genesis yet?"

"He's on speaker phone with me now," Billie said. "When will this go down?"

"As soon as they can make it happen," Dakotah said. "Likely by tomorrow morning. Genesis, are you okay working with your former boss?"

"Absolutely," Genesis replied. "We go way back and have a deep trust with each other. Besides, he's always wanted to work with tribal groups, unlike others who are just lip service."

"How soon can you be ready?" Dakotah asked.

"Billie and I were just talking about that," Genesis said. "The only snag is appointing someone as acting chief while we're tied up with this situation."

"Don't worry," Billie said. "We have it resolved with a second in command. It will not be divulged to others."

"Our cover is that I will be working with the Feds based on what has been happening and it may take a while because they are suspicious it may be occurring on other tribal lands."

"That will work," Dakotah said. "Jonas will call you shortly and give you instructions. Other than that, Billie will keep me in the loop. I suggest we keep our communications at a minimum and use Billie as the go between."

"And I thought I was paranoid," Genesis said, laughing.

"When you've worked in DC as long as I have, you need eyes in the back of your head if you want to survive. Good luck."

Chapter 7

Formalities had been explained in a cryptic manner to Genesis the day before by Jonas. "Something must be up," Genesis thought. "It was obvious Jonas didn't want to say anything over the phone." The plane touched down in DC and within a few minutes, Genesis was met by three FPF agents and whisked away to Jonas's office. The agents had been instructed to bring Genesis up the back way so that no one saw him come in. Jonas's assistant admitted them immediately to his office.

Genesis stopped dead in his tracks as the doors closed behind him. In front of him stood Jonas, surrounded by five FPF agents. The three who had escorted him from the airport joined their ranks. Genesis recognized all of them excepting his escorts and knew immediately that something was up.

"It is good to see you again my friend," Jonas said as he stepped forward and shook his hand. "You know most of the men. You will all be working closely together. Let's get to it. Raise your right hand and swear to uphold the oath."

Jonas administered the oath of service to him and when he had sworn to uphold the oath and duties required therein, Jonas handed him his badge and gun, a P226 as originally issued to the U.S. Navy Seals.

"I'll let you get reacquainted later," Jonas said. "We have a problem. Intelligence has picked up chatter that an outside force wants to take over a few of our power plants or do them harm. We have not ascertained which ones. Genesis, you worked with us a long time and were one of our best. I want you because you can give us access to lands we have not been welcomed on before. Whoever this is has been planning it for some time, apparently years. I have discussed it at length with the President who he wants us to keep it under wraps until we have more information and intelligence."

"What do you want me to do?" Genesis asked.

"First, I want this group, the nine of you, to get your skills up to speed. I'll give you three days to hone them. Work on firearms, entry, and tech skills, especially drones. When you are done, all of you will fly to Miami and help locate the two kidnapped individuals and free them. You'll be helping local law enforcement, especially the FBI and MDPD. Genesis, bring the men up to speed on what has happened there so far. This is to be a clandestine mission. The President and I feel we have a mole in our midst. Put this on Genesis, handing him a light jacket with the FPF patch on it. A van is waiting downstairs. Go now!"

As they were leaving, Jonas grabbed Genesis by the arm and whispered in his ear. "Thank you, old friend. Take care of yourself and the men. Show them how it's done."

Time passed quickly. The men in the training group had become fast friends. They were doing entry drills, which were old hat. It was a matter of re-imprinting muscle memory.

"Genesis," one of them asked. "Jonas told us you did entry a different way. Would you show us?"

"Sure," Genesis replied. "Before I do I want all of you to remove your mags and rack your bolts back. Good, now assume your entry position. I noticed that all of you are right-handed. Imagine you have just come through a door. Turn your rifle and body to the left to engage an assailant. How does that feel?"

"It feels natural," one of the men said, the others concurring."

"That's right," Genesis said. "Now, imagine the same situation but the assailant or perp is on your right. Turn to engage him."

The men started remarking to themselves, asking questions.

"You have noticed what most do not," Genesis said. "When a right-handed person does an entry and turns right, you need to turn almost the entire body to line up your weapon and engage, which usually requires placing the following leg further out into the room and shifting the leading leg right. This takes time because you are fighting biomechanics and you broaden your silhouette presenting a larger target to the assailant. Before I show you how I would do it, each of you go through the door and engage the perp, live fire."

All of them went through the entry engaging only the one target to the right. A kill shot time after time.

"You did well," Genesis said. "How did you feel as you turned right?"

"It was like you said," one of them said. "The initial part of the turn was easy, but the target was in the right corner. It seemed like I had to fight to get my body the rest of the way around by adjusting my front foot and back foot out. It didn't seem as natural anymore after you pointed it out."

"I felt the same," said another, others agreeing.

"Now I will show you what I do," Genesis said. "It works well for one-man entries. Reset and reposition the targets in different locations first then, get up on the catwalk so you can watch."

The men began moving the targets around, putting them in different places from before while Genesis waited outside the door, not able to see the new positions. After finishing, they walked up to the overhead catwalks of the firehouse, which was normally reserved for instructors giving instructions and grading them.

"John," Genesis called. "You are the head instructor. I will await your command. Time it as usual."

John turned his watch, which had a stopwatch as a function and set it to zero. All was ready.

"Go!"

Genesis kicked open the door, leaning about ninety degrees to his right as he looked left, then standing erect looking right, his head behind the frame. Scanning the room, he stepped through the doorway, engaging two perps' right away, one to the left and one to the right. A double tap to center mass on each. Across the room he shot a third target using only the gun in his right hand. There were two more doorways he had to clear. Re-holstering his left pistol, he used the same procedure for each door. One room was empty. The second room had two perps and two hostages. He engaged both in rapid fire, one shot each to the center mass then, another tap to the heads.

"Just under eleven seconds," John called down.

"Any questions?" Genesis asked.

"I have one," a team member said. "Why did you use two pistols and then re-holster one of them without using both all the way through the exercise?"

"The double pistols were for primary entry in case there was a perp on both the left and the right. It gives the body the ability to move more easily. The third perp was engaged with the strong hand. I could have used both pistols, but it was unnecessary."

"I noticed that you keep your pistol vertical and do not tilt it to the side as many instructors and agents do. Why?" another team member asked.

"Leaning a pistol to the side or turning it on its side promotes substantial inaccuracy when firing. Always keep your pistol's sights on the potential target and in a vertical position."

"I have a question," another team member called down. "Why did you shoot the last two perps center mass first and head last?

"It has to do with biomechanics again," Genesis said. "Imagine yourself as the conductor of an orchestra. You need to tell each musician what to do by how you move your conductor's baton. The last two perps were bending slightly down. Had I shot them in the head first, the bullet could have ricocheted into the hostage. I shot them center mass first so that they would be knocked away from the hostage, at least to some degree. I know what you are thinking that they could have easily shot the hostage before being shot again. However, that is often not the case. Why? Because the first thing every person does when thrown off balance is to attempt to regain that balance before doing anything else. They were in that state when I shot them in the head thus, eliminating their ability to shoot the hostages. Also, had they been wearing body armor, getting them each off balance before shooting them in the head keeps them moving in a manner from which they are unable to shoot back at me or the hostages. By the way, the method used to enter the room is termed limited penetration entry. Any other questions?"

"I noticed you did not extend your arms for firing, but both were bent, close to your face," John asked. "Is there a reason for that?"

"There is," Genesis said. "In close quarters, you are often unable to turn proficiently with your arms extended. A good example is a stakeout in a car where a criminal can walk up to you, and you cannot turn quickly enough to engage. I use what is called combat active reflex for shooting my pistol. It allows you to shoot in extremely confined conditions. Take your pistol and extend your arms like you would normally shoot it. Now, pull back so that your left elbow is at a ninety-degree angle, the opposite elbow if you're a lefty. You will still be able to focus on your sights, but the pistol is much closer to your face. Just make sure it's not so close when the slide racks back that it hits you. You will notice that you can turn very quickly and sharply this way. I believe that you should also practice it with your weak hand too, which can come in handy during a pinch. More questions?"

"Yes," another team member called down. "Any pistol handling tips for us?"

"Only one," Genesis said. "Many instructors and others teach you to turn your pistol to insert a fresh magazine. Never do that. You know where the magazine well is without looking at it. Pull your next magazine so that when it is going toward the well, the bullets are aligned in the proper direction. While doing so, never take your sights off target. Keep your sights on target as you change magazines. The same is true of your M-4. Keeping your sights on target saves valuable time that can mean the difference between life and death because you are eliminating the time needed to reacquire the target. This is something that you need to practice over and over so it becomes muscle memory."

"Is there a good way to practice this?" John asked.

"A good way is the six-second drill. Use snap caps and put two in each of two magazines to learn the mechanics. Put in your first magazine, shoot the first two rounds then, eject the first magazine and put in the second, remember to keep your pistol vertical and sights on target. Fire the remaining two rounds. The time allotted is six seconds. Of course, live fire is best since you cannot cheat the time that way."

"Holy shit," one of the men murmured to the others. "This guy is good."

"Well, we're here," John said. "Why don't we try it live fire while we have the chance. We're not going to get time to practice otherwise before we leave.

The squad walked a few yards to a short yardage pistol range and started the drill. Each time they tried, Genesis would blow his whistle as the time expired. The drill was more difficult than they had imagined. About a half hour later, most of them had the drill down well and took pride in their accomplishment. It was yet another tool for their tactical skills toolbox. The three days passed quickly as they honed their firing and communications skills, along with working with drones. Theirs wasn't the typical consumer drones found on the open market, but military drones designed for combat operations and stealth, quadcopters with unique capabilities. They had sound displacing blades that made the drone difficult to hear as it crossed beyond one hundred feet. Since they were not into aerial or cinematic photography the camera was primarily for surveillance, night and day, using a 3-axis gimbal with a 4K, 20x optical zoom lens, as well as wide angle and radiometric thermal lenses. The primary drone would be used for overwatch and had a range of almost twenty miles and a service ceiling of twenty-thousand feet. The networked drones had FLIR lenses with ten-mile range and would be networked together for grid searching at night. Nothing would be able to hide from them for long.

It was the third day when Jonas showed up. He briefed them on their mission and had all the documentation they would need for flights and rendezvous points. Genesis was assigned as security personnel to meet with a nuclear inspector to walk through the Port St. Lucie nuclear plant. The assignment promised to be informative if nothing else. They were not expecting danger but were to be brought up to speed with nuclear plant safety, security protocols, and related concepts. All information would pass through John to Jonas, no one else was to be included.

The flight to Florida seemed almost too short and found Genesis walking through West Palm Beach International terminal to the rental car agency. He picked up an innocuous sedan and drove the forty-five miles to Port St. Lucie, checking into the prearranged inn. He would meet with the inspector early the next morning.

Li Na was perturbed. Ting was proving craftier than she had given him credit for. The two men Ki had sent arrived, and they were doing drone searches day and night. The original information the President had provided them was no longer useful and she had altered their tactics to find where James and Dianna were being held. Then it struck her. Why not follow Ting with a drone? If she had dinner with him, they could be prepared to follow him directly after. By then, it would be dark, and it would be easy to follow him. He may be too crafty for that since darkness would allow a car to follow easily as well. No, best to invite him to a late afternoon lunch. He would be less suspicious. Time for the set up.

She had been correct. Once invited, Ting said he would be busy in the evening but could easily make an afternoon lunch. Li Na was sitting at the same table as before when Ting arrived, walking over to greet her, and taking a seat.

"It is good to see you again," Ting said, taking a seat.

"How is our hostage?" Li Na asked.

"He is fine. As a matter of fact, he has not given us any trouble. He loves playing video games and we have kept him occupied with that."

"What of the girl?" Li Na asked. "I don't have her if that is what you are inferring. My guess is that Cilatro has many enemies."

"If we could find her, the tribe would be in our debt. Ki has promised a substantial reward if we can."

"How much?"

"Upwards of two million dollars."

"I can look around and see what I can dig up. After all, we could each use the extra money."

"Please do," Li Na said. "It will help our cause. Be careful not to do anything to arouse suspicion."

"No problem," Ting said. "I know how to evade detection."

"Good. Let me know what you find out."

Li Na had observed every part of his face and eyes as he spoke. Intuitively and from her training, she was certain Ting was lying but he was a pro and didn't give anything away. He was a worthy opponent, her most formidable so far. They would have made a good long-term team if he were not double dipping with multiple triads.

Ting knew the lunch was over. That was his que to leave. Exiting onto the sidewalk out front, he motioned his driver to the curb and stepped into the back seat of the car.

"Drive in the opposite direction we came," Ting said. "At the first parking structure we come to pull in and we will wait."

Li Na had her men ready this time. A drone was up at three hundred feet directly above the restaurant, which tracked Ting's car until it pulled into a covered parking structure. To the naked eye and ear, it was both unseen and unheard. The remote pilot in command tracked the structure with the quadcopter until it ran low on fuel and had to return to base. It had tracked for twenty-eight minutes and barely had enough charge to get back. After thirty-five minutes, Ting's car pulled out and drove twenty-five miles north before doubling back and heading to his destination. They spotted the tail car Li Na had sent as an extra precaution and lost it as well.

"Yes," Li Na said.

"We lost them," the voice said. "He must have spotted us. The drone had to pull off as well."

"Damn!" Li Na exclaimed. "This is getting frustrating. Let's meet at the next rendezvous point and come up with a new plan."

"So, he had dodged them yet again," she thought. "He must have suspected the drone and presumed theirs was the typical consumer type. He had waited long enough in the garage that he knew the drone wouldn't be able to stay aloft and then left. Very resourceful. At least she had put the bug in his ear about the reward if the girl could be found. The question was would the amount be enough to sway him to betray Xu Lo. How would she handle it if she were in his situation? If Xu Lo had promised him a long-term payoff as a percentage moving forward, the amount would not be enough. She would find out soon enough because if he decided to take the reward, he would need to enlist her help to make it look like he was working only with them."

As she began to plan her new strategy, she needed to assess multiple angles of attack to solve her problem. The President had initially given them the identity of one safe house. She was wondering if it were possible for him to do it again. At the same time, she knew from Morgan that Billie had more training in the transparency than the President and wondered if there was a way to solicit his help? Her potential solutions were slipping away one by one. Because Ting had double crossed them, she had limited options. And if the girl died it would severely complicate matters.

Ting was smiling as he got into the car and gave the driver his orders to wait in the parking garage. He could sense that Li Na was on to him. Working with the other triads was proving to be just a lucrative and while the reward money was substantial there would be no way to collect it. Ting knew that if he produced the girl, it would be evidence that he had taken her and held her all along, especially since Dianna had seen him at each safe house during her captivity. No! The reward money from Ki would be certain death.

Knowing how Li Na and her intelligence group worked, Ting was certain he would be able to stay ahead of them. "They must think I'm an amateur to fall for their obvious tracking ploy," he thought. He would bounce them around for a few hours each time to make certain if they were using drones, even multiple ones, that they could not track him to his destinations. A few decoys here and there would do the trick. In the meantime, he would play the loyal employee. "You have met your match Li Na."

Genesis arrived at the Port St. Lucie nuclear plant and along with the inspector, was admitted through security to walk through the plant. Despite having drawings and construction plans for the entire facility, they were accompanied by one of the plants engineers. Occasionally he would point out various valves and other parts of importance to the inspector, but Genesis felt he was a bit nervous at their presence.

"Tell me Fred, how long have you worked here?" Genesis asked.

"I've been here about ten years," Fred said. "Why do you ask?"

"Just curious because you seem to know so much about the plant." Genesis said.

"It's his job," Roland interrupted. "If it weren't for men like Fred, our job would be much more difficult, and this plant would be much less safe."

"So, I'm guessing you know almost every bolt, circuit and piece of pipe in this place?" Genesis queried.

"I study the plant every day," Fred said. "I have to know as much as I can about it."

"Would a terrorist find it easy to sabotage?" Genesis asked. "It's part of my job to understand the security risks."

"There are dozens of places you could attack to accomplish such a task," Fred said. "However, you would need to understand the systems as much as Roland and me. And you would need the schematics he's holding in his hands to pinpoint the best places. Besides, the FPF would be difficult if not impossible to get past. You would know that better than I would."

"Well said," Genesis replied. "But if they could get past us, they could be successful."

"They could be," Fred replied. "That's why we have so many safeguards and fail safes. Look, I have a short meeting. Will you two be okay on your own for a while?"

"No worries," Roland said. "I've got this. Catch up with us later."

Genesis watched Fred as he made his way back toward the main control center. He sensed Fred was nervous about their visit. The question was why? Surely, he wasn't like this every time an inspector showed up. He shoved the thoughts out of his mind momentarily as he walked along with Roland who was explaining the basics of operations and the purpose of the major components of the plant.

"Does plant personnel such as the engineers get so nervous when you guys come around?" Genesis asked.

"Sometimes," Roland said. "We have the authority to shut them down for a more thorough inspection if we find something wrong. Unfortunately, due to politics, when we find something wrong, heads normally roll. Why do you ask?"

"Oh, it just seemed Fred was pretty nervous," Genesis said.

"I would be too if I were him," Roland responded. "His head would be the first on the block since he is chief engineer."

What Roland said seemed completely logical and could explain Fred's tense, nervous manner, but Genesis knew that nervousness in such a critical area was an emotion that most professionals would and could mask. He made a mental note to have his intelligence team check Fred out when he got back. They continued to inspect the plant.

Roland was explaining the systems and regulations as they continued. Genesis listened intently to all he had to say. For a commercial nuclear power plant to operate in the U.S., it needed to obtain a license from the U.S. Nuclear Regulatory Commission (NRC). To accomplish that, each plant was required to undergo regular safety reviews and an assessment of their essential structures, components, and systems, as well as security. Such inspections were particularly important if the plant's operating license was to be revalidated or renewed for operations beyond the originally intended life of the facility, known among the industry as 'Long Term Operation'. While that wasn't the situation for this plant, it could potentially explain Fred's nervousness.

"Something is up," Fred said.

"What do you mean?" Morgan asked.

"The NRC sent an inspector," Fred replied.

"That is not unusual, is it?" Morgan asked.

"No, but this time, he has an FPF agent with him."

"What's odd about that? Aren't they the ones in charge of security protocols?"

"Yes, but I've never known of one to accompany an inspector," Tom said.

"Don't lose your cool," Morgan replied. "You work at one nuclear plant; these guys have many to protect. Maybe he's just accompanying the inspector to get a better handle on how to strengthen security by understanding more about the systems."

"I hadn't thought of that," Fred said. "Maybe you are right."

"Keep an eye on them and if anything out of the ordinary occurs, let me know."

Morgan was not a man to panic. Weighing the conversation, he needed to make sure that there were no potential risks that would occur due to this inspection. He had a friend at the Ginna nuclear power plant in New York and would hit him up with a few questions. He didn't think there was anything to worry about but decided to err on the side of caution. It was his job to protect his boss's investments. Right now, his job was to retrieve Cilatro's daughter, and he had absolutely no leads. It was like a dead end he was thinking as his phone began to vibrate.

"Morgan."

"How much can you tell me about Billie Panther and his ability with this transparency ceremony?" Li Na asked.

"I have dug up all I can," Morgan said. "No one will divulge how the ceremony works. However, it appears that Billie is the best at it on BC, excepting the Medicine Man. You can forget the latter. It is unlikely we will meet him. Why do you ask?"

"As you know, the identity of the safe house the President gave us is of no further value. We have the choice of getting him to try again or talking Billie into it. I would suggest getting Billie if he is the best, but I'm not sure how to approach him about it."

"Let me look into it and I'll get back to you."

The power plant was in full operation and the day a bit cooler than normal for which Billie was thankful as he walked around the plant, admiring its design and efficiency. It promised to be a real money maker for the tribe, as well as providing sorely needed jobs. The reservation was just too far away from any towns. Driving to them for a minimum wage job was a waste of time. The two closest towns were Immokalee and Clewiston, both about forty miles away, and had scarce job opportunities. Billie walked over to the new office checking in with the plant manager. The construction trailers that had been so prominent during the entire project were gone and Billie had workers spruce up the entire outside area.

"It's looking mighty nice," Billie said as he entered the office.

"Yes, and it purrs like a kitten," Tim said. "Say, how long do you think it will be before they begin the second phase to enlarge the plant?"

"I'm not sure," Billie said. "But given how well its working, I'm guessing three or four months at most. We were not expecting it so soon, but it'll be good for everyone."

"That's what I wanted to talk to you about," Tim replied. "I don't want to sound greedy or anything, but since I'm going to be managing twice as much production, do you think I could get a raise once the second phase is completed?"

"I don't see why not," Billie said. "Why don't you do some research on what managers make for comparable plant sizes in the state and let's sit down and discuss the figures. I won't promise you double or how much, but once we decide on a figure, I'll present it to the council and see what we can do."

"Fair enough," Tim said. "Tell me, and I don't mean to intrude, I'm just concerned. How are things going finding your son?"

Billie let out a big sigh. "We don't seem to be any closer than when we started. Every time we think we have a lead it disappears. The police and FBI are stymied, but they keep trudging along."

"I heard the kidnappers wanted to take the place over," Tim said. "Is that true?"

"That's what they demanded," Billie said. "But after looking everything over we think it was a ploy. Stalling for time or something. Who knows? I've given up trying to think why. Thanks for letting me look around, but I have to run."

"No worries, Billie. Anytime."

Tim felt for the man. He had three boys of his own and could not imagine how he would feel if one of them were taken. Billie was just opening the door of his truck when Tim saw Morgan pull in. "Talk about a character," he thought.

Morgan's car pulled right next to Billie. He effortlessly, slid from the seat and stood looking over the top of the car at him. "What brings you out this way?" Billie asked.

"I'm looking for you," Morgan said. "Got a minute?"

"Sure, how can I help you?"

"Hmmmm. I'm not sure how to bring this up so I'll just be blunt and say it. We need your help."

"What kind of help?" Billie asked.

"The transparency," Morgan said flatly.

Billie looked quizzically at Morgan for a few seconds that seemed to stretch into minutes.

"I wasn't aware you knew about that," Billie said guardedly.

"Your culture has been fascinating to us so I took the liberty of trying to learn all I could about it," Morgan said. "I would not have known about this had it not been for the President."

"He told you about it?" Billie asked incredulously, not believing what he was hearing. "That part of our culture is sacred."

"I realize that," Morgan said. "But hear me out. When we all formed the partnership, none of us could have foreseen what would happen to your son and Dianna. We're still not sure of their ploy, but we have gotten close to finding them."

"How? Billie asked. "Law enforcement has hit a dead end so far?"

"You are familiar with Li Na and her previous intelligence work, right?" Morgan asked.

"Yes," Billie said. "I am quite impressed with her skills."

"As am I," Morgan said. "Let me put it bluntly. The President used the transparency to identify the house where James and Dianna were being held."

"You found it?" Billie said, trying to keep the excitement out of his voice.

"Yes," Morgan said. "But they had already moved to another safe house. The information was accurate, we just got there too late."

"Damn!" Billie exclaimed. "So, you want me to do the same thing, try to find it using the transparency?"

"Yes," Morgan stated. "I've been told you are the best at it."

"Thank you for the compliment," Billie replied. "I'm surprised the President used it to help you. As far as I know, the transparency was never meant to be used for such purposes, which is why I haven't tried it myself."

"Do you think you could help us?" Morgan asked. "It's in all our best interests and your sons."

"Since the President used it for this, I will consider it," Billie said. "Let me talk to the Medicine Man and determine the best option."

"Alright," Morgan said. "I'll wait for you to get back to me. Meanwhile, we are continuing our search using high-tech drones. They haven't panned out yet, but they are efficient. If we could pinpoint the location, the feds and MDPD can take it from there. Regardless, we need to end this debacle now."

"I couldn't agree more," Billie said, climbing into his truck. "I'll call you soon."

Billie's heart was racing. He had never thought of using the transparency to find James. As far as he knew, travel through the vortexes was limited to where you knew someone, or something was. He called Christina and filled her in on what was going on. It was still early morning as Billie raced to his airboat to find the Medicine Man, his hope renewed.

The room was darkened, only the glow of cigarettes visible as the three men talked. They made certain their identities were concealed.

"How is our strategy going?" the first asked.

"We hit a snag," Xu replied. "As soon as Ki realized what happened, they redrafted the partnership agreement. It now makes it impossible for us to take over as partner."

"Why don't we just threaten to kill them all?" the third man asked. "That has always worked in the past."

"I would normally agree," Xu said. "The problem is that Ki knows who I am. We are in no condition to start a turf war with the most powerful triad in Hong Kong and southern China. Even in this meeting, we are at a risk of exposing our group."

"Granted," the first man said. "We do risk exposure but there is much to gain. What about working the same deal with the other tribes?"

"It's too late," Xu said. "They have already signed agreements with them using the redraft as a template."

"What do you suggest?" the third man asked.

"Our best strategy would be two-fold," Xu said. "First, we demand ongoing ransom from the partner Don Cilatro for all plants. Second, we threaten sabotage continually to gain our demands."

"Do you think that will work with Cilatro?" the first man asked. "After all, he is like one of us. He may decide to cut his losses and move forward."

"Then his daughter will die," Xu said smiling. "We have spent too much time and effort to just walk away. Otherwise, our long-term strategy will not be implemented."

"That may be," the third man said. "But it is better to be alive than dead. Ki is not someone to cross and remain safe. He has eyes and ears everywhere. Labor and loyalty are his most valuable commodities and we have already broken the code."

"Perhaps," the first man said. "Let us move forward carefully. Does your man in Miami have the packages in a safe place?"

"Yes," Xu replied. "They are moved every couple of days. Finding them will be nearly impossible."

"Good," the first man said. "Let's play the shell game a little longer. If we decide to pull out, terminate them immediately. We can find another way to implement our long-term plan."

The man had headsets on as he fine-tuned the comm frequency, making certain he would not miss a single word. He had accidently bumped into Xu on the street and had dropped a small microphone in his pocket. It was constructed in such a way that after two hours the small battery would ignite and melt the inside, disforming the outside so that it resembled a hard raisin. Even if Xu found it, the likelihood he could recognize it for what it was would be remote. Other men were stationed nearby and as dark and remote as the meeting location was, their identity was no longer a secret. The men slowly exited the room. About every ten minutes, one would leave, picking up their bodyguards as they departed. They were in an old area of Hong Kong harbor with wet wooden walkways and junks, small boats used for fishing and transport. In the event one needed to disappear, private transport was never far away. As the men passed beneath the small, hooded lamps, far apart, their faces were recorded for posterity. Ki's eyes and ears were at work.

Wind whipped his face as the airboat sped across the sawgrass. The sound of the Lycoming aircraft engine loud in his ears. Now and then he would glance at the prop, at one point smiling. He remembered how the President had remarked that all the new people moving to Florida had begun to call them fan boats. He had scoffed at it.

"It's not a damn fan," the President said vehemently. "It's a prop attached to an airplane engine and the air from the prop propels the boat. It's an airboat, not a damn fan boat."

Though the two men often disagreed on things, that had not been one of them. Billie was excited as he slipped through the water amidst lily pads and sawgrass and maneuvered through cypress flats filled with water and around hammocks. Wildlife was abundant. Everywhere he looked there were deer, otter, turtles, egrets, turkeys on the edges of hammocks, alligators, snakes, and an abundance of wildflowers, air plants, and mosses and ferns. The trip seemed much longer than usual as he finally reached the hammock. The warriors had heard him coming and two were present to greet him as the boat came to a stop at the hammocks edge. Sandwiched between the two warriors, it was only a couple of minutes before Billie reached the chickee. The Medicine Man was in his usual seated position next to a small fire. He motioned Billie to join him as the warriors took up positions just out of ear shot.

"Why the unexpected visit, young warrior?" the Medicine Man asked.

Billie caught the Medicine Man up on everything since his last visit and then rehearsed everything that Morgan had told him. He carefully watched the Medicine Man's face and eyes as he spoke. They were blank, as if the news were already known.

"I suspected such," the Medicine Man said. "What is your concern?"

"Can we use the transparency to find my son?" Billie asked earnestly.

"That is a misuse of its power," the Medicine Man said unflinchingly. "Yes, it could be used for that purpose. But once you begin down that path, what is to stop you from using it to search for wealth and riches of the world that serve only to corrupt the soul?"

"I don't follow," Billie said.

"Remember your training," the Medicine Man said. "When you want to help, you know where the person is you are trying to help or where the person is you are trying to listen in on to help another or others. What is the difference?"

"You would be trying to find someone without knowing where they are."

"Precisely and that is the problem. If you try to find a person when you do not know where they are, you are breaking the guidance of the Great Spirit," the Medicine Man said. "It is part of the beginning of telling time and looking both to the past, into the present, and then, the future. The Great Spirit only allows us to use a small portion of his power. Having the ability to do the other is flirting with the powers of darkness that have such control you know not. To give us his full power is something none on this earth are ready for. It would corrupt them totally and then they would need to confront the Great Spirit in person."

"Then what the President did was a violation?" Billie asked.

"Yes," the Medicine Man said. "Although I'm sure he meant well. However, as you know, the road to hell is paved with good intentions. You must remember young warrior that the lives of many have greater value than the life of one."

"I understand," Billie said. "But that does not help me find my son."

"Tell me, gazing into Billie's eyes, "What is of greater value? The life of James or the lives and future of the entire tribe and turning them to the Great Spirit."

"That is a hard question," Billie said.

"No!" the Medicine Man exclaimed. "It is better that one perishes than a whole tribe or nation fall into unbelief. The battle is for the spirit and soul, not the cancer of money. That is why we are not allowed to do what the President did. I feel for your son, but the welfare of all the people is more important. You must understand this above all else."

"I do," Billie said. "I guess it's just a selfish wish for my son."

"It is not selfish," the Medicine Man said. "It is the love of a father. But fear not, there is a way, but not your way."

"A way to what, find James?" Billie asked.

"Yes, but only the area, not the exact location."

"How?"

"Leave that to me. I can do it twice, but no more. To do more is a transgression and to find an exact location breaks the law and the bond with the Great Spirit. That is why the President did not see the exact location. The Great Spirit blocked it for his own wellbeing."

"What can I do?" Billy asked.

"You will wait, and I will tell you where," the Medicine Man said. "Most things inside a house don't do well with bullets. Work with Li Na and her people. They will be more surgical and can call the police at the appropriate time."

"How long will it take?"

"Worry not, young warrior. Go now and I will prepare."

He motioned Billie away then, turned back to his fire, looking over his shoulder while the warriors escorted him to his boat. The burden Billie had was a great one, which he knew and understood. But the welfare of the tribe was too important to let the sorrow of one take precedence over many. The President had learned more than he anticipated. Good for him as long as he used the power wisely. He began the ceremony to make a special request and only he knew how to do so at this time. The day would come when Billie would also be taught. He waited until nightfall. The warriors stood watch to guard over his body once he separated his spirit.

The Medicine Man began to chant softly and slowly squeezing the dii potentia. He was instantly transported to the tree of life. His amazement never ceased as the wonder of the cosmos spread across space behind the tree that sat on the grassy green hill, which stood in stark contrast to the darkness of space beyond. The eyes were present as before, except this time, they were as flames of fire. The Medicine Man bowed himself low to the grass.

"What is it you desire my servant?" the penetrating voice asked.

"Forgive me Great Spirit," the Medicine Man implored. "A project of considerable long-term significance has been established for the tribe. But darkness rears its head in the quest for money and power. One of our members, a young boy, has been kidnapped, along with a woman."

"I am aware," the voice boomed louder. "What is it you seek?"

"I dare not overstep my bounds and usurp more authority from your power, Great One," the Medicine Man said. "Would you allow me to locate the boy and woman using dii potentia?"

"One of you has already attempted to do so."

"I have just become aware of it. I'm sure the President meant no harm and I will speak to him about it."

"You have great power my servant, the power to act in my stead, yet you have chosen to ask for that which would increase your power and potentially corrupt you. Because you have done so, I will reveal unto you in a vision, the location of the two you seek."

"You know where they are?"

"Of course. An insect falls not to the ground that I do not know about on the earth on which you live. Go now. Be patient and wait for the vision. You will receive it in due time."

The Medicine Man sat up. He was back in his familiar surroundings. Situating himself in front of one of the small fires, he began to think about the short conversation. The fact that he could locate James and Dianna was irrelevant but the fact that the Great Spirit would reveal it in a vision made him ponder. He realized that his soul was at stake because the temptation to locate a person or object done once successfully, would constantly present itself over and over and giving in a second time would surely bring his soul to destruction as he yielded to the enticement of the negative side of the spirit. He would speak to Billie and explain what was going to happen. As he thought more deeply, the President had located the house, but not the number. "Why had the Great Spirit protected him?"

The two men sat quietly as the food was placed before them and slowly began eating. Silence was sometimes a virtue but in this case it was unbearable.

"Since neither one of you is going to speak, I will Christina said. "The police have no leads, and this situation is becoming more unbearable each day. What are we going to do about it?"

"I spoke to the Medicine Man today," Billie said. "He can perform the same thing the President did and locate James and Dianna."

"Why didn't he already do it?" Christina asked.

"He is doing it now and will get back with me," Billie explained. "He cautioned me that the life of many was more valuable than one."

"That doesn't sound promising," Genesis said. "What did he mean by that."

"Exactly what he said," Billie replied. "I agree. The wellbeing of an entire tribe is more valuable than one of its members. What he said doesn't mean that James is not going to be found. As he explained, a sequence of events must be allowed to occur to ensure no interruption in a future timeline."

"So, he will help us?" Christina queried.

"Yes, when the time is right, we will know," Billie said. "Despite what is happening, we must remain patient. I know that doesn't help much, but we will find them."

"It will give us all an opportunity to prove our worth," Genesis said. "I spoke with the Medicine Man at the Green Corn Dance. He told me specifically to exhort all of those in authority to display an air of solidarity, trust, and example, not for the adults, but for the children to learn from."

"That makes sense," Christina whispered, frowning. "It's not his child caught in the crosshairs, but I see the wisdom in it."

"What else did he say?" Genesis asked.

"To work with Li Na and her small group," Billie said. "It is not that he does not trust the police, but that too many bullets may begin flying at one time. As he put it — most things in homes don't react well to bullets. It makes sense because of Li Na's clandestine experience in operations more complex than this one."

"There is only one problem," Christina said. "We need to find them first."

"Trust me," Genesis said. "We will. Everyone is working around the clock. Every time they move James and Dianna to a new safehouse, they become exposed and eventually we will find them. Sooner than you think. The noose is slowly tightening."

"Do we even know what they want?" Christina asked.

"I'm afraid it has become more unclear," Genesis replied. "Right now, we are waiting on another call with new demands."

"Let us each consider every potential scenario we can think of why they want James and Dianna specifically," Billie said. "If we can pinpoint the potential strategy, we can anticipate the next move. Right now, nothing makes sense because we don't know why?"

The voice on the phone was angry. Ting has not made contact for several days.

"You are placing us in jeopardy through lack of knowledge," the voice said. "How are the triads reacting?"

"They have no idea of our operation," Ting said. "As far as they know the hostages are leverage for a different purpose. They are not privy to the information we are collecting about the entire network of people and the contacts associated with each."

"Very well," the voice said. "Stay on course. I'll report to our man in the north and get back to you."

A stiff breeze was blowing as the two sat in the lounge of the gently rocking yacht a dozen miles off Miami's shore. They were in the process of doing exactly what Billie had prescribed, trying to determine why the kidnappers wanted James and Dianna.

"What do you want to cover first?" Morgan asked.

"Did you find anything out about the inspection visit?" Cilatro asked.

"Yes," Morgan said. "I spoke with my friend at the Ginna nuclear plant, and he said that what happened was routine and that it had been prescheduled far ahead of time. There is nothing to worry about."

"Good," Cilatro said. "We can't afford this thing coming back on us."

"Agreed," Morgan said. "What next?"

"The sixty-four-dollar question," Cilatro said. "Why do they want James and Dianna?"

"I've thought about that after my discussions with Li Na," Morgan said.

"And?"

"This is my theory so far. James was taken initially to coerce both the tribe and partners to give in. The redraft of the partnership preempted his value to them. Next, they took Dianna for greater leverage. They know that outing one partner and bringing in another also is not going to work."

"So, what does it mean?" Cilatro asked.

"They have only one play that I can determine. We have already signed similar agreements with multiple tribes. I have been told that another group of investors is working with other tribes that we have not scouted. My guess is that group is the same group that took Dianna. They know the value of energy so they will make agreements with the other tribes if they can. This leads me to believe there is only one purpose now for kidnapping your daughter."

"What reason?"

"To extort you specifically," Morgan said. "They have no leverage on the tribe or the other partner. Given the number of plants we will install, and the amount of money involved, their plan is probably simple extortion. You either pay or both are dead."

"That seems pretty shallow," Cilatro said.

"Perhaps, but think about our old protection rackets, you pay, or your business gets burned down. If that didn't work, they were killed as an example. Isn't it the same?"

"I suppose you're right. So, if we assume that, they will want a sum for each plant moving forward and guaranteed."

"Correct," Morgan said. "But it may not be money."

"What else would it be?"

"Electricity into the grid so they can sell it."

"Damn, I hadn't thought about that."

"Regardless," Morgan said. "You will make an agreement with them, and they will release Dianna and James. If you don't, they'll get rid of them and come at all the partners from a different angle."

"Probably exactly like our old protection racket. I'm not sure I see a way out."

"You know that there is only one way," Morgan said. "Find out who these people are and get rid of them."

"How do we proceed?" Cilatro asked.

"Work with Li Na," Morgan said. "I'm pretty sure that she has already guessed who they are?"

"Another triad?"

"Exactly. But from discussions with her, I suspect more than one because of their fear of Ki."

"Very well, let's put the plan into play," Cilatro said. "Work with her to flush these people out. Give her whatever resources she needs and both of you make it happen."

"She has already given me some information," Morgan said.

"I'll keep working with her."

"You know," Cilatro said. "For the first time in the dark life I was born into, I see light at the end of the tunnel. I have yearned for so long to be a legitimate, respectable businessman that it has consumed me every day. Now that it is about to happen, it seems as if it's all a fairy tale."

"I have the same dream," Morgan said. "When you get our age, the time for killing has to stop. We will make this happen my friend. Hopefully, . . ."

"Yes, I know. It'll be the last time."

Trembling hands full of excitement grasped the manilla envelope that Akio handed over at the Miami executive airport. As she carefully opened it and pulled out the photos and documents, she discovered her rationale was right on target. Akio glanced over her shoulder as they rode in the back seat of the limo.

The first picture was of Xu Lo, which she already knew about. He was leader of the 24K triad, the second largest triad operating out of Hong Kong. Active internationally, it had 20,000 members separated into thirty subgroups. He was her boss's main rival.

It should have surprised her, but it didn't. The next photo was Peter Chow, head of the Ho Wap To triad, fourth largest in Hong Kong. They specialized in protection rackets and had expanded to San Francisco in the late 1990s. He was supposed to be affiliated with her boss. There would be hell to pay for his cooperation with these other men.

As she fingered to the last group of photos and documents, she was surprised. It was a photo of So Wing Wo leader, Chi Wong. They were the king of extortion, drug trafficking, gambling, and prostitution. Like the other triads, they had established a base in the U.S. in San Francisco, Los Angeles, and New York decades ago and had a base of operations in Miami for more than ten years.

James Tindall

Like many of the triads and criminal organizations in general, most were attempting to establish legitimate businesses that were the most lucrative they could find. The main reason was due to increasing technology and skills of law enforcement in their ability to infiltrate such organizations and bring them down after sometimes, years of inside law enforcement work. What law enforcement did not realize was that the leaders they supposed were the kingpins of such groups were in fact, scapegoats. They were proxy's that ran the organization under the direction of the real leaders where numeric codes differentiated between the positions and ranks with the organizations. Only upper-level triad members knew who these leaders were, and they were never involved in dirty work. They kept far away from getting tainted by the soldiers in the triad who carried out the criminal activities. Long before terrorists' groups in the Middle East learned their lessons of communicating through phone and other technologies, the triads were masters of deception and nothing of significant importance was ever discussed over a phone. Honor demanded face-to-face.

In translation, triad means a triple union society. When most triads had formed, it referred to the union of earth, people, and heaven. Still, law enforcement, especially the British in early Hong Kong, speculated that triad means triangular imagery. Since the White Lotus rebellions, as well as the Boxer Rebellions in the 1850s in Shanghai and Xiamen, triads had embedded themselves in Asian culture. But Li Na knew from her intelligence work that triads were merely organized crime groups. Once the communist Chinese took over and cracked down in mainland China, triads were forced to operate out of Hong Kong, Taiwan, and Macau, as well as Singapore and other cities. Triads had made the transition to white collar crime years ago. The first triad had formed in the 18th century, the Heaven and Earth Society, in the mid-1760s. Two such groups were originally founded to restore the Ch'ing dynasty and the Ming dynasty. Though unsuccessful, they helped lay the groundwork for the successful and continued formation by separation of disgruntled members of other triads. In the beginning they had been intent on helping Chinese immigrants resettle into new locations and other Samaritan activities.

Sadly, the lure of money proved too powerful to resist and the triads became embedded in every type of criminal activity. It wasn't that long ago that law enforcement had found ties of two major triads to the Sinaloa Cartel, smuggling billions of dollars' worth of methamphetamines from Indonesia into the United States, Europe, and Asia. "Yes," Li Na thought bitterly. "These were her mortal enemies, those who had killed her parents and brother. She had been closing in on them for years and soon, she would have her revenge. Total revenge would be accomplished when the last leader was dead!"

Li Na had tried the lawful way without success. The crooked lawyers and judges always let the real culprits go. She had vetted Ki for seven years and knew that his triad was not responsible. By embedding herself in the See On Yun triad, and coupling their intelligence with hers, she had amassed a mountain of information that would lead her to her goal. She was only too happy to work with American law enforcement because they had the same goal. Her agenda was to move one more step up the ladder and now, she was within reach of the top rung and would soon be standing on it. All she lacked was one loyal partner.

"Are we sure of this information?" Li Na asked.

"Yes," Akio replied. "These photos were taken directly after their meeting. Here is a copy of the recording. It's a little muddled, but clear enough to understand."

Li Na listened to the recording through an earpiece. A smile began to appear on her face.

"Why are you smiling?" Akio asked.

"Because two of these men and their triads are supposed to be loyal to Ki," Li Na said. "They are exposed. When their heads roll, their members will swell our ranks during times we need to work in unison. We will become almost three times larger. Just think of it, more members, more money, more power, and more intelligence."

Akio wondered why she was so elated at the prospect. He didn't know that she could care less about anything other than more intelligence. It was not simply more information, but useful intelligence that had been eluding her. Li Na would chop off the heads of each snake and she would also find the three men she had watched kill her family. Their death would be merciless.

"Do you know where any of these men are now?" Li Na asked. "We know where all three are," Akio replied. "Lo and Chow are in Hong Kong. Wong is in Columbia. Our informants say he may be coming to Miami on his return to Singapore."

"Very well," Li Na said. "Keep me posted on Wong. Now, let's get down to the other business at hand. We need to find the hostages before the Americans. You know why."

The Seminole PD SUV was parked in a small lot at the end of the commercial pier adjacent to Lauderdale-by-the-Sea Beach. Genesis was leaning against the front fender when Horatio pulled up. The two didn't speak as they walked out onto the pier. A friend let the two past the security gate. When they reached the end of the second building, they turned, leaning against the south facing railing.

"What's so important we could not meet at your place?" Genesis asked.

"The electrician told me that what happened may not have been a lightning strike," Horatio said. "He couldn't prove it, but he thought the voltage was too low once he repaired it. I just thought it best to be more private from now on because I think we may be in over our heads."

"How so?"

"We have picked up communications from a triad and cartel south of the border," Horatio said. "We know the cartel is Sinaloa, but we are uncertain of the triad at the moment."

"How does that concern us?" Genesis asked.

"Do you believe in coincidences?"

"You know I do not."

"Then how do you explain the fact that the men who kidnapped James and Dianna are Asian from the surveillance videos? Then, you have Li Na from Hong Kong, where one of the partners for the power plant resides and look at these photos of Li Na meeting an Asian privately at a restaurant."

"She told us she has an intelligence man here in Miami Dade so it' no surprise."

"I agree but think of it. Asian, Asian, Asian, there's a connection. I'm just not sure about what, yet."

"I agree," Genesis replied. "But what is this about? We're not into illegal activities."

"No," Horatio said. "But the triads and cartels are trying desperately to expand into legitimate businesses. Our electronic tracking, drones, satellites, communications, and related technologies are significantly hampering their illegal enterprises. We have also infiltrated most of their organizations. If my suspicions are true, they have moved into Miami consolidating legal business ventures and are looking for new, more lucrative ones."

"Hmmmm," Genesis mused. "Lunadi said two of the most lucrative industries are water and energy, followed by food."

"There you have it," Horatio said. "It's not a far stretch to imagine what they could be involved in. But we have the same problem as everyone else on this case, what's their strategy?

"Indeed," Genesis said. "Before you find out from someone else, I'm working with another federal group now."

"Your old boss?" Horatio asked. "Yes. Keep it to yourself. I may be able to use you and feed you information. We will get these bastards, one way or another."

The water levels in the deep swamp surrounding the power plant were slowly increasing. Billie had presumed they would and had put up a canal with the sugar sand fill on the outside of the small canal away from the plant. A large twenty-four-inch pipe and diesel engine guaranteed that no matter how much it rained that the power plant area would remain dry, despite it sitting atop crushed shell rock. Still, Billie wanted to be certain, so he looked at extending the small canal deeper into the swamp and was scouting the best location. He was on his swamp buggy. Even with five-foot tall tires, the water covered the tops of the treads as the buggy pushed a small wave of water in front of it, making its way slowly around a large cypress head, exposing a lily pond. On the far side, the Medicine Man was sitting in his canoe, making his way toward him. As always, the muscular warrior was poling the dugout. Billie pulled his buggy beneath the shade of a cypress tree draped in Spanish moss as he waited for them. The dugout bumped into the edge of the buggy as the warrior brought it to a stop. Sitting in his elevated seat, the water around his boots, Billie and the Medicine Man were almost eye-to-eye.

"It is good to see you great one," Billie said, a smile on his face. It was a wonderful break to his day.

"And you," the Medicine Man said. "I did as I told you and you are not allowed to use the dii potentia to find the boy. It will be your downfall if you do."

"Is there any way to find him without it?"

"Yes, I will give you instructions now. You must listen carefully because it is only the vicinity, not the precise location."

Billie took a note pad and pen from his pocket. "Tell me what to do."

"I talked to the Great Spirit who gave me a vision three times," the Medicine Man said. "Where the location is, I cannot tell. I can only give signs. Over and over was the ocean with an arrow pointing away from it and the number with airplanes flying all around. The planes would go over the water and return. I saw several at one time that formed the shape of a long arrow."

"That's not much to go on," Billie said.

"Let me finish young warrior. There is much more. Next, I saw the number nine on the bottoms of the planes and then the planes would evaporate in my vision. Afterward the great spirit took me high in the air and I could see a fern leaf or what appeared to be a fern leaf surrounded by water like many little canals. The leaf appeared made of pieces of stone because it wasn't green. The fern was bordered to the south by a diagonal line, and I saw semi-trailers going along it with the number 595 on their tops then, they disappeared. Next, the spirit took me down to the ground and I was moving atop a canal that ran along a big highway to my left and the semis with the numbers appeared again and disappeared. Then, I was flying along to the right and I stopped on a small darker cross within a big white cross. At my feet were the letters WRMC in a circle. A man with a helmet walked by and took off straight up in a rotor bird."

"You mean a helicopter?" Billie asked.

"Yes, a bird with circular wings. Then I turned and was looking over the sawgrass. I was up in the air again looking far below into a green fern surrounded by the concrete fern and I started falling. On the green fern were white balls and people chasing them. It was all far away. As I got closer, I saw the semis again on the big road and then another smaller road going north. Toward the ocean side at the juncture was a big red topped house with a roof and pool sitting in the middle of a small pond with houses on the side of the pond by the semis. The pool was a big 'L' shape on the sawgrass side. Next, I was in my dugout and paddled along the big road to the ocean. That was the end of my vision."

Billie sat looking at him. "I'm not sure that gives me a lot to go on. This could be anywhere in Ft. Lauderdale or bordering towns."

"That was my vision. Work with Genesis and the woman. You will find the boy and woman."

"How can you be so sure?" Billie asked.

"The vision was given for a purpose; The Great Spirit does not lie and wants you to find them. Do all you can."

Billie noticed the muscular warrior moving his right hand very slowly. Suddenly he threw his long Bowie knife in one smooth motion. It thudded into the wood beneath his seat. Billie startled, jumping up.

"You scared the daylights out of me!" Billie exclaimed.

Beneath him, between where his legs had been, was a writhing cotton mouth moccasin. The knife blade had pierced the upper jaw and anchored the head against the plywood beneath; the mouth lay open exposing the fangs. Billie pulled the knife out, the snake still stuck to it. Holding the knife handle, he made an outward throwing motion. The snake sailed through the air falling into the water. Billie swished the blade in the water then wiped it off on his pants leg, tossing the knife back to the muscular warrior handle first. He caught it and slipped the blade back into the scabbard on his hip.

"I am much indebted," Billie said. "I owe you my life."

The warrior's nod was barely perceptible as he turned the dugout and began poling away.

"Remember, Genesis and the woman," the Medicine Man yelled over his shoulder. "You should contact them soon."

Billie's hands were shaking from the scare with the snake. It was over five feet long and bigger than his calf. It would have certainly delivered a lethal dose of venom. As watched its writhing body in the water, it was taken below by a four-foot-long alligator. He cranked his buggy and made all haste back to the power plant and his truck.

Chapter 8

Rain was falling hard off Miami's coast. The sea was relatively calm as Cilatro sat looking out the window. The yacht would be his home until the kidnapping of his daughter was resolved. The numbers for the multiple power plants looked very good. He would make millions in legitimate money. Finally, he could get out of the dark business he had been recruited into when he was a young teen, in which he had no choice. It was a life he had never wanted and in which he always felt trapped. Three times he had tried to leave and each time they kept him in by threatening him. The last time they had murdered his son.

The son he lost haunted him and he kept wondering if there was something he could have done to prevent it. The only option was to turn himself in and seek witness protection, but he knew the minute he did they would kill his daughter and him. It was then that he had been introduced to Ki who promised to rid him of his enemies if he cooperated with him in this new business venture. He slept little and his mind was always troubled at what he had been forced to do during his life. Being raised a staunch Catholic, he always had his sins absolved by his priest. If he gave him money, he could be forgiven any sin. What bothered Cilatro most was that deep down, he knew the only one that had the authority to forgive sins was God and that both good and evil on earth happened in God's name. He had vowed to leave his life of crime.

"I guess this is God's punishment for me," Cilatro muttered under his breath as he sat staring at the rain.

"We should get back to this," Morgan said. "At least we will have the numbers if extortion is their game."

"You really believe it is?" Cilatro queried.

"I don't see a more logical explanation," Morgan stated. "Also, Li Na said that one of the triads that looked like it was involved is an expert at extortion on a global scale."

"Damn," Cilatro swore. "It's like the protection rackets we got out of long ago. Such suffering we caused; God forgive us. Are you looking forward to getting out of this business?"

"You know my feelings," Morgan said. "We've both wanted out of this for a long time. It's time to slip away into a relaxed life. We have many more years behind us than ahead of us. I'd like to live them out in peace without looking over my shoulder. Besides, Ki will uphold his end of the bargain and we won't need to live in fear everyday."

"Agreed," Cilatro responded. "And from the numbers of each of the plants, even if we are extorted, we will have enough to lead a comfortable life. Still . . ."

"What are you thinking?" Morgan asked.

"As long as we are involved in this, whoever is behind it will always pressure us for more money," Cilatro said. "It's like a bad divorce that never ends."

"Understood sir," Morgan said. "What would you propose?"

"We will need to get our hands bloody once more and this time they will be deserving of it. Get Frank and Kelly and a few more men. Have them ready."

"For a takeout?" Morgan asked.

"Yes," Cilatro said. "We will take them to dinner. First let's get Li Na's opinion. It may be that her group will do it. After all, Ki told me they have been insubordinate. But just in case we need to stay under the radar."

"I'll have the men sharpen their skills," Morgan said.

Administrative assistants always knew the temperament of their boss, especially their mind set and demeanor. They could detect when things were going well and when they were not. Lately, there had been a deluge of unsavory characters in and out of his office. Since Akio had left for the U.S., it was particularly so. The three men who just walked in were as unsavory as they came. Oh, they dressed well, but they were pure evil. She could sense it, as certain as if she could see a black aura around them. There was little sound emanating from behind the doors to Ki's office. She knew they were planning something important and deadly. No matter, she was a triad member herself and to divulge any information about a leader or boss meant certain death. Although Ki was as deadly as a cobra, he was an honorable man in his dealings. If you didn't cross him, you would remain alive.

The three men, Fa, Chou, and Kang, sitting in front of Ki held hi rank in the triad. Fa was Deputy Mountain Master as designated by his numeric code (438). Chou, also a 438 was Ki's Incense Master, and Kang, the deadliest of the three was a Red Pole, a 436, military commander overseeing offensive and defensive operations for the entire triad. He relished dealing death and always chomped at the bit, like a horse racing to the stables.

"You have the latest intelligence reports," Ki said. "The question now is what to do with them?"

"There is no question about what," Kang retorted. "They have turned on their obligations and biggest triad leader. The penalty for this act of treason is death! They know that."

"Although I understand their reasoning and strategy, I must concur." Chou said.

"Fa, what do you think?"

"I do not disagree with Kang or Chou," Fa said. "The main problem is if we take them out, how to we do it without a war between the triads?"

"I can make it happen," Kang said. "I just need your order to carry it out."

"What I want is to swell our ranks," Ki said. "We can do that by absorbing all three triads. However, we will need the support of their remaining masters to do so."

"Agreed," Fa said. "They know the penalty for what their heads are doing. My guess is that they do not know, but because their lives are in jeopardy from the action, they would probably go along with us."

"What you say is true," Chou stated. "All we need to do is tell them to join us or die."

"We need to be a bit more diplomatic," Kang said. "The best way is to give them two choices. The first is that the head turned against their responsibility and agreement and as such, must be killed. The second is that because of what their bosses did, they can either cooperate or be killed as well."

"That's not much of a choice," Ki said.

"But it is true," Fa said flatly. "They either get killed along with their bosses for what they did or, they join us and have a new boss."

"It's a simple proposition," Chou said.

"Kang, what is the best way to make it happen?" Ki asked.

"They are not the only ones good at extortion," Kang replied. "If we ask them to a meet, they will likely tell their bosses. However, if we kidnap a son, wife, or someone else close to them and tell them to keep their mouth shut, they will do so and will show up."

"What if they don't go along with the new structure?" Chou asked.

"We keep their family's hostage until all is settled," Kang said. "That will coerce them. But I do not think it will go that far. They are aware of the punishment. If they say no outright, they will be killed on the spot."

"Sounds about as succinct as it can be," Fa said. "I agree. We have no choice. Honor demands it."

"Are we all in agreement to move forward?" Ki asked.

The three men nodded agreement.

"Good. Kang put the plan into action. I will contact Li Na. We will find their leader in Miami, and she will take care of him. But make sure she captures him alive and brings him back here. This is not something we want others involved in."

The hotel room had a spectacular view of South Beach. It was a shame it wasn't under better circumstances. They sat down on the two sofas in the room with a small table in the middle.

"Do you like puzzles?" Billie asked.

"I've never been great at them," Genesis said.

"What do you have?" Li Na asked.

"The Medicine Man had a vision that he related to me," Billie replied. "Because of the dii potentia, I was not allowed to do what the President did. Hopefully, this will narrow it down and we can find James and Dianna."

Billie began to relate the entire vision to them. Remembering all the Medicine Man had said, referring to his notes. Then, went over them a couple of more times.

"This is more complex than I thought it would be," Li Na said. "I think we should draw it out and then try to decipher it."

"Why don't we print off a few pages from the satellite feeds," Genesis said. "I can have some large ones here in a few minutes. We can draw on them and narrow down the area, hopefully."

"Good idea," Billie said.

Genesis sent a text to his team members who were in their command vehicle in the hotel parking lot.

"Let's make a basic sketch while we wait," Li Na said. "You both know the area much better than I do. Let's start with that. What do we know so far?"

"We know that the general area is north, but adjacent to I-595,"

Genesis said. "He mentioned planes a few times and flying back. I'm guessing that may be Fort Lauderdale-Hollywood International airport. We all know planes take off into the wind so, they go out over the ocean and slowly circle back toward their destination heading."

"That gives us three points," Billie said. "Right?"

"I believe so," Genesis said. "So, we have this line as I-595, the coast here as the east border, and the airport basically here, *drawing as he went.* Let's put the sawgrass of the Glades as the west border."

"That gives us the bottom of a slanted box," Li Na said, opening her computer so that the area was displayed via satellite image.

"That's an awfully large area," Billie said. "Including only one-half mile from the freeway will give us four and a half square miles. We need to narrow it."

"Agreed," Li Na said. "What about the recurring number nine? What significance would that have?"

"I don't know," Billie said. "Oh wait, what if it is the distance from the airport?"

"Good thinking," Li Na replied. "That would make sense."

There was a gentle knock on the door.

"Sir, here are the maps you wanted," the FPF member said. "We printed them out in one-square mile increments from the coast to the Everglades boundary."

"Thank you," Genesis said. "This will be a big help."

Spreading the satellite maps on the table so that they overlapped, they had a clearer picture of what they were looking at.

"Let's suppose that the number nine means nine miles from the airport," Genesis said. "If we follow I-595, assuming it begins at the airport, that will put us approximately here. But let's also measure it from the ocean so we have two adjacent areas. What are the other keys?"

"According to Billie's notes there is a helicopter, a cross, and the letters WRMC," Li Na said. "It's still a big area. Maybe it's a church with the letters WRMC on it?"

"There's also the canals and people chasing white balls," Billie said.

"But this entire area has canals among the homes," Genesis said as he circled it. "The white balls would mean a golf course, I think. Let's draw it out. Then we have a circle and in the circle a cross and another cross in front of that. Any suggestions?"

"Let's put WRMC around the top of the cross and circle," Li Na proposed.

The three were frustrated. Three hours had passed, and they had not been able to solve the puzzle. There was a knock on the door. Li Na had ordered sandwiches from room service. "Where do you want this ma'am?" the waiter asked.

"Bring them here and place them around the table where there's room," Li Na responded. "Be careful not to spill anything on the maps."

"Are you guys' helicopter pilots," the waiter asked.

"No, what makes you think so?" Billie responded.

"That circle there on the blank paper," the waiter said. "It's like one I drew when I helped my brother study for his FAA helicopter exam. It's a medical helipad or to get technical, heliport."

There was immediate excitement as the three glanced at each other.

"Do you know what these letters mean?" Li Na whispered, almost too excited to hear the answer.

"I'm not sure," the waiter said. "My guess is the last two mean Medical Center. The first two are abbreviations for the name of it. Will there be anything else?"

"No thank you," Li Na said. "You've been most helpful." She handed him a fifty-dollar tip and closed the door behind him virtually on a dead run back to the sofa.

"That's a great clue," Genesis said. "Li Na, look for medical centers on the satellite feed in this area."

James Tindall

It took her about ten minutes before she found it.

"Westside Regional Medical Center," she yelled excitedly. She had enlarged the electronic satellite image and began moving the map from left to right. "Here it is and look, *enlarging the image*, there it is, the helipad with the dual cross and the letters. We found the biggest piece of the Medicine Man's puzzle."

"Great work," Billie said. "Now we need to scrutinize this area for the smaller details.

"We need a golf course near a house with a red roof and 'L' shaped pool surrounded by the other small parts of the puzzle," Genesis said.

It took another two hours to finally solve the puzzle and locate what they thought was the house.

"Should we bring in MDPD and the FBI on this?" Billie asked.

"You said the Medicine Man advised against it," Genesis replied.

"I agree with Genesis," Li Na interrupted. "Besides we can handle this ourselves. We may want them to cordon off the area. I'll leave that up to you."

"Okay," Billie said. "We leave them out for now. How do we proceed Genesis?"

"I have my men outside," Genesis replied. "First, we will do a drive by then, a walk by, followed by a drone flyover. Finally, we wait until dark and make sure we know who is in the house."

"I have an idea," Li Na said. "We presume the men in the house are Asian. Lets' find the nearest Asian fast-food establishment and I'll knock on several doors around them and give them a flyer for home-delivery orders. Then, I'll knock on their door. It's unlikely they'll answer, but it will allow me to get closer than your men."

"That could be risky," Genesis said. "If they get suspicious, they'll move to another safe house."

"Agreed," Li Na said. "But if they don't open the door, I'll leave the flyer on it. When they look the first thing they'll do is call to make sure it's a valid establishment. Once they do, all their suspicions will be alleviated."

"Sounds like a plan," Billie said. "What Li Na proposes is common. If she doesn't loiter and proceeds to the next couple of houses down, I think they won't think anything of it."

"You're right," Genesis said. "Let's get on it."

Cilatro raced to the phone, so it didn't go to voicemail. The shower, still running, a water trail leading to the counter. "Yes," he said, panting heavily.

"We think we found them," Morgan said. "I just got off the phone with Li Na. She's with Billie and Genesis. They're about to begin the recovery operation."

"How did they find them?" Cilatro asked.

"A vision from the Medicine Man," Morgan said. "I know it sounds supernatural, but so far all the elements have been identified."

"Do you trust them?

"Yes. They will be using high-tech equipment. But first, Li Na will do a walk by with restaurant flyers. I'm certain if this is the location, they will find Dianna."

"Are they going to involve the police?" Cilatro asked.

"Only if necessary."

"Damn, they sound like us. May I ask why?"

"Apparently the Medicine Man thought that there may be too much anxiousness to let bullets fly."

"Sounds like a very wise man," Cilatro said. "What happens after the walk by?"

"The men from Li Na and Genesis will move in under cover of darkness utilizing night vision, as well as FLIR on the drone," Morgan said. "I suppose if they can identify the men and hostages, they'll move in."

"Good. Keep me posted. Have our men standing by for backup just in case."

Cilatro walked back to the shower and turned it off. He felt a little better now that his daughter was potentially located. Their own plan needed to go into action but not until his daughter was recovered. As hard and brutal as he had become during his life, his heart was as soft as any parent when it came to their children. "Therein lay the problem," he thought. "Children were a treasure and a curse, a weakness and a strength. They were so easy to use as leverage under the right circumstances. I don't know if I would do any differently if I were doing it to the Chinese."

The three men had all received calls from their wives who then handed the phone to the dark-clad leader in each of their homes. In each case the message was the same.
"If you want your family to live go to Kowloon Park Chinese Garden, north of Victoria Harbor, west of Shoppers Boulevard. You have one hour. Make no calls. Come alone. Understood?"

Men in their position had no choice. They knew that if whoever they were going to meet wanted them dead, they would be already. This would be a negotiation. A meeting that could not be refused. Apprehensively, the men arrived at the destination, walking through the park. They strolled down the brick walkways seeing guards posted here and there, each one armed. The guards would point the direction they should go as they went. After the last man passed, the guards fell in behind. Fearful, the three leaders looked nervously about. Directly ahead of them was the centerpiece of the park A wrought iron, three sectioned skeletal artwork with the star of China on top. It was surrounded by a small circular garden rimmed with marigolds and an elevated seating area that circled the entire garden.

The walkway going around either side of garden was blocked by five persons on either side, all armed. The men were ringed behind with no less than a dozen more guards. In front of them, sitting on the stone sitting area surrounding the centerpiece were two men. One wore a silk neckerchief around his face with only his eyes showing. When the three men were about six feet away, two armed guards stepped between them and the seated figures. The figure without a mask lit a cigarette., the glow from the lighter immediately identifying him. Their eyes widened in surprise as they were directed to sit down. Assuming a seated position they were at once ringed by the two men who had been sitting and the guards. Looking at each other they gulped knowing full well they were likely covered by snipers from the high-rise buildings to the north northwest and east of them. There was no escape and no need for questions. The head of See On Yun was smoking his cigarette, his back to them. The clear night revealed the smoke rising into the air as he exhaled. They immediately realized they would either be shot or make a life and death decision. They gulped.

"Do you know the penalty for betraying an oath to the triads? Ki asked, turning to look at them. Several of his men shown flashlights into their faces. The light was green to maintain night vision and not draw attention.

"It is death," Cai Wei said, the other two nodding in agreement.

"Would you support someone you knew had broken this oath?" Akio asked through his mask.

"Of course not," Liu Hui said. "To support that person would be like breaking the oath yourself."

"I agree," Cai Wei said. "What is this all about?"

"It is about breaking an oath and committing subterfuge against the triad," Akio replied. "Let me ask you another question. Would you punish the guilty with the prescribed judgement if you knew who they were?"

"We would have no choice," Fei Bence said. "We either punish the person or the triads involved go to war, which is always a waste."

"Yes," Ki said. "A terrible waste. It's so difficult to get good help these days, especially with experience."

"I have not broken an oath," Liu Hui said.

The other two murmuring in agreement.

"Ah," Ki said. "You speak with truth. Indeed, you have not, or you would not be sitting here. Thus, you have a choice."

"To live or die?" Fei asked

"Exactly," Akio replied. "Join them or join master Ki Luo."

"Our bosses broke the oath?" Cai asked.

"Yes," Ki said. "They colluded together. We have proof; secret meetings, pictures, and recordings."

"What are you proposing?" Fei asked.

"It is simple," Ki said. "We can either kill your bosses and you if you support them, along with your families. Or, as second in command, you join See On Yun as a branch and continue running your operations as you are. Occasionally we will collaborate."

"You do not leave us much choice," Liu said.

"I think it's a great choice," Akio stated. "You become the boss and continue as normal. You merely become an affiliate to us, and we can cooperate now and then on various business dealings. Everyone is spared a war and only three need die. Perhaps more importantly, you three will become the new bosses."

"I suppose you need a decision before we leave?" Cai asked.

"Honor demands it," Ki said.

"Understood," Fei said. "Would you mind if we conferred for a moment?"

"Certainly," Ki said, motioning his men out of hearing range.

"I don't know about this," Fei said. "If we go against our bosses, we will be killed when they find out."

"And if we don't, we support them and violate the oath by proxy," Cai said. "We cannot support them. The penalty is the penalty and will not be lessened."

"I agree," Liu said. "I did not break the oath and, it is better to be a leader in charge than a dead follower. I suggest we accept the offer."

"There is no other choice," Fei said. "Do we all agree?"

All shook their heads affirmatively then looked toward Ki and his men.

"Have you made your decision?" Ki asked.

"Yes," Cai said. "We need clarity on one point. You said we could lead our groups as they now are. What exactly do you mean?"

"Exactly what you were told," Akio said. "You control your groups and your books. We will not interfere. You are an affiliate that will swell our ranks and as opportunities arise, we will work together as a unified triad."

"Before you ask, there is strength in unity," Ki added. "Our separate ventures will be large and lucrative. The promise will be to support the union."

"Then we all agree," Fei said. "What do you want us to do?"

"Nothing," Ki said. "We will take care of everything in due time. Go about your normal activities as if nothing has happened. You will be apprised when the time is right. It will be soon."

The three men arose to leave and gave Ki and Akio the old Chinese greeting, bowed slightly, and walked away, glad they still had their heads. They looked forward to a new era in the triads.

Darkness was falling as the FPF command vehicle, a box truck disguised as a bread truck, readied for operations. It was stationed in the parking lot of a small park a quarter mile from the target area. The truck had prepared all its communications and the team was standing by, awaiting orders from Genesis.

"Is the drone ready?" Genesis asked.

"Ready to deploy sir," Sergeant Striker said. Seeing the frown on his commanders face he was concerned. "What's wrong sir?"

"It is awfully calm tonight," Genesis replied. "My worry is that they will hear the drone. If they do, they'll automatically assume it's the law."

"I can keep it up at two hundred feet sir," Striker said. "They won't be able to hear it that far away and we will still get good image quality on the infrared. I can also zoom in up to eight power optically with this mini drone."

"Ok, we will risk it," Genesis said. "Send it up to two-hundred fifty feet. Bravo team, assume final assault positions. Remember, non-lethal force."

The FPF squad had separated into two, four-man units, hidden behind shrubs on either side of the house about fifty yards away. They were awaiting orders to execute. Genesis was worried that things could go wrong still, he had confidence in his men and equipment. The drone was a real game changer. First gaining use in the military to reduce fatalities on the battlefield, they had and continued to save lives. Though there remained a great controversy about the government using drones, mostly because of the predator type that could deliver heavy weapons such as hellfire missiles, they were a godsend to special operations teams using them for surveillance and counter surveillance.

Genesis thought back to fifteen years before when he had helped Lunadi experiment with them and had used one called the Silver Fox to help the DEA, FBI, and U.S. Border Patrol, and Homeland Security surveil the border and identify people, drugs, guns, and many other items beneath the canopies of trees through what he called a black box deconvolution process. The professional paper that Lunadi had written had garnered a six-million-dollar grant for the company who developed the Silver Fox, and the game was on for smaller drones that could be used more efficiently for law enforcement purposes. The big controversy was always about collateral damage by the drones used by the military; such damage was unavoidable in warfare. Mere mention of the word drone tainted the air anytime the word was mentioned. He sometimes wished he could get the bleeding-heart liberals in DC to the sands of Afghanistan. They'd sing a completely different tune when it was their asses on the line instead of the innocent kids they sent over to be killed by an enemy they themselves had created, giving no thought to the consequences.

Although Genesis believed that drones were the most profound innovation for battlefield and law enforcement surveillance in the past fifty years, he was still old school and preferred eyes on. He was anxiously watching the monitor, seeing exactly what the drone was seeing. Their men were clearly visible on the street. Shadows began to appear near the front windows of the house. Suddenly, flood lights illuminated the front lawn; he ordered his men to pull back further.

"What do you see?" Genesis asked through his comm.

"There are several people in the dining room and kitchen," the team leader responded. There appear to be about half-a-dozen people that we can see with our infrared."

"Hold in place," Genesis said. "I hate to do this but bring the drone down to about thirty feet. Track around the entire house as a point of interest and let's see what we can through the windows."

"That's pretty low sir," Striker said. "They may hear the drone. I can back it off to a hundred feet or more away from the house as it tracks. That will help, but there will be trees in the way of the camera in a couple of places."

"Do it please," Genesis said. "I feel something is wrong. There are more people inside than we expected."

The pilot in command brought the drone down to about thirty-foot elevation and just over a hundred feet out. The quadcopter slowly began tracking around the house, viewing into every nook and cranny. The FLIR camera revealed seven people, most congregated in the living room and kitchen from the floor-plan schematic they had pulled of the property. Two were adjacent to the pool. One of those appeared to have something several feet long in his hands.

"Anything visible on the ground?" Genesis asked, speaking again into his comm.

"Nothing sir," the voice responded. "It looks and sounds quiet except for the movement in the kitchen area. The garage has been open since we arrived. It's dark with two SUV's inside. No sign of movement."

"I don't like it," Genesis said. "There's too much movement and the fact the garage is open at night in an affluent neighborhood is a red flag."

"Are you thinking what I'm thinking?" Sergeant Striker asked.

"Yes. They're ready to flee at a moment's notice."

"Bravo Team," Genesis said. "Try to get better eyes through the windows. We're going to move the drone in just a little closer."

"Do you have obstacle avoidance on that drone?" Genesis asked.

"Yes," Striker replied.

"Good. Move down to twenty-five feet and one hundred feet out."

"We won't be silent sir."

"Yes, but they likely won't notice and being inside should muffle the sound enough."

"Roger sir. Moving to twenty-five feet elevation and one hundred feet out."

"Do you hear that?" the thug asked, putting his cigarette out.

"Yeah," his companion said. "Sounds like a big mosquito."

"That's because it's not close."

"What do you think it is?"

"It has to be a drone, which is what I have this for."

"What the hell is that?"

"A semiautomatic 12-guage magnum, three-inch chamber, equipped with a suppressor and number four buckshot."

"What have you been expecting? A bear?"

"No, a drone. Go tell the others. We need to leave. Walk casually. Tell them to ease into the vehicles and wait for me."

His partner walked casually into the house and informed the others. Each slowly walked toward the living room and then, eased over to the side door entrance into the garage.

"Sir," Bravo Team leader said. "It looks like they're sitting down to eat. They all moved from the kitchen into the dining room area. I can't make them out anymore but they're around that vicinity."

"Roger," Genesis said.

As the two were talking, the men moved one by one silently, through the door to the garage and into the vehicles. Dianna and James had their mouths taped shut and hands tied behind them. They were quickly and quietly shoved into the back seats, one into each vehicle.

"Any movement?" Genesis asked.

"None outside that I can see," Striker said. "One of the men by the pool went inside a minute ago. The other one is still there smoking his cigarette. Wait, he's moving a little. There's a large flash. What the hell?"

"What's going on?" Genesis asked

"The drone's camera is out. It may be down."

The man ran from the pool and was in the closest SUV in seconds. Both cranked at the same time and sped down the driveway, tires squealing as they burned rubber on the driveway. Bravo Team leader heard them and raced toward the house from cover just as the vans passed. Li Na, carrying her sword cane, was at the rear of the second squad; she drew her sword. As the second SUV raced past them, she went into a lunge position and let her blade tip travel the entire length on the outside of the vehicle, penetrating the metal in several places and breaking the left rear taillight. The rest of the team fired rubber bullets, doing little damage.

"That sword won't stop a car," a member said, standing next

to her as he watched the vehicles race away.

"It wasn't meant to," Li Na said. "I merely marked it, hoping we can recognize it later."

"Hmmmm," the man said, walking toward the house.

"What the hell happened?" Genesis asked.

"They shot down our drone," Sergeant Striker said. "I'll launch the second one."

The second drone came to life with a high-pitched buzzing as it shot straight into the sky, gaining altitude quickly up to four hundred feet.

"There they go," he said. "I'll follow as long as I can."

"Keep me informed," Genesis said as he jumped into a waiting car and quickly arrived at the house.

"It looks like they've been here since the last safe house," Bravo team leader said. "The hostages were definitely here and from what we can tell there were five men, maybe six."

"Anything of value for us?" Genesis asked.

"Only this," Bravo Team leader said, holding out an empty shotgun shell.

"So, this is how they took down the drone," Genesis said. "They're savvier than we thought. We won't underestimate them again."

"I found it sir," one of the men said, coming through the back door, holding up the downed drone.

"Double check everything," Genesis said. "Make sure we don't miss any clues."

"Roger sir."

"What do you think Li Na?" Genesis asked.

"They're still a step ahead. We need an edge."

"I underestimated them," Genesis said. "It won't happen again. Hopefully we'll get a lead on them."

"Sir," Striker said. "I have them heading north on Nob Hill Road. They just crossed over West Sunrise Boulevard."

"Excellent," Genesis said. "Bravo Team, get to your vehicles and reposition per command."

The men raced to their vehicles around the corner, following directions from command.

"I don't mean to offend you," Genesis said. "You know the culture of these men better than we do. What do you think they will do now?"

"I'm not offended," Li Na said. "Think what you would do if you were nearly discovered a couple of times. Tell me."

"I'd go somewhere I could see you coming," Genesis replied. "But I'd maintain an exit strategy."

"Exactly," Li Na said. "Where would you go in this area?

"To the Glades," Genesis responded. "It's basically a sea of grass. Easy to hide in, but difficult to approach unseen or unheard."

"Did you get that Striker?" Genesis asked.

"Yes sir. I'll put up Dragon 1 momentarily."

"What's Dragon 1?" Li Na asked.

"It's a surveillance drone that gives us a wider search area," Genesis said. "We have three of them that will be on rotation. Assembly takes a few minutes, but they can stay up two hours at a time and have a range of 30km, about 20 miles. Hopefully, we don't lose these guys before we get eyes on them again."

"What if we do?" Li Na asked.

"We will begin a grid search from the last location. We will need your help. You know their thought processes better. Even in an open expanse like the sawgrass, they likely tend to go one direction more than another."

"I agree," Li Na said. "Tell me, you're a smart guy. How is it you're not married?"

"Because these very people had my fiancé killed when we were installing the landfill. It's one giant pit of snakes and I intend to find the king viper."

Li Na realized she had touched a nerve but also that she may have a better ally than she thought, the loyal colleague she sought. They were both after the same thing. Perhaps when this was over, they would pursue their own operation.

"I understand how you feel," Li Na said. "They took my parents and brother."

Genesis stared at her, deep into her eyes. He could read people well. He saw the same pain and torment he felt, the drive, commitment, and focus that would accomplish that which she pursued. There was much more to Li Na than he had realized. Both fell into silent thought as they stared across the front lawn, the last agent turning off the lights, closing the doors behind them.

Akio was near the airport when he had phoned Li Na that Wong had arrived and was staying in a five-star hotel along South Beach. His orders were clear. Take Wong alive and get him back to Hong Kong. Akio, along with the two assassins Ki had sent and some of Li Na's men, had been surveilling Wong all day. They had friends at the hotel who worked as waiters from the kitchen. Akio was certain that eventually, Wong would call for room service. Tonight would be the only time they had a chance to capture him alive. It was about 8:00 pm when Wong finally ordered a juicy T-bone steak. When it was ready, the kitchen sent it up along with meals the guards had ordered, one of Li Na's men posing as the waiter. Four more of her men crept into the hallway, two from each end, positioning themselves close to either side of the door, out of sight from the men in the room.

The waiter gently knocked and was allowed to enter. Getting a quick picture of all five men in the room he quickly drew a suppressed 9mm from the cart and killed one of the guards. The other guards pulled their guns, but it was too late as the four men at the door entered the room like a SWAT team killing them where they stood. Wong panicked because he realized who the men were. They quickly zip-tied his wrists behind him and led him out of the room closing the door, quickly moving to the exit stairway and down to a waiting vehicle. Within thirty minutes they had arrived at the private jet and loaded their prisoner.

"We have him," Akio said. "We're taxiing to the runway."

"Thank you," Li Na said, smiling.

The Hong Kong rush hour was as busy as ever, trains, ferries, motorcycles, and cars rushing their passengers to their jobs.

"We need to find the hostages so that we can implement our strategy," Ki said.

"I realize that," Akio replied. "Li Na told me they almost had them, but they slipped away once more."

"Does she have a plan to find them?"

"Yes. They are working on that now. She assured me they would be found soon."

"Good. What of the other matter?"

"Once we find the hostages, so they are of no consequence to them, Li Na and I have devised a strategy for pick up of the masters. We have Wong already. We will be there in about ten hours. Once we have the rest, we execute the nuclear plant sabotage and the insertion of the new leaders."

"How long after we retrieve the hostages before that happens?"

"Immediately sir."

"Alright," Ki said. "We cannot afford any more slip ups."

Cilatro sat despondent, gazing across the water, the yacht swaying gently. It had become like a prison. He yearned to see his daughter and hoped that she was okay although he realized that she probably wouldn't be harmed if they did what they were asked. What was strange was that there had been no more demands from the group. He was getting restless as he picked up the ringing phone.

"Yes."

"We had them and lost them, again," Morgan said. "I know it's not what you wanted to hear. The good thing is we have a better lead on them now."

"How?" Cilatro asked.

"Genesis has some high-tech law enforcement group backing them up. Li Na said it is a matter of time."

"Who is behind this?" Cilatro asked. "They always seem to be one step ahead. There is a leak somewhere."

"According to Li Na, she believes she found it. She said it's a delicate matter and must be carefully dealt with, so no suspicion is aroused."

"Understood," Cilatro said. "What about our other plan?"

"We can implement as soon as we have Dianna back," Morgan said. "I would recommend doing it now, but that would likely tip our hand and doing so could cause these guys to up the ante."

"We do not want to do that," Cilatro replied. "According to Ki, three other triads are behind this."

"That's a lot of enemies sir," Morgan said. "We don't have the manpower to go to war with them."

"True. But we do have Ki on our side who has the largest triad. Let's hold our cards close. We'll play them when the time is right."

Billie sat in his office, not wanting to go home because he would feel useless. He was thinking about James as he tried to get through the paperwork on his desk. He was glad to hear the phone ring because it would take his thoughts elsewhere.

"Genesis," Billie said. "Any news?"

"We had them," Genesis said. "They slipped away a few seconds before we went in."

"Damn it!" Billie exclaimed. "How did that happen?"

"They're cleverer than we gave them credit for," Genesis said. "It's my fault. I should have gotten MDPD to lock down a perimeter."

"Maybe," Billie said. "But if they had, lead would have started flying and we could have dead hostages instead of live ones."

"Perhaps it was best we didn't," Genesis replied. "Next time they will not get away."

"Do you have any leads on them?"

"We believe so. We have two drones up in the air searching as we speak. Li Na and I both believe that we can narrow the search area so that we can determine their relative location and move in. It may take some time, but we're already on it."

"What are you thinking?"

"She thinks they have left the city and are in the open somewhere so that they can spot an approach at greater distance."

"Makes sense," Billie mused. "But that means they would have less chance of escape if they were found."

"Correct," Genesis said. "But I think that's what they want. It will be the best way to force a negotiation."

"Yes, but with who?"

The two triad leaders were sitting around the small table. As they smoked their cigarettes in the dark, only a candle burning to illuminate the small room, they stared at the cell phone on the table. The third man in the room had given them the low down on the operation. Having flown from Miami to deliver the news, they could no longer afford to wait. Nothing, including going to war with See On Yun could change the course of what was happening.

"As I was saying gentleman, there is no way around the agreement," Ting stated succinctly.

"What are our choices in your opinion?" Xu Lo asked

"There are only two," Ting responded. "We either let the hostages go or kill them and wait for better timing or, we extort money from Don Cilatro for all power plants he is involved in."

"The problem I see is that he is affiliated with Ki," Peter Chow interjected. "If we extort him, it is like extorting Ki."

"That ship has sailed," Xu Lo said. "We have already broken the code. Besides, Cilatro does not know that it is us, so we have an edge. It's just another extortion scheme."

"Agreed," Peter said. "It looks like we agree but it would be better if Wong were here to voice his opinion. However, the question becomes how much do we extort?"

"I would say twelve percent," Xu Lo said. "We do not want to do less and if we do too much, there may be no agreement."

"The real question is how much does Cilatro love his daughter?" Peter responded.

"He's a hard-core boss," Ting said. "His wife was killed by another rival group when they attempted to murder him. Then, his bosses murdered his son. Since then, his daughter has been his entire life."

"What are you implying?" Chow asked.

"That he is as ruthless as any of you," Ting said. "There is a line in the sand and if we step over it, he will never stop coming after us."

The group sat silently for a few moments pondering what Ting had said. Knowing how ruthless they were, they grew even more silent.

"I'm afraid Ting is correct," Xu Lo said. "Including the fact that Cilatro is an ally of Ki, it may be better not to push the issue, be all business."

"I agree," Peter said. "Perhaps we should adapt the adage of the stock market — greedy pigs get slaughtered."

"We don't need to go there," Xu Lo stated. "Let's go with twelve percent. With the dozen plants Cilatro will be involved with, as well as our own, there will be plenty of money. We can always address the issue later."

"Agreed," Peter said. "And we don't need a war with Ki."

"It's settled then," Ting said. "I'll make the demand when I get back. It wouldn't be wise for the call to be traced to the Hong Kong area."

Li Na's men had been waiting for Ting to return from Hong Kong. As before, the meeting had been recorded and pictures taken. Once Ting landed at Miami International Airport, he was surveilled the entire time. This time the team had multiple drones they launched as Ting made his way home. Finally, they had discovered where he lived and within a day or so would know all his travel routes. Darkness covered their movements as they let the drones do the work, taking videos and still shots of the residence, layout of the area, parking garage next door, and other points. Within a few hours Li Na had all the information that had eluded her several times before. She was counting that jet lag always seemed to make a person think less clearly.

As she went over the drone videos and surrounding area, she looked for a location where her men could see the residence and parking area from a distance through a spotting scope. If they could be far enough away, a drone could be launched, and they could surveil Ting without him becoming suspicious. The car tailing him could be several blocks behind and never spotted, letting the drone do the work. She decided to call Genesis. They had the same goal in mind, and both had been dealt severe emotional blows and losses because of these people. It didn't take long for him to arrive.

Li Na was dressed in a silk robe tied around her waist. She exuded sexiness without realizing it. When she opened the door, Genesis gasped.

"Did I come at a bad time?"

"Oh, sorry," Li Na said. "A force of habit. Let me change really quick."

While she was changing, he looked around her hotel room. It was clean and well kept. Everything seemed in perfect order; nothing was out of place. He noticed the papers and computer on the table and started thumbing through the maps finding them interesting. They were all the Ft. Lauderdale and Miami areas. Satellite views of various locations. He had two in his hands when Li Na came out of the bathroom.

"I apologize," he said. "Force of habit. I did not mean to be nosey."

"It's okay. I was going to show them to you anyway. Do you recognize the two you're holding? Where they are I mean."

"Yes," Genesis responded. "This one is just south of us, and this area is between Ft. Lauderdale and Miami. Are they significant?"

"I believe they are," Li Na said. "I have been suspicious of one of our operatives for a while. I now know that he is working with the other triads to undermine us."

"Is he responsible for the kidnappings?" Genesis asked.

"Yes," Li Na said. "I mentioned a couple of things to him and that is how he has stayed one step ahead. He returned from Hong Kong a few hours ago and I finally found his location. Look at these. I suspect if we can follow him, he will lead us to the hostages."

The two watched all the videos the drones had sent back as Li Na caught Genesis up on her side of the operation.

"I need not tell you that my boss is most displeased," Li Na said. "We will handle Ting after we locate the boy and woman. If he happens to be with the hostages when we find them, it is imperative that I take charge of him without your law enforcement getting in the way."

"I can make that happen," Genesis said. "What can we do to help you? Do you really think that he can lead us to the hostages?"

"Yes," Li Na said. However, we must avoid all suspicion otherwise, we're going to keep playing this hide and seek game of his and trust me, he is Master of It. What I need is better drone capabilities. They must be able to stay aloft longer. What about this dragon you told me about? Can we task it to follow Ting?"

"Definitely," Genesis said. "After the last fiasco, we have set up all three of them so we can cover a larger area and always have one up in the air over target. We can keep them aloft 24 hours a day on rotation if needed. The airspace is a consideration due to the FAA, but it looks like they're far enough away from the two major airports that we only need to worry about class C, D, and G airspaces. I'll let the pilot in command (PIC) determine that."

"How soon can you have one ready?" Li Na asked.

"How soon do you need it?"

"By 5:00 am."

"It will be ready. I assume that you want it near the residence initially?"

"Yes. We need to track Ting all day or at least until we can figure out what he is doing and where he is going."

"How do you plan on doing that?"

"He thinks I consider him an ally, a colleague. He was, but now he is a traitor. I'll meet with him again tomorrow at the same restaurant. That will give you time to swap out drones if you need to. The meeting will be lunch for about an hour."

"So, you want us to follow him and nab him?" Genesis asked.

"No!" Li Na said, adamant. "We need to get his habits down. Somewhere tomorrow he is meeting a go between. We need to find out who. Once we do, that person will lead us to the hostages or to someone else who will. No matter what happens, we need to keep eyes on Ting."

"You need to bait him somehow," Genesis said. "Some disinformation is in order."

"I'm already ahead of you," Li Na smiled. "He has no idea that I know."

"How did you find out anyway?" Genesis asked.

"We have eyes and ears all over Hong Kong to gather intelligence," Li Na said. "We were surveilling the other triad leaders when he showed up to have a meeting with them. Quite fortunate."

"Indeed," Genesis said. "Do you need anything other than the drone?"

"Not at this time," Li Na said. "I cannot emphasize enough that this needs to stay between us."

"Clearly understood," Genesis said. "Do you mind if I ask you a question?"

"Go ahead," Li Na said.

"It looks like we have the same purpose. Do you have any idea who was behind the murder of my fiancé?"

"I do not know exactly," Li Na replied. "It is not who you think. Cilatro is cooperating with the triads. It was before my boss approached him. They are the ones who gave the order ahead of time."

"They knew about Mary Jane?"

"Not specifically. They have standing orders to get rid of anyone that may become a liability. I'm afraid she was taken as that, as were my parents and brother. However, I do know we seek the same people. To us it is personal, not business!"

"You don't know who they are?"

"No, but I have my suspicions and I am getting a little closer all the while. There is a good chance that when this is over that a new lead will point us in the right direction."

"But you're certain it was the triads?"

"Yes," Li Na responded. "You see, just like the cartels began cooperating with gangs and transnational terrorists, the triads were right behind them, but were smarter about it. The feds had put great pressure on what was always called the Mafia or organized crime. Because of their organizations that are still in place, though they have minimized their avarice and were pushed back into the shadows, they were a perfect union for the triads who could help back them and move them out of the shadows again. The triads came to the U.S. decades ago and are now embedded in most large cities and have strong unions with organized crime that your FBI thought was near death. Far from it."

"So, you're telling me that most organized crime is controlled by triads now?"

"No. That's not what I'm saying. They are partners with each, scratching each other's back. They still control their own organizations, but they cooperate, which makes them very powerful compared to years past. They should not be taken lightly."

"Hmmmm," Genesis mused. "That can explain some things I've been wondering about. Are you saying they are more dangerous?"

"Of course, they are," Li Na said. "If you look at organized crime, some issues to them were just considered business and they would eliminate problems as needed. To the triads, any potential problem is connected to the vitality of the business and is eliminated without thought. They take no chances and no prisoners They have the same goals, but no one interferes with triad business and lives. If one doesn't get you the other will."

"Then how do you deal with them?" Genesis asked.

"You become a ghost and stay a ghost," Li Na said. "Just like with Ting, when he goes out, it will look like anyone other than a triad or someone seeking revenge did it. It's the only way. When the opportunity is there, it must be taken. You must be prepared to get your hands dirty because the law will not hold them."

Christina had just finished teaching school and was on the phone when Billie pulled up into the school parking lot. She had been trying to reach him and had called Genesis.

"I've been trying to reach you," Christina said. "How come you haven't answered?"

"My phone is dead," Billie said. "I dropped it in the water and it's drying off in a jar of rice. I just wanted to stop by and say hi before I head into Hollywood."

"Well, I have Genesis on the line," Christina said.

"We're the only ones here. Put him on speaker."

"I wanted to give you the latest update," Genesis said. "I

James Tindall

believe we can find James and Dianna again within the next forty-eight hours."

"Are you sure?" Christina asked, lighting up.

"We have a lead on the guy that Li Na's intelligence group says is behind this," Genesis said. "It appears it's all about money. Anyway, we have eyes on him as we speak."

"You think he will lead us to them?" Billie asked.

"Not him," Genesis said. "He's too sneaky but we're fairly certain he has a go between that will."

"That doesn't seem too certain to me," Christina said. "I really need to have my son back."

"It's more certain than you think," Genesis said. "Billie, do you remember how the Taliban in Afghanistan quit using phones and began meeting face to face?"

"Yeah. They became relative ghosts."

"Well, the triads and many Asian gangs have long been doing that and that's why we're almost certain the go between will lead us to them. He or she will be the man passing messages between those watching James and Dianna and the boss. The boss is the man we're following."

"You're certain?" Christina asked.

"Yes," Genesis said. "I heard a meeting with him with triad leaders in Hong Kong, as well as pictures of them coming and going. The information is solid."

"Genesis," Christina pleaded. "Please don't let this guy get away. I need James in my arms."

"Don't worry. I won't. We are watching his every move with drones. These are not your average commercial type. Wherever he goes, we can see him. Once we find his meeting place, we will identify the go between and then, follow them both."

"Do you have any idea where?" Billie asked.

"Yes," Genesis said. "Li Na and Detective Yuen identified some early on. Li Na has placed one of her men in each just in case."

"It sounds almost too good to be true," Christina said. "We are counting on you Genesis."

"Not really," Genesis reassured her. "The man we're following has been seen in each location. One thing we know is that he never meets in the same place twice. We have identified three other locations as well. Look, I must run. Don't fret Christina. I won't let you down. We'll get James back. Have faith."

The cat and mouse game had begun. Ting didn't leave his residence until about 10:00 am. Genesis had a man on a rooftop garage about twelve hundred yards away. Dragon 1 was already on a preset circling route tracking the building when Ting emerged.

"PIC," Genesis said. "Make sure we have the next drone in place before this one runs out of energy."

"Will do sir," the PIC said. "Dragon 2 is on standby and will launch thirty minutes before fuel is out. I'm sending video to your monitor now."

Genesis and Li Na were sitting on a nearby park bench, not twenty meters from the command post. Every movement Ting made was visible. Passersby were waved on so that the small parking lot remained empty excepting FPF vehicles.

"How are we going to handle the locations he visits?" Genesis asked. "After all, it would be easy enough for him to hand a piece of paper with instructions to anyone inside."

"I have a man inside each location," Li Na said. "When he leaves, we make sure the drone covers front and back with the video. If someone else leaves, we need to also follow that person. My hunch is that if he makes contact that person will exit out the back."

"What would you do if you were him?" Genesis asked.

"I'd discretely pass instructions to someone inside as you suggest," Li Na replied. "After that, I would continue making another stop or two just to throw us off."

"Sergeant," Genesis called. "How long will it take to ready the third drone and have it on station?"

"It is ready now sir," Striker responded. "It could be on station within five or six minutes."

"Send it up," Genesis said. "If we need to split off, I want one to be able to follow each suspect."

Ting had made two stops and went inside for about twenty minutes each time. Li Na's contacts reported in saying he was sitting at a table having a drink but made no contact. Two drones were now overhead tracking him. As Ting left the second location, he stood by his car looking up, obviously suspicious that someone may be tracking him from above.

"I don't like this," Genesis said. "He may see something."

"Your sergeant assured me he could not hear or see the drones at their cruising altitude," Li Na said. "They are also made of plastic materials, so they won't glint like a Predator. But you are correct to be suspicious. Ting is very crafty."

At the third location, Li Na's man called in.

"He passed a piece of paper to the waitress," the man said.

"Watch her carefully, tell me what she does," Li Na replied. "We may be getting a break Genesis."

"She passed it to a man at the end of the bar, who's nonchalantly sipping a beer."

Time was ticking by as her man held on the phone, waiting to see if the man made a move.

"Ting is leaving," the man said. "Wait. The man at the bar is also, going out the back. He has on khaki pants and a light blue shirt, dark hair, about five feet ten inches and shades. I'll walk out slowly and see if I can get a clue about what he's driving."

"No!" Li Na said. "Stay put for now, we have that handled."

The drone footage revealed Ting exiting the front and the other man going out the back getting into a small gray sedan.

"What do you want me to do sir?" Striker asked.

"Follow the sedan with one drone and keep on Ting with the other."

"Roger that."

The gray sedan got onto I-95 heading north and just kept going. He pulled off and headed toward the ocean ending up at Bark Park Dog Beach. He lowered the windows in his car and sat. The drone overhead was tracking in a circle as they waited to see if he got out or if someone approached the car. Meanwhile, Ting was making a fourth stop. The man inside watched him carefully. The third drone was sent up to replace the one on station surveilling him. Immediately upon landing, the batteries were changed out and the drone quickly inspected. It was ready for the next flight.

"I don't like this," Li Na said. "Something should have happened by now."

"We just need to be patient and watchful," Genesis replied. "This is the most stressful part."

D on Cilatro was waiting on his yacht, anxiously waiting for news of his daughter when his phone rang. Anticipating good news, he raced for it.

"Hello," Cilatro said. "Tell me what is happening?"

"It is simple," Ting said. "What is happening is that you will give us twelve percent net from your share of each of the power plants you are partner in."

"If I don't?"

"Your daughter dies."

How do I know you will keep your agreement?" Cilatro asked.

"You don't," Ting replied. "But we are honorable. You have thirty-six hours to give me your answer."

T he drones had been up and rotated for hours while Ting made additional stops. The FPF squad was beginning to tire, hoping that something would have happened by now so they could become more actively involved. Somehow, they knew that something was amiss, that the man in the car was a decoy.

James Tindall

Chapter 9

Dakotah was sitting at his desk, late. A close friend warned that a secretive meeting was occurring in the Directors office. The apprehension in the air could be cut with a knife. "This is awfully suspicious," he thought as he contemplated what the meeting could be about.

"Dakotah, I'm surprised you're still here," Hal said. "Could you come to my office for a few minutes?"

"Certainly," Dakotah replied. "I'll be right there."

As he walked down the hall to the director's office, he noticed his assistant was gone. He tapped lightly on the door.

"Come on in," the director called out.

The two Asian men with Hal stood up as he entered.

"Dakotah," Hal said. "I'd like you to meet Jian and Hua from Tài Yáng Power out of Hong Kong."

"Good evening gentlemen," Dakotah said as he shook their hands. "How may I be of service?"

"They have contracts with several groups in Myanmar," Hal said. "Due to unrest issues in several areas, they will not be renewing contracts for their power stations. They entered the energy market expecting an influx of foreign direct investment because of economic reforms in the country. That just has not happened and they are pulling out of various power plants they invested in."

"How can I help them," Dakotah asked. His guard up as he remained wary since foreign investment was not allowed in infrastructure projects on reservations, especially water and energy.

"They would like to know how we arrange partnership agreements with the tribes so that everyone benefits," Hal stated. "Their company is hopeful this could be a pattern for future success for them in other locations."

"Would you like me to explain the process?" Dakotah asked. Jian and Hua were staring at him, not looking overly friendly."

"If you don't mind," Hal said. "Please."

For the next hour Dakotah explained the process and how it worked and used the recent example on BC. During the explanation, while the two men displayed some interest, he kept thinking their minds were elsewhere, as if they didn't really care about the agreements or how they worked. When he had finished, they pretended to be very excited, but Dakotah knew that something was off.

"Thank you," Hal said. "Do you gentleman need any clarification?"

The two men shook their heads.

"Very well," Hal responded. "Thanks so much for your help, Dakotah. I may need to speak with you tomorrow about some follow up questions."

"No problem, sir," Dakotah said. "I'll be in all day."

He excused himself and made his way to the door. Catching their reflection bouncing off the office windows onto a nearby mirror, he could see them smiling at each other. Something was up, but what? He walked down the hall, closed his office door, and made his way to the parking structure to his car. He grew nervous when he saw a shadowy figure leaning against a support column smoking a cigarette a few yards away. Climbing in, nodding at the man, Dakotah cranked his car and was out of the structure quickly. He was nervous, gripping the steering wheel so hard his knuckles turned white. Making his way to Pennsylvania Avenue NW and 11th Street NW, he reached one of his favorite restaurants. Inside, he was escorted to a table by the hostess and seated. It was near the back side of the restaurant giving him a clear view of the street. The low lighting would make it difficult for anyone outside to notice him. He ordered a salad, seared Aki Tuna, and a bourbon. Not the best match for fish, but he needed to calm his nerves. As he waited, he replayed the brief meeting over and over in his head. He began to wonder if there was something more sinister happening that he was unaware of.

Glancing at his watch, he realized it wasn't too late. Looking furtively about he pulled his phone from his inner coat pocket.

"Do you have a minute?" Dakotah asked.

"Certainly dad," Billie replied. "What's going on?"

Dakotah explained all that had just happened reasoning that something was very odd about it.

"You know," Billie said. "We have found out that it is a couple of triads from Hong Kong that are trying to muscle in on the power plant deal. That's what Li Na has told us. Because of the agreement, they have nowhere to turn and thus we believe, kidnapped James and Dianna for leverage. She said there is an outside group separate from the three she has been gathering intelligence on. Do you think it's possible these guys represent them?"

"I'm not sure," Dakotah said. "However, they didn't seem much interested much in what I had to say. It was as if the director was deflecting to have an out. After all, I have never known him to stay so late."

"Hmmmm," Billie mused. "He probably figured you would be curious if you saw his lights on. I'm not sure I can do anything, but I wouldn't take it for granted."

"I'm not," Dakotah said. "I will contact my friend later. Anything new with James since this morning?"

"Genesis and Li Na think they have a good lead on things,"

Billie said. "Right now, they are following the main person they believe is responsible for the kidnappings. If it works out, we have Li Na and Genesis to thank."

"I hope they don't lose him again," Dakotah said.

"They won't," Billie replied. "They've taken extra precautions and have him under the surveillance of multiple drones."

"Keep me posted son," Dakotah said.

"Will do."

The meal came quicker than expected. Dakotah loved its warmth, aroma, and taste. He saved the bourbon until after he had eaten. It helped him relax as he began to wonder what was going on. He knew it had to do something with power plants and energy, but what and how? Could this explain the unworkable ploy of taking the hostages? It was either the strategy behind this or the money, not likely both.

"You'll help us then," Jian stated.

"I cannot afford not to with what you're offering," Hal replied. "Besides, it's just a business deal that will be good for all concerned."

"Yes," Hua said. "There will be enough money for all."

The Medicine Man had seen in his transparency that things were beginning to go sideways. He would not interfere, but he and his young warriors would watch. A dozen of them poled their dugouts across sawgrass, lily ponds, cypress flats, and open water as they headed south. They had already been poling for hours, taking turns as others slept. Time was of the essence; progress was slower than anticipated.

The Medicine Man thought back on his vision and what he had seen while in the transparency. Occasionally, he would direct a slight course change as his group moved forward. Just when the sun peaked the horizon, they reached the destination that he had seen in his vision. At one time it had been a hammock but was now an old water treatment plant, long closed as newer technologies had come along and the treatment plant had fallen into disrepair and been abandoned.

The cabbage palms that marked most hammocks had been left when they built the facility, shell rock having been pushed around and leveled over the muck to form a solid foundation for the structures and a road. There were three buildings. One was open with only a roof. Several vehicles were parked inside. The other two buildings were a valve and pipe house that had been used to control water flow to the open aeration ponds around the facility. The third building was a small office with several rooms. The Medicine Man and his warriors took up positions around the north side of the buildings and remained out of sight as they sat and watched. The number of men surprised him. He thought there would be only a couple of them, which is what he had seen in the transparency. Why would they need so many to restrain two people? Suddenly, he heard a helicopter. It landed between the cabbage palms about one hundred yards away. Its blades kept turning at a low idle. It was an odd color, a mix of blues, greens, browns and black. It was not camouflaged but difficult to see in the air and on the ground. An Asian man got out and walked to the main structure. The pilot stood beside the copter, having a smoke. He was well armed with a pistol on his side and a semi-automatic carbine cradled in his arms. He also was Asian.

The Medicine Man knew something was going on. His heart began to beat faster when he saw James and Dianna led out the front door of the office hemmed on all sides by several guards. Their hands were tied in front of them, and they had tape on their mouths. He didn't like what was happening. It looked like they were going to be taken away. All they could do was watch to determine what course of action they should take.

The day had drug on and Li Na's men were still following Ting who had made several more stops. At the last stop a man had come to his table, spoke with him very briefly and took a small note that had been placed beside his drink. Ting picked up his glass and tipped it toward the man in mock salute as he walked to the restrooms and came out a few minutes later. He then walked out the front door, cautiously looked right and left and walked across the street, getting into his car.

"He made contact," her man said. "The guy just walked out the front, well dressed. He got into a white sedan across the street. What do you want me to do?"

"Follow him," Li Na said.

"I gathered," Genesis said. "Damn it, the first man was a decoy, wasn't he?"

"Yes," Li Na said. "We have a problem."

"Damn right we do," Genesis said. "One drone is covering the other suspect who hasn't moved, one drone is returning low on fuel, and we only have one drone left. Striker, how long will it take the other drone to get to this location so we can cover both subjects?"

"About ten minutes sir."

"Make it happen, now," Genesis said. "Hell fire. You told me he was crafty."

"Look," Li Na pointed. "Ting is leaving. We cannot follow both."

"I say we pull off Ting and follow the sedan," Genesis said. "I don't think he is a decoy, but the timing is all wrong."

"Agreed," Li Na said. "Sergeant, follow that sedan."

"Roger that ma'am."

The sedan cruised along, merging onto I-95 north. About ten minutes later it pulled onto Commercial Boulevard going east and a few minutes later headed north on NW 12th Avenue.

"I don't believe it," Striker said. "He's at FXE."

"What's that?" Li Na asked.

"It's Ft. Lauderdale Executive Airport," Genesis said. "It's pretty busy too; about four hundred to five hundred flights per day."

"Is that a lot?" Li Na asked. "Compared to Ft. Lauderdale International, no, but for us yes because its twenty-five or more flights per hour, a difficult number to cover."

"Bravo team leader."

"Go ahead."

"Send half your team to FXE. We'll direct you as you get closer. How far out are you?"

"About ten minutes."

"Roger," Genesis said. "We do not have a choice. We have lost Ting. This guy is our only lead. Hopefully he is not another decoy. I hate to say it, but we probably need more men."

"Yes," Li Na said. "I'll let you do the explaining to the Feds and MDPD."

"Let's wait until we get a handle on this guy."

Li Na looked at him knowing he was trying to do the right thing.

When the FPF team arrived about ten minutes later, they were directed to the northeast corner of the airport near a group of airplane hangars. Outside one of the hangars were several helicopters. The sedan had pulled up near the side of the closest hangar and the driver walked into the building. He emerged a few minutes later and stood beside his car, obviously waiting for someone.

"It's time," Genesis said, pulling his phone from his pocket, flipping it open.

"Phil," Genesis said. "Hold one moment and let me merge Sergeant McAllister. Okay, this is what we have. I have my FPF team doing surveillance and we think we may have the suspects identified. We didn't want to waste your resources, so wanted to make sure before we called."

"Who is the primary," Phil asked.

"The man's name is Ting, at least that is our position based on what we have seen."

"Do you know where the hostages are," Sergeant McAllister

asked.

"Negative," Genesis said. "We don't want to overstep jurisdiction, but I think we have gotten close enough to pool our resources. Right now, we have a suspect under surveillance at FXE. It appears he's going to be taking a helicopter somewhere. If he does, we will not be able to follow him for long. Our drone isn't fast enough."

"So, you really don't know where they are yet?" Phil asked.

"Not for certain, but we do know they are somewhere west of Sunrise and likely out in the Everglades."

"That narrows it down somewhat," Sergeant McAllister said. "We've done quite a bit of work out there, not too many places to hide."

"I agree," Phil said. "Why don't we set up a command post at the Andytown exit on the Alley. Let's do that immediately."

"My swat team is preparing as we speak," Sergeant McAllister said. "We have great charts of the surrounding area. Genesis, if your drone loses sight of the chopper, can you give us a directional heading?"

"No problem," Genesis said. "Even if we lose site of it, we can stay on the heading and investigate potential locations. We are readying another drone and will have both searching a grid pattern if this guy takes off."

"I hope this isn't a false alarm," Phil said.

"We all do," Genesis replied. "We will move our command vehicle and meet up with you at Andytown. I have an eight-man squad equivalent to SWAT. If you each bring the same, that should give us enough men once we pinpoint the location."

"Keep us updated every twenty," Phil said. "We're on their way."

"What about Ting?" Li Na asked.

"I'll let you deal with him later," Genesis said. "He's even more crafty than you imagined. I believe this other man is leading his men; Ting seems far removed at this point. No matter what happens, we likely won't be able to build a legal case against him unless one his men talks."

"That won't happen," Li Na said. "They are triad; talking to the police is a dishonor. They'll die first."

"Then, Ting will be our problem afterward," Genesis said soberly. "Striker, can you follow a helicopter?"

"Yes, but they will be much faster. I won't be able to keep up. But I do have 20x optical zoom on this one. That will help until he completely disappears."

"Okay," Genesis said. "Don't lose the man at the airport, no matter what."

A few minutes later, the other drone arrived. They packed it up and headed to the rendezvous area. On the way, they replaced all the batteries in the two drones. The FBI and MDPD had already set up their command post by the time they arrived. Pulling their command vehicle close to the others, they opened the back cargo doors.

"Phil, McAllister, meet Sergeant Striker," Genesis said.

Sergeant Striker nodded at them as he quickly unloaded the drones and made them ready for takeoff.

"Damn!" Sergeant McAllister exclaimed. "What kind of drones are those? I was expecting quadcopters, those look like mini-Predator's."

"We call these Dragon, 1 and 2; 3 is airborne," Striker said. "They have an operational range of 20 miles for about two hours each and a service ceiling of 20,000 feet. Dragon 3 is currently monitoring the perp at FXE. Look."

Phil and Sergeant McAllister peered at the monitor displaying an image of a man leaning against a car. The visual was so good they could see several cigarette butts at his feet. As they watched the man appeared to be suddenly alert as another in khaki pants and shirt walked up and opened the door of the closest helicopter. He had a small bag. He opened it and took out a pistol in a holster and clipped it to his belt then, pulled out a semiautomatic carbine and inserted a magazine and racked the slide chambering a cartridge. Both men climbed into the helicopter and momentarily the blades started turning.

"Looks like they're on the move," Sergeant McAllister said.

"Can we track their direction?" Phil asked.

"Watch this," Striker said as he clicked a couple of times with his mouse.

The monitor on his screen split showing a live view of the drone footage tracking the helicopter and a tracking view of the drone overlain on the surrounding topography showing roads, lakes, buildings, and other geographic features. An MDPD officer brought over a map of the area and began following along.

"Sir," the officer said. "If I had to guess I'd say they're headed to this point or beyond."

"That's assuming they don't veer off," Sergeant McAllister said. "But you may be right. Hey, that's where we busted a meth lab a few years back."

"Yes," Phil said. "I remember it made all the news outlets. As I recall that's an abandoned treatment plant."

"Yes," Genesis said. "But let's not get out hopes up. Sergeant, launch Dragon 2 and up the altitude to twelve hundred feet. Place it on a straight-line intercept with Dragon 3. Make sure it's above it, we don't want a midair collision."

"Yes sir."

The blades on Dragon 2 began turning and two minutes later it was airborne. It's four foot plus wingspan became smaller and smaller as it lifted straight up and began a slow climb to its cruising altitude. Within a couple of minutes, the sounds from the propellers had faded and it was out of site. The officers watched the footage the drone was sending back, which had been put up on split screen so they could see the images and the location over the terrain.

"This is like sci-fi," Phil grinned. "I hope we can put an end to this hostage crises today."

Three assault teams prepared as Sergeant Striker kept

them up to date on the location of the drone. After a few minutes, it appeared that the helicopter was definitely heading toward the abandoned treatment facility. The drone was taken up to three thousand feet and headed toward the facility at a maximum speed of sixty-five miles per hour. Even then, it could not keep pace with the helicopter, quickly falling behind, losing the image.

"Sir," an officer said. "It appears this is the location."

"Thank you," McAllister said. "Well gentlemen, it looks like this is the place. Phil, unless Genesis objects, I think the FBI should assume jurisdiction and we'll deploy as you suggest."

"I have no objection," Genesis replied. "I was going to suggest the same."

"Alright," Phil said. "The FBI assumes jurisdiction. Let's gather the men. There's no time to lose."

Warriors stood among the sawgrass surrounding the facility. They had spread out for better visuals, looking toward the Medicine Man for a signal to intervene. It did not come. As soon as the man got to the door of the facility, he spoke a few words to another that appeared to be the leader of the small group and James and Dianna were led hastily to the helicopter and put in. The pilot threw down his cigarette, ground it out with the ball of his foot and climbed inside. The other man seemed to give additional instructions to the group and jogged back to the helicopter, its blades now spinning at almost full throttle. No sooner had the copter cleared the trees than it yawed right with a slight bank and was gone. The sounds of it blades diminishing in under a minute, indicating it was flying low at maximum speed.

The Medicine Man was worried. He had gotten to the right place, but now the hostages were gone. While the sounds of the helicopter had disappeared, the men seemed to be preparing for a full assault. They had taken up strategic positions around the structures inside and out; an ambush. The warriors and the Medicine Man recognized the tactics immediately. They wondered who was coming. The Medicine Man knew it had to be law enforcement and assumed Genesis and others. They were headed into a sophisticated trap. Even with a drone, it would be difficult to spot individuals in the ambush because they were hidden beneath structures that would make it impossible to detect, even with infrared.

He made a few hand signals and shortly his warriors had assembled and decided on a course of action that could help law enforcement. There was only one road in; law enforcement would naturally assume that once the drones saw no vehicles or movement, the coast would be clear, and they would race in on their vehicles. If they did so, they would find themselves in a horrendous crossfire. The Medicine Man decided his warriors would intercept them and guide them so that they could encircle the facility and flush the bad guys out.

The officers from the FBI, MDPD, and FPF had gathered around while Phil gave them instructions.

"Men," this is where we think they are," Phil said. "As far as we know, there are two hostages. A young man and woman, James and Dianna are their names. Sergeant McAllister, will you pass around their photos? Thank you. We need to extract these two individuals safely."

"That may be difficult," an agent said.

"Agreed," Phil replied. "Right now, the drone is tracking overhead attempting to locate them and determine how many men we're up against. This road, pointing, is the only way in or out excepting by air or airboat."

"It will be difficult to surprise them," Genesis interrupted. "There is a small curve in the rock road here. I suggest we move in on foot from that point. It's about four hundred yards out, which will prevent them from hearing us. We'll be beneath the top of the sawgrass, so they won't see us either."

"Good idea," Phil said. "Let's position our teams in these three locations and close from there."

"Sir," Sergeant McAllister said. "The last visuals of the drone show no helicopter and no vehicles. Is it possible we missed them again?"

"Not sure," Phil said. "According to the visuals they should be there. Assume nothing at this point. Let's move out and meet at the end of the road near Alligator Alley. It's only a few miles away. Once there, we will make final arrangements and give updated visuals."

The men loaded into eight SUV's and proceeded to the rendezvous point, followed by the FPF, FBI, and MDPD command vehicles. Sergeant Striker had sent up Dragon 1 to replace Dragon 3 on scene. It was no time to run out of fuel and go blind on target. Four miles later, all the vehicles had joined together. Opening the doors on the command vehicle, Sergeant Striker swung the monitor out so the men could see the live feed. Nothing had changed and there appears to be no activity. "Alright," Phil said. You have your assignments. Stay on comm and good luck. Be safe out their and watch for friendly fire. Remember, don't shoot the hostages. Let's roll."

The SUV's headed down the rock road, keeping the speed slow enough to avoid throwing up dust clouds. Four agents were standing on extended running boards, two on either side of each vehicle. It was seven miles to target. As they moved forward, each man mentally prepared himself for what he might face. Most had been taught or experienced it personally to never assume, to be prepared for the worst. This, after all, is what they had trained for. Training and adrenaline would kick in immediately as they jumped from the vehicles.

A few minutes later, they were nearing the bend in the road when one of the Medicine Man's warriors stepped in front of them. The caravan came to an immediate stop, throwing some of the men off the running boards, forcing them to jump and run. The warrior was dressed in a calico shirt with one feather in his hat, a bow in his hand, quiver of arrows on his back, and a long knife on his right hip. Despite the color of his apparel, he was almost invisible in the surroundings.

"Genesis," Phil called over the comm. "You need to get up here now."

Genesis jumped from the fourth vehicle and trotted forward. He saw the warrior immediately, waving a greeting as he walked trotted him. Phil and Sergeant McAllister, some of the other agents and officers had walked up as well, forming a semi-circle in front of the warrior.

"What is it?" Genesis asked in Miccosukee.

"It is a trap," the warrior said. "The Medicine Man sent me to warn you."

"What is he saying?" Phil asked.

"He said we're heading into a trap," Genesis said. "Give me a moment."

The men standing around were amazed at the warrior. They had heard rumors about them but knew only what they saw on TV. Standing in front of them was a true warrior seemingly steeped in a time past, but who was obviously acquainted with the present. His eyes were a fierce brown, unblinking as he stood wearing his reddish calico shirt with a half-moon silver breastplate and a possibles bag on his left shoulder and knee-high leather moccasin's. His hands held his bow in a relaxed grip. The knife on his right hip was obviously a Bowie knife. While he stood conversing with Genesis, his chilling glance encompassed the entire group and sent shivers up their spine. His air of confidence was overwhelming. His speech seemed to be melancholy, a calm rising and falling of intonation as they listened.

As quickly as he had begun, the warrior stopped speaking and backed up a few paces from the group, standing erect and alert.

"What's up?" Sergeant McAllister said.

"Gather the men now," Genesis said sternly.

The men responded in less than a minute.

"I want all of you to hear what the warrior said," Genesis began. "The helicopter that we tracked landed and took the hostages, heading northwest. However, there are at least a dozen armed men at the facility who have laid a trap for us."

"I knew something was up," Phil said. "We cannot let them remain."

"Roger that," Sergeant McAllister said.

"I thought you'd say that," Genesis said, grinning. "The Medicine Man and his warriors are onsite and have the facility under surveillance. He sent this warrior for us to go with him. Once we get another hundred yards down the road, we will meet two others and the three of them will guide each group to locations so that we can get as close as possible and remain hidden. It will then be up to us to move in and arrest the suspects."

"These guys know SWAT operations?" Phil queried.

"Close," Genesis replied. "They are masters at guerilla warfare. Trust them. They will not let you down."

"Okay," Phil said. "Let's move out."

The twenty-four members of the three teams followed the warrior as he walked in front of them. Within a few minutes, they had met the other two warriors.

"They will lead us to very similar assault positions that we discussed," Genesis said. "Phil, you and your men follow this warrior and Sergeant McAllister, you follow this one."

"How will we communicate?" Phil asked.

Genesis and the warriors laughed softly. "They speak English."

Phil and McAllister were a little red faced.

"Don't worry," Genesis said, smiling. "You aren't the first to make that assumption. Okay, we part here. Pass it along; everyone should put their gloves on if they haven't. Jagged Grass is a bitch on the skin and clothes."

"Jagged Grass?" Sergeant McAllister asked.

"It's the old timers name for sawgrass," Genesis said. "It can be rather sharp."

The three groups parted as they began working their way through the swamp. It took them almost an hour to get into position as they waded through knee-deep water, sawgrass slicing their gear and clothes. It was far removed from an urban assault when the major worry was getting around a structure unseen. Here, they had to fight the environment too. Finally, the warriors motioned them to stop, pointing to their eyes with two fingers and then to the facility. The men nodded in understanding. They began to surveil each of the buildings and turned to ask the warriors a question; they were gone. They had been led to perfect surveillance positions, able to see all buildings without hindrance. More importantly, they were concealed. They could see vehicles under the open sided structure, which the drone had missed.

"Bravo and Charlie teams call in locations please," Phil commanded.

"Charlie team on northwest of open-sided structure," Genesis said.

"Bravo team west, southwest of main building," McAllister responded.

"Alpha team north, northeast of main structures. We move in two minutes."

Two minutes later the three teams began to converge on the facility. There were four men near the vehicles parked in the open sided structure. One of them noticed movement in the sawgrass as a team member crept forward and began firing with an automatic weapon, hitting the officer in the shoulder. Almost instantly gunfire erupted from all over the compound as the agents and officer's dove for cover, face down in the water, moving forward using a basic sniper crawl as they engaged the hostiles.

The four hostiles near the vehicles were all killed as the agents continued to move forward but almost a third of the agents were down, wounded from squad automatic weapon fire coming from inside the main structure. The volley of bullets was unrelenting and lethal. One of the vehicles exploded and then another, sending agents and officers running as a deadly salvo of bullets continued from inside the main structure. More explosions from planted charges began going off around them as several hostiles took cover behind trees and short concrete walls outside. Agents lobbed tear gas into the windows, which bounced off because they were barred. The tear gas created a blanket of smoke that allowed the hostiles to take cover behind it and behind more obstacles surrounding the building. Phil and his men had worked their way up from the sawgrass and had split into two groups. He circled to his right moving toward the corner of the building trying to make it to cover. Bullets continued ripping the air and ground around him. The tear gas made it hard to see so he held his breath as much as he could, coughing all the while, until he could clear it.

He was about to leap into a dead run when a hostile emerged out of the smoke, unaffected by it, his gun leveled at Phil. As he began to squeeze the trigger an arrow pierced him from behind, protruding out the front of his chest. A look of surprise and horror clouded his face as he looked down, falling backward, several rounds from his automatic carbine shooting skyward. Phil looked up to see the Medicine Man, bow in hand, blending back into the sawgrass. He tipped his hand at him as he lunged for cover, eating shell rock and grass, hitting the ground hard.

"Son of a bitch," he moaned. Looking down, he had caught a bullet in his calf. "I'm hit he said, yelling into the comm. We need to work around to the corners; give them no targets."

"Roger that," McAllister said. "We need to get these guys out front first before we can approach. Where the hell did they get all these weapons?"

"Figure that out later," Phil said. "Move in."

The three squads began to converge as more explosions

went off directly in front of each, sending them for cover yet again, shrapnel tearing the air. There were still three men behind cover around the building. One had a 20mm grenade launcher and was deadly accurate with it. He had the men pinned down, most with no cover. As he exposed himself to shoot another grenade, an arrow pierced the bottom of his throat in the 'V' of the neck. He fell dead without a sound. The smoke began to clear, and the two other hostiles met the same fate.

"Holy hell," an agent exclaimed, raising his head a little. "We should have let the warriors take care of this from the beginning."

The hostiles inside were still firing. With no protection outside, the swat teams placed strip charges on the front and rear doors, breaching both doors at the same time, throwing in flash bangs right behind. Twenty seconds later, the well laid trap had ended. The all clear given, members of each of the teams began a search to check for wounded and dying.

"Get medical out here," Phil screamed into his phone. "ASAP!"

He hobbled over to the main structure. It was then that he noticed the Medicine Man, surrounded by his warriors.

"I don't know how to thank you sir," Phil said. "I owe you my life. We all owe you."

"Thanks is unnecessary," the Medicine Man said. "I wished we could have arrived sooner."

"Sir," an agent said. "Medical will be here shortly."

"Thank you."

When Phil turned around to talk to the Medicine Man, he and his warriors were gone. There was no sign of them. Finally, he saw them in the edge of the sawgrass just off the rock pad the facility had been built on. He couldn't hear what they were saying but the Medicine Man was pointing toward the northwest. Despite their casual nature, Phil couldn't help admiring how organized they were. He watched them until they were finished talking. Genesis walked back to him; the warriors now gone.

"He told me what the warrior told us," Genesis said, knowing Phil was curious. "The helicopter headed northwest. He said the sounds of the blades disappeared quickly. That means they were flying low. They'll burn more fuel that way and could be anywhere."

"They cannot hide the helicopter for long," Phil said. "They had to file a flight plan. But, flying low means they'll stay off the radar. What's our best option?"

"I've already got the sergeant flying grid search with Dragon 1 and 2 on a ninety-degree quadrant. Let's call Li Na, she stayed back to meet Billie and Christina. She knows how these people think."

"Li Na," Genesis said. "I need to ask you a couple of questions. I'm here with Phil and Sergeant McAllister."

"What happened?" Billie asked anxiously, interrupting.

"I'm sorry Billie and Christina," Genesis said. "We arrived too late. We had a shoot out with the thugs, but they had already moved James and Dianna. We just missed them. Before you ask, we are doing a grid search now over a larger area, which is why I need to speak with Li Na. Our main question is what are your thoughts on where they may have taken the hostages?"

"I'm guessing the helicopter left with them?" Li Na queried.

"Yes," Genesis said. "Not more than five minutes before we arrived. It is almost as if he was anticipating us."

"He was," Li Na said. "It's how he operates. You said he took off to the northwest?"

"Yes, that's right," Genesis said.

"My guess is he will not return to the city. He knows with certainty that we are onto him. He will have prepared an exit strategy that will be remote, away from prying eyes. Scan your maps for such a location. It could be anything."

"We're already doing that," Genesis said.

"Look for abandoned homes, hunting camps, anything like that," Li Na said. "That's where you'll find him. Also, look for the helicopter. He won't let it return because that is his exit strategy. He is loyal only to himself and will leave his men as bait."

"Genesis, you need to find James," Christina said. "I don't know how much more of this I can take."

Tears were rolling down her cheeks as she spoke. The anxiety and stress had taken its toll. She was on the verge of a breakdown.

"Sergeant McAllister," Phil called. "I have several wounded men; can you call for replacements?

"I do as well. I'll get right on it."

Morgan was nervous about how things were going. Although he had the evidence he needed on Fred, he knew from experience that the longer things drew on the more chances there were for something to go awry.

"Where are they on finding Dianna?" Cilatro asked.

"I spoke to Li Na this morning and she said a raid was planned on an old water treatment facility," Morgan said. "As it turns out, all their information was correct, but the hostages were moved just before they surrounded the place."

"How is this guy staying a step ahead of us?" Cilatro asked.

"Li Na said he has lots of experience and is a brilliant strategist," Morgan said. "They had a shoot out and several of the men were captured but she said they're triad and will not talk."

"What are they doing now?" Cilatro asked. "Any chance of finding them?"

"She thinks this guy has backed himself into a corner," Morgan replied. "Because of the helicopter, which she thinks he will keep close to save his own hide."

"How?"

"Because the feds are looking for the helicopter to turn up. If it does, they will nab the pilot who will likely spill his guts for a deal unless he is also triad. However, she thinks he's too smart for that and will hold onto it to save himself if they're found again."

"They'll just go back to the city and another safe house," Cilatro sighed. "They'll keep dragging this out until you give them your reply."

"Yeah right," Cilatro muttered. "Twelve percent for more than a dozen power plants annually. I don't think so."

"I must admit that is steep," Morgan began. "We need to find them before the deadline. We still have twenty-four hours."

"You think they'll be found by then?" Cilatro asked.

"There's a good chance," Morgan said. "And, if we have her back, they're done. From what Li Na said, this guy is in it for the money. He's not going to go down for them."

"Do they have any leads at all?" Cilatro asked.

"They know the direction they were heading and that the helicopter was hugging the top of the sawgrass. I must agree with her. They are looking for someplace to hold up. If he is as sharp as Li Na said, he already planned the location in advance and I'm guessing it'll be a last stand. They'll be armed to the teeth."

"That means we have a slim chance of getting her back alive," Cilatro said.

"Not necessarily," Morgan said. "These guys are pros. The FBI, MDPD, and Genesis's group, some kind of fed task force, are honed to a razors edge. They'll find them and they'll use as much non-lethal force as they can."

"How did they find them anyway?" Cilatro asked.

"Drones," Morgan said, grinning. "Eye in the sky small drones with intuition from Li Na. The drones followed him for a couple of days and Walla. This time, they only had a few minutes head start. I'm certain they'll find them."

"Hmmmm," Cilatro mused, staring across the waves toward Miami. Make sure the men are ready to take charge of Dianna and bring her to me when she is recovered."

He hoped that Morgan was right, that his daughter would be returned safe. But there were other pressing matters.

"What of our project?" Cilatro asked. "Are we ready?"

"Yes," Morgan said. "We've been ready, and I don't need to tell you that the longer we wait the greater the potential we will be discovered."

"Quite right," Cilatro said. "Let's set the schedule for forty-eight hours, whether we recover Dianna or not. After all, the project doesn't have anything to do with her."

"I'll arrange everything," Morgan said.

"Finally," he thought. "The operation would be carried out and the monkey would be off his back."

"Do you want me to get rid of the engineer when it's done?" Morgan asked.

"Has he seen the tape where he supposedly committed the murder?" Cilatro asked.

"Yes."

"Have you met with him in public?"

"No, only on a deserted beach."

"Then, it is his word against yours. Killing him would only arouse suspicion. When it happens, they will look for a scapegoat which will be him. They'll fire him. Sweeten the pot some and arrange for him to leave the country. He will be of greater value moving forward as a consultant."

"As you wish."

"Besides before they can sort anything out, he'll be gone, and they'll never find out what happened. Make sure he gives you the device, we'll make use of it later."

"Very well," Morgan said. "We will initiate the operation in forty-eight hours."

"One more thing; looks like a tropical storm moving in. Be ready to move sooner if it hits. It would be a shame to let such perfect cover escape our grasp. It will make for better cover for the engineer.

Command for the FPF had moved to the facility. Only two of the thugs who had fired upon the officers were able to talk. Several more were being rushed to the hospital in critical condition. Li Na had driven out to interrogate them.

"I have asked them where Ting went," Li Na said. "All refuse to speak."

"As you suspected," Genesis said.

"Yes. They'll die first. These men are not like Americans. They have nothing to lose and no families to go home to."

"Is there any way to make them talk?" Genesis asked.

"No," Li Na replied. "Torturing them would do no good. It's who they are."

"So back to square one," Genesis muttered.

"Not exactly," Li Na said. "I believe they are within twenty miles of where we are now, in a location type as I described. We just need to find them. Any luck with the drones?"

"All three are up searching from this location to thirty miles north and fifty miles east to west. Phil and Sergeant McAllister are pouring over maps of that area to find a potential hide out."

"Don't give up my friend," Li Na said. "We will find them. They are running out of places to hide."

"I hope you're right," Genesis said, cell ringing. "Excuse me, I have to take this."

"Yes sir," Genesis said.

"How are things going?" Jonas asked.

"We thought we had it wrapped up, but they outmaneuvered us again," Genesis said.

"Alright," Jonas replied. "I won't be able to cover the team much longer. As you know it is listed as a training exercise. Some outsiders are getting nosey. What do I tell them?"

"Tell them we are providing technical assistance with our surveillance systems to the FBI and MDPD on a kidnapping case they're working."

"Outstanding," Jonas said. "There may be a problem given the shootout I heard about."

"Tell them we were only used for support," Genesis said. "I'll talk to Phil and Sergeant McAllister to back us up on it."

"Very well," Jonas replied. "Hurry though, you need to be up at the nuclear plant for security drills. Let's wrap this up before I need to pull you off."

"Understood sir," Genesis replied, hanging up. "When it rains it pours."

"What was that all about?" Li Na asked.

"My boss is giving us little time to wrap this up and then will pull us off."

"We better hurry then," Li Na said, grinning.

Morgan's phone was ringing. He was almost to Port St. Lucie and pulled off to a gas station, the wipers clearing his windshield from the steady rain.

"Ki just informed me the plant is going to be conducting security drill and protocols in two days," Cilatro said. "We need to move at once. How soon can he plant the countermand device?"

"The engineer said its ready when we say go," Morgan replied.

"We cannot afford to wait any longer," Cilatro said. "Use the storm as cover. Go!"

"Yes sir," Morgan replied. "It will be today."

Morgan was wondering why there was suddenly going to be a security protocol check and drill. How the hell did Ki find out? He's on the other side of the world. No matter, there was no time to waste.

"Fred Clubine."

"How are you friend?" Morgan asked.

"Having a great day so far," Fred said. "How about yourself?"

"I can't complain," Morgan said. "Say, do you remember that remodel project we discussed recently?"

"Certainly," Fred said. "I was wondering when you wanted to get started?"

"This afternoon or early evening," Morgan said. "Would that

work? I could use the extra money. My boss won't like me moonlighting but need to pay the bills somehow."

"We can begin anytime," Fred replied. "Everything is ready."

"Very well," Morgan said. "Let's shoot for early evening, when you are off work, about 6:00 pm."

"Okay," Fred responded. "I'll look forward to it."

Morgan knew they needed to be careful. This Clubine was smart. He knew better than to implicate himself or insinuate any kind of plan on the phone. If someone was listening in, they would have heard a conversation about starting a remodeling project, nothing more. And there would have been insufficient time to trace the call. It would be a few hours before Fred initiated the operation. His guess was the device was already planted and simply needed to be activated. He kept thinking about how Ki had found out about the security protocols because those activities were highly classified. If he knew that, he knew a great deal more about Cilatro, himself, and their organization. The only way to know such things was to have an insider and that insider had to be in senior management level in DC — senior executive service as it was called among the federal agencies. He would worry about it later. Right now, he needed to prepare. Having chosen an out of the way location to meet, he slowly made his way to it. The day was turning out to be a rotten one as the deluge of rain continued. He pulled his car into the parking lot behind the bowling alley and billiards club west of U.S. Highway 1, just off Southeast Harper Street. There were few cars in the lot as he chose a space near the back to park.

Once he arrived, he opened his trunk. The small aluminum suitcase inside contained $500,000 in mixed bills along with a burner phone and two new passports for Fred. One from Chile and another from Brazil. His new name was Frederique Castillo. It was what he had requested. Morgan surmised that he must speak both Spanish and Portuguese. To sweeten the deal, there was an additional $100,000. If Fred decided to go back on it, they would be able to track him, and he would meet an early demise. Having no family or living relatives, which was why he had been chosen, there was little likelihood of that; he would remain on their payroll for his expertise. This wasn't the only plant they intended to sabotage. Assured everything was ready, Morgan had noticed a small Italian-Greek restaurant when he had turned onto Harper, so he walked over and ordered some takeout, rain dripping from the brim of his Fedora, cascading onto his raincoat. He would be careful not to look above one hundred degrees with his hat brim. It would keep the restaurant staff and any cameras from identifying him. About twenty minutes later he was back at the car, the rain cascading down his windshield in sheets. At least the car was cool. There wasn't much sun in the sunshine state today. He threw his hat and raincoat into the back seat as he climbed in the front. He was glad for the coolness; it reminded him of New Jersey. As he slowly chewed his food, he glanced at his watch, then pulled out a cigarette. It would be a while.

The sun had been replaced with ominous clouds threatening rain at any moment. The high humidity caused the group to sweat from every pore. The three swat teams were felt certain they would be able to find the hostages before dark. Replacements for the wounded had arrived and Billie had come out to join them in the search, hoping he could be of assistance.

"Damn the humidity!" Genesis exclaimed. His phone began ringing, his frustration making it apparent he didn't want to answer it.

"You gonna get that?" Billie asked.

"What?" Genesis asked, almost screaming.

"This is Robbie. Did I call at a bad time?"

"No, just a frustrating day," Genesis said. "How can I help you?"

"Well, I don't want to frustrate you more, but do you know

that bar pit out near the West Boundary Road and the Adventure Hunting Trail?"

"Yes," Genesis said. "That's where we do a lot of hog hunting. What about it?"

"I just wanted you to know that something seems odd," Robbie said. "This morning a helicopter flew over the area."

"Hold on Robbie, I want to put you on speaker phone, if that's okay?"

"Sure."

Genesis motioned with his arms for Phil, Sergeant McAllister, and the others to gather around. They realized something was up and listened intently. Billie had opened a map of the area. "Go ahead Robbie."

"As I was saying, this morning a helicopter flew over the place. I had noticed it once before a few days ago. Then, a couple of hours later, Joshua, the troublemaker called and told me he saw several pickup trucks with about twenty to thirty men in them, all armed. At first, he thought they were going hog hunting, but then told me that the guns they had didn't seem like hunting rifles. Oh, and he also said the men looked foreign."

"I will check it out," Genesis said. "Thank you so much for the information. Tell Joshua thanks for me."

"Billie, show the Sergeant Striker the map and tell him to get all the drones over there now. Land one and refuel but keep the others up until the third one is on site."

"What do you think?" McAllister asked.

"That area is right on the edge of the reservation," Genesis said. "It's a favorite hog hunting area and usually has a few hunters wandering around. I really think we got lucky."

"It has to be them," Phil said. "We should move shop closer."

"Agreed," McAllister said. "Ochopee Fire Control District has a station at the Collier County rest area. That's only a few miles up the road."

"You're right," Genesis said. "Also, the Florida Trail leads from there and we can get the vehicles to the target from that area."

"Load up," Phil yelled. "We're heading out. Quickly, quickly."

Within thirty minutes, the vehicles were heading west down Alligator Alley. They were perhaps a dozen miles away from the next set up area. With several hours of daylight left, they wanted to make the most of it. Li Na and Billie were in his SUV, close behind them.

"We need to rescue James," Billie said. "We cannot miss another opportunity."

"Tell me more about the transparency," Li Na said. "I find it quite fascinating."

"What the President did was wrong," Billie said. "We are best suited to use it when we know the location of our interests."

"Like now?" Li Na asked.

"Yes," Billie said, surprised she knew so much about the transparency. "Because we know the location, I can go in and have a look," Billie said. "If James and Cilatro's daughter are there, I can pinpoint their exact location."

"So how does it work basically?" Li Na asked.

"My spirit can leave my body and I can do good things with it," Billie said. "I will not tell you how I can do that, only that the basic premise is to help others."

"Can you also do bad things?" Li Na asked.

"Yes," Billie said. "But thwarting the power of the Great Spirit is not something anyone in their right mind would want to do."

"Can you find other objects around the location?" Li Na asked.

"You mean like vehicles or helicopters?" Billie asked. "Yes, I can circle the area very quickly and give details of all I see."

"How quickly?" Li Na asked.

"The speed of thought," Billie replied, watching her reaction.

"What power," she thought, looking out the window as they reached their destination.

The sky grew darker. Although the tropical storm was

supposed to make landfall around the Orlando area, it seemed to be more widespread than the news had portrayed. There would be rain. That was a certainty.

Ting had all his men in place. There were only a few hours left before the deadline. Whether Cilatro agreed to the twelve percent demand he had given him or not was moot. They could find an inroad into the power industry without him and create their own opportunity. He positioned his men around the area in a way to cover every potential approach. Two men were inside guarding the hostages which were in a large RV trailer in the middle of the open area in front of the bar pit. The open area was about one hundred yards wide tapering to a narrow point on the west end. It would be almost impossible for anyone to approach without being seen. If things went badly, his pilot was waiting at the helicopter about one-quarter mile away. All he had to do was wait. He had felt a strange feeling all day, since arriving with his men by truck. He decided he would not wait for time to run out. Cilatro was stalling, he could feel it. Ting would kill the hostages and fly away before they could be found. It was better to be alive than dead.

The tri-agency law enforcement group pulled to the far northeast corner of the parking lot that provided vehicle access to the Florida Trail. Striker had re-tasked the drones and was monitoring the location. As soon as they pulled up, he deployed Dragon 3 and returned Dragon 1 to base. His GPS coordinates listed him as being 7.23 miles from target. Dragon 1 would slowly gain height and arrive on scene in about 10 minutes. Fortunately, Dragon 2 had about an hour of fuel remaining. As each drone returned, it would immediately be refueled, inspected, and put on standby. Odd Striker thought about the term refueling; all they did was replace the two large batteries in each drone when it returned.

James Tindall

"Sir," Striker said. "The drones are on site. You may want to look at this."

The three leaders gathered around the monitor as well as Alpha, Bravo, and Charlie team leads.

"There's a few vehicles here," Striker said as he pointed out personnel and equipment. "As you can see, the men are scattered all over."

"That's going to make it difficult to approach," Bravo team leader said.

"I agree," Phil replied. "What do you two think?"

"I suggest we use a frontal assault," McAllister said.

"Agreed," Genesis replied. "We will need to make sure they don't flank us. But we also need to get to the hostages first."

"They have that trailer pretty well surrounded," Phil said. "Do you think that is where they are?"

"I'm not sure," Genesis replied. "But I know who can find out, as well as pinpoint all the men."

"Who?" McAllister asked. "And how the hell would he or she do that?"

"It's called the transparency," Genesis said. "It's Billie. He can map out all the positions for us, including the location of the hostages."

"How can we help?" Phil asked.

"All I need is for you to stay out of my way and protect my body while I'm out of it," Billie said, walking up to them.

"Genesis will help prepare the ceremony, which will take a few minutes," Billie said. "The men may watch. Phil and Sergeant McAllister can help Genesis."

They both nodded affirmatively.

Genesis was eager to see the ceremony that Billie talked to him so much about. It wasn't the first time he had witnessed the departure of the spirit from the body. None-the-less, it would prove very intriguing. There wasn't a lot of wood available for the two small fires, mostly cattails, dead sawgrass, purple thistle, and Seagrape branches. They laid the branches on top of each other from small to large for each of the two fires. The hint of rain was strong as the clouds grew darker. Satisfied that all was in order, Genesis walked around to the sergeant.

"How is everything?" Genesis asked.

"Dragon 1 is on site," Striker said. "The men are moving around here and there, but all seems quiet."

"Alright, keep your eyes on it. Come get me if you need to."

The three men watched as Billie sat down. He pulled something from inside the small messenger bag draped over his shoulder. They could not determine what it was as Billie grasped the dii potentia root firmly. Genesis lit the fires and carefully tended them for a couple of minutes until he was sure they would burn well.

"What's he going to do?" McAllister asked.

"Watch," Genesis said. "Do not be shocked. All I can say is you're in for a surprise.

Phil was staring intently at Billie as he lay upon the ground. He was so still it was as though he were dead. The men continued watching as Billie lay his right hand on his abdomen and squeezed it tight. Without warning, a golden fiery mist encircled the ground where they stood and gathered around Billie in a circular motion like the top of a hurricane. The eye portion was directly over Billie's chest and stretched skyward like an upside-down vortex. Li Na had walked around the edge of the command vehicles to watch. She gasped as the vortex stretched to what seemed a mile high, penetrating through and clearing the dark clouds in its path. No sooner had it ascended than it immediately came crashing down, in a flash, sending the golden fiery mist outward for a hundred yards in all directions. At once returning to reveal Billie standing before them in spirit form. The golden fiery color changed to an almost black like those of shadows cast by a full moon. Billie's spirit quickly sped away from them in a motion much like a snake crawling, but so fast they could not follow it.

"Damn," Phil whispered. "What the hell did we just see?"

"That was the initiation of the transparency," Genesis said softly. "Very few in the world have seen it."

"Will they detect him?" McAllister asked.

"No!" Genesis exclaimed. "He will appear as a shadow and can move through any obstacle."

"How fast can he move?" Phil asked.

"He can travel as fast as he can think," Genesis said. "The speed of thought."

"So, he'll be back very quickly," McAllister commented.

"It depends on what he finds," Genesis said. "He will stay on site as long as needed to get the layout of all the guards and where the hostages are. I expect maybe ten minutes or more."

"I've seen a lot of strange things in my days," Phil said. "But nothing like this."

While they had been talking, many of the men had slowly encircled behind them, curious about what was happening. The golden fiery mist had encircled them all and for some unexplainable reason, they seemed to feel a peace they had not known before.

Li Na also crept forward slowly, not wanting to interrupt the conversation. Since her family had been killed, she had given little thought to religion or a God, but this phenomenon caused her to think on things she did not want to think about. Genesis noticed the men and was going to ask them to return to their previous positions, but then realized no harm would come from their watching. If they wanted to talk about what they had seen well, it'd just give the tribe more Indian Power. He grinned at the thought. Besides, no one would believe them anyway. They had been waiting about ten minutes and the men were starting to walk away when the dark shadow returned to hover over Billie and slowly transform again to a recognizable shape. All of them could see it was him. The color changed from dark to an orange fire as it shot upward in a beam and then, collapsed as it turned to fiery gold like before. When it hit Billie's body, the mist traveled over them in a wave, turning to a purple-blue flame that cascaded back across the ground to Billie's outstretched body.

A gasp went up from the group as the mist disappeared and Billie sat up. All eyes were on him.

"Is it always like this?" Phil stammered, not daring to ask, but not able to help himself.

"No," Billie said, getting to his feet. "It is different for each person that performs it. Come, we have work to do."

The entire group was filled with shock and awe at what they had seen but also filled with a peace that they would succeed. Sergeant Striker turned the monitor so the group could watch. He had also linked a couple of others; all displayed the same picture. The images were infrared making it easy to see the vehicles scattered about, as well as the location of personnel on site.

"Okay," Billie said, everyone still staring at him instead of the monitors. "You can clearly see the vehicles and men. I counted thirty-three. Some of them are scattered along each side of the clearing as it narrows to the west southwest. They're not showing up on here but take note as I point where each was."

Billie pointed at specific locations around the bar pit where the men were, explaining that they did not seem to be moving about, but stayed in general locations they were likely assigned.

"I also found the helicopter here," Billie said pointing. "It's about four hundred yards away. The hostages are in the south end of this trailer. They have gags on their mouths and their hands are tied. As you can see on the images, there is a guard at each of the two east-side doors. There is also a guard watching videos in the north end of the trailer, just inside the door. That's as complete a description as I can give you without going back."

"That's more than we could have hoped for," Phil said.

James Tindall

"Genesis, McAllister, thoughts please."

"It's clear cut that the hostages are first priority," McAllister said. "Let's devise a plan to extract them before engaging the rest of these people."

"Agreed," Genesis said. "I think it's going to take an entire squad to do so, at least to ensure that we retrieve them alive."

"What we need is a distraction," Phil said.

"I can arrange that," Genesis said. "Let me make a call. Meanwhile let's load up. We'll need to use parking lights so that the glow from our headlights isn't seen."

"Right," McAllister said. "I take it we're going up Florida Trail and turning left on the Adventure Hunting Trail?"

"Yes," Genesis said.

"Alright," Phil said. "We'll head out and stop here, one-quarter mile away, lights out."

"That'll work," Billie said. "The trees and swamp are so thick they won't see you."

"I'll call in the calvary," Genesis said. "Once we reach our quarter mile limit with the vehicles, let's move to within seventy yards short of the trailer in the surrounding undergrowth. We will wait there until the distraction takes place."

310

Chapter 10

The three young men were sitting on their motorcycles at the convenience store on Big Cypress. The SPD had already gotten on them, again, for making noise in the community with their 2-cycle dirt bikes.

"Man, you just can't have fun anymore," Joshua said.

"Yeah, these cops have thorns up their butts," another said.

It was quiet as they sat listening, trying to figure out what they could do to have fun on a Friday night, far from any city. The chirping of crickets, buzzing of mosquitos, and flashing from lightning bugs, known to outsiders as firefly's, was interrupted by a heavy metal tune as Joshua's phone rang.

"Shit," Joshua said sullenly. "It's the head cop. Hello. We're not doing anything, your officers already told us to beat it."

"That's not why I'm calling," Genesis said. "How would you like to help us tonight and have some fun too?"

"If we do, will you cut us some slack?"

"Yes, we'll work a deal."

"Okay," Joshua said. "What do you want us to do."

"Do you know where West Boundary Road meets the Adventure Hunting Trail?"

"Yes," Joshua said. "We ride our bikes there all the time and hunt hogs."

"Good," Genesis said. "This is what I need you to do."

F red had set the countermand device and hadn't been gone from the plant long when he received an emergency phone call.

"Hi Joe," Fred said. "What's going on. I thought you would have left by now."

"The plant is overheating," Joe said. "Get back here right away."

"Holy hell," Fred said as he made a U-turn and headed back. "Pull out the checklist and let's go through it."

"I did," Joe said.

"Then, let's do it again," Fred demanded.

As they went through the list, Fred knew that everything would check out. When he pulled up to the gate, security was already advised of the emergency and waved him through. He hit the ground running, to thwart any attention from himself.

"Did you find anything?" Fred asked.

"No," Joe said. "All the controls appear to be functioning within specs. It's odd. There has to be something we overlooked."

"Alright," Fred said. "Let's follow procedure. Begin shutdown. Everyone get their hazmat suits just in case. Let me get my pack out of the trunk. You take the south side, I'll take the central, and have Paul take the north. Let's do a manual check on all the potentially affected valves in the system. Have the emergency group begin checking their areas of responsibility"

"Roger that," Joe said.

"If the temperature keeps rising at the current pace, we only have about forty minutes before reaching the initial critical level," Paul said. "We need to shut it down now."

Fred and Joe looked at each other. They knew Paul was correct, but neither wanted the responsibility. "Damn it!" Fred exclaimed. "Shut it down now."

The control crew initiated shut down of the nuclear plant, visions of what happened in Chernobyl and the Japanese tsunami in their heads.

The three senior engineers began walking the various portions of the plant in the pouring rain, wishing they were somewhere else. Emergency personnel were also in place. Making sure he was out of visual range of the security cameras and Joe, as well as Paul, Fred removed the countermand device and put it in his pack. It only took a couple of minutes. The rain obscured him from potentially prying eyes and would cover his tracks, a blessing in disguise.

Looking about and proceeding to check the components that were his part of the system, he slowly worked around until he was sure he would run into the other two engineers. Just when he reached them, the corroded water valve erupted, sending steam everywhere. The water condensing from it, short circuited many of the doors and equipment trapping emergency personnel on the wrong side.

"What a mess," Paul said, rain pouring down his face. "It looks like one of the main water valves failed. Our men are trapped on the inside."

"I that's where the problem was," Fred said. Shouldn't take long to fix once daylight comes."

"Won't matter by then," Joe said. "You know protocol. They'll tear this place apart and your head will be first on the block."

"Well," Fred said. "I'm surprised we made it this long."

"It's been nice knowing you," Paul said. "Guess you'll be the proverbial scapegoat."

"I'm gonna miss you buddy," Joe said.

"Hey, don't be so glum," Fred grinned. "It happens. There are lots of fish out there to catch. My retirement won't come through, but my boat is already paid for."

The three men laughed.

Paul was next in line and would assume Fred's position. It was just politics. They never suspected that Fred had arranged the whole thing and with the device gone, it would be attributed to a faulty valve, which would be replaced in a maintenance check to ensure all was working properly.

"Well, let's manually open the doors and let the men out and wait until daylight," Joe said.

After a couple of hours, the crises appeared over; Fred drove to the rendezvous point to meet Morgan.

"About damn time," Morgan said, as Fred climbed out of his car.

"I told you it would take a while," Fred said. "Actually, it went better than I expected. The pipe I told you about blew. Looks like a total accident.

"Great, do you have the device?" Morgan asked.

"It's in my trunk under the spare tire cover," Fred replied. "Do you have my money and ID?"

"Yes," Morgan said. "It's here."

He put the suitcase on the trunk, holding an umbrella while Fred opened it, checking the ID's and then, counting the money.

"Hey," Fred said, excitedly. "There's much more than we agreed on."

"That's because we want you to be happy with our business and because we will need your skills again," Morgan said. "Show me the device and how to operate it."

Fred opened the trunk of his car, pulled out the hazmat suit and removed the spare tire cover, pulling out the device. He explained its workings and handed Morgan a sheet of instructions in case he forgot, along with an electronic controller.

"What's this?" Morgan asked.

"Once you place the device, you can use that to activate it from a distance. Think of it like a TV remote," Fred said. "No trace will be left behind once you remove the device."

"Great," Morgan said. "Better than I expected. Give me your phone please."

"Why?" Fred asked, handing it over. He watched as Morgan stomped it to pieces on the asphalt.

"No one will be able to track you now," Morgan said. "Use the burner phone in the suitcase so we can contact you. "Get another burner phone when you get where you're going. You better head out. The pilot is waiting for you at Witham Field. Here's his number, passing a piece of paper. Another number is also on the paper. If you need anything, we can help. Stay low and don't blow all the money. If you arouse suspicion well, I don't need to tell you."

"Thank you," Fred said. "I don't believe I got your name."

"It's not important," Morgan said. "Call me Carl if you need to. Time to go."

Morgan watched him as he drove away. He was happy to get the money and a new life. He pulled out his cell.

"It's done," Morgan said.

"The engineer?"

"On his way; available when we need him. The pilot will call when they are airborne."

"Excellent," Cilatro said. "I'll let Ki know and we'll ramp up at the power plant. Are we clear?"

"Yes," Morgan said. "There's no trace of what happened. I have the device. Fred showed me how it works. He's excited about the potential extra money in a place that's so cheap to live."

"Very well," Cilatro said. "Call Li Na. They're about to move in. Keep me posted."

It was so dark you couldn't see your hand in front of your face as the three young men sped down West Boundary Road, kicking up dust with their lights on, yelling and screaming. The three bikes were loud and could be heard from a great distance in the still night air. Joshua was following Genesis's instructions to the letter. Wearing headlamps atop their caps, they pretended to be fire hunting as they shot across the woods. They were having the time of their life. Joshua wondered why they hadn't thought about this before.

Occasionally, they would jump a log or mound of dirt, their bikes sailing through the air, the bright glow of the headlights illuminating the swamp and night sky for hundreds of yards. Genesis had been adamant about the stopping point and promised them not to be so harsh from now on if they cooperated. Another quarter mile and they would be there. The turnaround point. As they twisted and turned, they shot at tree trunks yelling gleefully when they hit one. The young boys took their time, tracing figure eights with their back tires in the dirt road, kicking up clouds of dust while they sped on. The closer they got to the point Genesis had told them to stop, the more daring they became, jumping larger logs and skirting around trees off the road, screaming, shooting, and gunning their motors. The stopping point was about three hundred yards from the bar pit.

Ting and his men heard the commotion. They had been listening to it for a while as the sounds grew nearer. About a dozen men were standing by the road, looking toward the lights that shot beams through the dark night. They could hear sporadic gunfire and then, screams of fun as the three bikers closed the distance.

"Go check it out," Ting said.

A few more men gathered near the road. Ting walked over to the trailer to make sure the hostages were secured.

"If we come under attack, kill them both," he said, motioning to the hostages, turning when he heard one of his men running up, panting heavily.

"What is it?" Ting asked.

"It looks like three motorcycles," the man said. "I'm guessing they are teenagers out for fun. Looks like they have stopped where they are for now. They're just yelling and spinning circles in the dirt."

"Keep an eye on them," Ting said. "I'll go check the others. Have the men ready just in case."

Ting knew from experience that if an assault came it would

be without warning and bloody. He walked around checking his men, getting further away from the bar pit. There was an uneasy feeling in the pit of his stomach. After he checked the last one, he found the small trail that led through the woods to the helicopter.

"The distraction has gone as far as it can," Genesis spoke into his comm.

"Move in," Phil commanded.

Genesis called Joshua. "Return to the community. You did great."

The three teams had already positioned themselves in their respective quadrants while the retreating motorcycles held the attention of the men at the pit. As soon as the order was given, they began to move forward. Genesis's team would attack the trailer and free the hostages two minutes before the other two teams moved. Looking around, he saw no sign of Li Na. Maybe she had stayed behind. Quickly reaching their objective, the situation looked like it had not changed. There were no personnel in sight at the back side of the trailer. By the front were the two guards, one at each of the two doors on opposite ends.

Genesis motioned to his men, holding up one finger to go in one minute. He crept around the back of the trailer and then around to the front corner. Knowing he had to catch the guard by surprise, he found a small rock. About to throw, the rain began pouring. The guard jumped to his feet, peering upward as he put his hand above his eyes to maintain his view. Genesis immediately charged, kneeing the man in the groin as he slammed his left forearm beneath the man's chin in a long glancing upward strike, which shot the man's head up and to the left. At once, Genesis struck the man on the right side of the neck below the occipital bone with a right inward hand sword. He crumpled to the earth, out cold. Another team member took out the other guard at the same time. The sounds of the assault were obscured by the falling rain as three of his mean lined up at each door. The first agent slipped his special operations hallagan tool beneath the rib of the door. Genesis gave the signal and both doors were popped open. The second agent threw in a flash bang through the front door. The team poured into the trailer. The men entering the back door grabbed the two hostages and drug them out before they could get on their feet. The guard at the front was leveling his pistol at them when the first agent entering the door drilled him with two shots to center mass from his 9mm suppressed pistol. Half of Charlie squad escorted the two hostages back to the vehicles. "Hostages safe," Genesis spoke into the comm. "Advance."

The members of the other teams moved forward and were immediately noticed, despite the rain. All hell broke loose as bullets started flying, hitting the trailer, dirt, trees, and vehicles. Ting's men were better prepared than the team leaders had expected. Every man was armed with multiple smoke grenades and began throwing them in all directions. The entire area around the bar pit and surrounding trees was filled with thick smoke that blanketed the area to head height above the now muddy ground. The sounds of gunfire continued. Suddenly, there were what appeared to be yelps, Indian war cries.

One of Alpha teams' members gun had jammed. He was trying to clear it when an assailant emerged from the smoke, leveling his carbine at his head. The officer's eyes opened wide in horror when at once there was a yelp and the man's throat was cut so deep that his head almost separated from his body. The officer stared incredulously at the man as he fell then, noticed the warrior behind him who nodded slightly, disappearing into the smoke. The gunfire continued along with the yelping. The smoke hung, stagnant like a bad horror film. Almost as quickly as it had started, the rain stopped, moonbeams casting their rays through the breaking clouds.

Phil had moved his team slowly forward through the open

field and edge of the trees. He met resistance every step of the way. He was talking through his comm to his men trying to get them to flank the positions ahead. Moving around a tree, a bullet thudded next to his ear; pain shot down his right side. Rotating in a rapid twirling motion by corkscrewing his legs down toward the ground and reducing his height, he swung his M5 toward the direction of his opponent. Before he could complete the turn, he saw the warrior, the blade glimmering from the scant moonlight penetrating the scattered clouds, rain drops on the tree leaves glistening like diamonds. The cut severed the neck and arteries, blood gushing in a pumping motion. The thug was dead before his body hit the ground. "Move ahead slowly lawman."

It was then Phil noticed that, again, the Medicine Man had saved his life. He did as instructed communicating with his men to do the same. The assault continued as Ting's men dug in, throwing more smoke grenades to keep the smoke cover as long as they could. They were trying to get to the tree line and escape on foot. There were more of Ting's men than there was law enforcement. Taking any of them alive no longer appeared to be an option.

Li Na had slipped away when the teams began their assault. She knew that Ting would not stay because he had no backup. She circled the bar pit and was on the other side when gunfire interrupted the stillness of the night. Dressed in black, she was armed with both a pistol and Wakizashi, a short sword with an eighteen-inch razor sharp blade. It was so dark that she kept getting slapped in the face with wet branches and Spanish Moss hanging from the limbs. She knew she was close to the helicopter when she heard a metal clank a few yards away. There was just enough moonlight now to see a small meadow ahead of her. She ran at a dead run to the edge, the rain softened earth masking the sounds of her movement. The pilot had started the engine; the blades began turning.

Ting at once appeared from the shadow of a tree and

headed to the chopper, looking furtively about. Li Na engaged him before could reach the door. Noticing her at the last second, he spun raising his pistol. She swung downward with the sword, cutting off his thumb; the pistol dropped to the ground. He swung with his left hand, hitting her on the right cheek knocking her backward.

"Damn the darkness," she thought.

She recovered and came back at him with a right roundhouse kick, which missed. Ting retaliated with a stomping kick to her chest, knocking the wind out of her as she sailed backward landing on her ass. She attempted to land a kick as she fell back, which grazed his groin just enough to pause his movements as he sunk slightly to the ground. He raced to the rear door of the helicopter and was almost inside when the short sword penetrated between his left ribs and emerged from the center of his chest. He knew he was finished, blood dripping from the corners of his mouth, gushing into the cabin from the wound to his chest.

"You will be a traitor to Ki no longer," Li Na whispered into his ear, pushing him forward.

The pilot in horror, began drawing his pistol.

"Drop it," Li Na screamed over the full turning of the blades. She climbed up in the seat beside him.

"Turn your spotlight on and head to the pit."

The pilot did as commanded and within a couple of minutes they were landing in the clearing beside the trailer, illuminating the scene with the spotlight. The other vehicles had arrived, as well as multiple vehicles from SPD. The entire area was lit like noon day. Several members of the tactical teams cautiously approached the helicopter as the engine died and the blades stopped whirring.

"Don't shoot," Li Na yelled as she held her hands out. Phil and Sergeant McAllister ordered their men to lower their weapons as they got the pilot out, put on handcuffs, and led him away. Genesis walked up with a smile on his face.

"Somehow I knew you'd find him," Genesis said.

"How did you know he would go for the chopper?" Phil asked.

"It's who he is," Li Na said. "He had no other options if we moved in. He was just hoping Cilatro would cave. He had no loyalties other than to his money."

Sergeant McAllister had his men drag Ting from the helicopter to place alongside the others. He was inspecting the body.

"You killed him with a knife?" McAllister queried, surprised.

"Not exactly," Li Na replied. "With this."

She had retrieved the short sword from beside the seat and pulled it from the scabbard, slicing it through the air as it made a singing sound and then, re-sheathed it in one fluid motion."

"Damn!" McAllister exclaimed. "I hope I never piss you off."

The men smiled as they began issuing orders to rope off the area and headed toward the command vehicles.

"I'll have Seminole PD keep watch; we can finish everything when it's daylight," Genesis said.

"So, you got the hostages out alive?" McAllister asked.

"Yes," Genesis said. "Thanks to your men. They are being treated by medical right now and debriefed."

"That's great," Phil said. "It looks like we finally solved the case and caught the bad guys, at least the ones here. Genesis, I want you to thank the Medicine Man and his warriors for me. He saved my life for the second time today. I don't know how to repay him."

"That goes for me too," McAllister said. "I was a dead man until one of your warriors saved my ass. I would love to repay him."

"You can repay him by giving him your respect and trust," Genesis said. "Those are of greatest value to him, more than money or fame. Perhaps one day he will need your help."

"He shall have it," Phil stated.

The group fell silent as they walked through the swamp and trees to the command vehicles, which were now surrounded by generators and lights as medical treated the wounded. Miraculously, none of the men had been killed but ten of them were seriously wounded.

"How many men did we capture?" Genesis asked.

"None," McAllister replied. "We found eighteen dead and may find more at first light but looks like about as many got away."

"It will be difficult to find them," Phil said.

"Perhaps, but we shall try," McAllister replied.

Medics were working on the wounded team members. The area was buzzing with activity. FPF had packed up it drones and were tidying up the command vehicle.

"A call for you sir," Striker said, handing the phone over.

"Hello," Genesis said.

"Get to Port St. Lucie nuclear plant immediately," Jonas said. "There's been an incident. You'll be filled in on the way."

"Yes sir," Genesis said. "Just wrapped up here, successfully. We'll leave at once. It will take us about two hours."

"Phil and Sergeant McAllister," Genesis said, shaking hands. "It's been a pleasure. Duty calls. Let me know if you need anything."

"What's up?" McAllister asked.

"Trouble at the Port St. Lucie nuclear plant. Got to run. Men, mount up."

Within seconds, all that could be seen of the FPF force was the taillights of their vehicles. Billie had been standing next to his son as the medics checked him out while one of the officers debriefed him on what he had been through. Phil and Sergeant McAllister walked up while they were finished.

"I wanted to ask Genesis, but he left before I could," Billie said. "Is it okay if I take James home?"

"Certainly," Phil said. "He's been debriefed and appears okay. If we need anything, we'll call you."

"Thank you."

"Also, we told Genesis," McAllister said. "The Medicine Man

saved both our lives and I'm sure many of our men. Please thank him for us. It's been an honor sir."

The three shook hands as Billie led James away and drove off. Li Na was talking to Dianna and made a brief phone call. "Do you mind if I escort Dianna to her father?" Li Na asked. "Go ahead," Phil said. "I'm sure that he's anxious to see her. We'll be in contact if we need anything else."

The sun was cresting the tops of the cypress when Billie's truck pulled up into the yard at the camp. Christina was running out the door, grabbed James and hugged him so tight that Billie was afraid she would suffocate him. Mabel and Dakotah were walking quickly behind her.

"Welcome home son," Christina said. "Look who's here. Its your grandma and grandpa."

"It's nice to finally meet you James," Dakotah said. "I've been a stranger from afar, but now I'll be close by. How would you like to go fishing?"

"You bet, that's my favorite thing to do," James said. It was as if the ordeal he had suffered was already behind him. But, that's kids, they bounce back quickly from the greatest hardships.

"Let's eat first," Dakotah said. "We've got a surprise for you." Mabel and Dakotah walked to the door, each holding one of the boys' hands. James looked over his shoulder.

"Mom and dad, come on."

Billie was smiling at Christina as they walked arm in arm into the house, tears of joy running down their faces. On the table was James's favorite breakfast, pancakes and sausage links. It was good to be together again as a family. Smiling and talking excitedly as they ate, the fear of losing him was past.

The cigarette boat raced across the water at breakneck speed toward the yacht on the horizon. Aboard was Li Na, Morgan, and Dianna. Don Cilatro was standing on the foredeck, watching the boat approach through binoculars. Mist flying over the bow as the boat crested the wave tops. When his daughter climbed aboard with help from the crew, he pulled her off her feet in a bear hug, his eyes glistening.

"It's good to have you back Dianna," Cilatro said. "Is there anything you want?"

"Could I just take a hot shower and go to bed?" Dianna asked.

"Absolutely," Cilatro replied. "Whatever you wish. Frank and Kelly will take you to your stateroom."

The two men led her away, smiling and chatting excitedly with their arms on her shoulders. It had been a trial but was over; she was glad to be among friends.

"Come with me," Cilatro said.

They walked into the lounge and bar area and closed the doors, making sure everyone was out.

"I doubt Morgan had a chance to fill you in Li Na," Cilatro said. "We decided to move forward with the operation."

"Ah, the incident Genesis was called back to," Li Na said. "So, the shut down is happening, what's next?"

"Not only the Port St. Lucie plant," Morgan said. "Two other plants were also knocked out by the storm."

"Better than we expected," Li Na said.

"Dianna doesn't know anything about it yet and she won't know of our involvement," Cilatro said. "I'll get her to brush up the figures on our new energy cost per kWh and pass it along. We will have a meeting with the local press and announce we're there to help."

"Are you sure we cannot be tracked?" Li Na asked.

"Everything has been taken care of," Morgan assured her. "The engineer is already in South America, and I have hidden the device where it will not be found. We just need to stick to the plan."

"Excellent," Li Na said. "I will inform Ki. He will be most pleased."

"I need to ask you something," Cilatro said. "Kidnapping

Dianna and the boy was a triad operation; how do we know it won't happen again?"

"We are taking care of that," Li Na said. "It will not. However, I suggest when you travel and stay in a hotel to keep men on either side of you or your daughter's room, as well as a guard at all three of the room doors. That will stop what happened before from occurring again. As for the triads involved, that issue will be dealt with shortly. Do not worry about them."

Li Na had departed; Dianna was asleep. Cilatro wanted to cement the trust between the partners and the tribe. He walked over to his phone on the table and called.

"Billie," Cilatro said. "I'm glad your son is home safe."

"It's a big relief," Billie said. "Thank you."

"No," Cilatro replied. "Thank you for all of your help and thank Genesis for me. I'm so happy and relieved to have Dianna back. It would not have happened without you."

"Thank you,' Don Cilatro. "But it is Genesis and Li Na who deserve the credit."

"And the transparency," Cilatro replied.

The FPF team arrived at the nuclear plant finding it thriving with activity. They were admitted through the gate. Genesis deployed his men to look for anything suspicious and to make sure security protocols were functioning as mandated by policy then, he went looking for the head engineer.

"You must be Genesis," Paul said. "The director told us to expect you and your men. How can I be of assistance?"

"You can tell me what happened for a start," Genesis replied.

Paul described all that had happened the previous day and night, filling in every detail and answering questions.

"I was informed the head engineer was Fred Clubine," Genesis said. "Where is he?"

"Unknown," Paul said. "I'm in charge when he is not here. We have tried contacting him and even sent an employee over to his house. We haven't been able to find him."

"That seems strange given this emergency situation," Genesis said.

"Yes, it is," Paul replied. "However, given politics it's not."

"What do you mean?" Genesis asked.

"Whenever something of this magnitude happens, there is a long-drawn-out process of investigation," Paul said. "In the end, the head engineer, accident or not, becomes the scapegoat and is fired."

"So, you think he just took off to avoid the investigation?" Genesis queried.

"If you were going to face hundreds of questions in front of a DOE and likely congressional panel, as well as the press, knowing in the end you would still be fired, what would you do?"

"Hmmmm," Genesis mused. "Not sure I wouldn't just leave and disappear."

"Exactly."

"How serious is this situation?" Genesis asked.

"It could be damn serious if we let the temperature increase without shutting it down," Paul replied. "Our other main engineer, Joe, is checking valves and systems with the inspection team right now for the third time. It will take a week or more to determine what happened. We're almost certain it was a water valve malfunction, but it didn't show up on our system check so we need to check the primary valves one by one. We also found a corroded pipe to a water valve that ruptured. Looks like it was due to age and corrosion."

"What happens until you're done?"

"The plant stays shut down," Paul said. "It could be a week, a month, or even more. The investigation team will determine that."

"How will they provide power to their customers?" Genesis asked.

"They will need to buy it from other suppliers on the grid," Paul said. "That should bode well for your tribe."

"What do you mean?"

"Since they are operational and close by, our power company will buy as much energy as they will sell."

"Interesting," Genesis responded. "Alright, let me know if you find a smoking gun. Until then, my team will ensure all security protocols are in place and functioning. I had better call the director."

"Sir," Genesis said, walking off. "We're onsite and I've spoken with the acting head engineer who tells me the incident may have been caused by a faulty water valve. They are checking their systems now and will let me know what they find. It'll all be in their report."

"Did the incident seem reasonable?" Jonas asked.

"Yes sir. The explanation is plausible, but something did seem odd. The head engineer is missing."

"That would be Fred Clubine," Jonas said. "I've met him a couple of times, seems like a smart fellow."

"Well, it looks like he just up and disappeared."

"Genesis," Jonas said. "Listen to me. Not all men have your honor. He was in charge, and he will become the scapegoat. Given the last few incidents of this type, I would run if I were him."

"Is it really that bad?" Genesis asked.

"Worse. Welcome to the world of politics and power, electric power. Keep me apprised."

Local press had gathered at tribal headquarters, along with the partners of the power plant. The President was behind the podium and had been briefed on what was happening. The press, impatient, began to clamor as he stepped behind the microphone. He waved his hands, motioning for them to be seated. The room fell silent.

"Ladies and gentlemen of the press," the President said. "We have been made aware of the shut down of Port St. Lucie nuclear plant and failure of two others. I will tell you what we know and what we are doing with our own power plant. First, the power companies from the three plants have contacted us, asking for additional power. I will not divulge how much or what the agreed price is. Second, we will continue to serve our own customers. I'll take questions, but please, one at a time."

"Mr. President," a reporter asked. "It's been suggested this was a sabotage of the plants so that other companies could make money from it. Do you believe that to be true?"

"Certainly not. It appears to be a valve malfunction from what we have been told and should be repaired soon. A thorough system check is underway. The other plants appeared to suffer powerful lightning strikes."

"Mr. President," another reporter began. "How do you see this affecting your customers and the price of power to them?"

"As you have read in our policy statement, the price of power will remain unchanged to our customers even as we provide as much electricity to the other power companies as we can."

"Mr. President, is it true that you are planning a second phase of your power plant, doubling the current availability of electricity?" another reporter asked.

"Correct. That was suggested when the plans and agreements were first signed and has been a primary objective as stated on our website. It is not a secret."

"Why is the tribe and its partners pursuing this path?" yet another reporter asked.

"I would think it rather obvious," the President said. "Every week more than one thousand people move into Dade and Broward counties. Recently, we were told to prepare for one thousand migrants each month that will be sent to our counties from the U.S./Mexico border to alleviate a surge of immigrants there, and more than 33,000 people have just moved here from New York, due to the recent pandemic. Our state is beginning to burst at the seams from streams of new residents. And if we do not want to end up in a severe water and power shortage like California, with rolling blackouts for both, we must act now. That is why the Tribe, and its partners are pursuing the path we have started."

The sobering facts that the President had presented caused the room to fall silent for a moment as the reporters feverishly took notes. They were ready to ask another barrage of questions.

"Look, that's enough from me. If you have more questions, please direct them to our press secretary. That is all."

He walked away from the podium and out the door. Both Morgan and Li Na congratulated him.

"That was awesome," Morgan said. "Thank you. Now that we have James and Dianna back, we can move forward with the projects at breakneck speed."

"Well done," Li Na said. "I agree with Morgan. You make a great politician. I'll be in touch."

He watched the two walk away, a smile on his face. Yes, he had done a great job. More importantly, what he had said about the need for power and water due to population growth in the area was true. The news media would vet the information and for once, tell the truth about something. They were all in the clear; his life would return to normal, at least politically. With the safe return of the hostages, a great weight had been lifted from his shoulders and a feeling of calm settled over him.

A satellite phone began ringing on the mega yacht moored in Hong Kong harbor. More than a dozen guards armed with automatic weapons strode the decks.

"Yes," the voice said.

"We have collected the data you required," the man answered.

"So, the tribe and other triad have no idea why the girl was kidnapped?"

"None. From listening in, they remain stymied. We have all contacts and continue to link the network."

"Good, we are ready to proceed. I will inform our man in

Beijing. Come in; we will finalize our strategy."

Genesis had finished his duties at the plant and left his men to wrap up, driving to Hollywood from his visit with Billie and Christina who had thanked him for rescuing James and how dear he was to them. He mulled over the discussion he and Billie had.

"I've been meaning to talk to you about something," Billie said.

"What's that?" Genesis asked.

"I had a phone call before," Billie replied. "The caller said that I had cost them a great deal of money due to the landfill. I passed it off but got another call this morning."

"What did the caller want?" Genesis asked.

"The voice seemed computer generated but said that I was not out of the woods. That I owed the money and the episode with James was only the beginning."

Genesis stared at Billie for a moment, his mind racing, wondering if what had happened with the hostages was not over.

"Let me give this some thought my brother," Genesis said. "It seems suspicious and is something I will definitely look into. Give me a couple of days to catch up on paperwork and we will talk."

"I appreciate it," Billie said. "Is there anything I should do until then?"

"Do not tell Christina and keep an eye on James," Genesis said. "If this is a continuing saga, we need to keep him safe."

"I understand."

Genesis had shaken hands and climbed into his cruiser. What Billie had said was puzzling. "What was the connection?" he wondered. He was just pulling onto Alligator Alley when his phone rang.

"Hello Genesis," Li Na said. "Do you have time for lunch? I'll be returning to Hong Kong and even though I'll be coming back, I wanted to say goodbye before I left."

"Lunch sounds great," Genesis replied. "Where?"

"What about that restaurant surrounded by palms off A1A?" Li Na queried.

"Yes," I know the one. I'll see you in a little while.

Genesis was excited that she wanted to say goodbye. He had felt an attraction between them, but things had been so busy that he had brushed it off. Nothing may come of it, but it was always pleasant to think of possibilities. His mind was filled with such as he drove to the restaurant and entered. Li Na was sitting at a corner table. "A true security conscious soul," Genesis thought as he made his way to her and pulled back a chair.

"I'm honored you thought of me," Genesis said. "It's not often I cross paths with such a skilled woman warrior. The men are still talking about you."

"I'm flattered," Li Na replied. "I feel the same. You'll have to teach me some things as well. I heard how you took out that guard, most impressive."

"Thank you," Genesis said. "When does your plane leave?"

"About 1:00 am, which is why I wanted to meet," Li Na replied. "I'm not sure how to bring this up."

"Straight out," Genesis said. "Say what you mean, I'm a big boy."

"Well, there are two things," Li Na said. "You likely know that I have a physical attraction, as well as a mental one for you. We are much alike. She watched his expression as she told him, wondering how he would react. His face didn't change, but his eyes were excited then, he smiled slightly.

"And?"

"Besides getting to know you I have a question. I am almost certain I know who killed my family but have not been able to get close enough to them, yet. More importantly, they are the same people who ordered by proxy the death of your fiancé so, would you like to help bring them to justice?"

His eyes narrowed as he thought. She could see the wheels

James Tindall

spinning. Perhaps a struggle within.

"Do you know this for certain?" Genesis asked, whispering, leaning forward.

"I am fairly certain," Li Na said. "It will take additional investigation. The evidence is there. I need more time to make sure. After all, we do not want to go to the police."

"Certainly not," Genesis replied, looking around. "Count me in!"

The two sat and chatted as they ate lunch and then, walked across the street to the beach. Taking their shoes off, they strolled along just outside the reach of the incoming surf breaking on the sand, washing upward, its froth returning from whence it came. They walked along, talking, holding hands. The breeze was behind them, blowing Li Na's hair forward, hiding her face. The impulse was so strong Genesis could no longer resist. He reached out and pulled her close, his arm around her waist as he bent her slightly backward and kissed her deep, igniting the passion within. They kept walking and talking, kissing more often. Somehow, they wound up back in her hotel room and made exquisite love, exploring each other's bodies. The time passed too quickly as they said final goodbyes and Li Na boarded her non-stop flight to Hong Kong. She couldn't keep him out of her mind. Warriors at heart, she knew they would remain close; he was the ally she sought.

For almost a week, the lady dressed in tight black leather pants, white blouse, and black, red-bottom, high heels had enticed the two triad leaders, Peter Chow and Xu Lo. Her body and beauty were enough to make a playboy bunny jealous. Never having been loyal to their wives, she had successfully lured the two leaders to their captor.

It was 2:00 am, rain was falling on the isolated Hong Kong docks. They were empty except for seven figures standing in a semi-circle beneath a lamp, high up on its pole. A perfect circular shadow was cast by the light, surrounded by an almost impenetrable darkness. The only sounds were coming from the rain drops spattering onto the wooden planks. The droplets glowing like white orbs as they passed through the light.

The leader had watched as they dumped the headless body into the water. Now for the final task. Three others were brought forward and made to kneel in front of him on the blood-stained planks. He did not take pleasure in what was happening, but it was necessary to keep order.

"Do you wish to speak?" Ki asked.

"We know what we did was wrong," one of the men said. "Get on with it."

"You were all aware of the price to be paid," Ki said. "Too bad you were not honest at the beginning; we could have worked together. Stealing someone else's plans and labor is never wise. I deliver you into the capable hands of Sǐ Wáng Tiān Shǐ (Deaths Angel). The men had heard of Deaths Angel but had never seen the person. No one they knew had and lived to tell it. Despite the rain, sweat began dripping into their eyes, fear paralyzing them. The woman stepped out of the shadows and walked forward, stopping in front of the three.

"Look at me," she said. "I want you to know who did this."

The men looked up, eyes widening at her beauty. They recognized her instantly. It was the woman who had enticed them. The woman whose lure of potential sex couldn't be resisted.

Their eyes trailed from her to the sword gleaming in the light, the tip resting lightly atop the wood plank in front of them. It was not the sword from the leader's cane, but her own, a razor sharp, battle-ready Katana with a twenty-eight-inch blade. She picked up the sword and rested it gently across her right shoulder then, began walking away; the clop clop of her heels striking the wooden planks became feint. The men watched after her as she disappeared into the darkness, feeling relieved she was leaving. Suddenly the sound of her heels grew louder as she returned, emerging from the darkness back into the light. A great fear gripped the three when she walked behind them, stopping just to the right of the last one, stepping slightly back. She raised her katana to the high ready position. Ki nodded.

Death's Angel stepped forward into a left lunging lead, the blade slicing through the air, severing all three heads of the men who kneeled before her master, shoulder to shoulder. She slung the blood off the blade and then wiped each side on the dead men's clothing. She handed it to one of the men who placed it back in its scabbard. Walking around to the front, she grabbed two heads in her right hand by the hair and the third in her left, holding them in front of her face, peering into the lifeless eyes.

"Death is better than dishonor," she said, dropping the heads and grabbing her sword.

"Wei Cai, Bence Fei, and Hui Liu," Ki said. "You are now the triad leaders of 24K, Ho Wap To, and So Wing Wo. Lead them with honor as our subsidiaries."

It was unclear if they heard Ki. They were still sick to their stomachs, recovering from the horror of watching their bosses' heads fall, coating the planks with pints of blood. They hoped to never see Sǐ Wáng Tiān Shǐ again, their shock and horror subsiding.

The woman walked away, disappearing into the dark night while they talked to Ki, their eyes trailing after, as beautiful and sexy as she was deadly. The men could not resist watching, if even in fear.

"Thank you, Li Na," Ki called after her.

END

ABOUT THE AUTHOR

James Tindall is the author of Jagged Grass, The Transparency, Sun God's Treasure, Alas Omega, and other books, including two best-in-field textbooks. He grew up on a Florida reservation wrestling alligators and training horses to earn money. He is a U.S. Army veteran who served in intelligence and is an expert in sharpshooting and hand-to-hand combat. He has five martial-arts black belts of advanced rank including a 9th degree in Kenpo, as well as four college degrees. As a federal scientist, he specialized in water, energy, and food security, engaging him in the areas of homeland and international security and counterterrorism. His assignments have taken him from Latin America to Brazil, Mexico to Alaska, Turkey to China, and many points between. When not writing, he consults and helps solve tactical and strategic problems for international governments and SOGs.